DEAD AMERICA
THE SECOND WEEK COLLECTION
PART 1
BOOKS 1-6
BY: DEREK SLATON
© 2019 - 2020

BOOKS:

FOLLOW NEW RELEASES AT:

www.DeadAmericaBooks.com

DEAD AMERICA: THE SECOND WEEK

BOOK 1: MISSISSIPPI

By DEREK SLATON

© 2019

CHAPTER ONE

Day Zero +8

Vernon sat in the wooden chair on his front porch sipping a hot cup of coffee like he did every morning. He watched the first of the sun's rays peek over the horizon and warm his dark skin like he did every morning. He stood up and stretched his forty-year-old back, ready to head across the river for work like he did every morning.

Only unlike a normal morning, he wouldn't be heading from his home in Lula, Mississippi to West Helena to work on engines at the local mechanic shop. This morning his work was more suited to the survival mentality that had encompassed the world.

He sighed and downed the last of his coffee. "Well, daylight's a burnin'," he said, to nobody in particular. "Better get to it." He headed back inside his modest two bedroom home and filled up two travel mugs with the last of the camping coffee pot from the fireplace.

He headed down the hall and took a deep breath before putting his hand on the knob of the second door on the left. He cracked it open, letting a ray of bright sunlight cascade down onto the sleeping form of his own little monster.

She gave an almost inhuman groan and grimaced at the light in her eyes, pulling the covers up over her head.

"All right, Nadia," Vernon said gently, "it's time to get up, girl. Lots to get done today."

The sixteen-year-old grunted again, tightening the blankets over her. He chuckled and shook his head, opening the door wider to brighten the room.

"Daddy…" she whined, voice muffled as he poked her still form. "Why do you insist on starting every day at the crack of dawn? It's the end of the world. There isn't any time clock to be punched."

"That's true," he agreed. "But ever since we lost power a few days ago, the only light we have is the one the good lord put in the sky for us."

Nadia pulled the covers off of her face and wrinkled her nose, her shoulder-length braids disheveled around her head like a halo on her pillow. "Still don't see why *I* have to be up at this hour."

"Because we're going across the river today for some more supplies," Vernon replied, perching on the edge of her bed.

Her brow furrowed. "We just went two days ago."

"And we've had eight new people show up in town since then, which means we're runnin' through them supplies faster," he explained.

Nadia rolled her eyes. "That's right, we have eight new people in town. Which is why Mister Kenneth asked for my help this morning in getting them situated. Remember?"

"Ah, damn." Vernon scratched at the salt-and-pepper scruff on his cheek as the conversation from the night before came back to him. "I'm sorry. You're just so good on these supply runs. You know we need you, baby. Are you sure Mister Kenneth can't handle this one on his own?"

"He's busy helping the older ladies get the daycare set up," Nadia replied, finally shaking the sleep from her voice and sitting up. "There's a lot more orphans in town ever since we had to go to the casino."

"What about Solomon and Gregory?" her father asked. "I know they are a little younger than you, but they seem competent enough."

Nadia sighed impatiently. "They're helping those big trucker boys and the church handyman get some barricades set up on the north side of town. They don't have much to work with, but Mister Kenneth figures something is better than nothing."

10

"I would take those boys along…" Vernon pursed his lips. "But they ain't exactly what I'd call physically able."

She laughed. "Yeah, they'd probably pass out just walking to the bridge, let alone all the way to West Helena," she agreed. "Plus, from what I can tell, they aren't that bright, either."

"So, that makes you the last capable person in this whole town," he reiterated.

She shook her head. "Maybe not. I was up for a bit after you went to bed and I saw a car come into town. I could hear Mister Kenneth talking to somebody before they went inside. Maybe they'll be useful."

"Well, maybe you right, girl." Vernon shrugged. "Come on, now, throw some proper clothes on, grab your coffee, and we'll go chat with Mister Kenneth."

The father and daughter headed across the quiet residential street. It was an old neighborhood, most of the houses built in the sixties, and not incredibly well-updated. But they stood, and it was home, and that was what mattered.

There were four people milling about on Mister Kenneth's large porch, enjoying their own morning brew, dressed in form-fitting clothing and armed to the teeth.

"Mornin' Vernon," Marc greeted, waving. "Not like you to be the last one showing up.

He laughed and patted his daughter on the shoulder. "Had a little trouble waking the sleeping princess today."

"Hey." She pouted. "It's not my fault you neglected to bring me coffee in bed."

Vernon laughed again. "If I had done that, you'd still be there. At least when I leave it on the counter I know you'll get up before it gets cold."

"Making a tired person find their own coffee," Nadia replied, shaking her head in disdain. "Pretty sure the Geneva Convention would classify that as a war crime."

"Hear, hear!" Mandy agreed, holding up her own mug. "You coming with us today, Nadia?"

"I'm afraid I require the young lady's assistance here," Mister Kenneth announced from the doorway, heading out onto the porch in his conservative Deacon outfit.

The morning sunlight shone off of his pristine bald head, and his presence brought a calm over the group, as it always did. He stepped out of the way and a young couple emerged, the woman holding a gurgling infant.

"I'd like to introduce you to the newest members of our little community," Mister Kenneth said with a smile. "This is Phil, his wife Emma, and their baby daughter Olivia."

"Pleasure to meet you all," Phil offered with a nervous smile.

Tony winked at him, adjusting his baseball cap. "Well, you say that *now*," he said playfully, and the tension seemed to drain out of the young couple as everyone chuckled.

"Phil, my friends and I are about to do a run," Vernon piped up. "We're a man down today."

Nadia clucked her tongue. "Excuse me. A *man* down?"

"Apologies," her father corrected, giving her a bow and a flourish. "We're a *person* down today, and you look like you can handle yourself, sir. Would you be so kind as to join us on our trip?"

Phil glanced at his wife, and she looked up at him with a little nod. "These people have taken us in. The least we can do is contribute," she replied.

He kissed her forehead and then leaned down to do the same to the baby, who giggled and squeezed his nose in response. Mandy let out a little noise of delight and cooed at Olivia as Phil turned to Vernon.

"I have a handgun with our things," he said. "I'll go grab it and we can get underway."

Mister Kenneth put a gentle hand on his shoulder as he turned. "If you look beside the washing machine, there's a crowbar resting next to it. You would be wise to take it with you." As the younger man headed inside, the old Deacon turned to Nadia. "I really appreciate you helping me out today. As it so happens, I have a fresh pot of coffee that should be finished brewing about now. Why don't you go help yourself to another cup before we get started?"

"Thank you," the teenager replied, and then turned to her father. "Daddy, you be safe today." She put a hand on her hip.

Vernon felt a pang in his heart as he took her in, looking so much like her mother. "Don't you worry baby," he assured her, voice thick. "I'll come home to you just like I've always done."

"Well, this is the first time you haven't had me watching your back," she replied. "So you'd better be extra careful. And I'm going to have a walkie talkie on me all day long, so you'd better keep in touch and let me know you're safe."

"I will, baby," he promised, and pulled her into a tight hug. She kissed his cheek and then headed into the house, stepping around Phil who emerged back into the sunlight.

"All right, I'm ready," he announced.

Darrell pulled out his keys and dangled them above his head. "Hop into the back of the pickup and we'll get rolling."

Vernon gave Mister Kenneth a little salute and the Deacon nodded at him, clasping his hands in front of him as the group headed to the truck. Emma bounced the baby next to him, her lips pursed tight with worry.

CHAPTER TWO

Darrell swung the wheel to the left just before the bridge and pulled off to the side of the road, the tailgate facing their destination.

Phil's brow furrowed as the crew began to dismount with their gear. "Wait, why are we stopping here?" he asked.

"We've got a series of barricades set up," Marc replied, motioning down the two lane bridge.

The newcomer squinted, putting a hand to his forehead so he could survey the makeshift fencing and parked cars up and down the highway. "Why not just put a gate at the end of the other side?" he asked.

"Might have something to do with our lack of supplies," Darrell replied, clapping him on the back. "Not sure if you noticed or not, but we didn't have a big hardware store in town."

Mandy sighed. "Or a restaurant."

"Or a bar," Tony added.

"It's safer to go on foot," Vernon put in as he led the group down the road.

Phil jogged to catch up to him. "How in the world are we safer on foot than in a truck?" He tucked the crowbar into a loop on his jeans and decided to hold his gun in lieu of jamming it into his waistband.

"Trucks are loud, my friend," Vernon replied, adjusting his sun hat. "Our biggest fear is leading a large group of those things back to town. Outside of us and my daughter Nadia, there aren't too many others that would be capable of putting up a fight should the situation arise. So we take extra precautions, even if it puts us at more of a personal risk."

Phil nodded thoughtfully. Before he could open his mouth again, Mandy reached out and tugged on his arm to stop him. She pointed to movement in a long train of barbed wire that ran all the way across the bridge.

"Looks like we caught a couple," she said, and held up a long metal pipe. Darrell joined her, the two of them heading up to the wooden stairs built to get over the hazard. Tony stood directly in front of the two zombies flailing in the wire, moaning and reaching for a fresh meal even though the barbs tore chunks off of their rotting flesh.

"Yeah, come and get me, ya bastards," Tony teased, sticking his tongue out to keep the corpses occupied.

Mandy and Darrell skirted around behind them and, in unison, skewered their heads with the pipes.

"Nice shot, y'all," Tony said, and the duo high-fived each other at their silent but deadly attack.

Vernon led the group over the wooden stairs, double-checking the security of the gates as everyone passed. As he did so, Phil paused and headed over to the bridge railing, peering down at the rushing water below.

"First time seeing the Mississippi?" Vernon asked, sidling up next to the newcomer.

Phil shrugged. "First time outside of Georgia," he admitted. "Never seen anything like this."

"Where were y'all in Georgia?" the older man asked.

"Marietta," Phil replied, turning back to him. "Just a bit northwest of Atlanta."

Darrell let out a low whistle as the group began to walk again. "Atlanta, huh? I mean it was bad here and we only had a few hundred people in town, so I can't imagine what it would be like in a city that size. Especially with them runners."

"The day everything hit I was home with my wife," Phil explained. "We got to see a couple of hours of footage from downtown before the networks were knocked off the air. I don't know how anybody could have survived that."

Mandy shook her head. "So how did y'all get out?"

"Dumb luck, to be perfectly honest," Phil admitted. "About six months ago, we got a good deal on a house in this new neighborhood on the west side of Marietta. It was one of these planned communities that lost funding, so only a few houses had been built. Since nobody wanted to live in a neighborhood that looked like a perpetual construction zone, we got it on the cheap. So we were able to throw stuff in the car and get out of town without being overwhelmed. We spent the last week working our way west."

Tony nodded, cracking his knuckles. "Good a plan as any, I suppose."

"My family is still alive and I get to go shopping with you fine people," Phil replied. "In my book, that's a win."

There was a round of chuckles, and they continued in a companionable silence for a little while before Phil took notice of a gaudy-looking eight-story building in the distance.

"If y'all don't mind me asking," he began, "what in the world is *that*?"

Vernon barked a laugh. "That right there is our very own den of iniquity."

"I'm sorry?" Phil scratched the back of his head.

"It's a casino," Marc explained.

"Ah, gotcha." The newcomer nodded. "I mean, it looks pretty nice from here. Sturdy, too. Why haven't y'all moved in there? Wouldn't that be easier to defend?" A somber silence fell over the group, and he looked around at the stern faces. He raised his hands, palms out. "Apologies if I said something wrong."

Mandy shook her head. "We tried to move in there. It didn't go well." Still stone-faced, she broke from the group and picked up the pace, heading for a zombie tangled up in the final barricade. "Got this one."

Vernon put a hand on Phil's shoulder. "We thought of the same thing and tried," he said quietly. "Twenty-five of us went in, only nine came back out. Mandy's brother was among those who didn't make it."

"I'm so sorry," Phil stammered, face white as a sheet. "I had no idea."

"Mandy knows that," the older man assured him. "She's not mad at you. Just still very raw and doesn't want to think about it."

"Understandable," the newcomer replied. "I won't bring it up again."

Instead of skewering the trapped corpse, Mandy smashed it violently three times in the face, until its head resembled pudding.

Vernon nodded. "Probably a good idea, friend."

"Clear!" Mandy called over her shoulder, and headed up over the last barricade.

The group checked their weapons, readying themselves for the task ahead.

Tony stretched his arms over his head, grabbing one wrist and bending at the waist to warm up his muscles. "All right, Vernon, what are we hitting today and how do you want to get there?"

"I think we're gonna have to go all the way north to the Stop 'n Shop," the older man replied.

"That's one hell of a haul," Tony replied, lowering his arms and reaching down to touch his toes.

Vernon nodded. "Yeah, but we about picked clean the other grocery store."

"There were a couple of grocery carts worth of stuff left in there," Darrell cut in.

"Yep," Vernon agreed, "but it's there in case of an emergency."

"Well, it's your call, bubba," Tony replied, bouncing back and forth on the balls of his feet. "So, how you wanna get there? Highway? Or you want to go through the neighborhood?"

"We had some issues with the highway last time," the older man mused. "Let's stick to the neighborhood. It's a little bit longer around, but I think it'll safer."

"Neighborhood it is, then," Tony squatted a few times, and then stood up with a smile. "I'll try to lead as many of 'em as I can to the highway and meet y'all up at the store."

Vernon stepped forward and gave the younger man's shoulder a squeeze. "Be safe."

"Always, brother," Tony replied with a grin, and then shot off down the road like a bat out of hell, legs pumping like practiced pistons.

Phil raised an eyebrow as the group continued in a different direction. "Where's he going?"

"Tony is our decoy," Vernon explained, "he's going to clear the path for us so we don't have to deal with too many zombies."

"He's also the closest thing our little town has to a celebrity," Darrell added. "He had one of those internet video stations that got pretty popular. He made those parker videos."

"Parker?" Phil furrowed his brow. "I'm not familiar with that."

"You know, parker," Darrell repeated. "Like he'll run real fast and jump off walls and shit."

"Oh, you mean *parkour*," Phil corrected.

Darrell laughed and waved his hands around his head. "Well look at you with them fancy foreign words and shit," he joked, and smacked the newcomer in the arm at his worried expression. "Relax, buddy, I'm just fuckin' with ya."

"Haven't even been with y'all a day and I already feel like I'm a part of the team." Phil rolled his eyes.

"Whoa there, bud, how can you be a part of the team when you ain't killed nothin' yet?" Darrell asked, a wicked glint in his eye.

"The hell I haven't," Phil shot back, squaring his shoulders. "I left a trail of corpses through Alabama that would make even the baddest serial killer blush." He narrowed his eyes. "And I've killed my fair share of zombies in the last week, too."

Darrell's eyes widened, and he nearly stumbled at the sudden realization.

Phil's face broke into a wide grin, and he couldn't hold back a laugh. "Just making sure you can take it as good as you can dish it out." He pointed a finger at his new friend.

Darrell shook his head and punched the newcomer's shoulder playfully, blushing at his naiveté. "Fuck, buddy, that was a good one."

CHAPTER THREE

"All right, what's the plan?" Darrell asked as he peeked over one of the abandoned cars across the street from the store's parking lot. "You wanna just go up and hit 'em? They're spread out pretty good."

A dozen or so zombies shuffled aimlessly around the lot, as if waiting for a fresh meal to wander into their domain.

"It's still early," Vernon replied with a shake of his head. "Let's give Tony a little more time to catch up with us."

"Y'all talking about me?" Tony asked, and the group whipped their heads around wildly, looking for the source of the voice. "Look up," he instructed, and they did, seeing a waving Tony standing on the roof of the one-story building behind them.

Marc raised an eyebrow. "What in the hell are you doing up there?"

"Led a group of those things down towards the rest of 'em on the highway, and rather than risk leading any of them back, I decided to go by rooftop," he replied with a shrug. "Hang on, I'll be right down." He hopped up onto the ledge of the roof and sprinted across it with perfect balance. He leapt gracefully out, landing on a streetlight as if he were a spider monkey in a tree. He adjusted his stance and slid easily down to the ground, landing on his feet effortlessly.

"Tony," Phil breathed, blinking at the young man, "that was *impressive*."

"Thanks man." Tony grinned and winked at the newcomer. "But that ain't nothin'."

"You think you can help us clear a path?" Vernon asked, motioning across the street.

Mandy held out a bottle of water from her pack, and Tony took it with a grateful nod, unscrewing the cap as he surveyed the parking lot.

"Y'all ain't planning on going around back at all, are ya?" he asked before taking a long swig.

Vernon shook his head. "Nope, just straight in and out the front door."

"Okay," the young man replied. "I think the safest course of action is gonna be for me to get on the other side of em, get their attention and lure them to the loading docks. Should be a fire escape or something on the back there that'll let me get on the roof. I'll keep 'em occupied until you give me the all clear and then we'll be off and home by lunch."

"We'll wait for you," Vernon replied firmly. "Anything special you want us to pick up?"

"Energy drinks," Tony replied with longing in his gaze. "Any flavor is fine. Oh, and some of them girly magazines."

"Tony!" Darrell hissed. "There's a lady present!"

"Oh please," the young man scoffed. "She's dirtier than all of us combined."

Mandy shrugged as Phil glanced at her. "Well, he's not wrong," she admitted.

"All right, see y'all on the other side," Tony cut in with a wink, and replaced the cap on his water bottle. He tossed it back to the lady in question and then hopped the car in a single bound before walking casually into the parking lot.

Phil watched with bated breath as the young man produced a knife and a extendable baton. He smacked the baton down on the parking dividers as he walked, letting out a loud metallic noise that attracted the attention of all of the corpses. They shambled towards him, save for one that darted faster than the rest.

"Oh, looks like we got a jogger," Tony praised it with a smirk. "You must be a new addition to the undead." He fell into a loose bouncing stance, and as the zombie reached him he ducked and tripped it with the baton, falling down on the back of its head with his knife. He wiped the blade on a miraculously clean section

of the corpse's clothes and then sheathed
it.

He stretched his arms above his head
as he waited for the rest of the mini-
horde to get closer to him. "Give me five
minutes, y'all," he called over his
shoulder, and then began a casual jog
around the cluster of zombies. He led them
back towards the building, keeping a
twenty-yard head start at all times.

As he reached the corner of the
store, one of the zombies began to
straggle off to the side, and he knelt
down to pick up a rock from the asphalt.
He threw it with perfect accuracy at the
back of the deserter's head, and this
enraged it just enough to rejoin its
hunting brethren.

Behind the store, Tony found a
transport truck that looked like it had
been abandoned while unloading a delivery.
He peeked inside, finding the back empty.
He bounced on the balls of his feet as he
waited for his pursuers to get a little
closer before clambering easily up onto
the hood of the truck. He vaulted up onto
the back, fell into a somersault and
rolled into a sitting position.

"If y'all don't mind, I'm gonna take
a bit of a breather," he said, stretching
his legs out in front of him. "It's been a
hell of a cardio day so far." He leaned

back on his hands and closed his eyes
against the warm sun. "I swear if it
wasn't for the stench, this would be a
perfect picnic spot."

Vernon threw open the front door of
the store, and Darrell and Marc were first
to burst in, shotguns at the ready. Mandy
followed, crowbar raised, and Phil began
to line up shopping carts as he'd been
instructed to beforehand.

"Okay," Vernon said as he closed the
door behind him. "Y'all know what to find.
Bottled water, drinks, and canned food are
the priority. Nobody goes anywhere alone.
We need ten carts, let's do it, people."

Mandy, Marc, and Darrell headed off
for the non-perishable food, each towing
two carts.

"Guess I'm sticking with you," Phil
said as he pushed two carts towards
Vernon.

The older man nodded. "Okay, grab a
couple carts and come on, then. We're
gonna hit the pharmacy."

When they reached the first medicine
aisle, the two men started tossing boxes
and bottles into the carts, every over-
the-counter medication that could prove
useful.

A crash from the pharmacist's desk
made them both freeze. Vernon turned to

his new charge and brought a finger to his lips. He leaned around the edge of the aisle and spotted a man in a bloodied lab coat thrashing around behind the window of the enclosed prescription medication area.

"Dammit," he muttered, and pulled back behind the shelving. "There's some stuff in there we really could have used."

Phil shrugged and pulled the crowbar from his belt loop. "Let's go get 'em, then."

"Too big of a risk," Vernon replied, waving a hand in front of him. "Look how fast he's moving. Dealing with shamblers are one thing, but we ain't gonna be messing with no runner today." He turned back to his cart but Phil touched his arm.

"Vernon, how strong are you?" he asked.

The older man furrowed his brow. "Strong enough, I suppose. Why do you ask?"

"Come with me," Phil instructed, and waved for him to follow. He led them to the window. It was a solid sheet of plexiglas with a hole and a divot at the bottom to exchange medication. The zombie threw itself against the invisible barrier, tie fluttering as it screamed and gnawed.

Phil slid his hand through the medication divot, and clicked his fingernails against the metal bottom. The ghoul dove for it, and he drew his hand back quickly.

"Boy, what are you doin'?" Vernon snapped.

Phil put up a flippant hand. "Just trust me, I got this," he said.

He reached down again and clicked his fingernails, and this time when the zombie dove for his hand, its tie pooled in the medication divot. Phil scrabbled for the fabric and pulled tightly, narrowly missing having his fingers chomped off, put effectively pinning the zombie's head against the window.

"Grab it, grab it!" Phil cried, and Vernon sprung to action, gripping the fabric tightly and bracing his leg against the lower wall to hold the thrashing corpse tightly.

"I got it, what are you gonna do?" he grunted, and his eyes widened as Phil ran over and threw open the prescription area door. "Oh shit!" He pulled as hard as he could on the tie as the zombie struggled to turn around and get to the young man invading its office.

Phil stabbed his crowbar into the side of the zombie pharmacist's head, letting it fall limp from the tie. "I think you're good, Vernon," he said, and the older man let go of the tie in shock,

31

the fabric fluttering back through the window as the corpse fell to the floor.

He shook his head and walked slowly around and through the door, where Phil was already holding up a few bottles of pills.

"The good news is, if I gave you a panic attack with that stunt, I'm pretty sure we have the meds here to make it all better," the younger man joked.

Vernon laughed and scrubbed his hands down his face. "You are one crazy little motherfucker."

CHAPTER FOUR

"Coast is clear," Marc said as he came back inside from lining up the last shopping cart in the parking lot. "I think we're good."

"How are we supposed to signal Tony?" Phil asked.

Darrell grinned and produced a baseball from seemingly nowhere, under handing it to the newcomer. "How good is your arm?"

Tony squatted on the lip of the roof above the truck he'd been lounging on, doing some balancing stretches as he kept an eye on the cluster of hungry corpses below. "They better have found those magazines," he muttered to himself. "This whole being single in a small town during the apocalypse isn't exactly conducive to a healthy dating life."

There was a dull *smack* behind him and he turned to see a baseball rolling across the roof from the front of the building.

"Well, it's been real, y'all!" he declared, giving his zombie friends a wave. "But it's time for me to go." He jogged to the opposite end of the building, narrowly avoiding another whistling baseball before he reached the edge.

Phil froze in his windup as Tony waved down at him, and they watched the athletic young man swing over the edge and use a drainage pipe to slide easily down to the ground.

"Tony, you want to scout ahead and make sure we're still in the clear?" Vernon asked as everyone got their carts rolling.

Tony gave him a little salute. "I'm on it."

"Just stay within eyesight," the old man instructed. "We may need you to help out if wheeling these things attracts attention."

Tony grabbed a lime-flavored energy drink from one of Darrell's carts and unscrewed the cap, moaning as he chugged half of it. "Hey Mandy," he asked when he'd caught his breath. "Did you find any magazines for me?"

"I did, you pervy Energizer Bunny motherfucker," she replied.

Tony grinned. "I appreciate ya! Of course, you can come by any time and read 'em." He winked at her as he tossed the bottle back into the cart and she shot him a middle finger with a smile.

"Okay, let's get moving," Vernon said. "We've got a long walk ahead of us."

About an hour later, the group emerged from the abandoned neighborhood. Tony pushed one of Mandy's carts, as one of the wheels was a bit wonky and she'd had trouble keeping it straight with one hand.

"Holy shit man," Darrell complained, sick of the squeakiness of his own carts. "Next time we go by a hardware store, I'm stealing every single can of WD-40 they've got."

Marc laughed. "It ain't that bad, Darrell, just think of it as white noise."

"Man, I went to so many concerts back in the day, my hearing is like eighty percent white noise as it is." Darrell rolled his eyes. "This shit is just annoying."

They rounded the last corner, and the bridge came into view a few hundred yards away.

"Oh, thank the sweet baby Jesus," Mandy groaned. "It's about damn time."

"Hell yeah, there it is!" Darrell agreed. "Get this shit loaded up and get home. I'm starvin'."

Vernon clucked his tongue. "Settle down people, we still have a bit of work ahead of us."

Phil stopped short, almost causing a cart pileup.

"Come on, newbie, don't tire out on us, now," Marc joked.

Phil furrowed his brow, straining his ears. "Did y'all not hear that?"

"Dude is getting paranoid," Darrell scoffed.

The newcomer scowled. "Everybody just stop for a second, and listen."

Vernon held up his hand to facilitate everyone stopping, and a moment later there was an echo of a low rumbling. A high-pitched whine followed, growing louder and louder.

"What the hell is that?" Marc breathed.

Everyone instinctively flinched as three cruise missiles buzzed over their heads.

"Everybody take cover!" Vernon bellowed, and the group hurried into action. They sprinted as fast as their legs could carry them to the tree line as a series of explosions sounded in the distance. They dove into a ditch behind the thick tree trunks, scrambling to stay laying down while peeking up over the edge of the divot to see what was going on.

They watched in horror as three more missiles hit the bridge, debris flying everywhere as the structure crumbled into the rushing river.

The group stayed stock still, staring wide-eyed and in shock, and the world seemed to go silent. After a few moments with no more explosions, Mandy suddenly shot to her feet, startling everyone.

"What the fuck?!" she screamed. "How are we supposed to get back now?!"

Darrell threaded his hands through his hair and pulled. "Who would blow up the bridge?"

Vernon swallowed hard and rolled onto his back, pulling out his walkie talkie. "Nadia? Nadia are you there?"

"Daddy?" her scared voice came crackling back. "Are you okay?"

"Yeah, I'm okay, baby, we're all okay," he replied.

"What was that noise?" she demanded.

Vernon took a deep breath before pushing the button again. "It was the bridge. Somebody blew up the bridge."

"Who would do that?" her voice was thick.

"It doesn't matter right now, baby," he replied gently. "All that matters is that the bridge is gone and we're still on the Arkansas side."

"What?" she exclaimed. "How are you getting back?"

"You let me worry about that," he instructed. "I need you to do something for me. It's incredibly important or else I wouldn't ask you to do this."

There was a pause and then Nadia came back, sounding firmer and calmer. "Okay. What do you need me to do?"

"I…" Vernon took a deep breath. "I need you to get people to the casino."

"Are you crazy?!" Mandy shrieked. "You want to send your daughter to that death trap?"

Tony grabbed her arm as Vernon held up a hand to silence her. She seethed, jerking away from them all and turning to face the decimated bridge with a huff.

"The… the casino?" Nadia asked. "But it's overrun with zombies."

"I know, baby, I know," Vernon replied, wincing at his own words. "But you're gonna have to figure out a way to make that place as safe as you can. And you're not going to have much time to do it in."

She clicked the button, but hesitated before speaking. "Because of the explosion."

"That's right," her father said. "Because of the explosion. Every zombie within a hundred miles is going to be headed our way, and our little town is not going to withstand it."

"I'll take care of it, daddy." Her voice was so stern and so like her mother's that it made his heart feel like it was about to burst from his chest.

"Baby, I want you to listen to me, and listen to me good," Vernon said. "You don't take shit from nobody, you understand me? Nobody else in that town has been out there fighting those things. Only you have. You make damn sure that people know they need to take orders from you. I know some of them older white boys ain't gonna wanna take orders from a sixteen-year-old black girl, but you do whatever you need to do make them understand. Are we clear?"

"I won't let you down," Nadia promised.

"I know you won't," he replied. "Now you hurry, run and find Mister Kenneth. I'll tell him what's going on while you round up who you need to round up."

She paused, and he imagined her giving a firm nod. "I love you, daddy," she said quietly.

He pressed the walkie talkie to his forehead, closing his eyes for a moment. "I love you too, baby," he finally said. "Now you get going."

There was a moment of hesitant silence before everyone clustered around the man they trusted to lead them.

"So, what's our plan?" Tony asked helplessly.

Vernon squared his shoulders as he clipped the radio back to his belt. "We gotta go north."

Mandy immediately doubled over as if she were about to retch, and Darrell moved away from the group to drive his fist into a tree trunk. Tony and Marc went pale.

Phil's brow furrowed. "What's north?"

"The Helena River Park," Vernon replied.

The newcomer shrugged. "And that's... bad?"

"A shitload of people had that same idea early on," Marc explained, voice hoarse with worry. "Back when all these things were runners. Somehow they got the bright idea that they could get down to the Gulf and be safe. One traffic jam later, and the population of the town tripled, only with zombies."

"So why don't we just go south and cross the river down there?" Phil asked.

Tony shook his head. "The current will carry us miles downriver before we can get across."

"If we could even get across without drowning," Darrell snapped, turning back to the group. "Not sure how strong of swimmers y'all are, but my dumb ass would be fish food for sure."

"Fact is, we need a boat," Vernon cut in. "Our only hope is to head towards the

River Park and see if there is one left that we can get into the water. And time is not our friend."

The group seemed to calm down, accepting the fact that this was their only option. They rummaged around in the carts, filling their bags with food and water.

"Tony, I'll need you to get a hundred or so yards ahead," Vernon continued. "We're going to be moving at a brisk pace, so you direct traffic for us. You tell us where to go and we follow."

"Just try and keep that fancy jumping and climbing to a minimum," Mandy added. "Some of us ain't great with heights."

Tony saluted and sprinted up the road.

Vernon took a deep breath. "Let's move out, people. We can do this."

CHAPTER FIVE

Victor pulled up outside of Mister Kenneth's house, hopping out with James, Doug, and Luke, his posse of moderately overweight truckers. Nadia took a deep breath as they approached, offering a thin smile to Solomon and Gregory as they hopped out of the truck bed. The teenage boys gave her a little wave as the group headed up onto the porch.

"Mister Kenneth, why are we back here?" Victor asked as he pulled off his hat to address the deacon. "We still got a lot of work to do on the barricade you wanted."

"Something more important came up," Nadia declared.

The trucker stared down his nose at her. "Excuse me little girl, but the adults are talking."

She got up from her seat and stepped in front of him, her nose inches from his even though she was a half of a foot shorter than him. Something in her eyes cut through the older man like a knife, and he shrank under her gaze.

"As I was saying," she said, ice in her tone, "something more important came up."

"All right, girl," Victor muttered as he stepped back from her. "What is it?"

"That rumble y'all heard a few minutes ago?" she asked, waving her hand. "That was the bridge over the Mississippi being blown up."

The men all froze, eyes wide.

"But what about our people?" James stammered.

Nadia shook her head. "They're alive, but they're trapped on the other side of the river."

"Well let's go get 'em!" Doug cried.

"No," she said firmly. "We have another task we have to tackle, and we don't have a lot of time to do it in."

"Well, spit it out," James snapped. "What do we need to do?"

She raised her chin. "We have to clear out the casino."

There was a long moment of awkward silence before Victor barked a hysterical laugh. "Oh, is that all, little girl? We'll just go clear out the casino? Hell, while we're at it, we can build a rocket ship to take us to the moon!"

"You call me little girl one more time and I'm going to plant your bitch ass in the ground," Nadia growled. "And if you don't think I can, let me remind you that while your doughy ass has been lounging around, *I've* been out there on the front lines fighting these motherfuckers. Word around town is that you couldn't make the

43

cut because you get winded trying to find your own dick in the morning to take a piss. Which, given the size of that gut I imagine it's a two day trip for your hands to make it below your waistline to find that shrunken gummy worm you call a manhood. Now, you got anything else to say? Or are you ready to start tackling this problem?"

Victor's mouth opened and closed like a fish, shaking his head and unable to speak.

"Miss Nadia," James said, coughing nervously and raising his hand. "I have a question."

She raised an eyebrow. "Yes?"

"Why?" he asked. "Why do you have to go to the casino?"

"Glad you asked, James," Nadia replied with a smile. "Because that explosion is going to attract every zombie within earshot. I know you boys have been working hard on a barricade, but it's not going to be enough to withstand a horde of any size. If we can get people into the casino we might have a chance at surviving whatever comes our way."

Solomon stepped forward, his brother in tow. "I speak for both me and my brother when I say we want to do our part. I know we're young and that's why we've been left behind before, but we want to help."

"I'm glad to hear you say that, because I was kind of counting on your two," she replied gently. "Everybody who would normally being doing an assault like this is currently on the other side of the river, which leaves it up to us.

"Now, I can see the look on some of y'all's faces and I can tell you're scared. But there's only one thing you need to keep in the back of your head. If a sixteen-year-old girl isn't scared to do this, then I shouldn't be either."

The three truckers glanced at each other and shrugged, unable to argue with the logic that they'd just been guilted into a suicide mission.

"Well, miss, we're with you, but I have one more question," James said. "Do you have a plan?"

"I do," Nadia replied. "You and I are gonna run over to your workshop while the rest of these guys get any weapons they can. Mister Kenneth, I'll need you to start getting people ready to move, and packing every bit of our supplies into vehicles. It may be awhile before we're able to come back to town."

The old deacon stood up from his rocking chair and nodded. "I'll take care of it."

"All right, gentlemen," Nadia said with a firm nod. "You know what to do. We meet back here in ten."

CHAPTER SIX

Phil kept a white-knuckled grip on the barrel of his handgun as they headed up the road leading towards the docks. "What's the plan if there aren't any boats?" he asked.

"Well," Marc drew out the word as he scratched the back of his head, "we know for a fact there are going to be boats near the water since there was a traffic jam that got everybody stuck. The thing we have to be concerned about is getting a boat in the water without being eaten."

Phil raised an eyebrow. "That doesn't sound so bad."

"Yeah, just a massive pileup of trucks, some of which don't have keys and others have zombies trapped inside," Darrell cut in, sarcasm evident in his voice. "All we gotta do is clear the ones with busted boats out of the way and get one in the water while fighting off a few hundred of them pricks with what—twelve bullets between us? Easy as fuckin' pie."

Phil's breath caught in his throat. "Okay, that does sound bad."

"Guys, it's Tony," Mandy pointed ahead at the figure tearing towards them, frantically waving his hands for them to come to him.

Vernon sped up to a jog. "We should pick up the pace," he instructed, and his group followed suit. They huffed as they finally reached him, and he shook his head in disbelief.

"Don't y'all be getting comfortable, we gotta move!" he urged.

"What is it, Tony?" Vernon rasped.

The younger man waved him off. "Come on! Keep moving." He took off around a bend, along a tree-lined curb, and the group stopped short in shock as they caught up to him.

Shoulder to shoulder across the only road into town shambled at least a hundred and fifty zombies. They moved at an aimless pace, as hordes were wont to do, not having noticed the fresh meal clustered at the bend ahead.

"Holy fuck," Mandy breathed.

Marc's face was white as a sheet. "What do we do?"

"We'd better be finding a fuckin' hiding spot, that's for damn sure," Darrell hissed.

Marc shook his head. "Where? Where would we hide?"

"I don't know," Darrell snapped. "Up a damn tree, anything!"

"No, if one of them spots us, we're all dead," Vernon put in, shaking his head. "They'll just wait us out, it's no good."

Phil pointed to a metallic building to the right, with a large stone silo in the yard. "What's that building there?" There was a large metal construct that connected it to a neighboring building across the street.

"Holy shit, you're a genius, Phil!" Tony grinned. "It's an old processing plant and they have a conveyor belt that connects the two buildings."

"So we lure them into one building," Vernon said thoughtfully.

Tony nodded. "And cross over to the other side!"

"Okay, if we're gonna do that we'd better hurry the fuck up and get there before they do!" Darrell urged, and Tony took off like a shot. He led the charge across the street and up onto the grass, and a few of the approaching zombies began to notice the movement ahead of them.

Tony made it to the building just before a few of the faster zombies did, and tried to throw open the door, but it was locked. He frantically looked around, spotting a nearby window that was about eight feet off of the ground.

"Christ I hope this works," he muttered, and sprinted for the window. A trio of zombies moved to intercept him, and he leapt into a kick, catching the lead one in the chest and knocking the other two over like a set of dominoes. He thrust off of the zombie and did a spring up the wall, grabbing the windowsill.

He held on with one hand and drew his baton with the other, ducking his head as low as he could while smashing the glass with the metal. He glanced down the road to see the rest of the group closing in, and more and more zombies from the other side.

Tony took a deep breath and clambered up through the window, dropping down onto the ground floor and rolling towards the front door. He unlocked it and threw it open, a zombie there to greet him. He reached up and grabbed it around the throat as they tumbled backwards, and he managed to keep from toppling over even though the zombie was large. He smacked it a few times with the baton, avoiding snapping teeth as he pushed it against the wall. He dropped the baton and drew his knife, stabbing it in the forehead just as two more zombies burst in through the door.

He whirled around and fell into a fighting stance, when the two corpses crumpled to the floor, revealing Mandy and Marc behind them.

"Thanks for the assist." Tony grinned.

Mandy winked at him. "Anytime, sugar." The others bustled in and threw themselves against the door, but the horde outside was too much for them to push back.

"Where in the holy fuck are we going?!" Darrell screamed.

Vernon pointed up at the conveyor belt that led to the crosswalk. "There! Move!"

"Go, I'll hold this!" Darrell cried, digging his heels in as best he could. Vernon led Phil, Mandy and Marc up the conveyor, slow and steady as they could on such a thin ramp. Tony stayed at the bottom, watching their progress.

Darrell grunted under the strain as an arm shot past his face, flailing from the widening gap of the door. "Are they up there yet?!" he yelled.

Tony clenched his fists and shook his head. "They're getting there, man!"

"They'd better hurry the fuck up, cause I can't hold this much longer!" Darrell cried.

Tony took a deep breath. "Fuck." He watched his comrades struggling with the steep incline. He spotted a six-foot-long piece of rebar and grabbed it, taking a step towards his grunting friend. "Okay, I got an idea! I need you to run as fast as you can to me and start climbing, I'll take care of the rest!"

Darrell nodded and braced himself to make his move. "Okay, I'm coming, you'd better be ready!" he cried, and then pushed off of the door. As soon as he let go, the door practically exploded from the weight of the zombies. It caught his foot and he tripped, hitting the ground hard in a panic.

He screamed as he scrambled to get to his feet, but the mass of rotting flesh descended on him instantly, decaying teeth finding purchase in his soft warm body.

"Darrell!" Mandy shrieked from above, open-mouthed at her friend's disappearance under the flood of corpses.

"Goddammit," Tony cursed, blinking back tears. "Y'all get moving, *now*!" he screamed up at them, and leapt onto the belt, closing the distance between them quickly. As he caught up to Marc, he saw a row of zombies managing to work their way upwards. "Vernon, they're coming up! You gotta hurry, man!"

The older man looked over his shoulder and his eyes widened, and he picked up the pace as best he could while still finding good footing.

Tony readied his rebar and then fell into a controlled slide, all the way back down the ramp into the row of zombies. It slammed into the chest of the first one, skewering a few like a kebab.

"Don't know how much higher y'all would be able to get, but I ain't taking any chances," he muttered, and jammed his end of the bar into the metal grating on the side of the conveyor. The kebab worked as a temporary barrier, trapping the other zombies below from clambering up.

Satisfied, Tony turned and climbed back up, just as Marc managed to haul himself up onto the landing above. The group looked down onto the factory floor to see easily a hundred creatures flooding the space, reaching up to the fresh meat above.

"Everybody okay?" Tony asked as he pulled himself up, and received a series of somber nods. "I'm gonna go out first and make sure there's nothing else that is gonna cause us any issues. The two most important things from here on out is that you don't look down and you don't make a noise. We don't want to go through all of this only to inadvertently lure them into the other building. Everybody clear?"

There were another round of nods, and then he took a deep breath before heading outside. He peeked down to see a dozen or so stragglers outside, but none of them took notice of him. He crept cautiously across the walkway, the wind rustling his hair as he moved. When he reached the other side, he scanned the ground floor of the opposite building for threats.

He let out a deep sigh of relief when there was no movement whatsoever, and popped back out to the walkway to wave at Vernon.

One by one, the group moved slowly and quietly across the street, and climbed down to join Tony on the ground floor. They stayed as silent as they could for fear of alerting any of the horde, and gathered around a dusty window along the far wall.

Vernon wiped the glass and peered out. There was a dirt road running alongside the river, completely devoid of movement, alive or dead.

"There's our road, and it looks clear," he murmured. "Tony, you know the drill. You go on ahead. For the rest of us, stay silent and move quickly. Let's go."

CHAPTER SEVEN

Victor pulled his truck up to the casino parking lot, stopping at the edge. He hung out the window as the group in the bed stood up to survey the area.

Nadia pulled out a pair of binoculars, inspecting the barricades at the front entrance. She carefully scanned the cars in the parking lot, making sure there were no straggler zombies lurking about.

"Looks like our barricades have held," she reported, "and I'm not seeing any danger coming from the parking lot. But we should avoid the cars just to be safe."

"Where would you like me to go, then?" Victor asked. "Because I'm assuming we ain't doin' a frontal assault?"

She shook her head. "Head over to the old hotel," she replied, motioning to an older two-story structure just to the north of the main building.

"All right," he barked, "y'all hang tight." He put the truck back in drive and everyone sat back down to avoid falling out onto the pavement.

"Man I love this place," James commented wistfully as they pulled in front of the old hotel.

Solomon shook his head. "It's so old. Why did they leave it up?"

"Because, young man," Doug replied, "this place used to be one of the most popular destinations on the river when it opened in the early sixties. Rumor has it that the new owner just couldn't bring himself to tear it down, so he had it converted into extra hotel rooms while keeping the retro feel."

"That's right," James agreed, "back in our day all we needed to have a good time was a grill and a swimming pool."

Gregory's brow furrowed. "But who would want to stay in a place like this nowadays? I bet there aren't even any flat screens."

"Some of us old folks yearn for a simpler time," Doug admitted with a chuckle. "Ironically, with this apocalypse we ended up going a bit further back than any of us would have liked."

Luke shook his head. "You know, it's really a miracle this place is still standing at all. How many floods and hurricanes have rolled through here over the years?"

"They definitely don't build 'em like this anymore," Doug agreed.

Victor rolled to a stop and everybody hopped out. James and Luke drew shotguns, taking a defensive stance in case anything

ran out at them. Nadia jumped down next to
the driver's side door, and Victor
motioned to the large building.

"What's the play?" he asked.

Nadia turned to Doug. "You have the
room key?"

He grinned and pulled out a large
battery-powered drill with a twelve-inch
bit, giving it a few buzzes for effect.
"Yes, ma'am."

"All right," she replied. "Second
floor, pick a room. Preferably one that
isn't occupied by the undead."

Doug nodded and led the group inside.
They fanned out and covered him as they
headed up the main staircase, and he chose
the first room on the left. He jiggled the
handle and tapped on the wood, but there
was no movement or sounds from inside. He
drilled through the locking mechanism, and
eventually it popped open, allowing them
entrance into a hotel room that felt like
it had transported them back in time.

Solomon wrinkled his nose as he ran a
hand over the lime green linens that
matched the curtains. "So… interior
decorating wasn't a profession until after
the sixties, then?"

"Hey now, this reminds me of my
childhood," James replied, patting the
bright yellow fridge. "Show some respect."

"Pretty sure this means you forfeit any right to make fun of anything in our childhood," Gregory shot back.

James scratched the back of his head as he took in the pukey green ceramic tile in the bathroom. "Yeah, all right, I'll give you that one."

Nadia tossed her bag down on the bed and began pulling out supplies.

"So, you gonna let us in on your little plan, here?" Victor asked, voice impatient.

The young woman took a deep breath to keep herself from snapping at him. Instead, she took three screwdrivers out of her bag and tossed them down in front of him.

"What in the hell you want me to do with these?" he demanded.

"You and James are gonna go find the four heaviest doors you boys can lift," she instructed. "You're gonna take them off their hinges and bring them back to us. Just make sure they're solid."

Victor crossed his arms, not touching the tools. "What in the hell are you gonna do with doors?"

She smiled and tossed a handful of long leather straps down in front of her. "Are you familiar with the three hundred spartan warriors?"

"Do I look like someone who would?" he scoffed.

"Given how much of a fatass you are, I would have assumed you saw the movie," Nadia shot back, and Luke snorted, quickly covering it up as Victor glared at him.

"Oh, oh!" James cut in. "That was that comic book lookin' flick, wasn't it? Hey, you saw it man, it had that freaky tall bald dude with that nose earring chain thing."

"Oh," Victor replied petulantly. "Was that the one with all them shirtless dudes with spears?"

James nodded. "That's the one."

"Well, hell, girl, I know what you're talkin' about now," Victor declared, but his brow furrowed. "But… I don't know what that means for us."

Nadia sighed. "We're going to use the straps to make shields out of the doors," she explained. "You four are going to act as our spartan guards, while the brothers and I unleash hell on our enemies."

"Uh, Nadia?" Solomon raised his hand. "I don't think we have enough bullets for this."

She pulled out a series of long knives from her bag. "These beds should have long metal supports. We're gonna grab those and Doug is gonna make us some spears."

Victor nodded thoughtfully. "That's just crazy enough to work, girl," he said. "I just hope you don't expect us to take off our shirts to match them movie Spartans."

"If you even *think* about taking off your shirt, just remember I have a gun and I know how to use it," she warned.

James laughed and smacked his friend's belly on his way by. "I think she'd be justified in doing so."

"All right," Victor agreed, finally looking like he was warming up to the situation. "We'll be back soon with those doors."

Doug held out the drill. "Here, don't forget the room key," he said.

As the rest got to work dismantling the bed, Nadia dug through the desk to find a map of the casino floor. She took a deep breath and picked up a pen to plot her assault.

Phil skirted a fresh zombie corpse. "I'll say this, Tony is one hell of a proficient killer," he said.

"Nah, this ain't killing." Marc shook his head. "It's mercy."

"Well, whatever you call it, he's really good at it," Phil replied.

Vernon nodded to the figure ahead jogging back towards them. "Speak of the devil," he said.

"Probably a good sign that he's not waving his arms at us in a panic," Mandy muttered, resting her crowbar on her shoulder.

Vernon inclined his head towards her. "Tell me about it." He stopped to take a breather as Tony caught up with them. "Please tell me you've found something good."

"Maybe," the younger man replied, "but I'm gonna need some help getting to it." He waved for the group to follow him, and headed up the road a bit. There was a private dock bobbing on the river, with a small boat tied to the end.

And a quartet of zombies hanging out between the bank and the vehicle to freedom.

"Normally, if there's just a couple of 'em, I can handle it on my own," Tony said quietly. "But with four, I'd feel more comfortable having some backup."

"Understandable," Vernon replied.

Mandy cracked her neck. "I've got your back. What do you want to do?"

"We don't have to kill 'em, we just need 'em out of the way," Tony explained. "That dock looks wide enough that if one of us is pushing a zombie over, the other should be able to squeeze past and take on the next in line."

Mandy held up her crowbar, and Marc held his out for the young parkour fanatic. He took it and saluted the lady with it.

"I would say ladies first, but I feel like that would be impolite in this situation," he joked.

"Plus, you know I'd smack the hell out of you if you treated me differently because of my gender," Mandy warned.

He winked at her. "So *that's* what it takes to get a smack from you. Good to know!" He turned towards the dock and she shrugged at the distasteful looks on her companions' faces.

"Hey now, I don't judge whatever weird shit y'all are into," she said, putting up her hands. "I would appreciate the same common courtesy." Without waiting for a response, she jogged to catch up to Tony.

They crept along the dock, the zombies focused on the water and not their approaching attackers. Tony went first, hooking the end of the bar around the zombie's neck and flinging it into the water. The thing growled and as the next closest whipped around, Mandy darted forward and skewered it, wrestling it off of the edge of the dock.

The other two zombies closed in, but Tony leapt around her and pushed out with the rounded end of the crowbar, pushing it back against its friend. He shoved forward with all his might, using the first one to topple the second one over into the water. The current easily pulled the grunting corpses away from the dock, sweeping them downstream past the rest of the group standing on the shore.

"And *that's* why we're not swimming across," Marc declared, swiping his hands together is if to wash his hands of the situation.

Phil shook his head as the bobbing zombies disappeared in the waves. "That is deceptively fast," he marveled.

"Come on y'all, let's go check out our new ride," Vernon said, and waved for them to follow.

Mandy sat on the edge of the dock, dangling her bare feet into the cool water. She looked the perfect picture of relaxation, which made Vernon smile until he settled his eyes on a concerned-looking Tony standing over the boat with his hands on his hips.

"What's the good news?" the older man asked.

Tony shook his head and stepped back from the edge of the dock, motioning for the trio to look. Phil gasped and both Marc and Vernon visibly recoiled at the sight. There was a corpse draped over the outboard motor, blade lodged firmly in its torso. The bottom of the boat was a veritable lake of blood, though it didn't seem to have come from the present body.

Phil swallowed back bile. "Is it fixable?" he asked.

"Maybe if I had a week and my workshop," Vernon replied tersely. "That blade is lodged in his ribcage, which means it hit all kinds of bones and cartilage. Even if the blade is still in working order, something I highly doubt, then the engine itself is gonna be all clogged up with blood and guts. This boat is taking us nowhere."

There was a collective sigh of disappointment throughout the group as they processed that information.

"Well, at least we know we're getting close," Marc said, and pointed upriver.

About a thousand yards up was the tip of the Helena River Park Peninsula.

Vernon squared his shoulders. "Let's get going."

CHAPTER NINE

"Holy fuck this thing is heavy," Victor huffed as he dragged the door behind him, arms limp under the leather straps.

Nadia rolled her eyes at the other three men, who seemed to be able to carry their shield-doors with relative ease. She grabbed the bottom strap of Victor's door and lifted it, keeping pace with him.

"There you go, big man," she cooed. "You got a teenage girl helping you now, so it's all gonna be okay."

He snarled as the rest of the group chuckled, and jerked the door out of her grip, picking up his pace. "I was just playing," he snapped. "I got this."

"Mmm hmm," Nadia replied, not buying it but happy he'd ceased his incessant whining.

They continued across the walkway to the casino. The doors were barricaded with chains and a few boards, and Doug leaned his shield against the wall to get to work on the planks with his hammer.

"Okay guys, listen up," the young girl turned to face her team. "This hallway is pretty wide, so when we get in there, I want you to get in the center and form a V. Luke, Victor, I want you two on the right. James and Doug will be on the left. You guys decide who gets to be top and bottom."

James furrowed his brow as he leaned on his horizontal shield. "Wait, we're stacking the doors?"

"Yep," Nadia replied with a firm nod. "Unless you want those things to be able to lean over and bite you."

James put up a hand. "All right, stacking it is."

The last piece of wood clattered to the floor, and Doug noticed that the key was still in the lock that joined the chains on the door handles. "The key's in the lock whenever we're ready," he said. "But, if I might make a suggestion?"

"Of course," Nadia replied, waving for him to continue.

"If the hall is wide, why are we setting up the formation in the center?" he asked. "Wouldn't it be better to put us against the wall so we don't risk zombies getting around us?"

She nodded, accepting his concern. "My fear is if we do that, and then there are too many zombies on the second floor, we could get trapped. Setting it up in the center is a risk, but it at least gives us a chance at a retreat."

"Fair enough," Doug agreed.

Nadia turned to her fellow teens. "Solomon, Gregory, I want you two on either side of the formation," she instructed. "I don't want you to worry about headshots. If those things start coming around, I want you to aim for center mass and hold them at bay. I'll be focused on the frontal assault, but if you got one I want you to call it out." She focused on James and Luke. "And I know you boys have shotguns, but *please* don't use them unless it's a last resort. As soon as that first shot goes off, we're gonna be getting real popular real quick. Everybody good?"

There was a round of nods and affirmations, and the young woman stepped forward to grab the lock. She turned the key and left the padlock hanging on the end of the chain, looped through the left door handle, just in case.

She glanced at her team, at the ready, and then threw open the door. Her four shield-bearers rushed in and got in position. Luke and James slammed theirs on the ground, and Doug and Victor stacked theirs on top, the hinges on the bottoms providing a little resting place to avoid slippage.

The noise attracted the attention of a dozen zombies from down the hall, and they tore towards their prey.

Nadia gripped her spear tightly, surprised at the speed of these runners, having been inside for so long with their muscles in decent condition. "Here they come!" she cried, and the men braced themselves against their doors.

Solomon and Gregory each took up a side, putting on brave faces but both horrified at the sight of these creatures up close for the first time.

"Forty yards," Nadia called, watching over the tops of the barricade to warn the men behind. "Thirty. Twenty. Ten!"

The first corpse collided with the shields, thrashing its arms upwards, the barricade just above armpit height. The men held fast as Nadia lunged forward, lining up her shot and stabbing her makeshift spear directly into the zombie's eye socket.

It hit the floor as four of its brethren trampled it at the same time, the left side of the barricade buckling slightly under the added pressure. James leaned into it, bracing his legs to tighten it up again.

Nadia caught the side of a zombie's head, slicing open its forehead instead of braining it. She grunted and pulled back, lining up a shot before lashing forward again, getting a direct eyeball hit this time.

The remainder of the hallway zombies hit the barricade, and the shield men struggled against the weight. Solomon jumped into action as a zombie flopped around to his side, and caught it in the chest.

"I got one, help me!" he cried, voice high-pitched as he wrestled the flailing corpse to hold it in place. Nadia finished dropping a third corpse in the front and then pivoted, jabbing a direct shot into the trapped creature's temple.

"Gregory, step up!" Nadia cried, banging her spear on the center of the barricade to keep the zombies in the center of the funnel. "Solomon, call out if any are coming around!"

The first young man moved to her side and they began a stabbing spree, carefully lining up shots and shoving their weapons forward, like extreme spearfishing. One by one the creatures collapsed, creating a heap in the middle of the V and releasing the pressure on the men holding it.

Gregory lined up a shot for the last zombie, but Nadia pushed his spear down and waved Solomon to take her spot.

"Why don't you take him out?" she asked. "A little practice never hurt anyone."

He stepped forward and held up his spear, face determined as he lined up his shot. He thrust quickly, the blade sinking into the zombie's forehead like butter. As it fell, the sounds of the dead faded, leaving nothing but the panting of the living.

"I'll give you this, girl," Victor huffed. "That works a whole hell of a lot better than I thought it was going to."

"Full disclosure," Nadia admitted, "that worked a lot better than *I* thought it was going to."

They relaxed, the shield-bearers setting their doors aside. James groaned as he got to his feet, knees cracking.

"You alright there, man?" Luke asked.

"Yeah." James chuckled. "Just fucking old. If there's any ibuprofen and whiskey in town left, I call dibs."

"Pretty sure my dad has a stash," Nadia piped up. "Y'all get us back safely and the first round is on me."

James grinned. "Girl you are speaking my language."

"Good," she replied. "Now come on, let's move up."

Solomon and Gregory shoved a few of the corpses to the side, in case they had to make a hasty retreat, and Nadia led the way to the mouth of the hallway into the main casino atrium. It was a cavernous area, the eight floors above them completely open with balconies so the patrons of the hotel could look down upon the casino floor.

The group scanned the area studiously as they approached the balcony, and didn't see any movement anywhere.

"Let's go take a look at what we're up against," Nadia instructed quietly. "But be on guard." She crept to the railing and peeked over.

The casino floor was blood-soaked, zombies ambling about everywhere. The slot machines were covered in crimson handprints and there wasn't a single card table left green. On the far side, the escalator was out of commission, corpses stuck in different areas of the conveyor stairs.

"Mother of god, look at all of them," Victor breathed.

Luke swallowed hard. "How many to do you think there are?"

"Gotta be a couple hundred at least," James murmured.

"Girl, how in the holy hell are we gonna take all those things out?" Victor hissed.

"That's our spot, right there," Nadia replied, and motioned to the escalators.

"Uh, that's great, but there's still hundreds of fuckin' *zombies*," Victor scoffed.

She took a deep breath, willing herself to stay patient. "And that's a choke point. They are gonna have to file up to us one by one which will give-"

Before she could finish her explanation, a few zombies by the Keno machines noticed her wide-eyed stare and began moaning. The noise alerted more and more of their brethren, causing a chain reaction of groans and snarls throughout the atrium.

"Back to the hotel?" Luke asked shrilly.

Nadia nodded. "Yeah, that's a good idea!"

They turned away from the railing and began to move, but a few dozen zombies poured out of several nearby hallways, blocking their way to the exit.

"Against the railing!" she screamed, and the four shield-bearers leapt into action, creating a V like a snow plow this time, bracing the doors against the railing for support.

The teenagers began to frantically thin the horde as it crashed into the barricade, arms flailing and teeth snapping. The sound of cracking wood echoed, causing everyone's stomachs to drop.

"The doors are breaking!" Victor cried. "You gotta take them out faster!"

Gregory's panicked thrust continued to miss their target, and though Solomon worked a more deliberate approach, he wasn't fast enough. Nadia clenched her jaw as she watched a crack form through the middle of one of the bottom doors.

"Who has buckshot!" she yelled.

Luke raised an arm. "I do!"

She grabbed the strap and lifted it over his head and off of the raised arm, tapping Gregory on the shoulder. "Get on all fours!" she cried. He dropped his spear with a clatter and complied, and she stepped up onto his strong farmer's back. She planted her other leg against the railing, and aimed down into the largest portion of the horde.

She pulled the trigger, the kickback intense in her hands, but her heart leapt with hope as the lead spread out and dropped four zombies at once. She cocked it quickly again, aimed, and fired, taking out another small group. Three more shots, the gun was empty, but the little horde was easily half the size it had been when they got assaulted the first time.

She jumped down to the floor and slipped the strap over her shoulder, picking up her spear again. "How are the doors holding?" she asked.

"Better, I think we're good," Doug replied.

Nadia helped Gregory back to his feet and the two resumed their zombie stabbing,

Solomon joining in slowly but surely. After what felt like forever, the horde was a heap of unmoving corpses.

James and Victor began to stand up, but Nadia put her hands on their shoulders to keep them in position.

"Hang on," she said, and leaned over the barricade. "Come on! Anybody else want a piece of us?!" she yelled into the pile. "Huh? Do ya?" She waited a beat, but there was no movement in the heap. "Fucking thought so." She stepped back, and tapped her shield-bearers on the shoulders.

The men relaxed and adjusted their stance and grips, making sure that the pile didn't fall in on them as they moved the doors. Nadia turned back to the railing and glared down at the casino floor, the zombies down there still focused on the group of fresh meat.

"Let's get back to the hotel room," she finally said. "I think we're gonna need something a bit stronger than those doors if we're going to hold them off at the escalators."

CHAPTER TEN

"We have to be getting close now," Vernon said as yet another trio of corpses crumpled beneath the group's melee weapons. "Seems like every few hundred feet there's another cluster of these things."

Tony led them along the road, staying close this time with the bigger pockets of zombies being a much more difficult threat for just one person.

Mandy peeked through the tall grass along the river. "Guys, check this out," she said, and her companions bunched around her.

"Good," Marc replied quietly, surveying the lazier current of the hundred-yard-thick river. "Looks like we're only half a mile or so away from the turnoff."

"No, not that." Mandy shook her head. "Look further up."

His eyes widened at the sight of a mid-sized boat bobbing in the water, trapped against a fallen tree. "Oh hell yeah! We're in business!" he hissed excitedly.

"Settle down, we still have to get to it," Vernon scolded.

Marc turned to him. "I can swim over and get it, then come pick everybody up."

"No, no, that's too dangerous," Vernon replied, putting his hands up to stop the train of thought dead in its tracks. "We don't know what's over there."

"We don't know what's up ahead, either," Marc insisted, crossing his arms. "No matter what we do, it's going to be dangerous."

Vernon took a deep breath, eyes steel. "We stick to the plan." His tone was flat and commanding, leaving no room for argument. His friend begrudgingly backed down, and followed with less of a spring in his step as the group headed after their leader.

At the corner of a building, Mandy and Phil jogged forward to silently take out two corpses staggering around towards them. As they admired their handiwork, Phil caught movement out of his periphery and grabbed Mandy's arm in an iron grip.

She glanced up and her face went white as a sheet, the two of them retreating quickly to the group, fingers over their lips. Vernon opened his mouth to ask what the problem was, but then closed it again, shimmying up to the corner and peering around for himself.

There were about a hundred zombies congregating around the entrance to the boat park.

He let everyone get a look, and then waved for a retreat back down the road a ways so they could discuss their options.

"Tony, what do you think?" Vernon asked quietly.

He shook his head. "I think that would be a goddamn suicide mission, that's what I think."

"Isn't that what you do, though?" Marc raised an eyebrow.

"No, Marc, it isn't what I do," the younger man huffed. "I know the other part of this town like the back of my hand. There are also only a few zombies here and there when you compare it to that kind of a horde. And god only knows how many of those things are further down."

"So what are our options?" Phil cut in.

Marc stepped back and dropped his gear into the grass with a soft *thud*, unbuttoning his vest.

"What are you doing?" Mandy hissed.

"Well, Tony doesn't want to risk it, so if we're gonna get out of this, then one of us is gonna have to do something," he replied, dropping the vest and unbuckling his belt. "Which is exactly what I'm going to do."

"Hey, don't throw me under the bus like that," Tony muttered. "If it wasn't for me we wouldn't have even made it this far."

"You're right," Marc replied, eyes softening. "That didn't come out the way I wanted it to. You've done more than probably anybody in this group over the last week, myself included. All I'm saying is that if you leading them away isn't an option, then we gotta do something else. So I'm gonna swim over and get that boat."

"Are you sure about this?" Vernon asked, worrying at his bottom lip. "We don't know what's over there."

Marc forced a grin. "Well, I know one way to find out."

"All right," the older man finally agreed. "I wish you luck."

"Hey, if you can get that boat free, don't fire it up," Tony said. "There's enough of a current if you can get it away from that tree that you should be able to make it down to that dock we were at."

"Good call," Marc agreed. "Kinda defeats the purpose of me risking my life if I start that engine up and get you guys swarmed in the process." He dropped his jeans and stood, nodding to the group as he rolled his shoulders, clad in just a beater and boxers.

Phil slung the gear over his shoulders, and Mandy jammed the extra

clothes into what room was left in her
bag.

Marc took a deep breath and inched
into the cold water. "Here goes nothing,"
he muttered to himself, shivering as his
body adjusted to the chill. He shook his
head and then sank right down into the
river, figuring that would be the quickest
way to get used to it.

He used a quiet breaststroke for the
first half of the stretch, trying not to
make any splashing noises, but once he
felt he was out of earshot, broke into a
quick front crawl for the rest of the way.

The group watched with bated breath
as he pulled himself onto the grass on the
other side, eyes darting around as he
rubbed his arms to try to warm up a bit.
Mandy gasped as a zombie tore out of the
tree line, and barely stopped herself from
crying out as Marc took notice, turning to
dive back in the water.

Four more corpses darted out from the
brush, and all five descended on him
before he could make it all the way back
in, tearing at him. Mandy buried her head
in Tony's chest as Marc's blood colored
the water, half of his lifeless body
bobbing in the waves as the zombies had
their feast.

Phil shook his head in disbelief, Vernon clenching his fists in anger at himself for not stopping this.

Tony kissed Mandy on the top of the head and then gently pushed her away from him.

"So, y'all will pick me up at the dock, then?" he asked.

She shook her head vehemently, tears creating rivulets through the dust on her cheeks. "No. No, you can't go out there."

"It's the only choice we've got," he said.

"We can go south and look for another crossing!" she insisted, gripping his arm tightly.

"There's no time," he replied, eyes pleading with her. "Every minute that passes, more of those things are gonna be heading this way. If we don't get out of here now, we might not get out at all." He hooked a finger under her chin, forcing her to look at him. "Don't you worry about me, hon. You just be reading to take care of me once we get back home."

She bit her lip and blinked back her tears, giving him a little smile. "Oh, I'm gonna take care of you good, boy." She let go of his arm and gave it a light punch, and he laughed and winked at her.

"Where do you want us to pick you up?" Vernon asked hoarsely.

Tony shrugged. "That dock is as good a place as any."

"All right," the older man agreed. "We'll wait for you."

Tony nodded and then squared his shoulders, jogging off into the woods in an attempt to flank the horde. He waited until they couldn't see him anymore to let the fear show on his face.

CHAPTER ELEVEN

Doug shook his head as he inspected their shields. "I don't think these things are gonna be much use from here on out," he admitted, leaning the fourth one against the hotel room wall. "I'm honestly amazed they protected us as long as they did."

"They built stuff to last back then," James said.

"Unfortunately I don't think they had zombie apocalypse on the mind when they were crafting those," Doug replied, and to prove his point, snapped off a fairly large chunk of the door. "So, any ideas on how we're going to hold of hundreds of these buggers?"

Victor sighed, sitting up from his flopped position on the discarded mattress. "Why do we have to? Why don't we just move everybody into this hotel? We'd be just fine here."

"Except if a horde shows up," Nadia countered, shaking her head and crossing her arms. "There's a huge open courtyard and two main staircases that lead up to the second floor. We'd be trapped in the rooms to just slowly starve to death. Because once they realize people are in the rooms, they'll never leave. We have to take the casino."

Luke opened his bag and started tossing out packs of beef jerky and bottles of water to everyone. "So, how are we gonna stop these things?"

"Can we just get more doors?" Solomon asked as he tore into his food.

"We'd have the same problem we did with these," Doug replied. "They'd crack under the pressure."

"We could just double 'em up!" Gregory suggested. "Doug can nail 'em together and-"

"Boy, we had trouble moving these one by one, there ain't no way in hell we're gonna be able to do double the weight," Victor cut in.

Solomon clasped Gregory's shoulder in reassurance. "It wasn't a bad idea, bro."

Victor tossed his bottle of water back at Luke and headed over to the fridge with a grunt. The door stuck, and he had to yank hard on it before he could get it open.

"Damn, what kind of shitty hotel is this that they don't have complimentary sodas for the guests?" He slammed the door and then paused when he realized the thing was on wheels. "Well, I'll be a son of a bitch."

"Don't be talking about your momma like that!" James snapped.

Victor shook his head. "Well, she was a bitch, but that's another story. Check this out!" He grabbed the fridge and pulled, rolling it around the kitchenette with ease. "Those things can't climb for shit, right? We slide a couple of these bad boys down each side of the escalator and that's gonna block 'em off pretty good."

"And we keep doors and guards at the top to take out any of them that make it over," Nadia added, eyes lighting up. "Color me surprised, Victor, but that's a damn good idea!"

He puffed his chest out. "Hey now, I ain't as dumb as I look."

"Man, it it way too early in the day to be makin' bold statements like that," Luke drawled, and the room broke into relieved laughter.

"Fuck you, man," Victor said, but there was no venom in his voice and there was a goofy grin on his face. "I mean, you're right, but *damn*, son." He snatched up a few of the screwdrivers and handed one to his companion. "Come on, boy, let's go get us some fresh doors."

CHAPTER TWELVE

Vernon peered around the tree the trio were crouched behind for what felt like the thousandth time. "When Tony gets that path cleared, we're gonna have to move quick," he said quietly. "We don't have to kill everything we come across, just knock 'em to the ground and keep moving. Also, stay as far away from the cars as possible. There could be zombies in them, under them, and everywhere else."

"What about the ones by the boat?" Phil asked.

Vernon sighed. "Those we will have to kill. Including Marc." He swallowed hard. "In fact, he needs to be top priority since he's fresh."

"Can you show a little goddamn respect?" Mandy bristled.

"I'm sorry to sound crass," Vernon replied, "but we don't have time to mourn right now. My only concern is making sure we're on the same page so we can survive this. That's what he took the risk for, after all."

She pursed her lips, crossing her arms in defeat but not replying.

A few shots echoed in the distance, and the horde's groans grew with excitement, shambling off in the direction of downtown.

"Well, that's one way to get their attention," Phil muttered.

Vernon took a deep breath. "Be safe, Tony."

They waited a few minutes for the zombies to mostly clear out, leaving half a dozen or so in their path but very spread out.

Vernon nodded to the last two members of his present group. "Let's move," he instructed, and they darted back out onto the road, moving at a brisk and purposeful pace. It was a few hundred yards to the small driveway that would lead them to the dock, cars back to bag jammed, most with boats on trailers behind them.

Vernon lowered his shoulder and crashed into the first zombie like a linebacker, catching it off-balance and sending the thin creature flying into the side of a car. The rest of the zombies turned at the noise, but had trouble navigating the bumper-to-bumper traffic as the trio blew past it.

They headed down the driveway, turning the corner to the dock, slowing down at the sight of an overturned vehicle in the middle of the road. That had apparently caused the initial jam, and Vernon put up a hand to slow them down.

"Let's go through the woods," he said. "Be ready." They spread out and approached the tree line, footfalls as quiet as could be as they readied their melee weapons. It would only be twenty-five or so yards to the river, but with the dense wood it was difficult to see where the enemies were.

As soon as they hit the brush, Phil stepped on a branch and a loud *snap* caused an uproar of moans from all around them.

Mandy muttered a few choice curses under her breath, and the trio moved into a more triangular formation, covering each other's backs.

"Got one," she declared, and stepped forward, crushing the skull of a hungry corpse to her left. As soon as it fell, she froze in horror at the sight of Marc tearing full speed towards her. She dropped her crowbar, putting her hands out to grasp his bloodied shirt, her fingers intertwining with still-warm organs half torn from his belly.

The momentum of his movement toppled them over, and she stared up at her dead friend's teeth chomping putrid puffs of air into her face.

Then he went limp, and she shoved him off of her, adrenaline spiking through her shock. Phil held out his free hand to help her up, and she gave him a grateful glance before retrieving her own crowbar and turning to back up Vernon.

The older man lined up two shots in succession, taking out two zombies on either side of a gnarled tree. "Come on," he hissed as the corpses slumped into the branches, "let's get to the boat before reinforcements arrive."

The duo tore after him through the trees, this time more concerned with speed than quiet, rushing right down to the waterfront. The boat bobbed against the fallen tree, and Vernon motioned to the back step.

"Get on, and I'll push it out," he instructed. "Find something to maneuver with."

They clambered onto the boat and Mandy found the emergency oars, tossing one to Phil. Vernon jumped down into the water, giving a mighty heave to loosen the boat from the fallen tree's clutches. Phil reached down and grasped his wrist, pulling him up into safety.

The older man hit the deck hard, out of breath, soaked from the chest down, feeling utterly spent. Phil and Mandy went to work immediately, paddling into the center of the river.

"Holy shit," Phil breathed as the straggler zombies emerged from the tree line, screaming from the shore. "We timed that right, didn't we?"

"Hell yeah we did," Mandy agreed.

Phil looked down at the tired man on the floor. "Should we start up the motor?"

"No," Vernon huffed, pulling himself up to a sitting position. "We need to keep it silent until we don't have a choice. Last thing we want to do is draw zombies to the dock and make it more difficult for Tony."

As if on cue, a few gunshots cracked in the distance.

"At least we know he's still kicking," Phil said somberly.

Mandy paddled faster.

CHAPTER THIRTEEN

Tony took a knee in an abandoned storefront, holding his breath as a small horde of zombies wandered down the street past him. He let out a ragged breath as they disappeared around a corner, and pulled the clip from his handgun.

Four bullets left.

"I hope y'all have had enough time to get that boat," he muttered under his breath. "Because I don't know how much longer I can keep this up." He cocked his head and a zombie from the street caught a glimpse of him, turning to bang on the window.

Immediately a throng gathered around the storefront.

"Back on the clock," Tony sighed, and leapt to his feet, giving the group a salute through the glass.

He turned and spotted a busted roof beam leading up to a patch of sunlight above. He grasped the beam, giving it a shake to make sure it was sturdy, and then jumped up onto it, climbing it with relative ease to the roof. He wandered to the front of the store, peering down into the sea of rotting flesh below.

"Yeah, cry all y'all want," he declared. "You ain't gettin' this." He smacked himself on the chest and jutted out his chin, and then turned on his heel. He had to get his jollies somewhere in this hellhole.

He headed to the back of the building, noting that the path directly south was clogged with zombies, only a few feet between each one. The other corner was pretty open, with sparse corpses for a few blocks and then that looked like—he hoped—open space.

"Well." He sighed to himself. "Looks like I'm going that way." He peered down into the alleyway to make sure it was clear before hopping over the edge onto a drainage pipe. All he could do at this point was hope he could get behind the horde, and that he actually had a ride waiting for him.

He hit the asphalt noiselessly and then peered around the corner, spotting a few dozen zombies in the street heading towards the banging at the front of the store. He took a deep breath, and then took off running in the other direction.

Tony fled like the wind, though with speed came noise, and despite being quick as a bullet, some of the zombies turned and reached for him as he passed. He managed to dodge them, but there were several clustering ahead, closing the gaps between them to try to swarm him.

He sprinted as hard as he could, put his shoulder down and slammed into what looked like the thinnest spot in their line. He made it through the other side, but lost his footing. He dove forward as he stumbled, tucking his head into a combat roll to pop back up and spring forward, continuing his run.

The next half block was clear, and he tore up onto a large expanse of grass, dodging the random stragglers grunting about in the foliage. At the other end he turned east, running full tilt for the river.

He skidded to a stop in the middle of the road by the water, eyes darting up and down. "Fuck. How far down was that dock?" he muttered frantically, and then took a chance on heading south. He moved quickly down the road, occasionally peeking through the tall grass at the water to keep an eye out for the boat or the dock.

Around a bend he froze, a few dozen zombies tightly packed in the road about thirty yards away. They turned to face him almost in slow motion, and he could barely move as their gauzy eyes seemed to lock on his heaving chest.

"Shit," he breathed, and then one of the zombies screamed.

Tony turned and faced the river, rolling his shoulders and bouncing from foot to foot. "I swear y'all better fuckin' be there," he grunted, and then sprinted to the bank, throwing himself as far out into the water as he possibly could.

The chilly river was a shock to his system, but his survival instincts took over quickly and he breached the surface, taking in a deep lungful and focusing on getting away from the shore. He backstroked about twenty yards out, hoping that would be enough distance in case any of the zombies decided to take a dip after him.

The current picked him up, and he began to simply tread water, keeping his head up as the river did all the work of carrying him to what he hoped was safety.

Around a sloping bend, he caught sight of a boat ahead, and his heart leapt into his throat. "Mandy!" he screamed. "Vernon! New guy!" He waved a hand and then had to put it back down to keep himself afloat in the rapidly quickening current, but heard cries of excitement from his crew.

They managed to grab the dock on the way by, holding steady as Tony floated down to them. Mandy held out her oar and he gripped it with white hands, Vernon and Phil reaching down to help him into the boat.

Mandy wrapped a blanket around his shivering form, rubbing her hands up and down his arms frantically.

"Glad you made it," Vernon said, voice thick.

Tony smiled, teeth chattering. "M-me too."

Phil knelt down in front of him, raising an amused eyebrow. "You *do* know my name is Phil, right?"

"S-sorry," Tony replied with a trembling shrug. "The hypothermia must have killed that brain cell."

Mandy grabbed the shivering man's face and planted a firm kiss on his pale lips. "I'm going to warm you up proper tonight, cowboy," she promised.

Vernon shook his head. "One step at a time, you two," he warned. "We gotta get to the casino." He headed to the ignition and fired it up, his shoulders feeling a little lighter that they hadn't lost yet another member of their team. He popped the boat into gear and they headed towards their new home.

CHAPTER FOURTEEN

Nadia led the lineup of refrigerators along the wall on the second floor of the atrium, spear first. At every hallway, she leaned around the corner to make sure there were no surprises, and then her team of fridge-pushers followed behind her once the coast was clear.

It was a slow journey to the escalators, but a safe one, and they stopped against the far wall, staying out of sight from the zombies below. The shield doors leaned to their left, having been brought down already on their previous run.

"Okay, Doug, Victor, Solomon, you three take the right side," Nadia said quietly. "The rest of you take the left. As soon as you get the first one down, Victor and Luke grab your doors and plug the hole in case any of them climb over."

"I thought you said these things can't climb?" Victor worried.

She shook her head. "Depending on how the fridges land, they might be able to get by. I'd rather prepare for that possibility, right?"

"Fair enough," the older man replied.

"I'll take center position, call out what I see, and spear any that get too close to the top," she added. The group nodded and slowly wheeled the brightly-colored appliances forward, standing behind them and ready to heave. Nadia backed up where they could see her, and gave a silent countdown with her fingers. As she hit zero, they rushed.

The sound of thumping feet and squealing wheels alerted the zombies on the casino floor, and a few of the closest ones turned and tore up the escalator immediately.

"Push!" Victor screamed. The trio gave the fridge such a great heave that the appliance tumbled end over end, crushing several of the ascending zombies. About two-thirds of the way down, it wedged itself on its side, clogging traffic.

On the left side, however, Gregory, Luke, and James were having a hard time pushing theirs, as the zombies were pushing back on the other side. Nadia leapt up onto the center median, stabbing down into one of their heads.

"Keep pushing!" she barked at the boys, taking down another zombie in its eye socket.

"It's not moving!" Luke cried. "We're caught on something!"

James knelt down and wrapped his fingers under the bottom of the fridge, yanking upwards to flip the whole thing over. The momentum broke the three barrier zombies back, folding them in half, the appliance flipping twice before standing straight up on the escalator landing.

Nadia jumped down to finish off the mangled moaning corpses, and then scrambled back up just as Victor and Luke secured the top of the stairs with shields.

"How we looking, girl?" Victor asked as he ducked down, bracing himself against his door.

Nadia watched intently as the zombies struggled to get around the appliances. One managed to get on top of the one on its side, but leaned too far over and slid back down into the sea of its brethren below.

"I think once we get the next ones down, the zombies aren't gonna be able to get up here," she said firmly.

Doug and Gregory approached with their second fridge, and Victor moved his shield aside to give them access. They shoved it down, and it slammed into the other one on the right side, nestling in to create a nice big barrier.

"Yeah, they ain't getting over that," Victor said, peering over his shield.

Nadia shrugged. "If it's all the same, we're gonna stand guard," she said.

"Fine by me," the older man agreed. "I've had my fill of lugging heavy shit all over the place."

"You want us to get the other one?" Doug asked.

Nadia shook her head. "No, you two head back to town and start rounding up the citizens. Hopefully Mister Kenneth has them packed up."

"But where are we going to house them?" he asked, scratching the back of his head. "We still haven't cleared out the upper floors."

"We'll worry about that later," the young girl replied. "Right now, we need to get them out of that town before unwelcome guests start arriving."

"Fair enough," Doug agreed. "Come on, Gregory, let's roll." He waved for the boy to follow, and they headed back towards the hotel at a brisk walk.

James and Solomon stepped forward on the left side and sent another fridge down the escalator, this one creating a nice sideways barrier against the upright one at the bottom. Luke slid his door back into place, closing up the gate as the duo went back to grab another appliance.

"Miss Nadia," Victor declared, raising his chin. "I believe I owe you an apology. I completely underestimated you."

She grinned at him. "Yes, yes you did." She put a hand on her hip and he shook his head with a chuckle, holding up his hand. She gave it a loud high five.

"Alright, make room," James barked. "We're coming though."

Victor moved his door to let the next fridge roll through. It flipped a few times and smacked back a lone zombie that had managed to wriggle up on top of the other two.

"So… Nadia?" James asked as he took a breather, staring down at their handiwork.

She turned to him. "Yes?"

"What else do we need to do to secure this floor?" he asked.

She shrugged. "This should be it. The upper floors are secure because the emergency exits open towards the stairwell. Those things won't be able to get them open."

"And when the time comes," James continued, "do you have any idea how we're gonna clear those?"

"My plan was to wait on the raiding party to get back from Arkansas and let them handle it," Nadia admitted.

James laughed. "That is a good goddamn plan, lil' lady."

"I thought so too." She nodded.

The older man smacked Solomon on the shoulder. "Come on boy, we got one more of these to do." He motioned to the last fridge behind them.

As the final appliance tumbled down, cementing a barrier that would keep them safe, Nadia couldn't help the flush of pride at how she'd done what her daddy had tasked her with.

CHAPTER FIFTEEN

Vernon killed the engine as the casino loomed into view, spotting a dock in the shadow of the tall building.

"Man, it's crazy how many of those things have already gotten to the bridge," Phil breathed, gaping at the few hundred zombies clustered around the destroyed bridge on the city side.

Tony nodded, finally a bit warmer and drier. "Doesn't look like they've reached our side, yet. Hopefully Nadia and the others got our people to safety."

"If I know my girl," Vernon piped up, "she's probably shootin' craps on the casino floor while everybody gets settled." He forced his voice not to tremble with his bravado. Their last attempted at the casino had been a tragedy, and he feared for his daughter and everyone else.

"If anybody could do it," Mandy said gently, "it's that kid of yours."

Phil leaned out and grabbed the rope from the dock, securing the boat before hopping out to pull it right in. They readied their weapons and followed him, Vernon bringing up the rear and lifting his walkie talkie to his lips.

"Nadia, it's daddy, you there?" he asked.

The group waited at the shoreline as the silence dragged on.

"Nadia, baby, you there?" Vernon tried again.

His heart began to pound in his ears at the lack of response. Panic rose in the back of his throat, and he thought he might scream if-

"Vernon, good to hear your voice, old friend," Mister Kenneth drawled over the radio.

Vernon immediately clicked the talk button. "Is my daughter okay?"

"Why don't you come on up to the casino and see for yourself?" Mister Kenneth sounded nothing but jovial, and the group relaxed, for the first time all day.

"We'll be right up," Vernon replied, throat thick and eyes moist. He brushed past the group, leading them up the path to the casino.

As they came around the outer courtyard, they spotted a few dozen trucks lined up by the retro hotel. Several townsfolk unloaded supplies, leading the less mobile people inside and giving directions.

Tony grinned. "Looks like she did it, Vernon."

Mister Kenneth emerged from the front doors, pausing to direct a few men with big crates, and then waving at the approaching group.

"I'm so glad y'all made it back safely," he bellowed, spreading his arms.

Vernon pressed his lips into a thin line, and the deacon's gaze faltered when he realized they were two short.

"Are they?" he asked simply.

Vernon nodded in silence.

The group took a moment, finally able to just take that moment, and Mister Kenneth clasped his hands together.

"Their sacrifice won't be in vain," he said firmly.

Vernon took a deep breath. "No, it won't."

"Come on," Mister Kenneth urged, "there's still lots to be done."

He led them inside, up and across to the second floor of the casino. People hurried around, putting together makeshift bedding in the hallways. The whole place was abuzz, people everywhere with makeshift spears made out of knives and metal rods.

Mister Kenneth motioned to the railing, and the quartet peered down at the horde below. They milled about, around a mountain of refrigerators, a set of people at the top of the escalators standing behind a barricade made out of doors.

"What do you think, daddy?" Nadia asked from behind them. "Did I do good?"

Vernon whipped around and scooped his daughter into the tightest hug he'd ever given her. "Oh, girl, you did *so* good! How… how did you do all of this?" He pulled back and stared down at her. He was in awe of the young woman she'd become.

"You raised me to think on my feet," she replied with a sly shrug. "Which is exactly what I did."

He blinked back tears. "That's my girl."

"She did real good, Vernon," Mister Kenneth added. "If we take our time, we should be able to clear out the main floor within a few days. They don't have another way up here, and it sounds like we're gonna be stuck here for quite a while."

"We weren't able to bring over the supplies," Phil piped up. "Do we have enough to get by?"

Mister Kenneth grinned. "Don't worry, my new friend. We have about ten days worth of food, and running water. Once we get the floor cleared, there's months of food stocked up down there."

Fresh moans echoed, and the group looked up to see some zombies flailing their arms over the railing above.

"Looks like there's still some work to be done, girl," Vernon declared, feigning disappointment. "What was your plan for them?"

Nadia smiled sweetly at her father. "Wait for y'all to get back and delegate."

He let out a deep belly laugh and pulled her back into a hug. Some things would never change.

END

DEAD AMERICA: THE SECOND WEEK

BOOK 2: HEARTLAND - PT. 2

BY DEREK SLATON

© 2019

CHAPTER ONE

Day Zero +9

The train moseyed at fifteen miles per hour. Bill sat at the helm, keeping watch for any obstructions on the tracks ahead.

"Where in the hell are we, anyway?" Corporal Bretz asked, squinting out the window as the sun peeked over the horizon.

Private Kowalski shrugged. "Somewhere in South Dakota, I think," he replied, peering out himself at the desolate landscape surrounding them.

"Southwest Wyoming, actually, crossed over the line sometime during the night," Bill cut in, stretching his neck from side to side.

Bretz wrinkled his nose. "Well, that explains why there ain't a damn thing out here."

"Right, because South Dakota is known for its wide swaths of civilization." Kowalski snorted.

They all lurched forward, Kowalski nearly barreling into Sergeant Kersey next to him, as the train screeched to a stop.

"Christ, what now?" Bretz grunted, getting to his feet to stand over Bill's shoulder. "I'm getting real tired of clearing the tracks of debris. Can't you just roll through whatever it is?"

The engineer shook his head. "Pretty sure that ain't gonna work this time," he replied, motioning ahead.

The Corporal bent at the waist to look out, and his jaw dropped. About forty yards ahead sat a beastly train, stopped dead on the tracks. From what they could see from their position, it was a long string of cars, and they weren't able to see the end of it.

"What in the hell do we do about this?" Kowalski asked from behind them, letting out a deep whoosh of breath.

Bill pulled a paper map out of the little nook next to his seat, spreading it out on his lap. "If I'm reading this right —and I'd like to think that I am—we're about twenty miles south of Moorcroft, Wyoming. With any luck, they'll have a siding there."

"Siding?" Bretz raised an eyebrow.

"Yeah, think of it like a passing lane on a highway," Bill explained. "If there's one there, I can get this big bitch out of our way and we'll be back on track." He stretched his arms above his head and yawned. "Pun not intended." He grabbed his bottle of water from beside him and took a long swig, then splashed a little on his face.

"When's the last time you slept?" Kowalski asked gently, putting a hand on the older man's shoulder.

"Hell if I know," Bill replied, taking a deep breath. "All I know is that I'm definitely over my allotted hours for the week."

Bretz chuckled. "Don't worry, we ain't gonna report you."

"Well that's good," the engineer said with a toothy grin, "because snitches get stitches."

The Corporal's eyebrows shot up. "You'd actually stab me?"

"If it's any consolation, I'd feel bad about it afterwards." Bill shrugged, and he and Kowalski shared a laugh.

Kersey stood up from his quiet spot on the floor and cracked his knuckles. "Kowalski, Bretz, escort Bill up to the engine of that other train. I'm going to let General Stephens know about our progress."

"On it, Sarge," Bretz replied with a salute.

Kowalski put up a hand. "Wait, how in the hell are we gonna get *both* trains up to that siding, or whatever it's called?"

"You've been watching me to this for two solid days now," Bill said, pushing the throttle back and forth. "I'd hope you can step up and move this thing about ten miles an hour. You think you can handle it?"

The Private straightened, puffing his chest out. "Do I get a conductor hat?"

Bill shook his head and chuckled. He didn't bother correcting the young man that he wasn't a conductor, but an engineer. "Tell you what." He clapped him on the back. "First one I find is all yours."

"Let's do it," Kowalski replied with a firm nod, and the trio exited the cab.

Kersey turned away from the door and slid on a headset, leaning against the wall as he fiddled with the dials on his radio.

"Heartland base, heartland base, come in," he said. "This is Sergeant Kersey." He waited patiently for a few minutes, the silence stretching out on the other end. "Heartland base, please respond."

"This is heartland base," came the reply. "We read you loud and clear, Sergeant Kersey."

"I have a priority alpha update and need to speak to General Stephens immediately."

"Please hold, I will get that set up for you."

Kersey nodded. "I appreciate it." At the click, he turned and stared out the window, watching the horizon illuminating in the morning sun. After all they'd been through, he felt like he would never be able to truly relax, but the sight of the rolling hills with nary a corpse wandering around definitely gave him comfort. The train wasn't the most comfortable thing in the world, but it was nice to have a bit of a break from being on high alert.

There was a series of clicks, and then a familiar voice came through.

"Sergeant Kersey, good to hear from you," General Stephens greeted him. "What's your current location?"

"General, we're currently about twenty miles south of Moorcroft, Wyoming," Kersey replied.

There was an audible sigh on the other end. "You're going to have to pick up the pace."

"I understand," the Sergeant agreed. "Bill has informed me that we should be able to speed up for a while since there's not much between us and Helena, Montana. He's just been playing it extra careful since the last thing we want is to get derailed by debris."

"Level with me. Is he being overly cautious?"

"Well, we're currently stopped because there's an abandoned train on the tracks," Kersey informed him. "So I think he's taking the right amount of precaution."

"I know you boys are doing the best you can," Stephens came back, and his subordinate could almost hear the pursing of his lips. "But I can't stress enough that the pace needs to be quickened as much as possible."

The Sergeant's brow furrowed. "Has… has something happened, sir?"

"The order has come down from the top," the General said. "We have a target for the offensive against the enemy."

"And I'm guessing that since you haven't ordered me to reverse course," Kersey prompted, "that you were right all along?"

Stephens clucked his tongue. "Yes, that's right. We're going to Seattle."

"I always did want to go to the Space Needle," the Sergeant replied wistfully.

The General barked a bitter laugh. "By all accounts, it's still standing," he replied. "Which is more than can be said about some other monuments."

"Is there a timeline for the assault?" Kersey asked.

"At least a week, maybe more," Stephens explained. "Going to depend on how quickly we can move the troops up."

The Sergeant nodded, and then took a deep breath. "And how is that going?"

"Better than expected," the General admitted. "The path you boys cleared for us from North Platte to Salina has given us a staging area pipeline. We have a couple of trains running around the clock shuttling troops and supplies to North Platte. Although we could use another staging area further up the line, if you come across one."

"I think we're going to have to take some time in Moorcroft," Kersey said, "so we'll give it a good once over and see if it'll work."

"Sergeant," Stephens replied sternly, "what did I just say about picking up the pace?"

Kersey sighed heavily, and pinched the bridge of his nose. "Bill hasn't slept in two days, sir, we need to give him at least a few hours to recoup. And besides, it'll give us a chance to restock."

There was a pause.

"Understood," the General finally said. "You boys doing okay on supplies?"

"Food provisions are decent, but could always use more," the Sergeant said.

"And ammo?"

Kersey half-smiled. "Enough to make us dangerous."

Stephens barked a more genuine laugh this time. "I have no doubt."

"I'll be in touch once we head out of Moorcroft this afternoon," Kersey assured him.

"Safe travels, Sergeant," the General replied, and there was a sharp *click* as the line went dead.

Kersey removed the headset and took a deep breath, stretching his arms above his head. He watched the last bit of the sunrise, enjoying the feel of the rays on his face, and the little bit of tranquility that he could grasp in times like these.

CHAPTER TWO

Bretz led the trio, Bill nestled safely in between he and Kowalski, who brought up the rear. The Corporal stayed vigilant, keeping his weapon raised and pausing at each gap between the abandoned train cars to check for threats. His partner's head swiveled this way and that behind them, double-checking that they weren't missing anything.

Everything seemed quiet, but they knew better than to let their guard down.

"So, what do you think this thing is hauling?" Kowalski asked as they walked.

Bill knocked on the side of one of the train cars, resulting in a hollow echo. "I'd be willing to stake my reputation that this one ain't hauling shit." He chuckled and shrugged, pausing at the next gap. "Seriously, though, with cars like this and where we are, it's a pretty safe bet it was hauling coal."

Bretz waved the all-clear for that gap, and they continued up along the next car.

Bill knocked on the side of that one, the same metallic echo replying to him. "Good news for us, is that it looks like it's already dumped its load. We should be able to get this thing moving pretty quickly."

"All right," Bretz declared as he stopped them at the engine cab. "I'll check it out. You two stay here." He motioned to the closed door, and slowly climbed the ladder next to it. As he reached the window, a zombie smashed into it from the inside, startling the Corporal into raising his weapon. He held his fire when his rational brain kicked in, the corpse trapped inside the cab with no way out.

It had a pinstripe shirt on, common to train engineers, but donned a baseball cap so bloodied it was impossible to tell what team it had once been for.

"Hey Kowalski." Bretz tapped on the glass with the barrel of his gun. "I think I found you a hat."

The Private raised an eyebrow in distaste at the crimson-soaked garment. "Yeah, pretty sure I'm gonna pass on that one."

The zombie smacked a rotting hand wetly against the glass, gnawing as it tried to get out to its fresh meal. Bill stepped forward and wrapped his hand around one of the ladder rungs.

"Whoa there," Kowalski huffed, jumping forward to grab the older man's shoulder. "Stay down here until Bretz clears it."

"If it's all the same to you, I'd like to make sure he's aiming in the right direction," Bill replied, gently shaking his arm out of the Private's hand. "Last thing we need is for him to inadvertently hit something vital. Because I get the sense that you boys don't want to push this train by hand."

The Corporal pursed his lips for a moment, and then waved for Bill to climb up. He moved over to give him room, and the engineer flinched when the zombie turned its face hungrily towards him.

"Relax, it can't get you," Bretz assured him.

The engineer shook his head. "It ain't that," he said, swallowing hard. "Just recognize him, that's all."

"Oh," the Corporal replied, blinking a few times. "Sorry to hear that."

Bill waved him off. "Eh. Don't be. He was an asshole." He shook his head, and peered around the familiar rotting head into the cab to get the lay of the land. "All right. You're gonna have to line your shot upwards so that it goes straight through the other window. Think you can do it?"

Bretz nodded. "Gotcha covered." He climbed around the engineer, taking the space back at the window. He tapped on the glass with the barrel again, hoping to lure the corpse into position.

The zombie thrashed about a bit, screams muffled by the door, and then finally pressed itself against the center of the window. The Corporal squeezed the trigger, and the glass *chinked* as the bullet tore through it, the zombie's forehead, and into the window on the far side.

The trio waited a beat to make sure that the crack of the gun hadn't alerted anything else to their presence.

Finally, Bretz unlatched the door, stepping out of the way. "Watch yourself, Kowalski, it's coming your way."

The Private stepped to the side as his partner opened the door and the zombie fell down to the dirt with a wet splat.

"Yum," he muttered with distaste, and then took up a defensive position as his teammates entered the cab.

Bill checked all of the gauges, inspecting all of the panels. He had to wipe blood from a few to see clearly, but for the most part things didn't look broken.

"How are we looking?" Bretz asked.

The engineer nodded. "I think we're ready to roll." He leaned out the door to address Kowalski. "All right, you take it nice and slow. You don't move until we are out of your sight, and for the love of Christ, don't go above ten miles an hour."

"I think I can manage faster than ten miles an hour." Kowalski rolled his eyes.

"Ten. Miles. Per hour," Bill repeated firmly. "You may only have three cars attached, but it's still gonna take you some distance to bring that thing to a stop. You ain't drivin' your minivan today, you're drivin' a *man's* vehicle.

"So do as I say, because if you fuck it up and rear end us, I'm going to have to bust my ass switching engines. And if your stupidity makes me have to do that, I'm gonna have someone bring me a dog leash and I'll drag your ass for the next fifty miles." He raised an eyebrow. "And if you don't believe I can, well, I'd say you can ask ole Eddie Hibbert, but when we got to our next stop the only thing there was an empty leash."

Kowalski stared up at him, wide eyed, and nodded slowly. "Okay," he said hoarsely. "Ten miles per hour it is."

"Good boy," Bill replied. "Now you run along and radio up to us when you're ready to roll."

Bretz watched with bewilderment as Kowalski scurried off down the train tracks, and Bill casually went back to getting the engine fired up. He opened his mouth, closed it again, and then opened it again, then closed it again. He shrugged his shoulders and shook his head with a chuckle.

"All right, I gotta know," he finally said. "That story about Eddie Hibbert… that wasn't true, was it?"

Bill smiled sheepishly. "Well, not entirely."

Bretz let out a deep sigh of relief. They had enough to worry about with the flesh-eating zombies without a psychopathic engineer.

Bill shook his head. "Dog leashes aren't really long enough, so I had to use a horse lead line instead."

CHAPTER THREE

Bill pioneered the train slowly down the track, the weight making it difficult to get up to speed. He also knew that they'd need to stop short of the siding so they could flip the switch, so there was no use trying to go too fast.

His eyelids began to droop. Unfortunately driving a slow train was just as bad as highway hypnosis.

Bretz furrowed his brow as the engineer's shoulders began to slump, and gave him a sharp clap on the back.

"Yeah, yeah, I'm good," Bill mumbled as he straightened back up.

The Corporal shook his head. "The didn't sound very convincing."

"I didn't really buy it either," the engineer replied, voice thick and groggy.

Bretz crossed his arms. "I've got an idea," he said, "why don't you tell me about some of the crazy shit you've seen out here on the rails? Keep your mind active and awake."

"That could work," Bill agreed, giving his cheek a little smack and blinking back sleep. "Before I can started though, I gotta ask—you don't get grossed out easily, do you?"

The Corporal snorted. "I've spent the last week and a half fighting the undead.

If you find a way to outgross that, I'll consider it an achievement."

"Fair enough," the engineer replied. "But don't say I didn't warn you." He leaned forward to recheck one of the gauges, and then took a deep breath. "So, this happened a few years back. I don't remember what run we were on exactly, but it was one of the more scenic trips through the middle of nowhere. It was towards the end of August, so hot as a motherfucker outside.

"We weren't close to any crossings, so we had it opened up to about sixty miles an hour, just screaming down the tracks. Well, we came around this bend to a bridge over a lake and about shit ourselves when we saw forty or so cows just hanging out in the middle."

Bretz laughed. "What the fuck? What were cows doing in the middle of a bridge over a lake?"

"Hell if I know." Bill chuckled and shook his head. "I think the incident report said some car wreck nearby took out a farmer's fence, but at the time we didn't care why there were there, only that they were."

"So what did you do?" The Corporal cocked his head.

Bill clucked his tongue. "The only thing we could do. Kept rolling full steam ahead."

"Why didn't you stop?" Bretz asked, eyes wide.

"We had a full load," the engineer explained, "so even if we hit the emergency brakes we'd still be a mile past the bridge by the time we stopped."

The Corporal winced. "I'm guessing it didn't go well."

"No sir, it did not," Bill assured him. "Those cows exploded like a piñata at a kid's birthday party. And let me assure you, there wasn't any candy inside."

Bretz hissed a sharp breath through his teeth. "Ugh. Cow guts, everywhere."

"Oh, not just cow guts," the engineer replied with a maniacal grin. "Cow body parts, cow shit, cow heads, cow everything, everywhere. The impact was so severe that it coated the entire front of the engine in it. And thanks to the extreme heat, it pretty much fused to it, including the front windows.

"We had to spend the next six hours with our heads sticking out of the portholes just to be able to see where we were going. Now, I don't know if you've ever smelled roadkill up close, but I can guaran-damn-tee that you've never smelled a couple tons of roadkill cooking as you roll down the road."

Bretz blinked at him in shock. "Holy shit," he breathed. "That's horrific."

"I tell you how bad it was, it actually killed my taste for steak for about a month," Bill declared.

The Corporal shook his head. "I can imagine."

"Lucky for you, you really can't," Bill said, and they shared a laugh. He leaned forward and flipped a few switches, and began to pull back gently on the throttle.

Bretz furrowed his brow. "What is it? I don't see the town."

"Found a siding," Bill explained, motioning ahead. "Go on and radio back to Kowalski and get him to slow down."

The Corporal lifted his radio to his mouth and clicked the button. "Hey Kowalski, you copy?"

"Yep, I'm here," came the reply.

"Look man, we're slowing down, so go ahead and throttle back," Bretz said.

There was a crackle before Kowalski replied, "I'll make sure I stop plenty short of you."

As the train came to a full stop, Bill stepped over to the door and heaved it open.

"Whoa, hang on," Bretz gushed, grabbing his gun and running forward. "You aren't going out there."

"Wasn't planning on it," the engineer replied with an amused smile. "I was just being polite and opening the door for you."

Bretz shook his head and ran a hand through his hair. "What do you need me to do?"

"There's going to be a manual switch up there," Bill explained, pointing through the window. "I'll just need you to flip it so that the rail runs off to the left there. Once you do, I'll pick you up and we'll park this big bitch."

The Corporal nodded and leaned out the door, doing a quick sweep of the immediate area. There were no zombies in sight, no movement of any kind anywhere. He hopped down and headed towards the switch post quickly, gun at the ready just in case.

He cocked his head at the track and looked up at the large lever, finally grasping it in one hand and heaving it down. He watched the rails to make doubly sure that the track was all the way over to the switched position. The last thing they needed was a derailment.

Bretz nodded at his handiwork and gave Bill the thumbs up before taking a few steps backwards and waiting for his ride to approach. As Bill cleared the switch, the Corporal changed it back for Kowalski, and then jogged up the train to escort the engineer out to safety.

They waited patiently outside as Kowalski brought up their train. It inched forward at a snail's pace, the Private obviously nervous about parking in exactly the right spot. After a few minutes of this, Bill shook his head and waved Bretz forward, heading towards the door.

The engineer grabbed the still moving train's ladder, and climbed up, opening the door just as the transport finally came to a stop.

"How did I do?" Kowalski asked, excitement evident in his voice.

Bill shrugged as he headed over. "Well, you didn't hit the other train or run me over, so I'll give you a thumbs-up."

"Hey, I'll take it!" the Private exclaimed, holding up a fist of triumph as Bretz joined them in the cab.

"I'll get us back up and rolling," Bill said, taking his place at the helm.

"Moorcroft should be just up ahead," Kersey said, leaning over to peer out the front window. "When you see it, stop short of it. If there is anyone in town, I don't want to make it obvious we're here."

The engineer raised an eyebrow. "I thought we had to keep pushing through."

"You obviously need some sleep," the Sergeant explained, "and I talked to General Stephens. They're ready to start moving troops out and they need a layover spot. I told him we'd check out the town to see if it was viable."

Bill shrugged. "Fair enough. Next stop, Moorcroft."

CHAPTER FOUR

"Bretz, go wake up the others," Kersey instructed as the train came to a stop just outside of town. He surveyed the land before them, a few rundown houses in the distance and a large two-story building by a football field. It looked like there was a nice suburb across from that.

The Corporal saluted and opened the door. "On it."

"Kowalski, get on top of the train and sweep for potential threats," the Sergeant continued, and then turned to give his Private a stern glare. "No shooting. Just looking."

Kowalski feigned a pout. "You're no fun." He slipped out the door, leaving it open so they could hear him if he needed to call down.

Bretz wandered back to the first train car, gun raised in case of any surprises, and unlatched the door. As he slid it open, three sleepy-eyed soldiers squinted at him in the sun, looking for all the world like they needed a snooze button.

"Rise and shine, boys," Bretz barked. "We've got work to do."

Private Buck Johnson dragged himself up into a sitting position, stretching his arms above his head. "For the love of Christ Bretz, it's too damn early in the mornin'."

"Hey, come on now," the Corporal chirped. "I let you sleep in until the sun came up, that's gotta count for something, right?"

Private Ben Mason rubbed his eyes and yawned. "What we got this time?" he asked. "Another car in the road?"

"Oh no, we've already cleared an entire train off of the tracks while you sleeping beauties were off in dreamland," Bretz said.

Private Adam Baker rolled over so that his back was to the sunlight. "So why the fuck are we awake?"

"Because General Stephens needs a rest stop, and we gotta find him one," Bretz jabbed the lazy soldier in the back with the barrel of his gun. "So get your shit and come on." He walked back towards the cab as the three soldiers trudged to their feet.

"Ugh," Baker groaned. "I am not a morning person at *all*."

Johnson laughed as he picked up his rifle and jumped to the ground. "Then why in the hell did you join the army?"

"Eh, my dad was in it," Baker replied with a shrug as he wiped the last of the sleep from his eyes. "When I turned eighteen I figured, why the hell not?"

Mason slid down after him to the ground and brought up the rear. "Good a reason as any, I suppose."

Kowalski peered through the scope of his sniper rifle, getting the lay of the land. "Hey Sarge," he called, and waited for Kersey's head to pop up from the door. "Looks like the streets are pretty clear. Can't tell if there's anybody in the school or not, but ain't nobody outside as far as I can tell. Although I will say based on the look of the houses, we're definitely gonna want to stay near the school."

"How's the town layout look?" Kersey asked.

The Private shook his head. "Hard to tell from here, but looks like the bulk of structures are to the north and west of the school on that side of the tracks," he replied. "It's pretty much open field on this side of things."

The Sergeant nodded. "All right, let's get geared up." He lowered himself down.

Bill climbed out of the cab and locked it up tight, and headed down the ladder before Kowalski joined them on the ground.

"Okay, here's the deal," Kersey declared as the group converged in front of the train. "Bill, Kowalski, and I are going to take up residence in the big house directly across from the school entrance. Bretz, Mason, I want you two to head to the west, see what you can find. Johnson, Baker, I want you to take the north.

"If you see supplies, note it. If you see zombies trapped in structures, note it. If you see anything that might be of value, note it. I need to be able to tell General Stephens if this is a viable stopover point or not, so all info is welcome. Questions?"

Mason raised his hand. "What if we encounter locals?"

"Ignore them as best you can," the Sergeant replied firmly.

Johnson's face erupted into a wolfish grin. "What if it's a pretty young thing?"

Kowalski snorted. "Then she'll ignore *you*."

A chuckle rippled through the group before Kersey put up a hand.

"If you encounter locals, make damn sure they know we're just passing through," he said. "If they ask for help, tell them there's some on the way."

Baker cocked his head. "And if they're hostile?"

"De-escalate if you can," Kersey replied. "And if you can't…" He raised his rifle. "Make them de-escalate."

There was a chorus of somber *yessir*, and then the Sergeant turned to Bill. "How much sleep do you need?" he asked.

"A few hours will get me through," the engineer assured him.

Kersey nodded. "Four hour mission timer, then we rendezvous at the train," he declared. "Any questions?" At the shuffle of shaking heads, he took up an offensive position, facing the town. "All right, let's get it done. Move out."

CHAPTER FIVE

Kersey brought up the back of his trio, Kowalski leading he and Bill towards the school, guns at the ready and ears perked as they went. They jogged across the deserted football field, patches of grass sporting splatters of crimson. They came around the bleachers towards the parking lot, and the Private suddenly took a knee.

The other two quickly followed suit, Kersey shuffling around the engineer. "What is it?" he asked.

Kowalski peered through the scope of his rifle, taking in the school across the lot. There were a handful of cars with no action, but to the right there was an eight-foot fence surrounding a square of asphalt. There were a few dozen corpses trapped inside, milling about aimlessly, bouncing off of the chain link in vain.

"Looks like somebody rounded up some zombies and put 'em in a holding pen," he said quietly.

Bill blinked at his companions. "Why in the *hell* would anybody want to hang on to those things?"

"Right?" the Private agreed with a shrug. "Pretty sure they'd make shitty pets."

Kersey furrowed his brow. "Do you see any movement at the school?"

Kowalski studied every window facing them, but it looked like each one had the shutters closed tight. The doors were closed as well, and he lowered the rifle with a shake of his head.

"If there is anybody in there," he said, "they don't want us to know about it. Everything is shut up tighter than a school girl on prom night."

Bill snorted. "You and I went to very different high schools."

"Let's move quickly and along the edge of the parking lot," Kersey instructed. "Use the cars for cover and try to stay out of sight. If there are people in there, I don't want them to know we're here." He straightened his shoulders at their nods and then waved for them to move out.

Kowalski led them across the lot, staying ducked down as low as they could get. They dashed behind cars, hoping to avoid spooking the trapped zombies as well and alerting anything else nearby to their presence. They flattened themselves against the last sedan on the far end, and the Private did a quick scan through his scope again.

"Sarge, there's a whole lot of nothing between us and the house," he said quietly. "Hell, they even left the front door open for us."

Kersey drew in a sharp breath. "Something feels off about this." His heart skipped a beat, and his two companions seemed to be contemplating their gut feelings as well.

"I can sleep on the train," Bill suggested.

The Sergeant shook his head. "No, whatever it is, we'll deal with it," he insisted. "But we're going to play it safe. Kowalski, when we get to the house, we clear the front room, then you find a corner, put Bill in it, and stay there while I clear the rest of the house. Understood?"

The Private nodded. "Yes, sir."

"Let's move, then," Kersey said, and waved them forward.

They dashed out from behind the sedan and rushed across the street, busting through the open doorway with guns at the ready. The two soldiers swept the front room, finding it quiet and empty.

Kowalski grabbed Bill's arm and jerked him towards a plush chair in the corner, near tossing him into it. The engineer landed on his ass with a soft *oof*, but the soft cushions were a godsend to his sore body. The Private stepped in front of him and took up a defensive stance, shoulders squared and handgun ready.

Kersey moved through the house, easing open door after door and meeting no resistance. The feeling of foreboding and dread that had been gripping his heart began to loosen its hold on his stomach, and finally he returned to the front room, holstering his weapon.

"We're clear," he declared. "Kowalski, secure the front door, and I'll do the same for the back."

Bill raised his hand from the easy chair. "And me?"

"Master bedroom is down the hall," Kersey replied, inclining his head in that direction. "Looks pretty untouched, so you should be comfortable."

The engineer leapt up from the chair, a spring in his step. He'd been excited about the chair, but a comfortable bed? He practically dove into the master bedroom. "If y'all find coffee in the kitchen, for the love of god make sure you save me a cup."

Kersey smiled. "Consider it done."

"Sweet dreams!" Kowalski called in a singsong voice.

Bill shook his head in amusement, rubbing his eyes as he shut the door behind him.

"Man, now that he mentioned it, coffee would be fanfucking*tastic* right about now," the Private said, letting out a wistful breath. He reached over to the light switch on the wall and flicked it, but nothing happened. "Ah. A boy could dream."

Kersey shrugged. "I'll check the cupboard, maybe we'll get lucky."

"Not gonna do much good without power, Sarge," Kowalski said.

The Sergeant shook his head. "The stove is gas, so while the coffee might not be entirely up to your standards, it'll be a drinkable caffeinated beverage."

"Fuck, I'll take it!" The soldier grinned with renewed vigor.

Kersey rummaged through the kitchen cupboards, and in the cabinet next to the fridge he found a massive can of ground coffee. "Found some," he called, and heard a noise of triumph from his comrade. "While I brew it up, I want you to watch that school like a fucking hawk," the Sergeant instructed. "If those shutters so much as rattle in the breeze, I want to know about it."

"Got you covered, Sarge," Kowalski promised from the front door, raising his rifle. He peered through the scope like a hunter awaiting a deer, watching the eerily quiet building.

A few minutes later, Kersey brought a mug of steaming liquid to his companion, taking a seat on a bench beside the front door.

Kowalski took it, eyes lighting up as he took a deep sniff of the dark brew. "Nectar of the gods, this is," he purred, and then took a sip.

Kersey inclined his head towards the door. "How's the school looking?" he asked.

"Whole lotta nothing, Sarge," the Private replied, shaking his head.

"Keep watching," the Sergeant replied, and stood back up, stretching his arms above his head. "I'll keep an eye on the back."

Kowalski shot him a wolfish grin. "You just wanna be near the coffee."

"Benefits of a higher rank, soldier." Kersey winked and strutted back to the kitchen to pour his own cup of wake-up juice.

CHAPTER SIX

On the west side of town, Bretz and Mason strolled along a side street at a steady pace. The train tracks ran parallel to the sidewalk, within dashing distance if they needed to get away from any approaching zombies.

The coast had been clear so far, the quiet sleepy town living up to the reputation Kowalski had declared it as.

"Hey man, can I ask you something?" Mason broke the morning quiet.

Bretz raised an eyebrow. "What's that?"

The Private took a deep breath. "Do you think this whole Seattle invasion thing is a good idea?" He chewed his lip.

"That's the beauty of being a grunt, man," the Corporal replied with a shrug. "They don't ask my opinion on shit like that. They just tell me that it's a good idea and I roll with it."

Mason scoffed. "Oh come on, you gotta have an opinion on it." He waved a hand vaguely in front of him. "They're about to throw us into one of the largest cities in the country to take on hundreds of thousands of those dead things. Doesn't that make you nervous?"

"It's not like we have any other options at our disposal," Bretz replied, his shoulders rising and falling again, though he avoided his companion's gaze. "We can't stay in Kansas, too many fronts to defend. If we don't try something drastic like this, then the country is just going to segment into mini-kingdoms filled with handfuls of survivors. I don't know about you, but I'd rather fight and die for something bigger than myself, rather than simply fight to survive an extra day."

Mason let out a *whoosh* of breath. "I gotcha man, but it's just…" He swallowed hard. "I grew up in the city. Tight quarters with a shitload of people. Everywhere you went, just people, people, people. This… this isn't going to be pleasant."

"All out war isn't typically pleasant," the Corporal said quietly.

They approached a corner and slowed down, taking in their surroundings. There was a diner across the street with a hotel behind it, sharing a parking lot. They swept the area, but there was still no sign of life or un-life. They almost expected to see tumbleweeds bumbling down the road.

"What do you say, bud, you hungry?" Bretz asked, motioning to the diner.

As if on cue, Mason's stomach growled, and he chuckled. "Fuck yeah I am," he said. "If I have to eat one more MRE, I'm gonna puke."

They raised their guns and slowly moved across the street, senses on high alert for any movement. The quiet was almost foreboding, leaving a heaviness in the Corporal's stomach that he was having a hard time shaking. He ducked through the open door of the diner, leading a quick sweep of the old-timey space.

"Clear," he said as he inspected behind the counter.

Mason took in the black and white checkered floor and fifties-style decor. "Clear," he agreed, and followed his companion through the floppy doors into the kitchen.

It was a small space, but the whole back wall was all shelving. They were both disappointed to find that the shelves were completely bare, picked clean. There was not a single thing left, not even the refills for the soda machine.

"Motherfucker," Mason muttered. "Not a single thing left." He kicked at an empty bucket in frustration.

Bretz furrowed his brow in concern. "Yeah it sucks," he agreed, "but we have bigger issues."

"What's that?" the Private asked sullenly, the visions of fresh burgers that had been dancing in his head evaporating into thin air.

The Corporal ran a hand along one of the stainless steel shelves. "Someone cleaned his place out, which means more than likely there are people here," he explained. "An if they're this methodical, they might not like the fact that we're poking around."

Mason took pause, eyes widening with the revelation. "You want me to let Sarge know?"

"Yeah, that's a good idea," Bretz replied, waving for him to go ahead and then heading over to the back office. He half-listened to his companion filling in the Sergeant as he inspected the cramped space, which had curiously also been completely cleared out. Even the desk drawers were wholly empty.

He emerged back into the kitchen and something caught his eye out the window. "Mason, I need to talk to the Sarge," he declared, and the Private blinked at him.

"Hey, hold up a sec," he said into the radio. "Bretz needs to speak to you." He furrowed his brow as he handed over the device, and then followed the Corporal's gaze out the window. "What the fuck…" he breathed, and his jaw dropped.

Across the parking lot, there were eight zombies chained up in front of the main entrance to the hotel. Their makeshift leashes were secured to the metal handicap parking poles, with a few feet of give, giving them enough reach to cover a good semicircle guarding the door.

"We may have an issue," Bretz said into the radio.

There was a crackle and Kersey came back, "What you got, Corporal?"

"Everything seems to have been completely cleaned out," he explained. "Except for the hotel."

"What's in the hotel?" the Sergeant asked.

Bretz shook his head. "Not a fucking clue," he admitted. "Mainly because someone saw fit to have half a dozen zombie guard dogs chained outside the front door."

"Shit," Kersey replied, "somebody caged up a whole mess of them by the school, too."

"Have you seen anybody?" Bretz asked, running a hand through his hair. "Living, that is?"

Another crackle. "Negative," the Sergeant reported, "you?"

"Not a soul," the Corporal said. "So either they've abandoned the town, they're hiding from us… or…"

"They're just waiting to strike," Kersey finished.

Bretz pursed his lips. "How do you want to play it, Sarge?"

There was a moment of silence. "How much more of the city you have to look over?"

"Three, maybe four blocks until we hit the edge," the Corporal replied.

"Do a quick sweep and head for the house," Kersey instructed. "I'll tell Johnson and Baker to do the same. Make sure you enter through the back, and say out of sight of the school. If there is somebody out there waiting to strike us, we're gonna make sure they pay a high price for it."

"On it, Sarge," Bretz replied with a firm nod. "We'll be there soon. Over and out." He tossed the radio back to Mason, who barely caught it in his shock at the weird scene in front of the hotel.

"So fucked up," the Private muttered as he secured the walkie-talkie and raised his weapon once again.

Bretz nodded. "It'll be so nice if one of these days we can just have a leisurely stroll through town without someone or something wanting to kill us," he said wistfully.

Mason couldn't help but laugh. "One day Bretz, one day."

CHAPTER SEVEN

On the north side of town, Johnson
and Baker worked their way through the
kitchen of a middle-class quality house.

"Ugh," Johnson scoffed as he slammed
the last cupboard closed. "Fifth straight
house without a goddamn thing in it."

Baker scrubbed his hands down the
sides of his face. "I'm starting to think
we should just call it and head back to
meet up with Sarge."

"Yeah, I'm with ya, bubba," his
companion agreed. "Let's go hit that
church at the top of the street, and then
we'll head back."

Baker raised an eyebrow. "If all the
houses are empty, why would you think the
church wouldn't be?"

"I dunno," Johnson admitted as he
checked his gun, "just kinda hoping that
they didn't think to raid the communion
wine."

His partner barked a laugh. "You know
bud, you might have a bit of an alcohol
problem."

"Well I'm *trying* to!" Johnson rolled
his eyes. "This apocalypse is making it
pretty damn difficult, though!"

They shared a chuckle and headed
outside. As they turned up the road,
Johnson caught sight of a figure dashing

into the backyard of a neighboring house. He raised his weapon and froze, waiting for any more movement.

"What are we trying to kill, Johnson?" Baker asked, having followed suit with his gun at the ready.

His partner clenched his jaw. "I saw something run down the side of the house."

"Okay," Baker replied, clapping him on the shoulder. "Let's go get it, then."

Johnson nodded. "Follow me up, then flank me when we get to the driveway," he instructed, and they moved in cautious unison towards the driveway. As they hit the asphalt, Baker darted over to the other side, and they headed towards the garage door, which was slightly open. With the large wooden privacy fence enclosing any areas between houses, it was clear where their culprit had gone.

The Privates each took a side of the garage, and Johnson raised his hand, silently counting down from five. As he got to *one*, Baker curled his hand under the bottom of the door and hauled it up, his partner ducking underneath.

Johnson swept the room quickly, on high alert as his companion covered his back, and then honed in on a figure in the back. They were frantically attempting to open the back door, but it seemed it was locked from the outside.

"Hands up!" Johnson demanded, and the figure grunted in frustration, stepping away from the door. "Hands up!" he repeated, and took another step forward.

The figure whirled around, and pressed her back against the wall. She looked to be in her early twenties, her shoulder-length black hair tousled and eyes as wide as saucers. What used to be a simple t-shirt and jeans was in tatters, revealing cuts and bruises all caked with different shades of dried blood.

She raised her hands, the left firmly gripping a small paring knife.

Baker gently put his hand on his partner's rifle, pushing the barrel down.

"What are you doing?" Johnson hissed.

Baker pursed his lips. "Following orders."

It dawned on the spooked Private what his partner was talking about, and he slung his gun over his back. It was their job to de-escalate. That was their mission with the locals.

"It's okay," Baker held his hands out to show that he wasn't a threat. "We're not going to hurt you."

She shook her head, lowering her knife hand to point at them. "You try to take me back there and I swear to Christ I'll leave you with something to remember me by," she warned, voice hoarse and fearful.

"We're not going to take you anywhere," Baker replied gently. "You have my word."

She took a deep, ragged breath, but didn't adjust her stance. "How do I know you're not with Shawn?"

"Girl, we don't know who the fuck Shawn is," Johnson cut in.

Baker nodded. "And there's no way in hell we'd ever hurt someone like you've been hurt." He inclined his head towards her, and she absently reached up to touch her cheek.

The cut there looked fresh, and deep. Her eyes brimmed with tears, glazing over as if she were reliving something horrific. Then the moment was over, and she blinked rapidly, swallowing hard.

"Bullshit," she rasped. "We're in the middle of nowhere fucking Wyoming. You expect me to believe you guys just dropped in from the air?"

Baker shrugged. "We came in from the railroad, actually," he explained, lowering his hands. "We're on a mission to clear a path from Kansas to the Northwest so we can move our troops there."

She sucked in a breath, and seemed to contemplate their story. After what felt like forever, she finally lowered her weapon, shoulders relaxing a little.

"My name's Linda," she said, still eyeing them warily.

"Okay, Linda." Baker offered a smile. "I'm Private Baker, this is Private Johnson."

His companion offered a little salute, and she inclined her head in his direction.

"Well, now that we got the pleasantries out of the way, can you tell us what in the holy hell is going on around here?" Johnson asked, waving a hand around his head and then drawing his finger down his cheek. "Who did that to you?"

She took another deep breath, and let it out shakily before she leaned against the wall, avoiding their gazes. "The zombie outbreak didn't hit us too hard," she began. "We're pretty detached from civilization out here, so by the time people started getting sick, we were getting word of what was happening to them. Families that were healthy packed up and headed to Pine Haven at the reservoir up north, thinking they'd have a better chance at surviving with easy access to water.

"A small group of us decided to stay and defend the town. We went door to door during those first couple of days and secured all the sick people, old and young alike. Made sure they were locked away and couldn't do any harm when they turned. Our hope was that we could secure the town and ride it out until help came.

"But it never did. After the television and the radio went dark, some people started to panic. That's when Shawn happened." She stopped, pursing her lips and blinking rapidly.

Johnson clenched a fist. "Who the fuck is this asshole?"

"He's the town's golden boy," Linda spat the words. "Star football player that got recruited to play for the state university. He did okay for them, but wasn't spectacular, so after college he came back to town where he could be a big fish in a small pond. He holds a lot of sway around here, even ten years after his playing heyday. He was able to get a number of survivors to follow him, promising to lead this town into a new era, but it would only work if they listened to him."

Baker wrinkled his nose. "And people bought that line of bullshit?"

"It's a bunch of small town guys who had their pinnacle moment in life playing high school football," she explained. "It didn't take long for them to do his bidding. And it got dark pretty fucking quickly."

Johnson drew his bottom lip between his teeth. "Is that how you got that?" he asked, jutting out his chin towards her face.

Linda swallowed hard, nodding jerkily. "Shawn realized pretty quickly that a lot of his followers had, um… needs." She looked at the ceiling, blinking a few times and clenching a fist. "Thanks to the way the virus spread, the town's demographics were a bit skewed. Not in their favor. There were five of us who were attacked and locked up in the school.

"They treated us like their own personal harem, having their way with us whenever they wanted. I didn't take too kindly to it, and fought back." She pointed to her face. "I ended up a little worse for wear… but you should see the other guy." A bewildered laugh tore its way out of her throat, and she put a hand to her forehead.

Johnson shook his head, face pale. "How long have you been out here?" he asked.

"Two nights now," she replied.

"This is such a small town," Baker pointed out, "how have you stayed hidden? Have they not been looking for you?"

"Oh, they send out patrols every now and then, especially at night," Linda explained. "But I found the only safe space in town." She raised her chin at their blank expressions. "You want me to show you?"

They both nodded, stepping out of the way. She slipped past them, and they noticed that she was careful not to brush either of them on her way by. They kept a respectful distance from her, not wanting to cramp her personal space, especially given everything she'd been through.

Linda led them straight to the church, where they'd originally been headed, and stopped at the front door. "You may want to cover your noses," she warned, and then turned the knob.

The Privates each raised their arms, hiding in the crooks of their elbows, but as soon as she opened the door they both gagged at the putrid smell that hit them. Baker leaned over the stone siding to dry heave, and Johnson frantically pulled a bandana from his pocket and tied it tightly around his face.

The entire main floor of the church was stacked at least six dead bodies high, all genders and shapes and sizes, some rotting worse than others.

"What in the holy goddamn fucking shit is that?!" Johnson gasped, motioning for her to close the door.

Linda pulled it shut, cutting off the smell, but the soldiers couldn't seem to shake it from their nostrils. "That's Shawn's idea of preserving the town," she said bitterly. "A lot of the people in there were sick, but an awful lot of them weren't. When he realized that no help was coming and we had limited supplies, he decided that if you couldn't be useful, you didn't need to be living."

Baker shook his head slowly, face still green. "And you've been *sleeping* in there?"

"Yep," she replied. "I figured it was the one place his boys wouldn't think to look for me."

"Get on the line with Sarge," Johnson instructed, pulling off his bandana and fanning the air in front of his face. "Tell him we've got trouble."

Baker nodded and pulled out his radio. "On it."

"You have more people with you?" Linda furrowed her brow.

"Yeah, a couple exploring the west side of town, and we got a couple of people at a house across from the high school," Johnson explained.

Her eyes went wide and she lashed out to grab his arm. "The High School?" she demanded. "You gotta get them out, *now*! That's where Shawn is."

"Baker!" Johnson barked, and his companion nodded firmly.

"Sarge! Sarge! Do you read?" he yelled into the radio.

There was a tense moment of silence before a crackle responded from the other end. "Yeah, I'm here, what is it?"

"Hostiles in the school!"

CHAPTER EIGHT

Kersey darted through the house, pulling all the curtains and securing every window. Kowalski ducked down below the front bay window, keeping his scope on the school. He cursed under his breath, and the Sergeant skidded up next to him.

"How are we looking?" he asked.

The Private shook his head. "Got two on the roof that look trigger happy."

"Can you hit 'em?" Kersey raised an eyebrow.

Kowalski shrugged. "Let me see." He pulled the little string on the blinds to raise them a few inches, and there was the instant crackle of gunfire. The window exploded, and the two soldiers ducked, covering their heads as glass rained down on them and the blinds blew clear off of the wall.

The silence afterwards was deafening, and Kersey lowered his arms slowly. "Kowalski?"

"Yeah, I'm good," the Private grunted, "but to answer your earlier question… no, I can't hit 'em at the moment."

"Fuck." Kersey let out a deep *whoosh* of breath. "Keep an eye on 'em." He crawled away from the window and then jumped to his feet in the hallway, heading into the master bedroom. He grabbed Bill's arm and jerked him from the bed onto the floor, startling the poor engineer into sudden wakefulness.

"Wha…?" Bill moaned as his ass hit the hardwood. "You know, you could just wake me up with a light tap. Or breakfast." He yanked his arm out of the Sergeant's grasp.

"We're in trouble," Kersey snapped.

Bill blinked away the sleep, suddenly wide awake as adrenaline began to pump. "What's happening?"

"Pretty sure the school is filled with people who want to murder us," the Sergeant explained.

Bill's eyes flicked to the ceiling for a beat and then back again. "Oh, so just your average Tuesday. Fantastic."

Kersey stayed low as he moved under the window, and then threw open the closet. Other than a few old flowered dresses in the corner and a few old musty filing boxes, there wasn't anything else to be found. He knocked on the interior wood paneling, moving across until there was a hollow echo.

"Over here," he demanded, and then used the butt of his rifle to smash in the paneling. There was a crack and he dug his hand in, prying apart a few chunks of wood to create a space wide enough for a person to squeeze through.

Bill blinked at the dark crawlspace. "You want me in *there*?"

"Yep," Kersey replied with a firm nod. "I need you to stay in there until one of the others comes and gets you out. You don't make a sound. We don't know what these guys are capable of, but based on the panic in Baker's voice, I'm thinking it's bad."

The engineer nodded, and shimmied his way in. "Stay safe, Sarge," he said somberly, and Kersey nodded his thanks before shoving the panels back into place. He pulled the hanging dresses over to cover the worst of the damage, and then closed the closet door.

He hit the deck back in the hallway and crawled up beside Kowalski again. "How we looking?"

"Tried to keep an eye on them, but I don't have much of a view," the Private admitted. "Pretty sure I caught a glimpse of some of them moving around to the back."

The Sergeant nodded and crawled back down the hallway to the kitchen. He peeked up over the sink, and sighed at the sight of six armed men darting across the backyard, taking cover behind the shed and an old car.

"Got company out back," Kersey called quietly.

Kowalski leaned into the hallway. "How bad?"

"Pretty fuckin' bad," the Sergeant replied, noting the assault rifles. "Is going out the front door an option?"

The Private pursed his lips, and then noticed a bike helmet hanging next to the front door. He grabbed it and balanced it on the barrel of his rifle, slowly moving it up into the broken window. As soon as it crossed the threshold, a single shot rang out and the helmet exploded into tiny bits of sparkly plastic and styrofoam.

"Not unless we want to get shot in the face," Kowalski confirmed. "Looks like these boys on the roof can shoot."

Kersey shook his head. "Options?"

"Call in an airstrike?" the Private asked.

The Sergeant couldn't help but laugh. "Don't think General Stephens will approve that."

"Well, we have reinforcements in town," Kowalski pointed out. "Let's just start shooting and get 'em up here."

"Negative." Kersey shook his head. "We do that and we run the risk of Bill getting shot. Keeping him safe is the most important thing."

"Glad you're so concerned about us getting shot," Kowalski retorted.

"Whoever you are!" A loud bellow sounded from the backyard, and the Sergeant peeked to see an athletic-looking blonde man in his early thirties step out from behind the shed. "You are NOT welcome here."

Kersey ducked behind the counter, his back against the cupboards, and shimmied over to the screen door. "Don't mind us," he hollered back, "we're just passing through."

"Passing through?" the man asked. "Who are you?"

"I'm Sergeant John Kersey, and my friend up front is Private Kowalski," Kersey called out. "We're on a field trip to the Northwest, and stopped in your fine town for a bit of R and R."

"Military boys, huh?" the guy asked, sounding thoughtful. "Well, looks like I might have a use for you other than stringing you up and feeding you to my pets."

"While we certainly appreciate not being zombie chow," the Sergeant replied, "we really do need to be on our way."

"Nonsense, there's no rush," the man replied, and the firm tone of his voice left no room for argument. "You boys are going to be my guests for a few days."

Kersey took a deep breath. "That's very generous of you, and we are very appreciative of the offer, but we really do need to get back on the road."

"This is not a request, Sergeant," the man declared. "You boys are the meal ticket we've been waiting on. If y'all are way up in these parts, coming in via a locomotive, that tells me the military values your service. As a result, I have a feeling they're going to be more than happy to guarantee your safety by providing us with some supplies."

The Sergeant couldn't help but laugh. "Your plan is to demand a ransom from the U.S. Military, in a time of war? You haven't really thought that plan through very well, have you?"

"Thanks to their *negligence*," the man growled, "we've been backed into a bit of a corner here. See, we don't have the resources to grow our own food. Our supplier up the road in Gillette has been knocked out, so all we have is what we had left when this shitstorm began, which isn't a whole lot. And despite paying my taxes six out of the last ten years, I'm not seeing any return of that from the government. But with *you* boys here, I figure that's about to change."

Kersey rolled his eyes. "So, what, you want to give us a nice comfy room,

we'll call it in, and then wait for some
food to get delivered? That sound about
right?"

"It does indeed," the man replied,
sounding rather pleased with himself. "So
why don't y'all just come on outta there?
Just leave your guns in the kitchen, and
some of my boys will take real good care
of 'em."

Kowalski crawled into the kitchen,
shaking his head vehemently. The Sergeant
nodded slowly at him, and the Private
scowled his defeat. He shoved his rifle
across the tile floor and slowly got to
his feet.

"All right, we're coming out," Kersey
called, and put down his own gun. He
clapped his companion on the back and they
both raised their hands, moving slowly out
the screen door.

Several men descended on them
quickly, patting them down to secure the
prisoners.

"Which one of you is the Sergeant I
was speaking with?" the blonde man asked,
and Kersey inclined his head. "Well, it's
nice to meet you, Sergeant. My name is
Shawn. Welcome to my humble little town."
He spread his arms and grinned, pausing
for dramatic effect. Then he raised a
finger and waved to his men. "Take them to
detention."

"If I had a dollar for every time I've heard that, I could have retired instead of joining the military," Kowalski muttered.

Shawn chuckled. "You and me both, friend. You and me both." He inspected the soldiers' bound hands, making sure they were secure behind their backs. "Once you have them locked down, send out a patrol for their friends who are wandering around town. Tell the patrol that if they find resistance, they have permission to shoot on sight." He stared down his nose at the soldiers, whose faces had drained of all color. "We have what we need to make a deal."

CHAPTER NINE

Mason growled under his breath as he watched a group of armed men lead their bound Sergeant and Kowalski across the street towards the school.

"Settle down," Bretz said quietly, putting a hand on his partner's shoulder.

"We've gotta go get them," Mason protested, whirling on the Corporal. They'd found an empty house adjacent to the school, having managed to take refuge before the shooters from the roof started scoping out the area. "God only knows what they're gonna do to them."

"They can handle themselves for the time being," Bretz said calmly. "We've gotta figure out a way to get into that house undetected."

The Private threw up his hands. "Why?"

"Because Bill isn't being frog marched to the school," the Corporal explained. "Which means he's either dead and we're truly fucked, or he's still hiding in there. *He's* the priority, unless you've magically learned how trains operate."

Mason sighed his defeat, shoulders slumping. "What's the play?"

"First things first, we need to make sure that Johnson and Baker are still rolling," Bretz said, and unclipped his walkie-talkie from his belt. He changed the frequency and hit the button. "Johnson, Baker, you boys there?"

"Bretz, we got hostiles in town," Baker came back immediately.

"Yeah, thanks for the warning on that one," the Corporal replied, voice thick with sarcasm.

"Sorry, Sarge was priority since he was with Bill," the Private gushed.

"Kidding, man, you did the right thing," Bretz assured him.

"Where you boys at?" Baker asked.

Bretz took a deep breath. "We're a block away from the school. Just saw Sarge and Kowalski being marched over from the house by some armed douchebags."

"Fuck," the Private replied hoarsely. "And Bill?"

"No sight of him," Bretz said. "We're hoping he's still in the house."

"When you get him, y'all make your way north," Baker instructed. "There's a church that's up… hang on, Linda, what road is that?" There was a pause and the Corporal furrowed his brow at the radio, wondering who the hell Linda was. "It's straight up Carver Avenue. Just for the love of god don't go inside. We'll be in the last house on the left."

"Understood," Bretz replied, "we'll see you soon. Over and out." He clipped the walkie talkie back to his belt and then turned to peer out the window again. The guards had retreated into the building, but there were still two snipers hanging out on the roof. Bretz sighed. "Looks like we're going to have to take the long way around to the house."

After ducking in and out of houses throughout the suburb, the two soldiers brought up the rear of the house. They knelt behind an old muscle car, clearly someone's restoration project considering it was up on blocks with the engine half-built.

Bretz peeked up over the trunk, narrowing his eyes to look for movement inside. He saw a few silhouettes moving around past windows, and ducked back down quickly. He drew his knife and turned to Mason, putting a finger to his lips and then drawing it across his throat.

His companion nodded in understanding, drawing his own blade. Bretz peered around the back of the car, watching the windows for an opportunity to move. When he dashed forward, Mason followed close behind, and they silently pressed themselves against either side of the back screen door.

Bretz quietly pulled it open, waving
the Private in and gently closing it
behind them to keep quiet.

"Man, can you believe the nerve of
these soldier boys?" a guy was saying, his
voice echoing from the living room.
"Coming into *our* town thinking they hot
shit?"

"Shawn's gonna learn 'em some
manners, I can tell you that," another guy
replied, sounding closer to the master
bedroom.

Bretz motioned for Mason to head
towards the living room, and then moved
down the hallway towards the other.

The Private moved deliberately and
slowly towards the sound of rummaging, and
saw the back of a guy as he dug around in
the closet on the far end. Mason crept
forward, and as soon as his opponent
backed out of the closet, he lashed
forward and planted the knife directly
into his jugular. The Private clapped a
hand over his victim's mouth, silencing
him as the life drained from his eyes,
body falling limp back into the closet.

Mason clenched his jaw, hating that
the apocalypse had brought out the worst
in humans. He hadn't wanted to stab a man
to death today. But he had a mission.

"Man, I can't find shit back here, if they had somebody else they gone now," the other guy called. "Yo, did you hear me?"

Bretz pressed himself against the wall around the corner from the end of the hallway as the footsteps got closer.

"Goddammit stop slacking off!" The guy stomped into the living room, and froze at the sight of his dead friend. The Corporal took the opportunity to curl his arm around and stab him in the eye, burying the blade deep into his brain. The guard didn't even make a noise as his body slid to the floor.

Mason knelt and stabbed his own corpse in the head to prevent reanimation, shaking his head once again and what he'd had to do.

"Bill?" Bretz called. "Bill, you here, buddy?" He waited a moment and there was no response. "Check everywhere," the Corporal instructed, and they split up, searching every room. Bretz entered the master bedroom, noting the rumpled covers. "Bill?"

Knock, knock.

The Corporal furrowed his brow at the noise, and opened the closet door. "Bill?"

"I'm in the wall." The engineer's voice was muffled.

Bretz moved the set of floral dresses out of the way, noting the damaged wall panel. He dug his fingers into the top corner and tore it down, raising an eyebrow at the sight of his haggard and dusty companion.

"That's one hell of a hiding spot," he said.

Bill coughed. "You're telling me."

"Come on, we've gotta get the hell outta here," Bretz instructed, holding the wood out of the way. "It's not safe."

Bill rolled his eyes. "Yeah, no shit."

CHAPTER TEN

Shawn led the way down a long series of hallways, the two soldiers keeping pace with armed men at their backs. The school was an absolute mess. There was trash everywhere, doors hanging off their hinges, and spray paint covering almost every surface they passed. Lockers, tiled floor, ceiling, a plethora of colors depicting a logo that neither of the prisoners could quite make out.

"Man, nice place y'all got here," Kowalski drawled as he trampled a crumpled-up chip bag. "Do you start the tour off with the best, or do we still have something to look forward to?"

Shawn glanced over his shoulder as he walked. "You have quite the mouth on you."

"Bet you hear that a lot from your buddies in the locker room," the Private shot back with a wolfish grin.

The blonde leader narrowed his eyes and spun around. He inclined his head away from the stairwell and motioned to the hallway to the left. "You know, I think you boys would benefit from having the full tour. Let's go to the gym."

Kersey shook his head as his companion as they followed Shawn to a set of double doors. The muffled sound of heavy bass intensified as he threw them open, shredding metal music blaring and echoing. The graffiti was a lot more concentrated in there, with makeshift barricades and social areas built around out of broken desks and overturned lockers. In the far corner there was a crude cage put together out of chunks of the bleachers, a group of terrified looking people inside.

In the center circle was a thick knotted rope dangling all the way to the floor, surrounded by an eight-foot-tall fence. Out the side was a long narrow fence hallway that led all the way to another set of double doors.

"What kind of host would I be if I didn't show you our main entertainment attraction?" Shawn sneered, and whistled loudly as they reached the center pen. A few guards standing by the prisoners looked at him, and he raised a finger, prompting them to open the pen, aiming their guns at the terrified residents. None of them looked to be in particularly good shape.

"Get your ass out of there." One of the guards reached in to grab a balding middle-aged man that looked about forty pounds overweight.

"No, please!" he begged as he stumbled out of the pen. "Don't make me climb!"

One of the guards kicked him in the ass, sending him sprawling to the floor. "Oh, yeah, there is no way in hell this guy is gonna last long."

"If he makes it to the third knot, I'll be surprised," the first guard replied, grabbing the man's collar and jerking him up to his feet.

The second guard shook his head as he grabbed one of the prisoner's arms and they began to drag him along. "Nah, man, look at the fear in his eyes." He laughed cruelly. "That alone will get him at least to the fourth one."

"Wanna bet?" The first guard grinned.

"Please…" the prisoner moaned.

The second guard shoved him against the fence hallway. "Pack of smokes?" he asked, ignoring the pleas of their victim.

"You're on," the first guard replied, and opened a door into the fence hallway.

"Oh my god, please," the man blubbered, gripping his new prison with panicked eyes. "Please, Shawn, no, don't do this."

The blonde cocked his head, feigning sympathy. "Shh, it's going to be okay," he cooed. "You know the rules. You have the same chance as everybody else."

The man broke down into full on sobs, sagging against the fence. "Please… no…"

"Three minutes," Shawn declared. "That's all you have to do is last three minutes."

"What the fuck, this is sick," Kowalski muttered, and Kersey shook his head, prompting him to stay quiet. The Sergeant knew there was no stopping this at this point.

He raised his hand to a guard at the far end of the fence hallway, and his lackey pulled on a chain, opening the side doors. Moans immediately joined the guitar solo, and the man backed up against the closed gate to the rope pen.

"Oh god, open it, let me in!" he begged. "Open the gate!"

"Now now," Shawn purred as half a dozen zombies ambled into the gym, stumbling down the fence hallway. "Ask nicely."

"Please, please open it!" the man screamed.

The blonde maniac cocked his head, putting a finger to his chin as if in thought. "Well, okay, since you asked nicely," he motioned to another guard. "Open it."

One of the guards who'd made the bet pulled on a chain next to the rope pen, allowing the prisoner access. The rotund man rushed for the rope, and quickly wiped his sweaty hands on his tattered pants. He gripped it tightly, struggling to pull himself up, sweat already beading on his red face as he looked over his shoulder at the corpses a mere ten yards away.

"Come on man!" Kowalski cried, stepping towards the rope pen. "Just take deep breaths and concentrate, you can do it!"

The man turned his panicked eyes on the bound soldier, and then followed his instructions, taking a deep breath and securing his feet on the first knot.

"Fall, you fat sack of shit!" one of the betting guards yelled. "I got smokes riding on this!"

The prisoner grunted and gripped the third knot, pressing his feet together on the second, and managed to reach up to grip the forth in a desperate fist.

"Goddammit!" the guard snapped, and pulled out a pack of smokes from his pocket before tossing it over to his buddy.

"Nice doing business with you," his companion replied with a wink.

The other guard scowled. "Fuck you," he snapped.

"Two minutes," Shawn declared as the zombies reached up to brush the bottoms of the prisoner's shoes.

He shrieked and managed to get up another rung, safely out of reach, but his breathing was heavy and he looked like he was struggling to stay up there.

"Come on buddy, you've got this!" Kowalski urged, desperation in his voice. Kersey remained silent, using the distraction to survey the room. There had to be something they could use to their advantage.

"One more minute," Shawn said in a singsong voice.

Kowalski nodded. "Yeah, that's right buddy, you can do this! One more minute!"

The prisoner looked like he was about to pass out, the exertion of holding himself up there too much for his aging body. Several of the guards began chanting *fall, fall, fall*, but he held on, crying with the effort.

"And, time," Shawn said, sounding almost disappointed, and one of the guards reached up with a long cane to pull the rope against the top of the pen.

As soon as his legs hit the fence, the prisoner let go, and flopped down onto the gym floor with a scream upon impact. Kowalski knelt next to him, wishing he could help him up without his hands tied behind his back.

"That was a hell of a show, buddy," he said emphatically. "You pissed off a lot of people, I'm proud of you."

The man nodded, gasping for air. "Thanks," he rasped.

"Take him back with the others," Shawn snapped, and two guards dragged the poor prisoner back to the pen.

Kowalski got back to his feet as the blonde led his captive Sergeant over.

"You assholes really need to get laid," the Private grunted.

Shawn grinned. "Oh don't worry, we do."

"Guess I wasn't that far off with the mouth comment, then," Kowalski shot back.

"Oh, we have women." The blonde chuckled. "They're just… secure."

The soldiers paled, and exchanged a disgusted look.

"Who knows?" Shawn continued, waving at a set of guards. "If you're nice, I just might let you visit the pleasure palace before turning you over to your superiors."

"No thanks," Kowalski snapped as an armed guy roughly grabbed the back of his collar. "I prefer the old fashioned way of winning the attention of a woman."

"Suit yourself." Shawn shrugged and whirled on his heel, heading back to the stairwell they'd originally been aiming for before their little detour to the gymnasium. At the top of the stairs, there was a classroom door with a padlock on the outside, and a crude sign made out of cardboard that read *Pleasure Palace*. Kowalski clenched his jaw at the sound of sobbing emanating from within.

A few doors down, Shawn stopped and the guards shoved the soldiers into the detention hall.

"It's not much, but this should keep you comfortable while we run down to storage and secure some communication equipment," the blonde explained.

Kersey rolled his eyes. "So, you just expect me to call my S.O. and tell him to bring up some food so we can continue on our mission?"

"Pretty much, yep," Shawn replied with a nod, crossing his arms.

"It's not gonna work," the Sergeant assured him. "But you do you, man."

Shawn chuckled, shaking his head. "We'll see, soldier boy." He slammed the door and there was a dull *thunk* as they locked it from the outside.

Kowalski immediately went over to the window, shoving open the shutter with his shoulder to find bars on the outside. "You would think with this much open real estate they would have thought to build on the right side of the tracks."

"Who knows, maybe they did," Kersey replied with a sigh.

"Sarge, how in the hell did things get fucked up this quickly?" the Private demanded, shoving against the shutters in anger. "I mean it's only been a week and a half and these assholes have gone full on Lord of the Flies cosplay, complete with murder games and a goddamn rape room. Is this what the country *is* now?"

"Nah, these guys aren't the norm," the Sergeant assured him. "Still plenty of good people out there. And once we give them a place to go and a way to get there, we're gonna rebuild."

Kowalski rested his forehead against the dusty window in defeat. "I sure hope your right, Sarge. I sure hope you're right."

CHAPTER ELEVEN

Bretz and Mason tore out of the church, the former dry heaving over his own shoes and the latter full-on spewing over the side railing. Bill stood at the bottom of the steps, not having wanted to go inside to look. He plugged his nose with his hand as the putrid smell wafted from the door opening and slamming shut.

"Told ya that you didn't want to see what was in there," Linda said, arms crossed and foot tapping.

"Yeah, well, be happy that we did, because now we're *pissed*," Bretz said as he straightened up. "We are going to take these motherfuckers out."

"Come on, let's get back to the house," she waved for them to follower her, glancing up and down the street. "It's not safe out in the open, especially now that Shawn knows you're here."

"Agreed," the Corporal said, and motioned for the young woman to lead the way. He ushered Bill ahead of him, he and Mason bringing up the rear.

"Told ya these boys are fucked up," Johnson declared from the couch as the quartet entered the house.

Mason shook his head, still a little green. "Yeah, I could have went without ever seeing that."

"So, what's the play?" Baker piped up, leaning forward in his seat.

Bretz took a deep breath. "Don't know yet. They've got snipers on the roof, and god only knows how many armed men inside. Not sure we're going to have the firepower to take them out."

"Linda, are there any places in town where we might be able to find some ammo?" Baker asked.

She shrugged and crossed her arms again, taking a seat by the door. "Not that I'm aware of. They did a pretty good job of clearing everything out, at least on this side of town."

"What about the hotel by the diner?" Mason snapped his fingers.

Linda's brow furrowed. "What about it?"

"Well, the doors were shut and there were a mess of zombies tied up outside of the place," the Private replied. "It's like they were guarding it."

"It wasn't like that the last time I went by there," she mused. "Granted that was before they…" She swallowed hard. "Before they forced me to be their… guest."

Bretz and Mason shared a puzzled look, but then it dawned on them why she was beaten up in a way that looked a lot more calculated than just random apocalypse scrapes.

The Corporal clenched a fist. "Oh we are *definitely* taking these assholes out," he growled.

"Well, anybody here know how to pick a lock?" Bill asked, flopping down on the couch and wincing as his kneecaps crackled.

Johnson raised his hand. "My sister kept losing her keys, so she'd call me to come let her into the house whenever it'd happen," he piped up. "I kept telling her to just give me a spare, but she said she didn't feel comfortable knowing there was another key out there." There was an awkward moment of silence as the group stared blankly at the Private. "Yeah, I know, she wasn't the brightest bulb in the pumpkin patch," he said, waving them off. "Lucky for her, she was prom queen and had her a sugar daddy by the time she walked across the stage for graduation."

Bretz rubbed his forehead. "For future reference, a simple yes will suffice in the future."

"What can I say?" Johnson grinned. "I'm colorful."

"All right," the Corporal continued, "here's what we're going to do. Mason, I want you to take Bill back to the train. You sit tight and stay quiet. If there's trouble, reverse course. If you don't hear from us by sunrise, y'all continue on without us."

"Yes, sir," Mason confirmed.

Bretz glanced around the rest of the room. "As for all of us, we're going to figure out what's inside that hotel. If they're protecting something that much, it has to be something valuable."

As Mason and Bill stepped towards the front door, the Private grabbed the engineer and jerked him back, dragging him back into the living room. "There's a patrol," he said quickly, and everyone leapt to action.

A trio of armed men approached the house, sawed-off shotguns at the ready.

"Fan out boys," the lead one declared as they entered the front hall, "I'll take the living room. The front door was shut, so somebody's been up here." He parted from his companions and moved slowly up the hallway, heading into the living room. A shit-eating grin broke out over his face at the sight of Linda's slender frame on the couch, with her back turned to him. "Oh, there's that pretty young thing I like so much," he drawled, licking his lips. "You ready to come home to daddy, lil' girl?"

"She's not going anywhere with you," Bretz said, voice ice cold as he pressed the barrel of his assault rifle against the back of the guy's neck. Linda sat up, curling her knees into her chest and watching with wide eyes as the scene in front of her unfolded.

"Boy, you see this here shotgun?" the intruder sneered. "With this spread it's gonna turn you and everything around you into Swiss goddamn cheese."

"That's cute that you think you can do a forty-five degree turn, aim, and fire in the time it would take me to pull the trigger," the Corporal said.

The guy chewed his bottom lip, his trigger finger twitching a bit. "Hey, maybe you're right, maybe I'm right, or you know, maybe we both just need to kick it down a notch, talk about things instead of being in a Mexican standoff."

"Talk about things, huh?" Bretz asked, rolling his eyes. "Why so chatty all of a sudden? Is it because you think your boys are gonna come save the day?" As if on cue, the other two intruders appeared in the other doorway.

They entered, flanked by soldiers, who kicked their knees out from behind them.

"So, here's what's gonna happen," Bretz continued. "You move, I'm gonna shoot you. My friend here is gonna come grab that shotgun, and you're gonna keep playing statue, we clear?"

His prisoner sighed. "Yeah, we're clear."

Johnson stepped forward and grabbed the shotgun, shoving it into the side pocket of his pants. Bretz moved around so he could look at him squarely.

"You did the smart thing, there," the Corporal said, cocking his head. "Now, I have a few-"

Linda leapt up from the couch and kicked the prisoner between his legs.

He whimpered and dropped like a stone, rolling back and forth on his back. "Oh, you fuckin' whore," he groaned.

"Well. I guess I'll ask my questions in a minute," Bretz said, and took a step back to watch the show.

Linda's eyes went maniacally wide, and leaned over to undo the guy's belt. She tore open the gaudy American flag buckle and ripped the leather from the loops and then straightened up, kicking him in the thigh.

"Roll over, George," she demanded, but he continued to writhe in pain on the floor. "Roll the fuck over, fat man!"

He still didn't comply, and she brought her foot down hard on his crotch. Even through his protective hands, the force made him retch with pain.

"Stop, please stop," he gasped.

She stared down at him menacingly. "Roll. Over."

She raised her foot again and he complied, rolling onto his stomach. Linda leaned over and looped the belt around his neck, pulling it tight through the buckle to create a tight leash. He gagged as she jerked on it, gasping for air.

She lowered her mouth next to his ear. "You're my bitch now," she growled, and then loosened the noose a bit to allow George a breath. She handed the belt over to Bretz. "Hold this for a minute, please."

The Corporal took the belt in hand, staring down with amusement at his new prisoner.

Linda walked over to the other two on their knees, leaning over to study each of their faces. She squinted as they sweat under her scrutiny, and finally she straightened up.

"Kill the one on the left," she demanded. "The one on the right did us no harm."

"Oh god, please, no!" the one on the left begged, shaking his head frantically. "I'm so sorry for what I did to you. Please, I don't want to die."

Johnson pursed his lips and looked to Bretz with a questioning gaze. The

Corporal gave a little shrug, and his Private swallowed hard.

"Ma'am." Johnson cleared his throat. "I don't know if I feel comfortable-"

"Do it," Linda snapped, "or I'll do it my goddamn self."

The prisoner burst into tears, honking sobs like a terrified goose. Johnson ran a hand through his hair, and the woman snarled, reaching over to grab the knife from his belt. He stared, dumbfounded, as she whipped around and got down on one knee, pressing the blade against her offender's throat.

"You know, I could make this nice and easy for you," Linda growled. "Jab this into the right spot on your soft little neck, and bleed you out *real* quick. Just a tiny little prick…" She dropped the blade and tapped the flat of it against the front of his crotch. "Kind of like you." She cocked her head, returning the knife back up to his cheek. "But I think back to the times you visited me. How you didn't make it nice *or* easy for me. And when it was quick, you took your frustrations out on *me*." She reached up with her free hand and touched the still fresh wound on her cheek, baring her teeth in a soundless hiss. "I think turnabout is fair play, don't you?"

He shook his head, still sobbing. "No, please, no, I'm so sorry, I'm-"

She plunged the knife into his belly, right to the hilt, and he made a noise somewhere between a gag and a gasp. Blood gurgled in his throat and he groaned as she twisted the blade, crimson running out over his chin.

"I'd love to keep this up and make you suffer for as long as humanly possible," Linda said, jerking the knife back and forth in his soft flesh. "But my new friends and I have shit that needs to get done." She tore the blade hard to the right, slicing open his guts completely.

The body flopped wetly to the floor, innards spilling out onto the carpet, twitching a few times as the life drained out of him.

Linda wiped the blade clean on the back of his shirt and then stood, staring down her nose at the dying man. She spit on him, saliva hitting him square in the forehead, and then turned to Johnson, holding out the knife.

"Thank you," she said.

He shook his head, and unclipped the sheath from his belt. "Girl, you know how to use that thing better than I do. Why don't you hang on to it?"

"Much appreciated," she replied, and graciously accepted the gift, clipping it to the waistband of her pants. She turned to the other prisoner, still on his knees, pale and fearful at the sight of his comrade's innards all over the floor. "Don't worry," Linda continued, "I'm not gonna hurt you. I remember the only time these assholes brought you to us. They tried to force you to partake, and you didn't. You actually had the balls to stand up to them and do what was right."

"I'm so sorry," he blurted, quiet tears spilling down his cheeks as he stared up at her. "I wish I could have done more… I wish I could have stopped them…"

"If you had tried, you would have ended up dead," she cut in, shaking her head. "I'm not angry at you. However… I do have a question for you, and it's a real simple one." She paused for effect, bending to stare down at him. "Are you with Shawn? Or are you with the rest of us?"

"You get Shawn out of the way and I'll do whatever you want me to," he said immediately.

She nodded, straightening back up. "Good. Now, I don't want you to have any conflicting emotions, so we're gonna leave you tied up here nice and snug while we go take care of the Shawn problem at the school. You okay with that?" She waited for his nod, and then cocked her head. "I don't remember your name."

"Charlie," he replied, just as quickly as before.

She smiled. "Okay, that's good, Charlie. That's good. We'll talk soon." She turned away from him, and Baker and Johnson took him off to the back room to get him secured and comfortable.

Linda stepped over to Bretz, and took George's leash. He was much more terrified looking now, unsure of what his fate was going to be at the hands of the avenging angel. She jerked on the belt, causing him to gag and heel next to her.

"Mason, get Bill to the train and lay low," Bretz instructed after handing over the prisoner.

Linda motioned back towards the church. "There's an old four-wheeler path that starts about a hundred yards north of the church," she explained. "It runs east, then south towards the tracks. It's a bit of a hike, but you shouldn't have to worry about any patrols."

"You up for a hike, Bill?" Mason asked, rocking back and forth on his heels.

"Next time I say I can sleep on the train," Bill replied from his vantage point leaning in the doorway, "y'all do me a favor and let me sleep on the goddamn train. I was supposed to be getting some rest and now I'm going on a fuckin' nature hike."

Linda shook her head and leaned over to the Corporal. "He's a surly one, isn't he?"

"You have no idea," Bretz replied.

"I heard that!" Bill called over his shoulder as he headed out with Mason, and there were chuckles all around.

Bretz leaned down and pulled out a zip tie, securing George's hands behind his back. Linda yanked hard, choking him until he got to his feet, face red from lack of oxygen.

"Well, what do you say we take the new dog for a walk and head down to the hotel?" she asked. "See if we can't find out what's in there."

The Corporal bowed at the waist and motioned to the door with a flourish. "Ladies first."

CHAPTER TWELVE

"Goddamn girl, ease up, I'm moving," George gasped as Linda practically dragged him along the street, leading the trio of soldiers.

She narrowed her eyes and tightened the noose briefly to remind him who was in charge. "You'll speak when spoken to," she snapped. She let off a little bit and he coughed.

They reached the parking lot of the hotel, leaving a wide berth from the eight chained zombies in case one of them got loose. They'd been secured with four in the front and four on shorter chains in the back, giving a double line of defense.

Bretz furrowed his brow. "Well. Ideas?"

Baker scratched the side of his face and walked across to one side of the little horde, stepping closer than his group. He jumped up and down and they quickly moved over to him, grabbing at the end of their tethers.

"Is there enough room to sneak through behind them now?" the Private asked.

Johnson snorted. "You? If you're up for it. Me? Not a chance in fucking hell." He put up his hands. "I don't want to be zombie chow."

"We could just shoot 'em." Baker shrugged.

"No, we've gotta do this quiet," Bretz said. "I don't want to get into a firefight with these assholes until it's on our terms."

Johnson sighed. "So, you want to knife 'em?"

"I don't really see any other way," the Corporal confirmed with a shrug. "Do you?"

Baker pulled out his knife and stepped forward, trying to line up a shot to deliver a blow to a nearby corpse head. As he inched forward, one of the zombies knocked over another and snapped at him.

He leapt back, stumbling and ending up on his ass on the pavement. "Fuck!"

"You all right?" Johnson asked.

"Yeah," Baker assured him as he got back to his feet, "but that is not a viable plan. Way too fucking risky."

Johnson motioned over his shoulder. "Maybe we can find something useful in the diner?" he suggested. "Metal post or something?"

"Mason and I were in there earlier," Bretz put in, shaking his head. "It was gutted."

Baker sighed. "Do we *really* need to get in there?"

"They're protecting it for a reason," Johnson insisted.

Linda rolled her eyes at the back and forth, and gave George a shove forward. It dawned on him what she was doing, and he dug in his heels, pushing back against her.

"No, fuck no," he begged.

She grunted with the effort of pushing against his large frame. "Hard way it is, then," she warned, and reached down to grab his balls in her tiny fist. He shrieked and she used the distraction to shove him closer to the horde.

"Don't! You fucking bitch, *don't!*" George screamed, and the zombies perked right up, ready for their meal.

Linda gave him one last hard shove and he staggered into the group of corpses. He tried to roll away but they immediately tore into his legs, dragging him down to the asphalt.

The soldiers stared in shock, watching the screaming man struggle under gnawing teeth.

"Are you waiting for an invitation?" Linda snapped.

Bretz and Baker shook their heads and leapt into action, quickly stabbing the backs of as many heads as possible as they fed on their fresh meat. The whole ordeal took less than a minute, all of the zombies dispatched while George moaned and bled out on the asphalt.

Linda stepped forward, staring down at him with icy eyes.

"These guys really hurt you, didn't they?" Bretz asked quietly.

She jutted out her chin. "You have no idea." She pulled out her new knife and plunged it down into George's forehead, preventing reanimation and helping to get her revenge all in one fell swoop. She turned away to clean the blade and sheath it, taking a deep breath to steady her racing heartbeat.

"Johnson, you're up," the Corporal said, stepping aside.

Johnson nodded and clambered over the pile of bodies, making quick work of picking the lock. The door opened a hair and he stepped back, readying his gun as Bretz began a silent countdown to breach the door.

The Corporal reached zero and burst inside, flanked by the other two soldiers, Linda bringing up the rear. There was no noise inside, but it was very dark.

"Baker, hit the blinds," Bretz said, "let's see what we have."

The Private felt along the wall and opened the blinds, letting light bathe the hotel lobby. The quartet blinked at the piles and piles of blankets and clothing filling the place, with only a few narrow pathways heading through.

"Christ," Johnson breathed. "It's hoarders, Wyoming edition."

Bretz shook his head, reaching over to flip a button-down shirt over in his hand. "This explains why everywhere we went, we couldn't find anything of value."

"What's it all doing here, though?" Baker asked with a shrug. "I thought they were up at the high school?"

Linda took a deep breath. "Shawn is a bit of a control freak, so this isn't a surprise," she explained. "This is probably his rainy day supply cache. So when things get low, he can just off everybody and live comfortably for a while."

What a charmer," Johnson muttered. "Bet he's fun at parties."

"Well, if I get my way he's going to be the guest of honor at the party *I* throw," Linda said, selecting a red fitted t-shirt from one of the piles to replace her tattered tank top.

"Pretty sure if we dig, we'll find some party favors in here," Johnson suggested.

Bretz nodded. "Look around for anything useful. Guns, ammo. A hunting rifle would go a long way towards taking out those snipers on the roof."

They spread out, digging through the piles of fabric.

Baker lifted a cast iron pan from beneath a pair of khakis, shaking his head. "Man, you'd think in a rural town like this, there would be plenty of hunters."

"Lots of elderly people here," Linda explained as she emerged from behind a wall of junk wearing her new shirt. "So probably not as many hunters as you'd think. The group here in town would go up to their cabins by the reservoir up north most weekends, so they probably kept the bulk of the weapons there."

Johnson wrinkled his nose. "Either that, or there's a goddamn arsenal at the high school."

"That too," she admitted.

Bretz emerged from one of the back offices. "Anybody got anything?" he asked, and received a round of disappointed shaking heads.

"So, now what?" Baker asked.

The Corporal pursed his lips, contemplating, and then suddenly his eyes lit up, a sly smile curling his mouth.

"Oh hell," Johnson barked. "Last time he had a look like that, I ended up getting chased through some Middle Eastern shitberg by a bunch of pissed off locals."

Bretz ignored him. "Linda, how bright is Shawn?"

"Um, the highlight of his life is catching a ball," she scoffed. "You do the math."

The Corporal turned to Baker. "When you were getting supplies back at basecamp, did you pack any C4?"

Johnson threw up his hands. "And there it is."

"Wait, wait," Linda cut in. "Like explosive C4? You do realize I have to live in this town after we take Shawn out, don't you?"

Bretz raised a finger in the universal sign of holding on. "Just, bear with me, please," he said, and turned back to Baker.

The Private nodded. "Yeah, got C4, grenades, pretty sure I picked up a grenade launcher or two."

"Christ, did you pick up Stingers, too?" Johnson blurted.

Baker shook his head. "No, but I did look."

"Perfect," Bretz said, clapping his companion on the shoulder. "I want you to go back to the train and grab some C4."

"Hell, pick up the grenades, too," Johnson added. "Could come in handy if we get pinned down."

Bretz nodded. "Yes, good idea. Johnson, I want you across the street on the roof to keep watch. If a patrol comes this way, take them out however you can. Once they see the pile of zombies outside, they're going to know we're here."

The soldiers saluted and headed off to follow their orders, fist bumping as they parted ways in the doorway.

Linda tapped her foot, crossing her arms. "So, you want to tell me why you're going to blow up my town?"

"Don't worry, the only thing I intend on blowing up is the abandoned diner in the parking lot," Bretz assured her.

Her brow furrowed. "What good is that going to do?"

"Well, we don't have the numbers or the weaponry to do a full scale assault on the school," the Corporal explained. "Our sniper is a prisoner there, which means we can't take down their shooters on the roof. We'd be cut down before we could even get to the front door. So we're going to have to bait Shawn if we want to take him out.

"If he thinks we're going to blow up his stockpile, he'll negotiate with us for our buddies. That gets us close enough to the door to give us a fighting chance. If we can get inside, we'll cause a hell of a ruckus."

Linda drew in a deep breath. "Okay," she finally said. "I trust you."

Bretz pulled out his handgun and gave it a quick check. "You know how to use one of these?" he asked.

"Only fired one a couple of times," she admitted. "I wasn't very good at it."

"Well, they don't know that," he replied, and held the gun out to her. "If they see you pointing it in their direction, I guarantee they'll take cover. Could be useful."

She took it gently, and then offered him a smile. "Thank you. For helping me."

"It's why I became a soldier," Bretz replied. "To help people." He paused, feeling like he might have put a reassuring hand on her shoulder if not for her recent apocalypse experiences. Instead, he returned her smile. "Don't worry. We'll get your town back."

CHAPTER THIRTEEN

Kowalski tossed another pencil up into the ceiling, wrinkling his nose as it bounced off and clattered to the floor. "Oh, this takes me back."

"Spent a lot of time in detention, did you?" Kersey asked, spinning the teacher's desk chair around a few times before turning towards his companion. They'd found a nail file in one of the desks and had taken care of their plastic bonds. The file had broken, but at least they had their hands to occupy themselves.

"Yeah, my sophomore year I was a little hell raiser," Kowalski admitted. "Pretty sure I spent more time in here than in actual classes." He threw another pencil and it stuck fast, and he fist-pumped the air with a grunt of victory.

Kersey raised an eyebrow, shaking his head.

"What?" the Private asked. "It's the little things, Sarge."

Kersey chuckled, but the moment was short lived at the rattle of the padlock on the outside of the door.

"We have to buy as much time as we possibly can for Bretz to figure out how to get us out," the Sergeant hissed quietly.

Kowalski nodded. "I can handle that."

"Just don't piss them off too much," Kersey warned. "They need us alive but I don't think they'd have any issues smacking us around."

Kowalski just winked at his superior, and they both turned to the door as it opened. One of Shawn's lackeys rolled in a metal cart with some giant ancient communication equipment that looked like some relic out of a museum.

Shawn strolled in, standing next to it, and waved a hand as if to present them with their prize. The soldiers looked at each other and then back at the cart and then burst out laughing.

"What in the hell do you want us to do with this thing?" Kowalski gasped, wiping fake tears from his eyes. "Call in an air strike over Berlin?"

"It's old ham radio tech that one of our townsfolk upgraded to high frequency," Shawn explained, crossing his arms. "So if you wanted to, you could call Berlin, not just order an airstrike on them."

"Okay, fine, bring it over and let me see what I can do," Kersey said, and rolled around the teacher's desk to have a look at the machine.

The lackey rolled the cart over and plugged the radio into the large battery on the bottom. It whirred to life, giving off a low hum.

"Not often you can hear the radiation coursing through the air," Kowalski quipped, tossing another pencil at the ceiling and missing spectacularly.

Kersey leaned over and began tuning the dials. "So what do you think, Private? Who should we get in touch with?"

"You need to get in touch with the decision maker," Shawn declared.

The Sergeant rolled his eyes. "That's great and all, but in case you haven't noticed, there's a bit of a nationwide issue going on. Dead rising, and all?" He waved his hand over his head. "So, if you want your ransom for us, we're going to have to contact who we think we can get a hold of. They can run it up the chain of command from there."

The blonde huffed, but his shoulders relaxed.

"I don't know." Kowalski leaned back in the desk chair he perched in. "What do you think? General Bretz?"

Kersey raised an eyebrow. "General Bretz? I wasn't aware he had gotten a promotion."

"Yeah, field promotion," the Private replied, nodding his head in seriousness. "Very deserving if I say so myself."

"Okay," the Sergeant agreed, stifling a smile. "General Bretz it is." He dialed the radio to their emergency frequency, and reduced the radius to just a few miles. He lifted the mouthpiece to his lips. "Calling General Bretz," he said. "This is Sergeant Kersey, over." He paused and waited, but there was just silence. "General Bretz, this is Sergeant Kersey, do you copy?"

"Where the fuck is he?" Shawn demanded, eyes narrowed with annoyance.

Kersey waved him off. "Give him a minute, he's a busy man."

"He'd better fucking hurry," Shawn muttered, cracking his knuckles.

"Sergeant Kersey, this is General Bretz," the reply crackled over the old radio. "Status report."

"Sir, we are currently at the high school in Moorcroft, Wyoming," Kersey explained calmly.

In his best Stephens impression, Bretz replied, "What in the hell are you doing there?"

"Well General, we stopped for supplies and ended up getting a little more than we bargained for," Kersey said.

"Explain yourself, Sergeant!" Bretz exclaimed, and Kowalski coughed to stifle the laughter threatening to bubble up in his throat at how much fun it sounded like the Corporal was having.

"We've been apprehended by the town's leader, a man named Shawn," Kersey explained. "He wishes to trade our freedom for supplies. Food, water, the basics."

Bretz clucked his tongue. "So, just so I understand the situation, you failed your mission by getting captured by a bunch of civilians who have decided to wage war against the United States of America?"

"What?!" Shawn blurted, eyes going wide. "No, we're not waging war, we just want food!"

Kersey held up his hand to signal him to quiet down. "General, I don't know if they've declared war on the nation…" he began.

"Bullshit!" Bretz barked. "They kidnapped U.S. soldiers for their own selfish gains! And as you know Sergeant, we don't negotiate with hostile forces, be they foreign or domestic. Since you have sensitive information that could be used against us, I'm afraid we're going to have to Ripley this situation."

Shawn gripped his hair in both hands. "Ripley the situation?!" he cried. "What the hell does that mean?"

"It means they're going to nuke the site from orbit," Kersey said.

The blonde's mouth opened and closed like a fish. "What?! They're going to *nuke* us?!"

"It's just a figure of speech," Kowalski cut in, struggling not to look extremely amused at the situation unfolding before him. "It's more than likely just a barrage of tomahawk missiles."

"Well, General," Kersey continued into the radio, "what can I say? We had a good run. Had to come to an end at some point."

Shawn dove forward and snatched the mouthpiece from the Sergeant's hand. "Oh, General, don't blow us up!" he begged. "Please, we're sorry, we aren't waging war on the USA."

After a few tense moments of silence, Bretz suddenly burst into laughter. "Oh, stop shitting yourself man, we're just fucking with you."

Shawn's eyes widened in realization and as Kowalski dissolved into laughter, his eyes narrowed with menace. "Do you think this is a fucking game?" he growled into the radio. "I will straight up murder your men."

"No you won't," Bretz replied confidently.

"Oh really?" Shawn sneered. "Strong words from someone who doesn't have any cards to play."

"Why don't you come take a look out the window?" the Corporal asked.

Shawn shook his head. "Hell no, I'm not stupid."

"Jury's still out on that one," Kowalski quipped.

"Relax, Shawn," Bretz came through. "Nobody is gonna take a shot at you. We're not going to risk our men's lives like that. Especially when we know you're going to waltz them out the front door for us."

The blonde chuckled, but it sounded forced. "That would be one hell of a trick there, General."

"It's Corporal, actually," Bretz replied, amusement in his tone, "but the promotion was nice while it lasted."

"General, Corporal, I don't really give a fuck!" Shawn snarled. "You have ten seconds to give me a reason not to kill these two and send every man I have out to hunt you the fuck down!"

Bretz sobered quickly. "Find a window and look to the west," he demanded.

Shawn grunted and waved at one of the guards to open the shutters on the west side of the room. "What am I looking for?" he asked.

"We found your hotel stash," Bretz replied, and then an explosion rocked the building.

A fireball rocketed into the sky, from the direction of the hotel, and as Shawn regained his footing he let out a loud roar. "What the fuck?!" he screamed into the radio. "I'm gonna kill you and everybody you know! Starting with these two right here!"

"Relax, that was the diner," the Corporal said, as if placating a small child.

"What?" Shawn asked, bewildered as he scrubbed a hand down his face. "The diner?"

"Yeah, the diner in front of the hotel," Bretz explained. "Just a warning shot to let you know we weren't bluffing."

The blonde growled in frustration and sat down on one of the desks. "All right," he said finally. "What do you want?"

"We're going to be at the west side parking lot in ten minutes," Bretz said. "I want your men off the roof, all the shutters closed, and you alone are going to escort the prisoners out to us."

"No, fuck that," Shawn replied immediately. "I'm not coming outside alone. You get what you want and then I'm dead."

There was a pregnant pause before the Corporal came back. "Okay, you get *two* men by the entrance. And just so we're clear, we see movement on the roof, *you* die first. A shutter opens, *you* die first. Are we clear?"

"Crystal," Shawn growled into the radio and then threw the receiver down in frustration. "Fuck!"

"Watch yourself there," Kowalski warned, a shit-eating grin on his face. "Pretty sure there's going to be a shortage on high blood pressure meds."

"One more fucking word, and I'll kill you on principle!" Shawn roared, turning to the Private with fire in his eyes. He whirled towards his lackeys by the door. "Get 'em ready to move. You two are with me outside. Make sure your boys on the roof know what the deal is. Tell 'em to stay out of sight until my signal. And get a couple of the men from the gym up here, too. I don't want these fuckers getting away with this."

He kicked one of the desks with another scream and stalked out of the detention hall.

"Looks like they're following our orders," Bretz said quietly from their vantage point behind two back-to-back cars about twenty yards from the school door.

Baker peeked over the hood for a split second. "Looks like it," he agreed. "Although I got ten to one odds that they have shooters ready to go."

"No doubt," the Corporal agreed, "which is why we gotta stay frosty." He nodded to Johnson, who grinned at him reassuringly.

Linda kept her back to the car, controlling her breathing as she gripped the handle of her new knife. She closed her eyes at the sound of the building doors opening.

Bretz watched as two armed men came out, guns raised. They took up positions behind a nearby car, exciting the zombies in the pen off to the side of the parking lot. They began to rattle the fence, as if building up a cheer for the two soldiers stepping out into the sunlight. Shawn followed close behind, keeping his handgun firmly pressed against the back of Kowalski's head.

"Move it, you loud mouth piece of shit," he snapped, and then shoved him forward. As soon as they passed the car, the blonde ducked behind it where his guards were. "Here you go! Now get the fuck out of my town!"

"Where are the rest of the prisoners?" Bretz called out.

Shawn muttered something under his breath and then peeked up over the hood. "What are you talking about? That is all of them!"

"No it's not!" Linda shrieked, and stood up fully, squaring her shoulders at her abuser. "And you know it."

Shawn sighed and shook his head. "I'm sorry sweetheart," he said, condescension dripping from his voice, "but these two soldiers are the only ones leaving today."

Kowalski and Kersey continued at a slow pace, not wanting to draw too much attention to themselves during the tense standoff. The excited zombie groans echoed on, accentuating the stare down between the woman and her former captor.

"That's not the deal, asshole," Linda snarled. "Everybody gets free today."

"Why don't you sit back down, sweetheart?" Shawn sneered. "The men are handling this."

She clenched her jaw. "Call me sweetheart one more time and see what happens," she warned.

"Oh, feisty." The blonde laughed heartily. "I knew you were my favorite for a reason."

Linda grabbed the handgun at her side and Baker reached up to grab her wrist. Her face went white and she tore her hand away from him, but got the message to keep herself in check.

"Sorry," he whispered, after realizing he shouldn't have grabbed her.

Shawn stood up and raised his gun in the air. "That's far enough, soldier boys!" he called, and Kowalski and Kersey froze, about halfway across to safety.

"What's the problem?" Bretz called. "Thought we had a deal, here?"

"Well your bitch there wanted to renegotiate, so we're going to renegotiate," Shawn replied with an arrogant smirk. "You don't get your men back until I get *her*."

"Not gonna happen," the Corporal called back immediately. "She's not going back in there."

The blonde cocked his head. "You really don't value your men's lives, do you Corporal?"

"I promise you, I value their lives a whole hell of a lot more than I value yours," Bretz warned, voice like steel. "I assure you that this is not a road you want to go down."

Johnson narrowed his eyes at the sight of one of the shutters on the second floor moving ever-so-slightly, and the glint off of the tip of a barrel in the sunlight. "Contact!" he yelled, and leapt to his feet, opening fire immediately on the threat.

The shutters imploded, and the gun barrel disappeared inside.

Linda took the opportunity to point her handgun at Shawn and fire a few shots. She missed by a mile, but the offensive move sent him barreling back into the building to take cover.

Kersey and Kowalski skidded around the two cars, having sprinted as soon as Johnson fired. Kowalski felt a hard impact on his back and flew to the asphalt, bringing his arms up just in time to break his fall.

The Sergeant cried out and grabbed him by the back of his vest, dragging him behind cover. "Holy fuck, are you okay?" he demanded.

"I am gonna *kill* the motherfucker who shot me!" Kowalski snapped, clenching a fist.

Kersey shook his arm. "Are you okay?" he asked firmly.

"Yeah, it just caught my vest," the Private assured him, shaking him off. "Motherfucker!"

More guards came out of the woodwork in the school, opening fire on the soldiers ducked behind the cars in the parking lot. Shutters opened, and snipers popped up on the roof, a few more guards bustling out the front doors and taking cover behind their own cars.

"Great plan, General," Kersey drawled, raising an eyebrow at his Corporal.

Bretz shrugged. "Hey, you're out, aren't you?" he asked, holding out his handgun.

"We've gotta fall back," Kowalski said as he took another handgun from Johnson.

"Hell no!" Linda cried, slapping her hand on the side of the car in frustration. "We're not leaving my people in there."

"Lady, we're pinned down," Kowalski argued. "So unless you have a way to flank those ground shooters and keep them occupied long enough to take out the top shelf assholes, we need to fall back."

She pursed her lips in response.

"That's what I thought," the Private snapped.

Linda glanced down at Baker's utility belt, and snatched one of the grenades free. She held it up in front of Kowalski's face and pulled the pin out, giving him a wink before lobbing it over the car and straight towards the zombie pen.

The grenade smacked into the brick wall of the school, skittering across the pavement to rest a few feet from the chainlink.

The guards barely had time to react before the explosion racked the battlefield, shrapnel flying in all directions. As the smoke cleared, everyone peeked up from their respective cover to see the zombie pen in tatters. Quite a few of the corpses that soaked up the blast painted the pavement and walls with rotted goo, but the remaining ones from the back flooded out into the parking lot.

The guards ducked behind cars screamed and turned away from the soldiers, firing on the horde closing in on them. Many of them not being highly trained gunmen, they were unable to hit the zombies in the head, and couldn't fell enough of them to protect themselves.

"Help us, help!" one of them screeched up at the windows, but the angle was too hard for the second-floor shooters to hit anything substantial.

Two of the guards managed to make it to the front doors, but when they yanked on them, they realized they were locked. Shawn had barred the door from the inside.

They turned around just in time to meet the gnawing teeth of the rotted angels of death descending on them.

"Fuck this!" another guard threw his weapon and raised his hands, jumping out from behind his car. His partner followed suit, looking hopefully at the soldiers in hopes that they could surrender instead of facing such a grisly fate.

The soldiers held their fire, but one of the second floor shooters obviously adjusted his aim down at the two defecting guards. Bretz and Baker spotted it and shot them, shredding the shutters on that window and destroying the position. The rest of the soldiers stood up to join, but all of the shooters on the roof had retreated back inside as well.

Johnson and Kowalski dove out and grabbed the surrendering guards, shoving them back behind cover and pinning them facedown on the pavement.

"It's real simple boys," Kowalski grunted as he secured his prisoner's hands behind his back with zip ties. "You stand up, we're going to put you down. And if you think it's a good idea to go back on your surrender, just know that we're all about bullet conservation. So we'll feed you to those things rather than waste the ammo. We clear?"

The two bound guards nodded furiously, holding position and keeping their mouths shut with wide eyes.

Johnson and Baker kept their guns focused on the second floor, Bretz focused on the roof. Linda and Kersey kept their eyes on the small horde, still clustered around the door and feasting on their now-quiet meal.

"Looks like everybody retreated," Bretz mused.

The Sergeant turned to him. "So, what's your plan, General?" he asked, unable to keep the playfulness out of his voice.

"You know, keep calling me that and I'm going to assume it was a real promotion," the Corporal teased.

Kersey chuckled. "We can't have that now, can we?"

"So, what's the layout like in there?" Bretz asked, tone back to business.

"Long hallway when you get in, classrooms on either side," Kersey replied. "Gym is on the left and the stairs are straight ahead."

The Corporal sighed. "So basically a shooting gallery and we're the ducks."

"Pretty much," the Sergeant agreed.

Bretz pursed his lips. "Any idea on numbers?"

"At least five, based on who was shooting as us here," Kersey said.

Kowalski shuffled up next to him. "We saw at least a dozen or so armed men in the gym too, who knows how many more hostiles are in there."

"They aren't all hostile," Linda cut in.

Kowalski gave her the side-eye. "They looked pretty fucking hostile to me."

"Don't get me wrong, some of them are." She put her hands up, palms out. "But a lot of them are just afraid of Shawn. You cross him and you get selected to play the rope game."

Bretz furrowed his brow. "The rope game?"

"Gym glass from hell," Kowalski explained.

"Fun," the Corporal said flatly.

Kersey sighed. "So, any ideas on how to get them not to shoot us?"

"The principal's office is five doors up on the right," Linda suggested. "If you get me to it, I could make an announcement that Shawn's reign is at an end."

"How you gonna do that?" Johnson drawled. "There's no power."

"It's an old school system on a battery backup," she explained. "Also doubles as the town's tornado warning system, which is why they made it work without power."

There were some fresh excited groans as a few of the zombies finished their meal and turned towards the source of conversation in the parking lot.

"Baker, see what you can do about them, will you?" Kersey asked.

The Private stopped his second floor sweep, and drew a long knife from his belt. He kicked the first zombie in the chest, sending it tumbling back, and then slammed his blade into the second one's face. Before the first one could get back up, he descended on it and plunged the knife into the back of its skull.

The noise unfortunately attracted a half dozen more of their friends, and Baker backed up. "Shots coming," he warned.

"Just make them count," Kersey instructed.

Baker sheathed his knife and drew his handgun, carefully lining up each shot, timing his breaths and steps backwards as he dropped each corpse. Falling into the zen state was almost peaceful, and dropping zombies that wanted to eat him was always a source of satisfaction in this cruel world.

"Well, I think we have us a plan," the Sergeant declared as his Private came back around the car.

"Half of one, at any rate," Bretz corrected. "Not really looking forward to a run down a long hallway Those assholes aren't the best shot in the west, but I'm betting they could hit us in that scenario."

Kowalski glanced over at the remaining zombies approaching, and tapped Baker on the shoulder as he began to take them out as well. "Hey, make sure you leave one of them alive. I have an idea."

"Do I wanna know?" Baker asked.

Kowalski grinned. "Probably not."

"Well he might not want to know, but I sure as hell do," Kersey piped up.

"This thing is dinged up and probably isn't gonna stop another shot in the back," Kowalski said as he unclipped his bulletproof vest. "I figure if we put it on one of those dead fuckers we can use them to lead the charge, get some good use out of it."

Bretz shrugged. "Guess it won't really matter if a bullet cracks through it," he agreed. "And frankly if one of those boys manages to land a shot that goes through two kevlar panels and a torso, we deserve to catch a bullet."

"Kowalski, go help Baker," Kersey instructed.

The Private nodded and moved over to his reloading friend.

"Which one do you want?" Baker asked, motioning past the large pile of corpses.

Kowalski cocked his head and tapped his chin, then pointed towards a six-foot-tall zombie missing a significant portion of his face and neck. "Let's get that big boy over there," he said.

"All right," Baker agreed, and took out the last two on either side before holstering his gun. "Any thoughts on how to do this?"

Kowalski nodded. "Get behind him and secure his arms." He waited for his companion to flank the creature before clapping his hands a few times. "Hey big fella, come at me!" He stamped a foot and the zombie screamed, lunging at him.

Baker took the distraction and leapt forward, grabbing its arms and pulling them back hard. He was able to hold its wrists with a firm foot planted in its back, keeping its snapping jaws safely in the other direction.

Kowalski reached for his knife, and then remembered it wasn't there anymore. "Shit," he muttered.

Baker paled. "Shit? What do you mean, shit?"

"Hey lady," Kowalski barked, turning to Linda, who was closest to him. "I need your knife."

She headed over and drew it, handing it to him, hilt first. "Here you go, soldier boy."

The Private took it and braced a hand on the zombie's chest before gently shoving the knife up into the bottom of the corpse's chin. He was careful to angle it so that it wouldn't pierce the brain. The zombie tried to snarl but the knife held its mouth closed.

"Thanks." Kowalski grinned at Linda.

She shrugged. "Anytime."

"Hey Sarge, we got one," the Private declared. "Help me get the vest on him and we'll be good to go."

Kersey picked up the vest and headed over, Bretz on his heels. They managed to shimmy it over the confused and enraged creature, and then the Sergeant turned to Johnson.

"Go get that door unlocked, but leave it shut," he instructed, patting their new pet zombie on the shoulder. "We're gonna do this thing."

CHAPTER FIFTEEN

Bretz held fast to the back of the zombie's vest, the corpse struggling and unable to understand it didn't have the ability to bite. Johnson finished unlocking the door before moving behind the Corporal, holding tightly to the back of *his* vest, to keep him steady for their charge. The other four stood behind them, checking their weapons as they got ready to breach the door.

"Bretz, Johnson, Kowalski, you three push forward and get to the stairwell to secure it," Kersey instructed. "If anybody's hostile, don't be afraid to shoot them."

"That definitely wasn't going to be an issue, Sarge," Kowalski quipped.

Kersey nodded. "Baker, Linda and I are going to hit the principal's office. Hopefully when that announcement goes out, we'll have people laying down their arms."

"What are we going to do with them if they do?" Bretz asked over the frustrated grunting of his undead prisoner. "There's only a handful of us."

"There's a cage in the gym with people who need to be freed," Linda explained. "They'll be able to help out."

Bretz shrugged. "Good enough for me."

"Okay, let's do it," Kersey said, and nodded to Kowalski.

The Private reached around the zombie and wrapped his fingers around the handle of the door. He gave a silent countdown from three with his fingers, and then yanked it open.

The bulletproof zombie caught a shot in the chest as soon as it breached the door, followed quickly by several more cracks as Bretz maneuvered his meat-shield forward. There were only four men firing, two in the stairwell and one on each side of the hall, poking out of classrooms.

The soldiers moved at a swift pace, easily shoving the giant zombie with their combined weight. Kowalski and Baker leaned out from opposite sides of their single-file charge, firing downrange towards the guards. Their shots missed, but it forced their attackers to get back into their cover.

When they reached the principal's office, Baker dove for the door, taking cover there to lay down fire at the shooters. Kersey and Linda slipped by him into the office, the Sergeant sweeping the area quickly to make sure there were no straggling hostiles there.

"It's clear," he said, "get to the intercom."

Linda didn't need to be told twice, and rushed over to start it up.

Bretz pushed on, nearing the stairwell. The zombie was no longer walking, as most of its body had been completely shredded, chunks and limbs falling off in droves by the time they got closer to their attackers.

The Corporal yanked the knife from the zombie's chin before shoving it face-first into the stairwell door. Regardless of the fact that it had no working limbs, it was still starving and latched on to one guard's shoulder with gnawing teeth.

He screamed in pain and fell backwards against the other shooter, who leapt out of the way and lunged towards Bretz, gun raising. The Corporal batted the barrel to the side and buried the knife into the guard's bicep, causing him to drop his weapon and scream. Bretz drew it and then plunged it into the guard's throat, kicking the gurgling man back onto his companion and the pile of rotting flesh still feasting away.

Kowalski and Johnson hopped over the tangle of bodies into the stairwell, the former keeping post at the door frame to keep an eye on the hallway. Johnson fired three times, putting a bullet into each of the twitching bodies' heads.

"You two, secure the hall," Bretz said, moving past Johnson to the stairs. "I'll make sure nobody comes at us from above."

A loud beep echoed all around them as the Corporal headed up the stairs. There was a click and then the sound of Linda clearing her throat.

"All right, everybody, listen up, it's Linda," she began. "You all know what's going on here is wrong. My new friends and I are here to put a stop to it, and end Shawn's reign of terror. If you lay down your guns and step out of the gym and classrooms with your hands up, you get to live. You'll also have the opportunity to build this city back up. I've made a deal with the military and they're going to be bringing in food and other vital supplies so we can thrive. All you have to do, is put down your weapons and come out. If you're going to do it, do it now."

She released the intercom button and let out a deep breath.

Kersey raised an eyebrow at her, half-smiling. "We made a deal with you?" he asked.

"Not yet." She cocked her head. "But it sounded more believable than saying I got you to promise them hookers and blow. Whatever gets them to surrender, right?"

The Sergeant nodded. "Spot on, girl." He headed over to Baker, still guarding the door. "How we looking?" he asked.

"Clear on this end," the Private reported. "Should be save to move up to the stairwell."

The trio moved quickly down the hall, Linda in the middle, and as they reached the stairs Kowalski and Johnson stepped out, aiming towards the gym. The doors to the gymnasium opened and a dozen men stepped out, unarmed with their hands raised. Their eyes were wide and fearful, with a hint of relief when they saw Linda surrounded by soldiers. Bretz emerged from the stairwell, having cleared the landing above.

"I don't see Shawn," Kersey muttered.

She shook her head. "Me either, but I didn't expect to."

"Anybody else missing?" the Sergeant asked.

She studied the group, lips pursed. "Two, maybe three more, not including Shawn."

"Bretz, help Johnson and Kowalski corral these assholes," Kersey instructed. "Baker, you're with me. Linda, can you come with us? You know this place better than I do."

She nodded. "Let's go."

The three of them turned and headed up the stairs, pausing at the top landing. Kersey did a silent countdown before pushing on the door, and a hail of bullets immediately ripped through the wood. The trio flattened themselves against the concrete wall, staying stock still in hopes of playing possum.

After several seconds of quiet, tentative footsteps sounded in the hallway, moving closer to them. Kersey ducked down, laying on his side so that he could aim out the door. He gave Baker a thumbs up and the Private gave the latch a shove.

Gunfire ripped again, but it was at chest height, and Kersey fired from the floor, hitting his target in the face. As the body fell, the Sergeant caught a glimpse of Shawn and one of his lackeys diving back into a room. He remained on the floor, the door resting on his knee as he continued to aim at the room.

"Baker, move up," he whispered.

His companion stepped over him, keeping his gun trained on the offending door down the hall. Once he was clear, Kersey got to his feet, and began to move up the hallway, Linda quietly following.

"Give it up Shawn, it's over," the Sergeant called. "Your men downstairs have surrendered. You and your little friend there are all that's left. So why don't you be a good boy and come out with your hands up? Linda here might even let you live."

He glanced over his shoulder at her, and she shook her head. He offered her a smile and a wink, and then turned back to the door. His smile dropped immediately at the sound of a woman whimpering, and Linda realized what room they'd approached.

"That's the room where they kept us," she breathed.

Baker shook his head. "Fuck, they have hostages."

"Shawn, you may want to rethink the whole hostage taking," Kersey bellowed. "Didn't work out too well for you the last time."

The door suddenly flung open, and Shawn emerged, dragging a naked woman out by the throat. He held her in front of him, using her terrified form as a human shield.

"Put 'em down, boys, or else the whore gets it in the head," he demanded.

Baker scoffed. "Yeah, we're not doing that."

"Shawn," Kersey cut in, "you gotta understand something here. This ain't the good ole days where they'd lock you up in county for a few weeks until your lawyer could get you probation. There is a zero percent chance we're going to let you walk out of this. Too many other things to deal with than assholes like you."

The girl let out a ragged sob as Shawn pressed the barrel of his gun harder into her temple. Linda locked eyes with the lackey from the doorway, an overweight fellow that she recognized.

"Conner, it's Linda, you remember me?" she asked gently.

Shawn growled. "Don't listen to that bitch, it's you and me, buddy, stand fast."

"Conner," Linda continued, ignoring the blonde. "Shawn isn't going to be able to help you anymore. I'm going to be in charge. I know you're a great door guard, and I'm going to have people for you to guard."

The frightened man nodded.

"Goddammit Conner!" Shawn roared. "Don't listen to her, I'm the only one you need! Shoot that bitch *now*!"

"Conner," Linda said again, voice gentle and smooth, "I'll be forever grateful if you'll help us disarm Shawn." She licked her lips and batted her lashes. "And I *show* my gratitude."

The lackey's eyes widened with realization and he immediately stepped out from the doorway, aiming his handgun at the back of Shawn's head.

"You stupid motherfucker," the blonde growled.

Conner shook his head. "I'm sorry Shawn, but I'm with her now," he said, voice shaking.

The blonde let out a grunt of frustration, realizing wholly that he was defeated. He raised his arms, stepping back, and Baker quickly moved to him, snatching the gun and bringing Shawn to his knees. The girl staggered away, grabbing Kersey's vest, and he gingerly put an arm around her as she sobbed into his chest, shielding her body with his own.

Linda approached Conner. "You did good," she said.

He turned nervous eyes on her. "I did?"

"You did amazing," she assured him, and gently took the gun from his hand. He grinned at her, and she smiled back before smashing the weapon against the bridge of his nose.

He collapsed in shock, and she kicked him completely over, kneeling on his chest to continue raining blows down on his face. Kersey gaped at the scene, watching as she spit on the broken and blubbering man's face.

"Fuck you, you rapist piece of shit!" she screamed. "You're gonna get what's coming to you." She moved out of the way as Baker shoved a bound Shawn down onto the floor next to Conner. He produced another zip tie to secure the bloodied man's wrists, and Linda stepped over to join Kersey.

The Sergeant shook his head in awe. "That was one hell of a bluff."

"He's always looked at me like that," she said bitterly. "Even before this shit went down. Figured I could use it to my advantage for once."

"Good call," Kersey said. "Any idea on what you want to do with Shawn?"

Linda's eyes darkened, and she grinned deviously. "Oh yeah, I have one."

CHAPTER SIXTEEN

Shawn gripped the chain link fence in the gym, eyes wide with panic. He knew there was no point in trying to escape the fence hallway. He built it, after all.

"Please," he turned to Linda, injecting as much pain into his voice as he possibly could. "Please, I'll do anything you want."

She raised her chin and stared him down. "I want you to climb."

He clenched his jaw, shaking his head, knowing she wasn't going to back down. This was it.

"Johnson, if you wouldn't mind," Linda said, and the Private wandered over to the door and pulled the chain to release the zombies into the fence hallway. They locked on Shawn and staggered towards him, moaning and stumbling.

Shawn dove into the rope pen as soon as they raised the gate, grasping for the rope. He climbed frantically, screaming in fear as the zombies reached for him, barely scraping the bottom of his shoes.

"Looks like I owe you five bucks, Sarge," Kowalski declared.

Kersey grinned. "Told you he was gonna get above them."

"Yeah, but come on, they're touching his feet," the Private replied, motioning to the rotting fingers brushing the screaming man's shoes. "Can I get a judge's ruling on that? Because I feel like that counts."

Linda raised a hand. "Sorry, if they ain't eating him, it doesn't count."

"Well, fuck," Kowalski replied, but he didn't sound all that put out.

Kersey inclined his head to the cage at the far end of the gym, where they'd corralled the other undesirables. "What's your plan for them?" he asked.

"I figure we'll let them stew in their own shit for a day or two," Linda replied, not even sparing them a glance. "Then I'll take 'em out back and put a bullet in the back of their heads. Or the front, I haven't decided yet.

Kersey's brow furrowed. "Linda. You're not a killer."

Bretz snorted and shook his head. "Oh hell yes she is."

"Oh, well, I suppose the Corporal thinks otherwise," the Sergeant said. "Regardless, I can't let you kill them."

"With all due respect, *Sergeant*," Linda said firmly, "you guys are leaving. I have to do what I can to ensure my people's safety."

Kersey put up a hand. "I understand that. I'd like to make a deal with you."

"I'm listening." Linda crossed her arms, though she was still watching Shawn struggle to stay on the rope.

"The bulk of the surviving U.S. military is currently stationed in Kansas, and we're on a mission to clear a path to the Northwest," Kersey explained. "There's going to be a major offensive, and soon. Now, my General has given me orders to find a stopover point for troops being transported to the front lines, and I think your little town would be perfect."

She wrinkled her nose. "You want to flood my town with troops?"

"Being a troop hub will have its benefits," the Sergeant insisted. "Steady supply of food, medicine, doctors. Not to mention you'll never have to worry about someone like Shawn ever again."

She pursed her lips and thought for a moment. "Okay. I accept your offer. However, I don't see what that has to do with offing these assholes."

"We're about to go on a full war footing in this country," Kersey said, "and even though we've never fought a war like this in our nation's history, one thing remains the same."

Linda raised an eyebrow. "What's that?"

"We always have a use for warm bodies," the Sergeant explained.

She smiled as she imagined what would be in store for the abusive assholes if they became fodder for the military. "Okay. I'll spare the ones in the cage," she agreed. "But surely you can grant me a lone exception."

Kersey smiled, knowing what she wanted, and nodded.

"Hey Kowalski, you any good with that thing?" Linda asked, motioning to the sniper rifle on his shoulder.

He puffed out his chest. "I'm pretty good, actually."

"Fantastic." She clapped her hands together. "Now that I'm in charge, I've decided to make some decorating decisions. First of which, is that I don't think we're going to need a rope in the gym anymore. I don't know where the ladder is, would you mind taking it down for me?"

Kowalski grinned. "Not at all, ma'am." He tipped an invisible hat at her and unslung his rifle from his shoulder, aiming at the top of the rope.

"No!" Shawn screamed, clambering up another knot, white knuckled. "No, please no!"

The Private fired a well-placed shot, severing the rope and sending the shrieking blonde ex-leader down to his death. The group watched as the zombies descended on him, reaping the benefits of his own rigged game and tearing into his unwilling flesh.

CHAPTER SEVENTEEN

"Yo, Mason!" Johnson barked as the soldiers approached the waiting train. "You enjoy slacking off while the rest of us were getting shot at?"

Mason scoffed. "Slacking off? You have any idea how cranky Bill gets when he doesn't get enough sleep?"

"Fair enough bubba," Johnson replied, clapping him on the shoulder. "Fair enough."

"Where is Bill, anyway?" Kersey asked, stretching his arms above his head.

Mason motioned to the engine car behind him. "He's been sound asleep on the floor of the cab since we got here."

"He's been asleep on a metal floor this whole time?" Bretz laughed. "Did you at least get him a pillow?"

"Nope," Mason replied with a shrug. "He just rolled up a jacket and was out like a baby on NyQuil."

Bretz shook his head. "Son of a bitch, guess he wasn't lying when he said he could sleep on the train."

"Lesson learned," Baker declared. "I'd be quite content *not* making another stop like this one."

"Hey, Mason, why don't you head on back?" Kersey said. "Kowalski and I will take the first watch with Bill."

The Private in question gawked at his superior. "What the fuck, Sarge? I got the last kill, that means I get the first nap!"

"Technically *Linda* got the last kill, since it was her idea," Johnson cut in. "Plus, she gave you the order. It's like giving credit to the hammer instead of the carpenter."

Kowalski shook his head and climbed up into the cab. "Maybe Bill will loan me that jacket," he muttered.

The trio of remaining Privates headed off to the makeshift sleeping car, leaving just the Corporal and his Sergeant.

"That was a close one," Bretz said, tone serious. "Hit us pretty good on the ammo as well."

"Yeah, I know," Kersey replied, exhaustion finally seeping into his muscles. He leaned against the side of the train, scrubbing a hand down his face. "How bad is it?"

"Linda was able to spare us a few boxes of rifle ammo, so Kowalski is sitting pretty," the Corporal said. "Rest of us are really low. Like maybe eight full mags between us on the assault rifles, and about six shots each on the handguns."

"Well, we can't wait on a resupply," the Sergeant explained. "So we're just gonna have to hope we can find a gun shop along the route." He scratched the back of his head.

Bretz yawned. "And hope we don't run into much resistance."

Kersey waved his hands back and forth in front of his companion's face.

"What… what are you doing?" Bretz asked, brow furrowing.

"Wondering how you are keeping up a conversation while being asleep on your feet," the Sergeant said, "because what you just said is a pure *dream*." They shared a chuckle and he patted his friend on the shoulder. "You go get some sleep. I'm gonna call the town in to the General."

Bretz raised his hand. "Be sure to tell him about my field promotion."

"Sure thing." Kersey laughed. He watched the Corporal amble off to the sleeping car, and then hauled himself up the ladder into the cab.

Bill sat at the console, rubbing the sleep out of his eyes as he checked the gauges. Kowalski's form shuffled around in the corner, attempting to get comfortable with the jacket pillow.

"How are we looking, Bill?" Kersey asked.

The engineer made a circle with his thumb and forefinger. "Looking all right,

Sergeant. Everybody tucked into their beds?"

"They're about as comfortable as they're gonna get," Kersey said.

Bill nodded and cracked his knuckles. "Well, let's get this show on the road, then."

"Hey Bill," Kowalski grunted from the back, rolling over to face them. "Anyplace else we need to start worrying about? Please tell me that this place was the worst we're gonna see before Seattle."

"Well," the engineer drew out the word, rubbing his chin, "we still have to go through Helena, Montana, but the real ass-clenching run is going to be through Missoula."

Kowalski's brow furrowed.

"You know he has nightmares, right?" Kersey said.

"Well, he'd better, because it's gonna be a bitch and a half getting through it," Bill replied. "There's a huge train yard and it's the biggest city between here and Washington."

The Sergeant sobered. "Any chance we can go around it?"

"Nope." The engineer shook his head, popping the *p* as he said it. "It's the only viable path through the Coeur d'Alene National Forest. Unless you want to take a huge detour down to Idaho. In which case, we'd have to go through Boise which would be a hell of a lot worse."

Kersey sighed. "Well, we don't have to do that today, do we?"

"Nah, we're a few days out," Bill assured him.

The Sergeant stretched his arms above his head. "Good," he said. "At least I can get one more mediocre night's sleep before I die." He patted Bill on the back, and the engineer gave him a salute and hit the throttle.

END

DEAD AMERICA: THE SECOND WEEK

BOOK 3: EL PASO - PT. 2

BY DEREK SLATON

© 2019

CHAPTER ONE

Day Zero +10

Ten miles east of El Paso laid the sleepy town of Butterfield, Texas. Once upon a time, Leon Jones would have been one of almost a hundred people living on one of the sparse and spread out plots of land. Many joked that Butterfield had been a ghost town before the apocalypse. Who knew they'd be right one day?

Leon knelt down beside his camping stove, his tall fit frame casting a shadow over it. Though in his fifties with greying hair, he was still fit, and with the bloody military fatigues he wore, he didn't look at all helpless.

On this morning, however, just after dawn, he wasn't worried about looking helpless or not. All he cared about was the precious commodity in his frying pan—a lone egg. He was determined to fry it perfectly—not too little, not too much—because he didn't know when he'd be able to have another. *If* he'd ever be able to have another.

Food grew scarcer and scarcer these days. The Rivas Cartel had spent the better part of the week raiding every home and business close to El Paso, taking anything of value. And the most valuable thing in the apocalypse was food.

Leon inhaled deeply, enjoying the scent of the fresh egg he'd been lucky enough to find nestled in the old busted henhouse. "It's a shame I couldn't find any coffee to go along with this," he said under his breath.

He poked the egg gently to make sure it was as firm as he liked it, and nodded to himself in satisfaction. He turned the heat off and tipped the frying pan over a paper plate he'd liberated from the trailer behind him. As he stepped back up into the double-wide, he took one last sniff of the fresh morsel before settling on the grimy couch in the living room.

The place was musty as all hell, the kind of smell that made Leon think of an old folks' home. There was a thin layer of dust over everything, and he was willing to bet it was there from before the zombies considering the dry field in the surrounding area. He shoved a putrid-smelling beer can away from him, and sighed to himself.

"I feel you, brother," he muttered to the ether, half to himself and half to the ghost of the previous owner. "If I were livin' here in triple digit temps half the year, I would have given up on life too." He leaned forward and bit into the egg, gobbling half of it and chewing slowly, savoring the creamy yolk on his tongue.

The pleasure was short-lived, however, at the sound of a rumbling engine.

Leon immediately sank to his knees, crawling over to the kitchenette window. He gently pulled back the sheet that was a makeshift curtain and peered out at a white truck skidding to a stop at the small shack-like house across the field.

A trio of men jumped out of the vehicle, all carrying AK-47s with a swagger that was unmistakable.

"Motherfucking cartel," Leon muttered. He popped the other half of the egg in his mouth, and crawled back over to the couch to grab his scoped bolt-action sniper rifle. He double-checked the fresh clip was primed and ready to go, and gave the gun a loving pet. "Well girl, looks like we have another day of action on our hands. Starting early, too."

He headed back to the window, peeking out just as the cartel members kicked the door in to the tiny dilapidated house. A zombie staggered out, short compared to the cartel members, and they hooted at it, forming a loose triangle. They teased it, enraging it from behind every time it got too close to somebody. The confused corpse wandered back and forth, screaming and moaning in frustration.

Leon tore a bit of the sheet clear from the window, so he could aim his rifle through it but stay mostly hidden. He peered through the scope just in time for one of the men to get bored of the game and shoot the zombie in the back of the head, splattering rotted brain matter over one of his companions.

"We used to joke about how interrupting breakfast should be punishable by death." Leon chuckled to himself, low in his throat. "Took a while, but finally get to make it real."

The cartel member covered in zombie goo stepped up to the shooter, shoving him in anger at being splattered with guts for no reason. The third man simply laughed and watched as his friends argued, bumping chests in a classic display of testosterone.

Leon aimed carefully, and took a deep breath, his nerves relaxing and hand steady. As the grappling duo moved so that one's back was to him, he pulled the trigger. The bullet went through both of them, dropping both bodies to the ground, as the third man quickly fumbled with his radio, screaming frantically into it.

Once upon a time, Leon had been the fastest shot in his battalion, but years behind a desk after his years of service had slowed him a little bit. He put a bullet in the third man's forehead, but not before it seemed he'd been able to get a partial message to whomever was on the other side of that radio.

"Motherfucker," he muttered to himself, and sat back on his heels. He took a beat to begrudge his waning skills and the fact he was about to lose his hideout, and then snapped to action.

Leon leapt to his feet and ran to the bedroom to grab his two duffel bags. He threw them over his shoulder and peered out the window once again. He didn't hear any more vehicles approaching. He looked out the window on the other side of the trailer, noting a row of three houses closer to together about forty yards across the dusty field.

He burst out the front door, tearing around the back of the trailer just as the roar of approaching engines grew in a crescendo. He peeked back around the corner to see three vehicles cresting the horizon, and shook his head, taking off at a sprint for the houses.

He made a snap decision upon reaching them to head into the center house, figuring they'd start their search on either the left or the right side. The knob turned easily, miraculously unlocked, and he dove in, slamming it behind him. There was a moan and a shuffle as a zombie staggered in from the living room.

Leon jumped past it, giving it a shove in the back and heading down the hallway into the next room, closing the door behind him. *Hopefully they'll see that thing and call this place clear,* he thought as he took in the bedroom. *Hopefully.*

He dropped his duffel bags in the closet and knelt down in the corner, gripping his rifle tightly. He strained his ears to hear, and luckily with the thin walls he was able to hear some voices outside. They spoke in rapid Spanish, and though he was a bit rusty he could pick up most of what they were saying to each other.

"Go check that house out," one demanded.

A scoff. "Why should I do it? I went first on the last one?"

"Yeah, well, I'm driving," the first guy snapped. "So unless you want to walk back…"

The response was mumbled so low that Leon couldn't make it out, but he assumed it was likely something derogatory. There was a loud *crack* as somebody kicked the door in, and then a *thud* and a laugh.

"Hey, I found you a friend, man!" somebody said, and then there was a gunshot. Leon assumed they'd found his dead companion.

"Quit fucking around and search the place," the bossy one snapped.

"Nobody's in here," the other guy whined. "Or, what, you think the zombie had a roommate?"

The sound of the footsteps retreating made the hiding man let out a soft sigh of relief, though he knew better than to count his chickens before they hatched.

"Hey, that was awfully quick," another voice said from outside, sounding skeptical.

"Fucking zombie in the living room, man," someone protested.

"That wasn't my question," the other voice grew in volume and sternness.

"Hey, if you think someone was shacking up with a ghoul, then by all means, have a look," the other guy replied. "We're moving on to the next house."

"Fucking slack asses!" the stern one barked. "I guess I have to do your job for you!"

"Fuck," Leon muttered, swallowing hard. *The one time these guys are thorough.*

His muscles tensed up again at the sound of footsteps inside the house. There was a bit more chatter but it seemed more slang than anything, he couldn't quite make out what they were saying. The last word, however, was *bedroom*, and he crept behind the door, drawing his knife.

The door knob turned and he raised his weapon, waiting as the barrel of an AK-47 nosed its way through the crack in the door. It creaked as it opened, and a man entered slowly. Just as he was about to turn his head, Leon dove for him, batting his gun down and pressing the knife to his throat.

They grappled a little, and he noted the fear in the guy's eyes as he slammed him back against the dresser, knick-knacks clattering to the floor. He couldn't have been older than twenty-five, and Leon fought the churning in his guts at the thought of harming a kid less than half his age.

As another cartel member approached from the hallway, the older man spun his prisoner around and curled his knife arm around his throat, using him as a human shield.

"Put it down or I will gut him like a fucking fish," Leon warned.

The approaching cartel member lowered his weapon immediately, putting up a

tentative hand to try to defuse the
situation. "Calm down, friend," he said in
heavily accented english.

"I'm not your fucking friend," Leon
growled, "and if you take one more step
then I start slicing." He dug the blade in
a little harder, a bead of blood forming
on the top.

"Hey, you guys okay in there?"
somebody yelled from outside.

"Yeah, dumbass here slipped and fell
when he saw a dead body," the kid called
back, voice surprisingly steady. "Guess I
should be thankful he didn't shit himself
again!"

The guy outside laughed. "Okay, well
this house was clear so we're going to
move on up the road."

"Sounds good!" the prisoner replied.
"I'm going to piss and then we'll be on
our way."

"Take your time," his comrade yelled
back, "whoever shot our boys is probably
long gone by now."

After a few tense moments, when they
were sure the other men were out of
earshot, Leon pursed his lips at the
cartel member in the hallway. He slung his
rifle over his back, putting both of his
hands up.

The older man lowered the knife and shoved his prisoner away from him. "Go on, kid," he said.

"It's not too bad," the guy murmured in Spanish as he looked at the scratch on the younger man's neck. "Go get cleaned up in the kitchen, we're going to have to go soon."

As he headed off, Leon leaned against the dresser, crossing his arms as if he hadn't a care in the world. "Okay, you've piqued my interest," he said. "Why didn't you rat me out to your boys?"

"Because it takes skill, not to mention cantaloupe sized cojones, to take down three of our men," the cartel member replied with a shrug.

Leon furrowed his brow. "Yeah, well, they interrupted my breakfast."

"Understandable."

"Still doesn't explain why you didn't rat me out," the older man prompted.

His opponent shifted his weight. "Because I have a use for you."

"Sorry to burst your bubble, but I don't do work for the cartel," Leon spat, wrinkling his nose.

"There are some of us who don't like what's being done to civilians in El Paso," the man insisted. "We've set up a safe haven for them. A man of your particular skills could be very useful to them."

Leon cocked his head, studying him for a moment. "I'm really thankful you never sat across from me at a poker table," he finally said, "because I can't get a read on you."

"I just lied to protect you," the man replied easily. "If I had gotten caught, they would have made an example out of me. That alone should be enough to convince you."

Leon pursed his lips. "Perhaps."

"Well, consider the alternative," the man said. "Where else are you going to go? The closer you get to town, the more of us that are roaming around, so you can't risk heading back in that direction. You have one road to the east, but the next bit of civilization is about seventy miles away. If the elements don't get you, then the wildlife will."

Leon sighed. "So, what do you propose?"

"You do not leave this room and you don't make a sound until we are gone," the man instructed. "In a couple of hours, my man Francisco will be by to pick you up. Just be ready to move when he gets here." There was a moment of silence, and then recognition, and the man turned to leave.

"Hey," Leon said quietly, "you never told me your name."

"No, I didn't," the cartel member replied. "The fewer people who know who we are, the safer we stay. Good luck, friend." With that, he headed to the front door to meet up with the younger man, wiping the last of the blood from his neck. He and Leon nodded to each other, before the older man closed the bedroom door once again.

He sat down on the floor, out of sight of the windows, and sighed heavily. He looked at his scuffed watch and couldn't help but smile.

"Man, not even eight in the morning, and already a shit-filled day."

CHAPTER TWO

Leon rolled a pen across his fingers and back, checking his watch again. It had been about two hours, and he'd been able to fall into a zen-like trance while spinning the pen around his fingers a multitude of ways. He hadn't wanted to move from beneath the window in case of potential bad company, but it had remained quiet.

At the rumble of a single engine, he got up onto his knees and peeked through the blinds as an SUV approached the house. Leon grabbed his duffel bags and stashed them next to the front door, rifle at the ready as the vehicle came to a stop out front. He cracked the door, and watched carefully as the driver's side window rolled down.

The man behind the wheel looked to be in his mid-thirties, with chocolate hair and aviator sunglasses.

"Well, you coming or what?" he asked.

Leon opened the door a little wider. "You Francisco?"

"Who the fuck else would I be?" the man shot back.

Leon rolled his eyes. "Well, the first three who showed up today sure as hell weren't Francisco."

"And that's why I'm here." Francisco put a hand to his chest. "Now, do you want a ride to safety, or are you gonna start huffing it up the road?"

The older man shrugged, picked up his bags, and flung open the door, jogging down the front steps to the vehicle. He opened the hatchback and tossed his bags in before skirting the SUV to get into the passenger's seat.

He raised an eyebrow as he turned sideways, surveying the three people sitting in the backseat. There was a middle-aged couple clutching each other on one side, eyes wide with terror, and next to them a twenty-something petite but athletic woman with jet black hair.

"Folks," Leon greeted them with a tip of his hat, "how we doing?"

Francisco rolled his eyes and punched the gas, starting the next leg of their journey.

"Oh, we're doing just *peachy*," the young woman piped up, sarcasm dripping from her tongue. "Let's see, my best friend was shot in the street two days ago because he accidentally bumped into some cartel thug. My roommate vanished yesterday and I can only imagine what horrors she's dealing with. And now I'm fleeing the city with two people so fucked up they can't even speak and some over the hill dude in bloody army fatigues. Of course none of that even includes the whole dead rising to feast on the living bullshit."

Leon blinked at her and then nodded casually. "Well, you gotta look on the bright side of things. At least it ain't rainin'."

"Yes, mister military man, we are truly a blessed group of people." She rolled her eyes.

He shrugged. "We are more blessed than you know, assuming you believe in that stuff."

"Oh yeah?" She crossed her arms. "How so?"

He cocked his head. "Well for starters, we've outlived at least ninety percent of our fellow countrymen."

"Ninety percent?" Her jaw dropped, and there was a moment where it seemed nobody in the car could even breathe. "You can't possibly know that."

Leon pinched the fabric of his shirt and tugged it a few times. "The military garb isn't just for attracting the ladies," he said. "I'm military intelligence. At least, I *was* before this shitshow hit."

"So…" She cleared her throat, voice thick. "It's like this everywhere?"

"Worse in a lot of places," he replied. "Some of the major cities are on the verge of being completely wiped out. Even with our southern neighbors paying us an unwelcome visit, we're still ahead of the game."

"I thought you military intelligence guys were a bunch of geeks behind computer screens," Francisco cut in as he turned a corner. "How the hell did you take out three of my guys?"

"I wasn't always in intelligence," Leon explained, shaking his head. "Started my career as a sniper. Ran several dozen missions in various theaters over the years. Decided to make the career change after some dumbass nearly got me killed because they sucked at their job. I wanted to do my part to make sure the next kid who filled my boots didn't have to die due to negligence."

The young woman in the back leaned forward. "That was noble of you." She seemed sincere, her sarcasm gone.

"Eh, don't chalk it up to nobility. My black ass loves me some air conditioning, which in very short supply out in the field." Leon chuckled and turned to the driver. "So, you gonna tell us where we headed?"

Francisco nodded. "It's a little town called Fabens, about thirty miles southeast from town."

"What is this place, anyway?" the young woman asked, leaning forward.

"It's a refugee camp of sorts that was hastily set up by Rodriguez, the second in command of the Rivas Cartel," Francisco explained. "Some of us, like myself, have been rescuing people who would be eliminated or worse, and getting them to a place where they have a chance at survival."

"How many have you gotten out?" she pressed.

He shook his head. "Not nearly as many as I would like."

"And the cartel just lets 'em be?" Leon raised an eyebrow.

Francisco barked a bitter laugh. "The cartel doesn't know about them yet. Rodriguez is the one in charge of exploring the region, so he's been steering everyone to the north and east. But it's only a matter of time before he has no choice but to send people south."

"Well, nothing like a little impending doom to get the morning rolling," Leon said with a sigh. "I'm Leon, by the way," he said, turning again to the passengers in the back.

"Clara," the young woman replied, and shook his hand. She motioned to her companions. "No idea what their names are, they don't say anything."

Francisco made a hard left turn off of the main road, bumbling down a dirt path leading to the east. "Hang on tight, we're taking the long way around."

CHAPTER THREE

Detective Rogers walked down the main
road leading into Fabens, enjoying the
morning sun bathing everything in a warm
glow. It made even the dusty ground look
ethereal, beautiful, pre-apocalypse.

He reached up and made sure all of
the edges of the bandage on the side of
his head were secure. The wound where his
ear had been was taking its sweet time to
heal, and getting dust all up in there
wouldn't help anything along. He sighed
and smoothed back his thinning black hair.
For a man in his early forties, sometimes
he felt like he was twice that.

He approached the bridge over the
large drainage ditch. "Harry, Charlie,
what do you say boys?" he asked of the two
older men standing guard.

"Detective Rogers," Harry greeted,
lowering his makeshift spear that somebody
had fashioned out of a broomstick. "Good
to see you on this fine morning."

Rogers inclined his head, leaning on
the railing over the ten-foot-wide ditch.
"Any activity overnight?"

"Nothing too bad," Charlie replied,
shaking his head. "A dozen or so making
their way up to the cars." He motioned to
the vehicles lined up bumper-to-bumper
across the bridge as the barrier.

"About twice that much wandering up the ditch," Harry added, motioning over his shoulder.

Rogers stepped over to peek down on that side, noting about twenty or so zombies in the deep gully, reaching up in vain at the fresh meat.

"I figured after lunch we can take care of them," Charlie suggested. "The boys on the west side bridge have the extender to take them out from above.:

Rogers nodded, pulling back from the railing. "There been any other survivors coming up from the south side of town?"

"Not for two days now," Harry replied. "I'm pretty sure everybody who's going to make it out as done so."

Charlie straightened. "Although, you just give us the order and we'll get a team together and go door-to-door."

"This was a town of eight thousand people," Rogers explained, shaking his head. "Seventy-eight hundred of which lived south of this drainage ditch. We haven't seen anywhere near that many zombies wander our way, so god only knows how many are on the other side. I don't like the thought of leaving survivors over there, but for the moment it's going to have to stay that way."

Charlie nodded, shoulders slumping a bit. "I understand, Detective."

An airhorn cut harshly through the calm morning air, from the direction of the interstate.

Rogers sighed. "Besides, we have other issues to deal with at the moment." He put a hand on Charlie's shoulder. "I tell you what. Let me see what sort of chaos is at our doorstep, and if it's not too bad I'll see if I can't find a runner to get a message to any potential survivors over there. We got a deal?"

The older man nodded, eyes brightening. "Okay. Thank you."

Rogers smiled and gave his shoulder a reassuring squeeze before giving both men a wave and heading back off towards town. His smile fell from his face as he put distance between him and the men, guilt gnawing at his stomach from the lie he'd just told. There was no way in hell he'd be sending anyone across that bridge. It was far too risky.

The main part of the community consisted of a small line of building next to a strip mall. Rogers approached as an SUV pulled up, skidding to a stop in the dirt. As the dust settled, Francisco jumped out and approached him.

"Detective," he greeted as the passenger door opened, revealing a tall black man in military fatigues.

Rogers nodded. "Morning. What have you got for me today?"

"A shell shocked couple, a nice young lady, and a badass motherfucker," the military man declared as he skirted the hood of the vehicle.

"Humble," the Detective commented, raising an eyebrow. "I like him."

"Leon," the military man said with a grin, extending his hand.

Rogers returned it and shook heartily. "I'm Detective Rogers, welcome to Fabens."

A few locals opened the back doors of the vehicle, helping the frightened couple out and beginning to unload the bags. Clara thanked a man that helped her jump down from the SUV and then strolled over to the trio of men like she owned the place.

"And who might you be?" Rogers asked politely.

She planted a thumb on her chest. "I'm Clara."

"Welcome," the Detective said.

"So, how is the scouting going?" Francisco piped up as he stretched his legs.

"I don't know if you ever visited this area before the world came crashing down, but it's slim pickings out here," Rogers admitted. "We've gotten as far east as Allamore, but the communities are so small that most of them don't even have a gas station, let alone grocery stores."

"Well, what about this place?" Francisco shrugged, motioning in the general direction of the city. "There are hundreds of buildings on the other side of the bridge."

Rogers shook his head immediately. "And also potentially thousands of those creatures. We have maybe a hundred bullets in this town, so if somebody goes over there and attracts a horde, we could very easily get overrun. You get me some better weaponry and I'll risk it, but until then we're *not* going over there." His tone was sharp and final.

Francisco threw up his hands, undeterred by the stern Detective. "Do you not understand what's at stake here?" he snapped. "If the cartel discovers this place and you don't have anything to show your value to them, they will wipe you off the map. Not only that, but they will make examples of those of us who helped you. Rodriguez is doing everything he can to divert search parties away from this area, but it's not going to be long before he has no choice but to send people this way. A day, maybe two at the most."

"Well, if that's the case, then it sounds like you need to get on with

supplying us with weapons," Rogers
replied, crossing his arms.

Francisco narrowed his eyes. "Send
people to the other side of that bridge,"
he growled.

"No." The Detective jutted out his
chin. "It doesn't do us a damn bit of good
to find something useful over there if we
end up being overrun." He took a deep
breath to try to defuse the harsh energy
in the air. "My scouts are hitting Van
Horn today. It's a sizable town with a
grocery store, and with any luck, a liquor
store."

"You'd better make sure you find
something that will make the boss happy,"
Francisco warned. "Because if you don't,
it's *all* our asses."

Rogers let out a deep whoosh of
breath. "Trust me, nobody is more aware of
that than I am."

"Good luck," Francisco said, voice
softer, and offered his hand. They shook
firmly, a silent apology passing between
them as their gazes connected. He turned
and got back into the now-empty SUV,
making sure there were no locals behind
him as he backed up and peeled off back
the way he'd come.

"Well," Leon said as he stretched his
arms high above his head, "in the span of
an hour, I went from potentially dying

alone, to potentially dying in a group. I guess that's progress."

Rogers couldn't help but chuckle, shaking his head. "Sounds like you've had a fun day."

"Sniped three assholes, got into a Mexican standoff, and had a freshly cooked breakfast," Leon explained with a toothy grin.

The Detective raised an eyebrow. "Was there coffee with that breakfast?"

"Shit man, I wish," Leon replied with a snap of his fingers. "I haven't seen any of that in about a week."

Rogers clapped him on the back. "Why don't you come inside and I'll see if I can rectify that travesty," he said. "And we can talk about what you can help us out with."

Leon nodded and leaned over to grab his gear.

Clara cleared her throat in an overly dramatic manner. "And what about me?" she asked, arms crossed and foot tapping in the dirt.

Rogers motioned to an older woman at a nearby picnic table, speaking in low tones to the shell-shocked couple. "If you want to go talk to Helena over there, I'm sure she has something you can help her with."

The young woman glanced at the group and then back to the Detective, rolling her eyes. "So, you have an overabundance of able-bodied people who can venture out and find supplies, then?"

"No," Rogers replied slowly, rubbing his chin. He wasn't quite sure what to make of the petite woman as of yet. "We're quite short handed, actually. But do you really want to go out into zombie infested areas?"

"Fuck no I don't," Clara snapped, planting her hands firmly on her hips. "But you know what? I also don't want to become a prisoner of the cartel. You'd be lucky, they'd just put a bullet in your brain. You know what they'd do to me?"

He winced. He knew what she was insinuating, and she was absolutely right. He pursed his lips and looked her dead in the eye. "Are you capable of handling yourself out there?" he asked.

"I run marathons for fun," she replied, "so if I get into a situation where fighting isn't an option, I can certainly outpace them. I'm guessing that's more than you can say about the bulk of the residents here." She waved her hand in the general direction of a cluster of elderly people folding sheets on a porch across the street.

"Okay," Rogers said in defeat. "I'll introduce you to Trenton. He's my head scout. If he thinks you can be of use out there, you're in. If not, then you're staying here. It's his ass on the line, so it's his decision on who he brings. Fair?"

She nodded. "Fair."

"Well, come on then," he said as he turned back to Leon. "Let me show y'all the command center."

CHAPTER FOUR

"No offense Rogers," Leon said as he entered the old reception hall, "but I'm not sure this room lives up to the name *command center.*" He didn't look terribly impressed as he took in the cheap folding tables around the perimeter of the mid-sized room. There were various maps and white boards along the walls, with a smattering of people around studying documents and making lists.

"There's a fresh pot of coffee in the corner," the Detective said with a grin, motioning to the little camping stove in the corner.

Leon laid eyes on the happily bubbling percolator atop it, and snapped his fingers. "This is the best goddamn command center I've ever set foot in."

"Mister Rogers, would you and your friends like some coffee?" A woman with short bone-white hair walked up to them. She looked to be in her seventies, paper-thin skin crinkling as she smiled. "I just brewed it up."

"Thank you, Ethel," the Detective said warmly, taking her hand in his. "I think we'd all like one."

She turned her bright friendly eyes on Leon and Clara, who couldn't help but smile back at her. She shuffled off to check the brew as Rogers waved them over to a map of El Paso and surrounding areas on the wall. There were several red X marks over some of the smaller towns leading east on the I-10, a few with a circle around them.

"This is what we're working with," Rogers explained. "Antiquated, I know, but we're lucky we have a map that even goes out this far."

Clara leaned forward to study it. "What are the marks?"

"The X's are for places we've scouted, and the ones with circles around them are places we've cleaned out," the Detective explained. "I know you overheard me talking to Francisco, but we haven't found hardly anything that would be of value to the cartel boss."

"What has he deemed valuable?" Leon asked, scratching the back of his head. "Food? Medicine?"

Rogers shook his head. "Alcohol."

Leon's eyebrows shot to his forehead. "Let me see if I got this right. He's making you risk people's lives to go out on a beer run?"

"Tequila actually, but yeah, that's a pretty accurate description of the situation." The Detective sighed.

Clara's brow furrowed. "Why would he put *that* above everything else?"

"The cartel controls everything across the border," Rogers explained. "Rumor has it that they have a pretty sophisticated farming operation underway. And I would assume he doesn't give a shit if people get sick and die."

Leon scoffed. "Given the current state of the world, I'm guessing high quality tequila will soon be in extremely short supply."

"Bingo," Rogers replied, making his hand into a finger-gun and popping it off at his new companion. "Regardless of the absurdity of it, we need to locate some if we want to get on his good side."

Leon pursed his lips. "Or at least stay off his bad side."

"At least," the Detective agreed, and then turned his attention to an approaching man. "Trenton, good timing," he greeted the tall and muscular twenty-something. "I'd like you to meet Leon, and your new recruit, Clara."

The sandy-haired man cocked his head. "New recruit, huh?" He raised an eyebrow at the young woman. "You think you can hack it out there?"

"I survived a week living under the cartel," Clara replied, bristling a little.

Trenton shrugged. "Good enough for me. We're short-handed, anyway."

"We lose somebody else?" Rogers furrowed his brow.

"Carver wiped out on his bike," the younger man replied, rolling his eyes. "Pretty sure it's a broken arm, but Helena is tending to him now."

The detective rubbed the bridge of his nose. "Damn. Okay. Looks like he'll be on bridge duty for a while."

Ethel approached with a tray of steaming mugs of coffee and her warm smile.

"Ah, thank you, milady," Leon moaned with happiness, savoring the scent of the fresh brew. She chuckled as she set the mugs down on the table and retreated with the tray to a chorus of thanks from the others.

"So, you find anything of value in that last run?" Rogers asked as he sipped his steaming mug.

Trenton shook his head. "Nothing that's gonna help. Only found one bottle of tequila, but it's so cheap I think it would be better used to degrease my engine."

"Well then." The Detective shrugged. "You boys ready to hit Van Horn?"

"About as ready as we're ever going to be," Trenton replied. "The size of that place scares me."

Leon raised an eyebrow. "Scares you more than the cartel?"

"Bullet to the head is better than a bite to the neck," the younger man explained.

Leon nodded, and took a long sip of his brew. "Can't argue with that," he admitted.

"Well, it's an hour down the road, so y'all better get on trucking," Rogers cut in. "Francisco came by earlier and told us we're on a timetable."

Trenton paled. "How long?"

"A day, maybe two at most," the Detective replied.

"Fantastic," the younger man declared, sarcasm evident in his tone. He turned to Clara. "Okay, grab your weapon and let's head out."

Her cheeks pinked. "Um." She blinked a few times. "The cartel kind of frowned on civilians having weapons, so I don't really have one."

Leon unsnapped the knife holster from his belt, and held it out to her. "Here you go," he offered. "This baby served me well for years, hopefully it will do the same for you."

She took it gingerly, giving him a thin smile. "Thank you."

Rogers sighed and reached down to his ankle, lifting the leg of his jeans to reveal a snub-nose 38. "Ammo is really tight around here, so you'll only have the six shots that are chambered. Should be good in a pinch, though," he said as he held out the weapon.

Clara took it and stuffed it into her pocket with a somber nod.

"With where we're going, the last thing you want to do is make a lot of noise, anyway," Trenton piped up. "Being the center of attention is definitely something you don't want to be."

"Pre-apocalypse, I would have argued with you," Clara replied with a chuckle, and motioned for him to lead the way outside.

Leon watched them go, almost zoning out as he sipped his coffee. The dark liquid was more comforting than he'd ever known it to be.

"So," Rogers said, leaning against the table and drawing his new charge out of his reverie, "what do you bring to the table?"

Leon took a deep breath. "Well, for starters, I can shoot a motherfucker dead at two hundred yards. More importantly, however, I think I can help you out with your less than stellar mapping."

"Oh really?" the Detective asked, raising an eyebrow. "And how are you going to pull that one off?"

Leon drained his mug with a satisfying smack of his lips. "I tell you what, you grab me another cup of coffee, and I'll show you."

Rogers grinned. "Deal."

CHAPTER FIVE

Trenton led Clara through the parking lot towards two men on dirt bikes. They looked to be in the early twenties, fit and bronze in the sunlight. Clara raised an eyebrow. When he'd said that their buddy had fallen off of his bike, she hadn't assumed a motorized vehicle. He was lucky to have gotten away with just a broken arm.

There was a dune buggy too, housing another twenty something man, though he looked out of place of the handsome frat boys with his freckled skin and rounder belly.

"Hey, Trenton, you find yourself a girlfriend?" one of the dirt bike guys said.

The other one hooted and gave him a high five. "Yeah man, she's *all* kinds of hot."

Clara didn't even break stride, stalking up to the two of them with her chin high. She put a hand on her hip, staring them down as she tapped the hilt of her knife with a sharp fingernail.

"I…" the first guy stammered, "I think we may have gotten off on the wrong foot here."

She cocked her head. "You think?"

"Clara, I'd like you to meet Reed and Jay," Trenton said, obviously amused with the exchange. "From this point on they will be fine upstanding citizens. Gentlemen, this is Clara."

Jay gulped and smiled nervously, nodding at her. Reed gave her a little salute.

"And over here is Malcolm." Trenton inclined his head to the driver in the dune buggy. "He's going to be your ride to Van Horn."

Clara gave the duo a thousand-watt smile and then turned on her heel, heading over to the vehicle. She raised her eyebrow at the amount of duct tape holding the thing together. Every metal surface seemed to be buried in rust and there were even exposed wires sticking out from the engine.

"Hi." She gave the driver a wave and motioned to the hole where the windshield should have been. "Is this thing actually going to make it to Van Horn? It's looking a little worse for wear."

Malcolm smiled and patted the steering wheel. "This is a tough old girl," he said. "I've had her for years and she hasn't let me down yet." He reached into a compartment and pulled out a pair of goggles, holding them out to her. "You're going to need these. The windshield is… kinda missing."

Clara laughed and put them on, shaking her head as she slid into the passenger's seat. "All right," she said. "Let's do this."

He turned the key and the engine chugged a little before quieting down again. The dirt bikes started up no problem, rumbling to life, and Reed and Jay peeled out of the parking lot. Trenton wandered over.

"Starter trouble again?" he asked.

Malcolm nodded. "Yeah, she'll get going here in a minute," he replied. "Y'all go ahead, we'll catch up."

Trenton gave him a little salute and hopped on his own dirt bike, kicking it on and then speeding off after the others.

Malcolm tried again, but the motor just wouldn't turn over.

Clara raised an eyebrow. "Usually have this kind of performance issue?" she asked.

He blushed. "Only around pretty girls," he said, and then wrinkled his nose, as if he immediately regretted saying it.

Clara laughed it off, hoping to put him at ease, and this time the engine started up into a low rumble.

Malcolm sighed in relief and popped the dune buggy into gear. "All right, hang on."

CHAPTER SIX

Rogers headed back over to Leon, a fresh steaming mug in hand. The older man was setting up a heavy-duty looking laptop hooked up to a power bar.

"What…" the Detective trailed off, mouth opening and closing in shock. "Whatcha got there?"

"This, sir, is a state of the art communications laptop," Leon replied as he rummaged around in one of his duffel bags. "This allows me to the ability to tap into satellites currently circling the globe."

"Um." Rogers scratched the back of his head. "Does it require power?"

Leon nodded. "A shitload."

"Sorry to say that we haven't had power in this town since we got here," the Detective admitted.

"Not an issue, my friend," Leon replied with a toothy grin. "Be a pal and point me to a window that faces south."

Rogers furrowed his brow and motioned to one of the large windows on the south end of the building, watching with fascination as Leon pulled out a rolled up piece of black material. There was a cable attached to one end, and it flopped down as the tall man flung open the roll like a beach towel. He headed over and opened the window, hanging the material out the side of the building and then closing it to hold it in place.

"Perfect," Leon murmured as he ran the cable back to his power bar.

"Well," Rogers said, impressed as he shook his head. "What do we have here?"

"This here is a portable, flexible, solar panel," Leon explained. "It's capable of powering this laptop and pretty much everything else in this room. Although it's gonna take a little while for this baby to get up to speed."

The Detective let out a long whistle. "And how exactly did you acquire this stuff, if you don't mind me asking?"

"I was visiting for a training exercise at Fort Bliss, on the northeast side of the city," Leon replied as he opened up the computer. "When this shit went down, it didn't take long for the base commander to get the order to pull back to Kansas".

"Now, one of the perks of being military intelligence is that very few people have the clearance to know what my orders are, and the base commander was *not* on that list. I simply told him my orders were to take what I needed from the base and move to an undisclosed location. I don't think he really gave a shit if I was telling the truth or not, so he shrugged, threw me a set of keys and told me to go wild. Forty-five minutes later I had a jeep loaded down with gear."

Rogers rubbed his chin thoughtfully. "In the early days of this thing, there were some rumors going around about Fort Bliss. Is it really as bad as what people say?"

"I'll admit, I don't have firsthand knowledge," Leon said with a sigh. "Once I got out, I had no intention of going back. But a few days ago, I got in touch with a few boys from the base who decided that the military life no longer appealed to them. Based on what they told me, it's a complete and total shitshow there."

The Detective winced. "That bad?"

"According to them, the base commander didn't have the stones to do what was needed, which was to put down the infected men," Leon explained, voice hard. "Instead, he sealed the camp up tight and left them in there to turn."

Rogers' jaw dropped. "Christ." He shook his head in disbelief. "So there's a zombie army inside the base?"

"Unless the cartel has gone in and cleaned it out," Leon said bitterly.

The Detective let out a deep *whoosh* of breath. "That hasn't happened," he replied, thankful for small miracles. "Francisco said they sent a small squad to scope the place out, hoping there was some military grade gear in there. He said one guy was able to get to the fence, but had a dozen bites on him. After that, they doubled the locks and put some guards on it to make sure nothing got out."

"Well, that's a good piece of news, at least," Leon said. "Don't want the cartel to be running around with military shit."

Rogers peered down his nose at the flickering computer screen. "So your buddies… any chance they can come help us?"

"Not anytime soon," Leon replied with a sigh. "We're not supposed to chat for three more days, and besides, last I heard they were roaming around New Mexico. It's doubtful they could get here in a timely manner."

The Detective wrinkled his nose. "That's a shame." He paused, taking a sip of his coffee. "At least it's comforting to know that there are some people out there on our side."

Leon nodded, and raised his mug in a salute to the sentiment.

CHAPTER SEVEN

Francisco sped up the I-10, headed to
the cartel checkpoint just southeast of El
Paso. He passed heaps of corpses that had
been chewed up by the mounted machine guns
on the guard trucks defending the
checkpoint.

He slowed to a stop at the gate,
leaning out the window to the armed guard
standing there.

"Hey, can you let me through?" he
asked. "I'm on my way to report in to
Rodriguez."

"It's going to be a moment, sir," the
guard replied, putting up a hand. "We were
told this is a closed checkpoint, so we
have to get your clearance."

Francisco growled. "Do you know who I
am?"

"Yes, sir, mister Francisco, I do."
The guard swallowed nervously. "But I also
know who told me to close this checkpoint,
and I don't want to anger them either."

The driver sighed, leaning his head
back against his seat. "You're right," he
said, waving a hand. "Do what you need to
do."

The guard nodded in appreciation and
stepped away from the vehicle as he
pressed on the little communicator in his

ear. He turned around and spoke in quiet tones.

Francisco began to tap on the steering wheel a bit, but forced himself to stop. He needed to keep his cool. Cool as a cucumber.

The guard turned back to him. "Sir, if you don't mind me asking, what were you doing southeast of the city?"

"I do mind, actually," the driver snapped. He knew he had to be firm and unrelenting, even as his heart pounded in his chest. "I don't report to you. If you or whoever is on the other side of that little radio wants to know what the fuck I was doing, then they can go ask Rodriguez. *That's* who I report to. Now, if there's nothing else, can you kindly move the fuck out of my way before I run your ass down?"

The guard touched his earpiece, and then nodded, waving at one of the guard trucks to move out of the way. "Have a good day, mister Francisco," he said.

The driver huffed and rolled up his window, kicking up dust as he sped through the checkpoint.

As Francisco peeled out towards El Paso, two men stepped out of one of the guard trucks. Juan Pablo straightened his tie and suit jacket and strolled over to watch the truck disappearing into the distance.

"Hector, did you find any of that at all suspicious?" he asked, inclining his head to his tall partner.

Hector nodded his bald head. "Every single word of it, sir."

"I'm wondering if you'll run a quick errand for me," Juan Pablo said, crossing his arms.

His partner straightened. "Anywhere you wish, sir."

"Grab a truck and take a drive down the interstate here," his superior instructed. "Spend half an hour or so, and see if you find anything that might be of note."

Hector nodded. "I'll return soon, sir."

"Thank you," Juan Pablo replied, clapping him on the shoulder before sending him off. He stared at the cloud of dust still hovering where Francisco had driven off. "What are you up to?"

CHAPTER EIGHT

Francisco drove slowly through the streets of El Paso, surveying the ever-depressing scene. Cartel members walked the streets, chests puffed out and heads held high, guns always at the ready with their swagger turned up to a thousand. Terrified civilians peeked out through broken windows, meekly staying inside to avoid drawing attention to themselves and risk getting killed.

The zombies weren't the biggest threat here.

He turned down the main strip towards city hall, and slowed to a stop outside. He jumped down and furrowed his brow.

"Hey, you can't park here," a cartel member with a cigar hanging out of his mouth barked. "Can't you see we're setting up a celebration?"

Francisco shrugged as he sauntered over. He could see. There were at least a dozen civilians, climbing up ladders at gunpoint to hang decorations all over the street.

"Relax, I'm only going to be here for a few minutes," Francisco said.

"I don't care if you're just here to take a piss," the cigar man snapped. "You need to move that car, *now*."

Francisco steeled his gaze. "I'm here to meet with Rodriguez." The tone of finality and the name-drop seemed to tame the man, and he pulled the cigar from his mouth to hock a thick glob of spit onto the ground.

"Fine," he growled. "Just be back quickly. We have a lot of work to do."

Francisco waved his hand around his head. "What is all this, anyway?" he asked.

"It's a celebration of Tiago Rivas, the man who led us to the taking of El Paso!" the cigar man bellowed, spreading his arms, and several cartel members dotting the street raised their fists and hooted cheers in response.

Francisco shook his head. "Another celebration. What a waste."

"It's never a waste to celebrate our glorious boss!" the cigar man balked.

The shorter man turned towards city hall, or at least what used to be city hall. "Yeah, let's see if you're saying that when we're out of food." He strode into the building taking in the flurry of cartel members running back and forth like chickens with their heads cut off. He managed to snatch someone by the arm on the way by. "Have you seen Rodriguez?" he asked.

The young cartel member pointed down the hall to the right, where the door to a large office stood open. Francisco nodded in thanks and headed in.

Rodriguez stood over a large table, a map of the city spread out beneath him. He slammed his hand down hard, startling the four men standing at the other end of the table.

"I don't want to hear your excuses," Rodriguez said, voice low and menacing. "I want the asshole who gunned down three of our brothers found and brought to justice."

"Sir, we've checked the area twice," one of the men stammered meekly, wincing as his superior slammed his hand down on the table again.

"Well check it again!" Rodriguez boomed. "Burn the place to the fucking ground if you must, but this person needs to be found. Do *not* come back without them."

The four cartel members nodded before rushing out the door, eager to get out of the fire. Francisco shut the door behind them and chuckled.

"You know they're never going to find him," he said.

Rodriguez grinned, taking a sip of his coffee. "Of course, but it will keep them busy for another few hours." He sat down in his office chair, motioning for his friend to sit opposite him. "So, you were able to safely extract him?"

"Yes, he's with the detective in Fabens," Francisco replied.

"Good," his superior replied with a nod. "Have they made any progress?"

Francisco sighed as he took a seat. "No. They haven't."

Rodriguez pursed his lips. "Did you explain the situation-"

The door suddenly burst open, interrupting them proper, as a fuming young man in an Armani suit stormed into the office.

"Why are you sending my men back out to that abandoned town?" he demanded.

Rodriguez sighed, as if dealing with an insolent child. "Because, Angel, I want the man who killed our people found and dealt with."

"Fuck him," Angel spat the words. "He's probably in the middle of the desert dying of thirst right now. We need to be expanding our empire."

"In due time," Rodriguez replied, voice still calm and level.

The younger man snarled, resting his fists on the table and leaning forward. "The time is *now*. You have dragged your feet and held us back long enough. It's time for us to move down the I-10 and claim it for ourselves."

"We will head that way when I say we're ready to," the older man explained, as he had what felt like a hundred times before.

Angel sneered. "My father-"

"Your father put me in charge for a reason," Rodriguez cut in, setting down his cup. "I don't care if you're the boss' son, if he wanted you to have a decision-making position he would have given it to you. But he gave it to me.

"So go and do as your told, and take your men back to the Butterfield to find the person who murdered three of our brothers in cold blood. If there is resistance in the area, we need to quash it."

Angel grunted and turned on his shiny leather heel, stalking to the door. He paused in the frame as he wrapped his hand around the knob.

"I know you're stalling for a reason," he warned, a mischievous sparkle in his defiant eyes. "There's something down the interstate that you want to keep to yourself. I don't know what you're hiding, but I will find out. You can guarantee that." He slammed the door behind him, leaving a deafening silence in his wake.

"I can't keep them at bay much longer," Rodriguez admitted quietly, pinching the bridge of his nose. "If the Detective doesn't find something, and find it soon, it's not going to be good."

Francisco shook his head. "Angel might not be our most pressing issue."

"Christ, what now?" his friend demanded.

He took a deep breath. "I got stopped at the checkpoint on the southeast side of town. Someone was in one of the trucks, relaying questions to the guard. If it was someone loyal to Angel, they might put two and two together."

Rodriguez sighed, shaking his head. He picked up his mug again, swirling the brown liquid around instead of taking a sip. "Did the Detective ask for anything that could be helpful to them?"

"He said they're short on guns and ammo, but it's too risky to get into the armory," Francisco said with a shrug.

His friend pursed his lips, seeming lost in thought for a time. "I'm afraid we don't have a choice," he said finally. "We're out of time. See what you can get to him, just make sure you take the long way around to avoid that checkpoint."

Francisco got to his feet and nodded. "I won't let you down." He headed for the door, taking one last glance back at his superior's contemplative face before he exited the office.

CHAPTER NINE

Trenton skidded to a stop a half-mile away from Van Horn, leaning on one leg as he pulled a set of binoculars from one of his saddlebags. He surveyed the area as the others pulled up behind him. One by one, everyone turned off their engines, and he lowered the binoculars.

"Okay, looks like there's a string of buildings on the north side of the interstate that leads into the main part of town," Trenton said. "I'm only seeing a handful of shops, none of which look like a liquor store."

"Well hell, there *has* to be one." Reed threw his hands up. "How the hell can anybody live out here and not drink?"

Trenton shook his head. "If there is one, I'm not seeing it."

"You know," Jay piped up, "I went out on a couple of dates with a girl from Van Horn. She lived in a pretty nice house."

Reed snorted. "Bitch, nobody that lives in a nice house would ever go out with you."

"Okay, a nice house for the *area*." Jay rolled his eyes. "Nicer than anything else I saw driving through the town. I figure if we can't find a liquor store, that might be our best bet."

"It's thin," Trenton mused, "but I've heard thinner." He rubbed his chin.

"Goddammit," Malcolm muttered, furiously tapping one of the gauges on the dune buggy.

Trenton raised an eyebrow. "Problem?"

"I'm almost out of gas," the younger man replied sheepishly.

"Jesus Christ man, can you not keep up with this shit?" Reed snapped.

Malcolm scowled. "I filled up with you guys! I should still have half a tank." He shook his head. "Must have sprung a leak again."

Trenton sighed and put the binoculars to his eyes again, trying to find a gas station. "Looks like there's a truck stop on the south side of the interstate," he said. "You two get filled up, then circle around the east side of the city and see if you can find a liquor store."

Clara raised her hand. "How are we going to fill up if there's no power?"

"It's a truck stop in a small town in the middle of the desert," Malcolm replied. "More than likely, they have a generator. If a storm rolls through and knocks the power out, they're not exactly at the top of the list to get it fixed, so they have to be prepared."

Trenton got off of his bike and walked over to them, putting a firm hand on the young man's shoulder. "Do *not* go through the center of town, do you understand?" he asked. "God only knows what's in there."

"Yeah, of course," Malcolm replied, blinking rapidly. "I'm not stupid."

Reed snorted. "Says the man who's out of gas."

"Fuck you!" Malcolm snapped, narrowing his eyes.

Trenton clapped his hands together sharply. "Drop it, both of you," he warned. "Malcolm, Clara, the three of us are going to go around the west side of town and check out the houses on the north side. We're going to be on frequency thirteen. Call only if there is an emergency or if you locate our target." He held up his walkie talkie and gave it a little shake.

Malcolm pulled out his own and handed it over to Clara. "Here, you'd better hang on to this," he said. "I have a tendency to misplace them."

"If something goes wrong and we lose contact, meet back at this spot in two hours," Trenton instructed. "Any questions?" He waited a beat, but nobody said anything. "Okay, let's do this." He strode over and got back on his bike, kicking it back to life.

He watched the dune buggy trundle off towards the truck stop, and he turned to lead the others along the west edge of town. They found a dirt trail, likely a walking trail for the locals, and though it was a bumpy ride, it was a lot safer than going through town.

Trenton slowed to a stop when he spotted a row of relatively expensive-looking houses through the trees. "Is that them?" he asked.

"Yep," Jay replied with a nod. "That's them."

"What's that building over there?" Reed asked, pointing to a fairly large structure on the far side.

Trenton pulled out his binoculars, surveying a football field with bleachers next to it. "Looks like a school," he said.

"If there's nothing in the houses, we could give that a shot," Reed suggested.

Jay's brow furrowed. "You think we're going to find the booze we're looking for inside a school?"

"Shit man, every teacher I know is a borderline alcoholic," Reed replied, rolling his eyes. "I mean, wouldn't you be if you had to deal with dozens of assholes like us every day?"

Trenton shook his head. "Have you ever seen a teacher's pay stub?"

Reed shrugged. "Nope."

"Let's just say they aren't going to be buying top shelf stuff," the older man replied, and turned the binoculars back to the houses.

They were out in the open, no fences lining any of the yards. A few zombies roamed about behind the eastern-most house, but that seemed to be the only activity.

"Route looks pretty clear," Trenton reported. "Just two of those things outside the house on the left."

Reed crossed his arms. "So, we start on the right?"

"No, we should take them out." Trenton shook his head and got off of his bike, rolling it down into the bushes. "If we draw their attention and they start making a racket, they could bring the whole town down on us."

Jay reached down for the long metal pipe he'd secured to the side of his bike before walking it over next to Trenton's. He made sure the kickstand was secure and then got out of the way so Reed could join them. The latter took off his button-up overshirt, leaving him in a beater with his weapon harness housing a mini metal baseball bat.

Trenton pulled up one of his pant legs to free his machete, and turned to the duo. "Okay, which one of you wants to pick the lock?" he asked.

The two younger men turned towards each other and immediately engaged in a quick game of rock, paper, scissors.

"Dammit," Jay muttered as his friend cut his flattened hand with his finger scissors.

Reed scoffed. "It's just one zombie, man, you can handle it." He clapped his companion on the back.

"Last time I swung this thing, I pulled a muscle," Jay whined, giving the pipe a few *whooshes* through the air.

Trenton waved for them to follow him through the trees. "It's a bit of a walk, so you have time to limber up."

"Everybody remember where we parked," Reed said, making a beeping noise with his mouth as he mimed using an auto-lock clicker.

When they reached the tree line, they crouched in the bushes behind the backyard. The zombies stared up at the house as they ambled back and forth, not paying attention.

"You get that door open quick," Trenton whispered to Reed, "we don't know what else is around here."

The younger man nodded, and got ready to spring.

Trenton dove out of the bushes first, leaping for the zombie on the left. His footsteps alerted it just in time for it to turn to face a machete to the mouth, the blade cutting its head in half. As it crumpled to the ground, Jay lowered his shoulder and caught the other one in the back, sending it crashing to the ground.

Before it could get up, he landed his pipe onto the back of its head twice in quick succession. The creature twitched once and then fell still, and Jay rotated his shoulder a bit, switching the pipe to his other hand.

"You good?" Trenton whispered, and the younger man gave him a thumbs up.

They approached Reed, who was still working on the lock, digging around in there for all he was worth. Jay tapped him on the shoulder and pointed at the met he knelt on. His friend moved and they lifted it, finding a silver key beneath.

Jay smacked him on the shoulder and grinned, and Reed shook his head, shooting him the bird before sliding the key into the lock. He gave a silent countdown before pulling the door open, and Trenton rushed in first.

Something collided into his side, and he flopped to the tile floor, a snarling corpse on top of him. He got a hand up around the creature's neck, bracing his elbow to keep the snapping jaws at bay. More moans came from the hallway, and he waved frantically at Jay.

"I've got this, clear the house!" he commanded.

Reed slammed the door and locked it, the two of them heading quickly across the kitchen. Jay slammed the end of his pipe into the eye of a shambling zombie in the hallway, and Reed slipped past to check the living room. The duo made quick work of the bedrooms at the front of the bungalow, finding nobody else.

"Clear!" Reed called as he emerged from the bathroom, and Jay nodded at him.

"Great!" Trenton grunted from the kitchen. "Y'all wanna come help me, now?"

Jay's eyes widened and he barreled back. "Shit, sorry man!" he blurted as he and Reed each took an arm of the older man's attacker. They jerked it back and pinned it against the wall, holding it still so Trenton could stab it in the forehead with his machete.

As he wiped the blade on the corpse's pants, Trenton waved his free hand around the large kitchen. "Reed, you check in here," he instructed. "I'll do the living room. Jay, you scour the bedroom closets and dressers."

"Just in case they have a secret stash?" Jay asked.

Trenton nodded. "Or ammo. It's not our primary target, but damned if it isn't a close second."

They split up to search the house, and the only sound was the creaks of opening cabinets and the *clickety-clack* of rummaging items. Within a few minutes, they reconvened in the kitchen.

"Not a goddamn thing in here," Reed reported as he stood up from beneath the sink.

Trenton held up a half-full bottle of whiskey. "Found a bottle of cheap shit by the recliner," he said. "Guess the previous owner got tired of standing up for his drinks."

"I found a box of nine mil, no gun though," Jay said as he stuffed the ammo into one of his side pockets.

"Well, it's better than nothing," Reed said with a shrug.

Trenton settled his backpack on his back. "Okay, let's get geared up for house number two."

CHAPTER TEN

Malcolm pulled up to the first pump, about fifteen feet away from the main truck stop building. They unbuckled their seat belts and got out of the dune buggy.

"We need to find the generator," he said, pointing around the building. "Should be around the back, there."

Clara furrowed her brow. "Aren't you going to turn this thing off?"

"With as temperamental as it's being, it's best to leave it up and running," he replied, shaking his head. "Last thing we need is to get it gassed up and then not be able to start it."

She pursed her lips, a million concerns springing to her lips, but she bit them back. These guys were the experienced ones, not her. She was just along to help, and helping meant doing as she was told.

She drew her knife and headed around the building, her new companion following behind her. Around the corner was a tall wooden privacy fence, creating a small cubby nestled right up against the wall of the truck stop.

Malcolm peeked through a crack in the wood. "Bingo," he said as he spotted the generator inside. He looked around, spotting a tire iron leaning up against a pile of scrap metal nearby. He picked it up and made quick work of the wooden door, prying open the lock. As the door sprang free, he handed the tire iron over to Clara. "Here, you should hang on to this," he said. "It'll give you a little more reach than that knife."

She took it with a nod, sheathing her knife. "Thanks." She turned the tire iron over in her hands a few times as he stepped into the cubby and pulled the cord on the generator a few times.

It sputtered and then roared to life, drowning out the sound of the dune buggy out front.

Malcolm turned back to her. "We should make this quick," he yelled, "I don't like how loud this thing is!"

Clara nodded and gave him a thumbs up instead of replying. The duo froze on the spot, breath catching as they spotted movement across the road. An old run-down trailer park stood there, and close to what looked like eighty zombies emerged from the thick of it, staggering towards the source of the noise.

Malcolm tore to the pump to refuel as fast as he could, but Clara stayed rooted to the spot, mesmerized at the size of the horde lumbering towards them. This was the biggest group of zombies she'd seen so far, and she blinked slowly, her brain suddenly sluggish. She couldn't help but wonder what the hell she'd gotten herself into—if she were in over her head with these guys.

Malcolm quickly popped off the gas cap and inserted the nozzle, but the trigger popped back when he tried to dispense gas.

"Fucking hell," he muttered, and pulled a credit card from his pocket. Even in the apocalypse, big brother still wanted every last cent. He entered his pin, and then tried the trigger again, but still no gas.

The screen on the pump flashed *Would you like a car wash today?*

"No, I don't want a fucking car wash!" Malcolm screamed, and hit the decline button. Finally the gas started to flow, and he turned to signal for Clara to run to him. As her glazed-over eyes registered him, her mouth opened in a scream that he couldn't hear over the cacophony of noise around him.

He didn't realize what she was saying, but the intent was clear when a warm and gooey hand wrapped around his bicep.

Clara leapt forward, but as Malcolm struggled with the zombie, the hose came free of the tank and spewed liquid all over the place. The gas ignited from the running dune buggy, and liquid fire bathed the ground in a freakish glow.

She turned tail and quickly pounded the emergency pump shutoff button on the side of the building, and then the fire suppression button next, sending a thick white cloud from the awning down onto the flames.

She pressed her back against the brick wall, holding her tire iron at the ready, holding her breath as she waited for the cloud to dissipate.

"Malcolm?" she croaked, and swallowed with fear as the silhouette of a staggering corpse appeared in the smog. Two more flanked it, and then she could make out the shape of the dune buggy. Next to it, there appeared to be three shadows feasting on a fallen fourth, and a sob ripped its way out of her throat.

Clara didn't have much time to think. The trailer park horde had caught her scent, and everything under the awning was fire-singed but still dangerous. So she ran.

She pumped her legs as fast as she could into the street, and made a snap decision to run under the bridge towards town. She didn't think that running for the interstate would help her, and if she ran into a horde with no cover she'd be screwed. At least in town she could hide as she moved.

On the other side of the bridge, there were a few handfuls of corpses scattered about, moving slow. Nearby there was a row of semi-detached houses, one end shrouded in dense tree cover.

She took off as quickly as she could for that end, using the bushes to hide from any staggering dead. She hit the back door of the end house, and wiggled the knob. It didn't appear to have a deadbolt, so she jammed her knife into the latch and jiggled it until the lock came free. She dove in and slammed the door behind her, raising her tire iron in a defensive position in case anything came at her from the dark.

After a few moments of silence, she let out a deep ragged breath and locked the door again, pressing her back against it and sinking to the floor. What the fuck was she supposed to do now?

CHAPTER ELEVEN

"Motherfucker." Reed slammed the kitchen cupboard shut in frustration. "Doesn't anybody drink in this town?"

Jay put a hand on his shoulder in an attempt to calm him down. "Dude, you need to relax, we'll find something."

"This is the fourth house we've searched," Reed grunted as he swatted his friend's arm away. "If we don't find anything the cartel is going to murder us all."

Trenton walked into the kitchen and leaned on the island, facing them. "Jay's right," he said gently. "You need to relax, man. We still have another rich person's house to hit, and we haven't even gone into town yet. Plenty of opportunity to find what we need."

"Besides, if we don't find anything, we can always say *fuck it* and just head east," Jay added, a lopsided grin breaking out on his face. "It'll be like *Easy Rider*, just on dirt bikes… with zombies."

Reed couldn't help but laugh. "You know they died at the end of *Easy Rider,* don't you?"

"Dude, spoilers!" Jay clapped his hands over his ears, gasping dramatically.

Trenton peeked out the back window. "Looks like the coast is clear, let's move," he said, back to business, and the trio got ready to move. At this point darting across the backyard and standing guard while Reed picked the neighbor's lock was routine.

"We're in," he hissed as the bolt clicked, and he turned the knob.

An ear-splitting alarm blasted into their faces, echoing with jarring clarity through the air.

"What the fuck, man?!" Jay screamed, eyes wide. "There's no fucking power, how is this thing going off?!"

Reed rushed inside. "Fuck if I know, but it is!" he yelled back, nearly drowned out by the bleating alarm.

Trenton shoved Jay in and motioned for them to keep their eyes open as he slammed the door behind them. They split up and ran through the house, being cautious in case of zombies but trying to hurry to find the source of the insanely loud alarm.

Trenton skidded down the side hallway, and spotted the attic trap door in the ceiling. He pulled it down and hurried up the ladder, finding a car battery hooked up to a series of electronics. He grabbed a handful of wires and yanked them free, finally silencing the alarm.

He let out a deep breath, ears ringing from the sudden silence, and slid down the ladder.

"What the hell was it?" Reed asked from the other end of the hallway, speaking louder than necessary over his own ears.

"Fucking jury rigged job," Trenton replied as he strode over to him, "hooked it up to a car battery."

Jay hollered at them from the living room, staring out through the bay window overlooking the front yard. "Holy fuck man, we gotta go! We gotta go and go now!" he yelled, motioning wildly to the window.

Several dozen zombies emerged from the houses across the street, pouring around the corners with no sign of stopping.

"Jay, we need to-" Trenton began, but the younger man dashed past him before he could finish, tearing for the back door.

Reed made a mad grab for him, but missed. "Jay!" he cried, and tore after his friend.

Jay burst out the back door, right smack dab into a zombie on the deck. His momentum sent them tumbling down the stairs, and he let out a high-pitched scream as the ghoul sunk its teeth into his shoulder. He struggled to roll away, yelping at the feel of his flesh tearing away.

He pulled out his gun and fired right into the zombie's temple, spraying brain matter across the grass, but before he could get up another rotting body fell on him from behind. This one bit into his throat and he fired into its eye socket. He rolled over onto his back, expecting another zombie, but seeing only Reed staring down at him from the deck, eyes wide with fear.

Jay gargled and smiled, as if telling one last joke, and then put his gun to his own head, pulling the trigger.

Reed screamed in agony, leaping forward, but Trenton grabbed him around the waist and all but threw him back into the house. He slammed the door and locked it, pressing his back against it just in time for the smacking of dead hands against the window.

Trenton knelt down in front of his companion, putting a hand on his shoulder. "We can mourn later, but we've gotta get the fuck out of here now," he said firmly.

Reed nodded jerkily, swallowing hard and getting to his feet. He followed Trenton to the front window, watching through the bay window as the yard flooded with zombies. It was like a rotted mosh pit on the lawn, smashing up against each other to get to the house.

Trenton shook his head. It would be no good trying to get out the front. He hurried to the east side bedroom, peering out the window on the side of the house. There were only a few zombies between the two structures, and he could see the street from there. The backyard was a no-go, completely swamped all the way across.

He turned to Reed, whose eyes were beginning to glaze over.

Trenton growled and smacked him in the back of the head. "Focus. We gotta go and go now. Are you with me?"

Reed nodded again, blinking back tears. "Yeah," he replied hoarsely, and cleared his throat. "Yeah."

"Okay, we've gotta get to the street," Trenton continued. "We get out this window and run like motherfuckers."

The younger man shook his head. "But to where?"

Trenton pursed his lips for a moment, and then straightened his shoulders. "To the school."

"The *school*?" Reed balked.

"It's big, and there are lots of potential exits," Trenton explained.

Reed scrubbed his hands down his face and tightened his grip on the bat in his hands. "Okay. Good enough for me."

Trenton nodded and went back to the window to make sure they still had a path. He carefully unlocked the window and eased it open as quietly as he could, the moans of the horde outside floating into them. He gave a silent countdown and then vaulted out the window, lowering his shoulder into a zombie's chest.

It stumbled into two of its brethren as Reed hit the ground and the two of them tore over the fallen trio towards the road.

Hundreds of zombies flooded the street, all ambling towards the house that had been the source of the dinner bell. A few stragglers turned to head towards the duo as they navigated the deadly obstacle course of oncoming corpses.

A cluster in the middle of the road clogged up their path, and Reed held his bat out like a jousting lance and rammed it into the sternum of the lead zombie, knocking it into its pack like a set of bowling pins. The living duo leapt over the surprised fallen, tearing and ducking and weaving around sluggish zombies.

As they got further from the house, the crowd thinned a bit, though more and more were turning around to pursue them. By the time they hit the school parking lot, there were at least a hundred in pursuit.

"Give me your bat," Trenton huffed as Reed knelt down in front of the front door to the school. The younger man tossed it to him and got to work on the lock.

Trenton turned and feinted side to side, trying to cluster the two fastest zombies as they power walked towards him. His movements caused them to stumble closer to one another, so that when he crushed the first one with a bat to the skull, it tripped up the second one. Trenton took a knee and bashed the back of its head into the pavement, springing back up to his feet.

"You've got about ten seconds or we're gonna have to make a run for it," he said, eyeing the horde about thirty yards away.

Reed grunted. "Yep," he replied, still digging in the lock.

Trenton glanced from him to the horde, keeping watch for any quick power walking stragglers. "Six seconds." He looked to the right, mapping the best escape route around some dumpsters. "Four seconds." Zombies flooded around the left side of the building, blocking any hope of getting away on that side. "Fuck," he muttered as more swarmed the right side, leaving them completely trapped. "Fifteen seconds and we're dead."

317

He backed up next to Reed, drawing his gun. He had no desire to know what it felt like to be eaten alive—and he sure as hell was going to make sure that neither of them would ever know.

The metallic *click* of the lock was music to his ears.

"Got it!" Reed cried as he yanked open the door, and they pulled it closed behind them in the nick of time. They pulled it shut as the horde descended on them, banging on the double doors in frustration.

Trenton locked the doors for good measure and tossed the bat back to Reed, raising his gun.

"Do you hear something?" Reed asked, eyes wide.

His companion shook his head. "No, but if I do, we need to be ready," he said, moving slowly and purposefully down the hallway. All of the classroom doors were closed, and neither of them felt the need to open them. Upon finding one that was half-open, Trenton covered it while motioning for Reed to open it all the way.

The room was empty, several desks overturned and pools of blood on the floor. Reed quietly shut the door behind them and Trenton headed for the windows, opening up the metal shutters a sliver to see outside.

"How's it look?" Reed asked, keeping his voice low.

Trenton shrugged as he surveyed the grassy area. "Well, it looks better than what was chasing us, that's for damn sure," he murmured. His eyes widened at the sight of a large smoke plume in the distance towards the interstate. "Oh, fuck me."

"What is it?" Reed asked, swallowing hard.

Trenton opened the shutter a little wider and pointed. "Come take a look."

Reed peered out and paled. "Fucking Malcolm, man, what did he do?"

"Let's see if we can find out," Trenton replied, and closed the shutter up tightly before pulling out his walkie talkie. He held it up to his lips. "Malcolm, Clara, either of you copy?" he asked, and let go of the button. There was nothing but static. "Malcolm, Clara, can you hear me?" He paused, pressing the radio against his forehead.

He sighed and headed for the nearest desk, setting the walkie talkie down and flopping back into the chair.

Reed pulled up a chair next to him. "Keep the faith man, they could just be avoiding zombies like we were," he said, though his voice sounded desperate in his own ears.

"Here's hoping," Trenton replied, scratching the back of his head.

There was a moment of silence, and Reed leaned forward, resting his elbows on his knees. "Do you think the cartel will really wipe out the town if we don't get back with something?"

Trenton took a deep breath. "I don't know," he admitted. "But at the moment, my only concern is finding a way out of *this* shit."

CHAPTER TWELVE

Rogers thrummed his fingers on the table, staring at the military laptop. The screen simply read *Connecting...* in green letters on a black screen.

"Does it usually take this long to connect?" he asked.

Leon nodded. "Unfortunately, yeah. I've only been able to tap into one satellite and it has a ninety minute clock to circle the globe," he explained. "When I do get it, we'll only have in-range imagery for about five minutes. I mean I could tap into another one, but I really don't want to draw attention to myself. I'm assuming there's a functional government working somewhere, and would rather them not getting upset with me."

"I can understand that," Rogers agreed, and then perked up as a loading bar appeared on the screen and began to rapidly fill.

"About damn time," Leon muttered. "Let's see what we can see."

The screen flickered and then went live, showing a top-down view of south Texas. Leon began typing to zoom in, centering on El Paso.

"Look at city hall," Rogers said, leaning over his shoulder. "That's where they said they were setting up."

Leon tapped a few more keys. "One trip to city hall, coming right up."

The screen focused in on city hall, showing dozens of people moving around on the street.

"What the fuck are they doing?" He furrowed his brow. "Looks like they're playing tag."

Rogers squinted and pointed to a few figures carrying something big and white across the street to a telephone pole. "Looks like they're setting up for a party."

"Shit." Leon shook his head in disbelief. "No wonder they have us out here risking our lives for booze."

The Detective nodded. "It's really a shame this thing doesn't have drone strike capability."

"Well, if we can ever get into Fort Bliss I might be able to make that a reality." Leon chuckled.

Rogers blinked at him. "Good to know," he replied, impressed.

"Okay, well, this ain't doing us a whole hell of a lot of good," Leon said with a sigh. "Where are your boys at?"

"A town called Van Horn," the Detective replied. "It's about ninety miles east on the I-10. Can't miss it, as it's the biggest piece of civilization on that route."

Leon clicked away at the keyboard again. "All right, let's take a trip." As he zoomed in on the town in question, they noticed a large smoke plume rising from the south of the city. "That can't be good."

"No, no it can't," Rogers agreed, blinking rapidly. "I mean, maybe they did that as a diversion?" He put a hand to his jaw as he took in the zombie horde on the north side of the city.

The two men stared at the screen in mild shock for a few moments, barely blinking when the screen went black.

Satellite out of range scrawled across the black monitor.

Rogers took a deep breath and straightened up. "Leon, I know we just met," he said firmly, "but I have a huge favor to ask of you."

"The tone of your voice makes it sound like you about to ask something that's gonna make my black ass hitchhike outta here," Leon said as he leaned back in his chair.

The Detective took a deep breath. "It doesn't look like our scouts are gonna make it back." He licked his lips and crossed his arms. "So when the cartel comes, I'm going to need you to pose as the town's leader."

Leon closed the laptop and stood up, shoving cables back into his duffel bag. "Man, it's been a boatload of fun, but I'm gonna get on up outta here."

"I'm serious," Rogers insisted.

"And I'm serious too, motherfucker!" Leon snapped. "Why in the hell would I wanna act like this town's leader? You want me to get shot in the fucking face? Why don't you man the fuck up and do it your damn self?"

"Because I'm supposed to be dead," the Detective replied, pointing to the bandage on the side of his head. "Rodriguez, the second in command of the Rivas Cartel, did this to me in order to save my life. There are others in the cartel who think I'm dead. If they see me alive, they'll butcher this town on principle."

Leon stalked to the window and all but ripped it open, pulling his solar panel back inside. "So why the fuck should I stay, then?"

Rogers shrugged and let out a bitter laugh. "Because dying in a group is better than dying alone?"

The taller man took a deep breath as he stuffed the equipment back into his bag, zipping it up with an air of finality. He scrubbed his hands down his face and turned on the Detective.

"Why me?" he demanded. "Surely there's somebody else who can do it."

"Most of the people in this town were exiled out of El Paso," Rogers explained, "deemed useless and a waste of resources by the cartel. If one of them steps up to speak for us, they're not going to be taken seriously. You, on the other hand, being military intelligence, would make it seem like there is competent leadership here."

Leon sighed. "Well, based on our current conversation, it would be nice to have the appearance of competency in this town."

They shared a chuckle, diffusing the moment a bit, and Rogers stared up at him, hope in his eyes.

Leon scoffed and shook his head. "Okay." He held up a hand. "I'll do it, on *one* condition."

"Anything," Rogers replied quickly.

Leon puffed his chest out. "From here on out, you call me Mayor Leon."

The Detective burst into laughter, the stress of the day suddenly bubbling over into the only thing he could do. He held his gut as Leon clapped him on the back to make sure he was all right, and finally straightened up, gasping for breath.

Rogers shook his head and wiped a tear from his eye. "You got it, Mayor."

CHAPTER THIRTEEN

Rodriguez pointed to an area due east of the city, but before he could open his mouth to explain, one of the cartel members stepped forward.

"Sir, if I may," he began, "I spent a lot of time on this side of the border before this, and that area you want us to explore is vacant."

Rodriguez internally rolled his eyes, but schooled his expression into a glare and turned to the younger man. "Are you questioning my judgement?"

The cartel member gulped. "No-no sir," he stammered. "It's just… my cousins and I used to go dirt biking out there. So I speak from experience. I know you have a difficult job to do and I just want to help in any way I can."

Well, fuck, Rodriguez thought, realizing that he had no way out of this without raising suspicion. He sighed and turned to the group fully.

"Thank you for your input," he said, crossing his arms. "I tell you what, you and your men have been working hard for me. Go get some food, put your feet up, and come back to me in an hour and I'll have a new destination for you."

"Thank you, sir," the cartel member replied, grinning in relief. The group hurried to leave, and Rodriguez assumed they were eager to use every second of their restful hour.

Angel Rivas strolled in past the bustling group, and sneered at the older man. "Rodriguez." He drew out the name as if he were testing it in his mouth. "Still sending our men out on wild chases, I see."

"Just being thorough," Rodriguez replied with a flippant sigh, "something you were never good at. Which explains why I'm in charge and you're not."

Angel smirked. "Well, we'll see about that," he said, and snapped his fingers.

His superior lost all color in his face, not liking the smug look. His stomach dropped like a stone as Hector shoved Francisco into the room and onto the floor, bound and bloodied.

"What the fuck?" Rodriguez roared. "How dare you do this to one of my men!"

"*Your* men?" Angel sneered. "Oh, so they're *your* men now? I'm guessing that's going to be news to my father."

The older man stalked forward, inches from the cartel leader's son's nose. "You speak to me like that again, and the next words out of your mouth will be coated in your blood."

Angel's smug expression didn't falter, and he simply stepped away from his fuming opponent and kicked Francisco in the stomach. The bound man let out a *hoof* and a groan of pain, unable to even rise to his knees from the beating it looked like he'd endured.

Rodriguez stepped forward, shoulders squaring, but Angel drew a massive handgun. He cocked his head as well as the gun.

"You need to sit down," he demanded, and watched with glee in his eyes as the man that had been his superior sank slowly into a chair. "That's it, sit like a good little puppy."

Rodriguez clenched his fists. "I demand to know the meaning of this."

"I caught him stealing weapons from the armory," Juan Pablo announced from the front door.

"You dense motherfucker, he has armory clearance," Rodriguez snapped. "He has the right to get whatever he wants."

Juan Pablo pushed off of the doorframe, strolling forward with his hands clasped behind his back. "But not for *whomever* he wants," he drawled.

Rodriguez schooled his expression but beneath his heart pounded and there was a massive knot in his throat. He didn't like this situation at all. They could be well and properly fucked.

"You see, I was at the southeast checkpoint when he came back this morning," Juan Pablo explained as he paced back and forth. "He was acting, shall we say, suspicious. So I had my friend Hector here take a joy ride down the I-10." He motioned to the man standing proudly behind the hissing Francisco. "Hector, would you like to tell our friend here what you found?"

Rodriguez closed his eyes, taking a deep, calming breath. They were well and properly fucked.

Hector grinned. "Fabens."

"And they brought this information to me!" Angel cut in, sounding positively chipper. "Which cleared up why you kept sending our men to areas we know contained *nothing* of value."

Rodriguez opened his eyes, and shrugged as if he hadn't a care in the world. "So. What are you going to do? Shoot me?"

Angel shook his head, the curl of his lips animalistic. "Not unless I have to," he cooed. "I wouldn't want to rob my father of one of his favorite pastimes."

Juan Pablo spread his arms dramatically. "Hector, if you'd be so kind as to assist Mister Rodriguez to his feet." He grinned. "We're going to pay Tiago Rivas a visit."

CHAPTER FOURTEEN

Hector pressed the barrel of his
rifle against the back of Rodriguez' neck
until he reached up and rapped on Tiago's
office door. A bodyguard cracked the door,
peering down his nose at the group.

"Who is it?" The cartel leader's
voice carried from inside.

The bodyguard surveyed the motley
crew in front of him. "Rodriguez, your
son, and a few others," he replied,
sounding almost bored.

"Oh, I didn't realize the party was
starting in my office today," Tiago
replied and clucked his tongue. "Very
well, send them in."

The bodyguard opened the door wide,
stepping aside. Angel swept past Hector,
who held Rodriguez at arm's length by the
collar. Juan Pablo dumped Francisco onto
the floor, leaning against the wall and
crossing his legs at the ankle.

Tiago looked up from cutting his
steak and his eyes nearly bugged out of
his head. He shoved his chair back and
glared at his son.

"Angel, have you lost your mind?" he
demanded. "What are you doing, leading my
second-in-command around like a dog?"

His son raised his chin. "Juan Pablo
and I caught Rodriguez and this piece of

shit organizing a resistance movement against you."

Rodriguez scoffed and rolled his eyes.

Tiago pursed his lips, reaching down for his silk napkin. He dabbed daintily at his mouth and then skirted his desk, stalking over to his second-in-command. He raised an eyebrow.

"A resistance movement?" he asked, voice level.

Rodriguez shrugged, trying to seem casual though his heart throttled his chest. "Hardly."

"Then explain yourself," Tiago said with a wave of his hand, "against these serious accusations."

His second took a deep breath. "In the town of Fabens, I set up a safe haven for the undesirables who are expelled from the city. They are of no threat to you or any of us."

Tiago clucked his tongue and turned to his desk, lifting his glass of fine tequila and swirling it. "So, who am I to believe? My son, or my second-in-command?" He downed the glass and then pulled out his gold-plated handgun, whipping around, wide-eyed. "You two have *always* butted heads, but I thought you could work through it like mature fucking adults.

Apparently, I was wrong." He raised the gun to his second's forehead.

"Wait!" Francisco cried, scrambling to his knees as best he could.

Tiago laughed at the state of the man, and leaned over to accentuate how much lower his beaten subordinate was. "Oh? You wish you say something?"

"Fabens was… my doing," Francisco said, voice hoarse with pain.

"Your doing?" Tiago threw his hands up with mock exasperation. "And why would *you* think that was a good idea?"

"I…" Francisco gasped and then cleared his throat, catching his breath, "I thought that putting the undesirables to work venturing out into the infected areas to retrieve supplies was worthwhile. They risk their lives and we reap the benefits, costing us nothing."

Juan Pablo snorted, raising his hand. "Then what about the weapons you were stealing?"

"You were stealing weapons?" Tiago snarled. "To give to *those* people?"

"A few rifles and handguns, nothing that would pose a threat to us," the beaten man insisted. "Just something to help them get what we need."

"Enough," Rodriguez cut in, glaring down at his friend. "Francisco is attempting to cover for me. Fabens was my idea, and he was just following orders."

Tiago barked a few choice Spanish words, and then turned back to his second, tapping the barrel of his gun against his temple. "Why would you betray me like this?" he asked, voice rising in pitch and volume. "After everything I've done for you? Everything I've done for your family?"

"We have a lot of territory to hold, and our manpower isn't going to be increasing," Rodriguez replied, battling to keep his voice steady. "And as your second-in-command, it's my duty to make sure we have the things we need to withstand any threat."

Tiago narrowed his eyes. "And you thought that sneaking people out of the city was the way to do that?"

"These people were discarded," Rodriguez insisted. "I found a use for them. Think of it like a human recycling program."

The cartel boss laughed, lowering his gun hand and resting a hand on his stomach. "That's a good one. Human recycling." He paced slowly to Francisco, like a lion stalking its prey. "So. You were just following orders, huh?"

"Yes..." the beaten man stammered. "Yes sir."

"And why did you follow his orders?" Tiago asked.

Francisco swayed back and forth on his knees. "Because I'm loyal, sir."

"Oh, you're *loyal*?" The cartel leader sneered, and Rodriguez' heart skipped a beat at how similar his son resembled him in that moment. "Loyal." Tiago stepped back, tapping his handgun on his thigh. "So you're loyal to Rodriguez, then?"

"Yes, sir…" Francisco gasped. "I'm… I'm loyal."

Tiago's eyes hardened. "You're supposed to be loyal to ME!" he roared, and fired his gun, putting a bullet in the broken man's gut. "You're not supposed to be loyal to anyone else! Only me!" He fired three more times into the moaning man, and then took a deep breath, running a hand over his hair before turning to his second. "We're going to take a field trip down to your little pet project," he said, voice smooth as silk once again. "If it has borne fruit, you may yet live to see another sunrise. If it has not… then you will wish you met *his* fate." He motioned to Francisco, who bled out on the floor, twitching.

Rodriguez blinked down at his friend, trying not to show his emotions, but inside he screamed and thrashed with each ounce of the life draining from Francisco's body.

"Juan Pablo, get the car," Tiago barked. "And get someone in here to deal with this mess! I want this cleaned up, and this piece of shit traitor hanging from a lamp post by the time I get back."

Juan Pablo nodded and headed for the door. "Yes, sir."

Tiago holstered his golden gun and skirted his desk, sitting down to resume eating his steak as if he hadn't been interrupted in the first place.

CHAPTER FIFTEEN

Clara rose up onto her knees and peeked out the window, surprised that the horde hadn't come knocking for her yet. There were a smattering of zombies roaming about, but nothing even close to the crowd that had swarmed around the truck stop.

She let out a deep sigh of relief and then glanced at the kitchen. "Well, if I'm here, I might as well see if I can find what we need," she muttered, and got to her feet. She bounced on her toes for a moment to loosen up her joints and then headed for the cupboards, opening and closing every one.

She found a handful of canned goods, and an open bag of chips that was more ants than chips. The pantry and the fridge also stood empty, and even the freezer had been picked clean. She slammed the door shut in frustration, and then paused at the sight of a flyer stuck to it with a University of Texas magnet.

20% OFF LIQUOR SALE, the flyer boasted, and Clara ripped the paper free. She stared at the picture of an unmarked building, no big advertising, just a small hand-written sign in the window. She closed her eyes.

"Son of a bitch," she breathed. They'd passed that building on their way into town. It was one of the first ones they'd come across on the outskirts.

She reached for her walkie talkie, and hit the button to speak. There was no sound, not even static, and she examined the device. It was powered off.

"Good job there, Malcolm," she muttered. "Dumbass." She paused and shook her head, berating herself for making fun of a dead man. She hadn't known him well, and he hadn't been the brightest bulb in the box, but he deserved her respect.

She took a deep breath and powered the radio on, turning it to channel thirteen and whispering a quiet prayer to whatever deity would listen before pressing the talk button.

"Trenton," she said firmly and clearly. "Trenton, are you there? It's Clara."

She held her breath as she waited for a few tense moments.

"Clara!" Trenton came back, voice bursting with excitement. "You're alive! Is Malcolm with you? We saw smoke coming from the truck stop."

"He's… he's gone," she replied. "So is the dune buggy."

"Ah," came the somber reply. "Are you okay?"

"I'm a little scared, but I'll live," Clara assured him.

There was a moment of quiet and then another click. "Where are you?"

"I'm in some small house just north of the interstate," she said.

"Are you able to get out?"

"It looks like it," she said, heading back to the window to double-check. "There's only a handful of those things around."

"Okay," Trenton said quickly, voice like stone, "I want you to get back to the interstate and head back towards Fabens. About ten miles up the road is a town called Allamore. Go north and you'll find a safe house we set up. Food, water, everything you'll need to be comfortable for a while. Reed and I will meet you there when we can."

"I have a better idea," Clara cut in. "I figured out where the liquor store is."

"You did? How?" Trenton blurted. "Wait, forget that, I don't care. Where is it?"

"You're not going to believe this, but it's one of the first buildings we passed when we came into town," she replied, scrubbing a hand down her face in frustration. "It's a small concrete building with a handwritten sign in the window. That's why we missed it."

"Fuck, fuck!" Trenton barked. "Fuck!"

"Are you okay?" Clara asked immediately. "What happened?" She imagined the guys being gored by zombies. "Trenton, what's going on?"

"I fucked up, that's what's going on," he moaned. "I fucked up and two people died."

She calmed down, realizing he was beating himself up, and shook her head. "Hey. It's not your fault. We all missed it." She decided not to ask about Jay, whom she assumed had fallen given the fact that he said *two* people died, and mentioned he and Reed would meet up with her.

"Yeah, well, you all weren't in charge," Trenton said quietly.

"Well, don't make their deaths be in vain," Clara insisted. "We have a chance to protect Fabens, so let's figure out how to do it."

There was a quiet moment, and she hoped that Reed was comforting him proper on the other end.

"You're right," Trenton finally said. "Okay. How do we do this… how… I got it, I think. Can you get to the liquor store?"

Clara peered out the window again. "I think so. I can see the main road, and it's just like a mile or so run to get to the store."

"Okay, get there as quickly as you can," he instructed. "Get in, find what we need, and sit tight. Reed and I will take care of finding transportation. We will come get you."

Her heart leapt for the first time since she'd left El Paso. *Is this what hope feels like?* "Okay. I'll radio you when I'm in."

"Be safe," Trenton said firmly. "Over and out."

Clara pocketed the walkie talkie and checked her weapons, making sure her gun was loaded and accessible. She gripped her tire iron, knowing it would be her best bet to stay as quiet as possible.

She watched the zombies from the door's window, taking a deep breath. "Don't think, just go," she muttered to herself, bouncing on the balls of her feet. "Go now. This is just like any other run. Go as fast as you can and don't look back."

She took a deep, steadying breath, and then threw open the door, darting outside. She flew past two zombies before they could even register her presence, and ducked under the clawing arms of a third. The last one in the yard managed to catch her shirt on the way by, and she stifled a scream as she spun around.

341

She smashed the tire iron down on the ghoul's wrist, shattering it into pieces and sending the frustrated zombie staggering back. She tore free and took off running to the road, too afraid to look over her shoulder to see how far away the quartet of corpses were.

"Don't look, just run," she huffed as her legs pumped against the ground. "You're faster than they are. They can't catch you." She focused on her path along the road, even as moans grew louder behind her. They straggled up onto the pavement from the shoulders, and she zig-zagged as fast as she could across the lanes to avoid them. Stopping to fight would be death—she needed to keep moving.

Clara reached the parking lot of the liquor store as her calves began to scream in agony, and jerked hard on the front door.

It was locked.

"Shit," she muttered. At this point, she finally turned around, eyes widening at the sight of the horde that had gathered to stagger up the road. Even at a hundred yards away, it was an intimidating sight, and she fought the panic rising up in her throat. "Shit!" She turned and yanked on the door again, though her rational brain knew it was futile. "Fuck it," she grunted and took a step back from the door, drawing her revolver.

This definitely counted as an emergency, and since she already had the attention of almost a hundred zombies, it didn't really matter how much noise she made. She aimed at the latch, turned her head away, and fired.

The door fell open, the wood falling away, and she tore inside, pulling it shut behind her. Having completely destroyed the latch, Clara looked around wildly for something to hold the door closed. She spotted a string of Christmas lights in the window and ripped them down, wrapping the cord around the door knob several times. She pulled it taut, testing the strength, and then stretched it out and tied it around the leg of a heavy metal shelf nearby.

She plucked the cord to make sure it was secure. If somebody were pull hard on that door, it was likely that the whole thing would come free, but she had no other options, and hoped that the zombies wouldn't be that smart. They tended to just bang on stuff, not pull open doors.

Clara ran behind the front counter, scanning the back wall for anything worthy of the cartel boss. She clambered up onto the counter to reach the top shelf, finding a mini-case of tequila priced at $250.00 per bottle.

She raised an eyebrow as she pulled it down. "Hopefully that's retail and not an insane markup," she said, shaking her head. The bottles were dusty, but intact.

As her feet hit the floor, the thunder of zombie hands smacking the front of the building made her heart leap into her throat. The moaning permeated the walls, and she froze stock still, waiting to see if the Christmas lights would hold.

When the door stayed put, Clara lifted her walkie talkie to her lips. "Trenton, I found it."

"That's great!" he replied immediately, the sound of an engine in the background. "Sit tight, we're headed your way!"

She took a deep breath and pocketed the radio, wincing as the windows rattled in their frames under the violent hunger of the creatures outside. "Not going anywhere."

CHAPTER SIXTEEN

"You got anything?" Trenton called across the classroom as he peered out one of the windows.

Reed made a noise of dissatisfaction. "Not seeing *shit*, man."

"All right," Trenton replied with a sigh, heading for the door. "Let's try across the hall." They crept across to the closest door across the way, pausing with their weapons at the read.

Reed gripped the knob and then threw the door open, allowing his companion to rush in, machete raised.

"It's clear," Trenton declared, and headed for the window as the door gave a soft *click* behind him.

They scanned the zombie-filled landscape, dozens of corpses staggering around the main parking lot.

"Holy shit," Reed said, pointing. "I think I got something, look at the far end there."

Trenton shifted his focus to the side his friend surveyed, and honed in on a bright cherry red extended cab pickup truck. "You have any idea how to hot-wire a truck?"

"Afraid picking locks was as far as I got in my criminal career," Reed admitted.

His companion rubbed his chin. "What are the odds the keys are in the building?"

"Let me see those binoculars," Reed said, holding out his hand. He raised them to his face and scrutinized the truck, seeing a few plastic barrels in the back full of basketballs and soccer balls. There was a pile of baseball bats and some other sports equipment. "Check it out," he said, handing the binoculars back over. "Either that's the P.E. teacher's truck, or somebody was stealing equipment."

Trenton nodded as he lowered the device, shoving them back into his belt. "To the gym," he declared, and they headed out of the classroom.

They were cautious but brisk as they headed down the hallway, easily finding the double doors of the gymnasium. A thick metal chain held them shut with a lock. Reed grunted as he inspected the lock, realizing it was a combination instead of a key.

"Fuck," he dropped it and shook his head.

Trenton motioned to the sign for the locker room. "Hey, Reed, let's hit the showers," he said, and headed around the corner.

The duo quickly ducked back around at the sight of two zombies banging on the door to the locker room. Trenton did a silent countdown and they crept up behind the corpses until they were within arm's reach, and struck in unison. The zombies crumpled to the floor without so much as an extra groan to alert anyone of their presence.

"Looks like they were after somebody," Trenton said as he wiped his blade clean on one of the fallen creature's shirts.

Reed pushed against the door, and met resistance. He pushed a little harder, whatever was bracing it from the other side giving a squeaking noise as he managed to shove it across the tiles.

"Definitely after somebody," he grunted, pushing harder. Trenton helped him and they managed to get it open wide enough for Reed to slip through.

The offending item blocking the door was a metal desk, and Reed wrapped his hands around it to move it out of the way enough so that Trenton could follow him in. He turned at the sound of shuffling feet and his eyes widened at the sight of a large zombie staggering out of the locker area.

It looked like at one time he may have been a bodybuilder, with broad shoulders and a thick neck. Now he just looked like swiss cheese, missing large chunks out of his enormous biceps. Before Reed could react, the gigantic zombie crashed into him, slamming them both back against the concrete wall.

"Fuckfuckfuck!" Reed screamed, pushing up against the corpse's chest to try to keep its snapping jaws away from his tender flesh.

Trenton managed to wriggle just far enough through the door, and brought the machete down into the thing's head. It stuck halfway, but far enough to sever the brain, causing the zombie to slump forward.

"You okay?" Trenton asked.

Reed grunted and heaved the heavy body off of him, throwing his arm over his eyes to catch his breath. "Y-yeah."

"Holy fuck, that was close, man," Trenton let out a relieved laugh, scratching the back of his head.

His companion shook his head and couldn't help but huff his own laugh. "Next door we come across, you're going in first."

"That's a deal," Trenton replied, reaching down to help his friend to a standing.

Reed finally got up, liberating the machete from the corpse and handing it back through the door before finally shoving the metal desk clear. He slowly made his way through the locker room as Trenton patted down the attacking corpse.

"We're clear," Reed called.

Trenton shook his head and walked into the main locker area. "No keys," he reported, and then they both fixated on an open door in the corner. "Maybe the office?" he suggested, and they wandered in.

Trenton rummaged through the desk drawers while Reed checked the filing cabinet, chuckling at the sight of a hidden bottle of scotch in there.

"Eighteen-year-old scotch," he said, pulling it out and giving it a wiggle.

Trenton shook his head. "Here's a man who took his alcoholism seriously."

"Yeah, I can respect that," Reed said.

His companion opened the last drawer, and the jangling of metal made both of them hold their breath. Trenton grinned, reaching in for a keyring. The black car key matched the brand of the truck.

"Looks like we're in business," he said, and shoved them deep into his pocket.

They headed out of the locker room, re-inspecting the hallway before heading quickly to the back exit of the building.

"Is this the right door?" Reed asked.

Trenton scratched the back of his head. "I think it's the closest one to the truck, but let's see how bad it looks." He gently pushed on the metal release bar, ever-so-slowly opening the door a hair's breadth so he could get a good view of the parking lot.

Zombies staggered about, but the first ten feet or so out the door is pretty clear, and most of them were spread out instead of in groups. He carefully and silently closed the door again.

"So… you want the good news, or the bad news first?" he asked, trying to sound cheerful.

Reed rolled his eyes. "When the fuck did we start getting good news today?"

"Fair enough," Trenton chuckled. "Okay, there's enough room to get the doors open and for us to get up a head of steam."

Reed raised an eyebrow. "But?"

"But, there's like a hundred zombies between us and the truck," Trenton finished.

His companion let out a deep whoosh of breath. "Fantastic."

"Just channel your football days, put your head down, and run like a motherfucker," Trenton instructed.

Reed couldn't help but laugh, scrubbing his hands down his face. "Not loving this plan."

"Yeah, me either, but it's the best we've got," his friend replied with a helpless shrug. He put his hand on the release bar. "Ready? On three. One. Two. Three!"

He flung the door open and they burst into the parking lot. The sound of the metal door coupled with the quick movement drew the attention of every zombie within earshot, and they all turned towards the source.

Trenton led the charge, crashing apart two zombies that were close together, sending them stumbling back into a domino effect against other corpses. He continued like a lead blocker clearing the path for his running back, Reed hot on his heels.

The surrounding zombies began to swarm around the disturbance, and the two men ducked, bobbed, and wove through a sea of rotting flesh and grasping hands. Trenton kept his eyes on the truck, that cherry red beacon of hope, trying to ignore the cold dead fingers brushing every inch of his flesh as he flew past them.

As they managed to break free of the thick of the horde, the truck was about twenty yards away, and Trenton mashed the unlock button on the key fob. Nothing happened.

"Fuck, it's not unlocking!" he screamed.

"Keep trying!" Reed huffed from behind him.

Trenton hit it over and over, but still the truck stayed silent. As they reached the doors, they jerked on each handle, but everything remained shut tight.

"Christ, do we even have the right keys?!" Reed cried, voice carrying a panicked edge.

"I fucking hope so!" Trenton fumbled to switch to the actual key, but when he tried to shove it into the lock, he found a wad of dried bubblegum had been shoved into it. "Are you fucking *kidding* me?!" he cursed, and looked over his shoulder at the horde that was only ten yards away. "Into the truck bed!" he yelled.

The duo jumped up into the back, using the tires for leverage, and flung themselves to relative safety just as the wave of zombies reached them.

"The key didn't work?" Reed asked as they backed up into the center of the truck bed, back to back to avoid the reaching hands.

Trenton shook his head. "Fucking pranksters shoved gum in the lock. God only knows how long it's been like that."

"No wonder the coach drank," Reed quipped as he smacked the arm of an overzealous zombie with his bat.

Trenton reached down and grabbed one of the baseball bats from the equipment cages and smashed it a few times against the back window of the cab, finally shattering it all over the backseats. He ducked inside, careful not to catch on any of the jagged glass, and slid into the driver's seat.

"Oh, you'd better fucking work," he muttered, and slid the key into the ignition. He turned it, and the engine sparked to life, the satisfying rumble of a working vehicle like music to his ears. "We have life! Get in!" he called back.

Reed dove inside, taking up a defensive position in the back window. "Don't gotta ask me twice," he declared.

Trenton popped the truck into gear and punched the accelerator, flattening several zombies as he peeled out of the parking lot.

His walkie talkie crackled and then Clara's voice came through, "Trenton, I found it."

Relief washed over him. "That's great! Sit tight, we're headed your way."

Hope burned in his chest. They might just have a chance.

CHAPTER SEVENTEEN

Clara leaned up against the front
counter, staring at her makeshift door
lock. She couldn't help but imagine it
breaking, a hundred zombies flooding in to
tear her flesh from her bones with their
teeth. She shuddered, fingering the stock
of the revolver secured to her side.

"Clara, you still with us?" Trenton's
voice through the walkie talkie broke her
morbid thoughts, and she immediately
raised it to her lips.

"Yep, just me and a hundred of my
closest friends," Clara replied dryly.

"Yeah, we can see that," Trenton
replied. "We're about a hundred yards away
on the frontage road. You certainly know
how to draw a crowd."

She sighed. "Any idea on how to get
me out of here?"

"There are too many for us to drive
through, so we're gonna have to lure them
away," he explained.

She took a deep breath, picking at
the hem of her tank top. "You're gonna
have to take them in the direction of
Fabens, because there's another horde down
by the truck stop. Wouldn't be good if you
ran into them."

"Yeah, no kidding," Trenton came
back. "Okay. We're gonna do a drive by and

see if we can't get them onto the frontage road. Sit tight, and just be ready to move, because we may not have much of a window."

She jumped down from the counter and gripped the six-pack of tequila tightly. "I'll be ready," she promised, and shoved the radio back into her pocket.

Trenton popped the truck into gear and drove slowly up the road towards the liquor store. The tiny building was buried in a plethora of zombies at least twenty deep. He turned and backed up so that the bed faced the horde, and then laid hard on the horn.

The loud bleat got every creature's attention easily, and the mass of rotted heads turned, mouths open in excited moans as they ambled towards the truck.

"Well, that worked pretty well," Reed said.

Trenton moved the truck forward at a snail's pace, so that he wouldn't outrun the staggering zombies. "Let's hope so," he said.

Reed peered overtop of the heads, scoping out the store. "Shit," he muttered. "There's still about twenty of them around the store."

"We can deal with that," Trenton declared. "Are the rest still following us?"

His passenger nodded. "Yep, you're still the zombie pied piper."

"Let's get 'em down the road a little bit," Trenton said, and led the throng about a half a mile before punching the gas. He sped towards the next interstate ramp, and then did a quick one-eighty, screaming back down the freeway towards the liquor store.

He got off just before, stopping in the middle of the road about fifty yards away.

"What are you thinking?" Reed raised an eyebrow.

"I'm thinking curbside pickup," Trenton replied, inclining his head to the passenger door. "What kind of wingspan does that door have?"

His companion opened the door wide and then slammed it shut with a shrug. "Five feet, maybe?" he said.

"I can work with that," Trenton declared, and put the radio to his mouth. "Clara, do you copy?"

Clara tightened her grip on the tequila, and lifted the radio to her mouth. "I'm here."

"Which way does the front door open?" Trenton asked.

"Um," she replied, brow furrowing. "It opens outwards. Why?"

There was a pause. "Okay, this is going to sound crazy, but when I tell you to, I need you to open the door for me."

She almost dropped the alcohol in her shock, and stared at the walkie talkie as if it had offended her. "Uh, yeah, that does sound crazy," she said. "You got any particular reason, or do you just like to challenge me?"

"We've gotta get as close as we can to the building to shield you from the zombies still outside," Trenton explained. "We have to be five feet away from the building in order to get our door open."

Clara nodded, finally grasping the idea. "Yeah, yeah, I'm tracking."

"You have bullets left?" he asked.

"Five shots," she replied.

"Okay, you get that door open and shoot whatever you need to shoot," he instructed.

She barked a laugh. "Thanks for the permission, but that wasn't going to be an issue."

"Fair enough," he replied with a chuckle. "You let me know when you're ready."

Clara walked over to the door and unwrapped her Christmas light lock, holding the knob tightly to keep the door shut. "I'm ready," she said into the radio. "You just tell me when." She shoved the walkie talkie back into her pocket, and tightened her hand around her gun.

She heard squealing tires outside, and the road of an engine growing closer.

"NOW!" Trenton's voice echoed in her pocket.

Clara threw the door open, and then took a step back, firing carefully into the closest zombie's face. Its forehead exploded onto its brethren, a trio of creatures that rushed forward to take its place, ambling through the door.

The truck smashed over the rest of the group, taking the front door right off of its hinges.

Clara dove behind the counter, putting a hard surface between her and her pursuers. She took her time aiming her weapon, acutely aware of how little shots she really had to get this right. She dropped first one, then two zombies, and as the third hit the counter and opened its mouth to scream, she put a bullet point-blank into its eye socket.

She didn't waste any time darting around to the door, rushing towards the truck with the alcohol in hand. Reed stood against the passenger door, firing at the zombies wedged against the other side.

Clara lunged forward, shoving the case of tequila across to the middle seat before clambering up herself. Reed immediately slid down into the passenger's seat and slammed the door.

"Go go go!" he cried, and Trenton hit the gas for all he was worth.

Once they were back on the frontage road heading towards the entrance ramp, the three shell shocked civilians stayed silent. It was Reed that broke the quiet, spotting the horde they'd led away, still ambling after a long escaped target.

"Christ, they're still walking," he breathed.

Clara swallowed hard. "We're going to have to keep an eye on that." She crossed her arms, happy to be in the presence of live human beings.

"First things first," Trenton said hoarsely, nodding to the box of liquid gold at Reed's feet. "We have to get that tequila back to town. Not going to have anything to protect unless the cartel is happy with us."

CHAPTER EIGHTEEN

"Man… that's one hell of a haul to get to," Leon said, and let out a low whistle.

Rogers shrugged as he circled a few more places on the large map on the table. "Pretty much everywhere is going to be a hell of a haul from where we are."

"This is true," Leon replied.

The Detective inclined his head towards the duffel bags. "How detailed can that satellite get?" he asked.

"If I push it?" Leon pursed his lips, and shrugged. "I can get down to twenty feet above ground level. I mean, we ain't gonna be able to look in stores or nothing, but we can at least scout out hordes."

The loud bleat of an air horn sliced through the air, and the two men straightened up.

Rogers turned to his new companion. "If we survive the day, that'll be useful," he said, and then patted him on the back. "Are you up for this?"

"Don't worry man, I got you," Leon replied, offering him a reassuring smile. "I spent half my career learning how to please the higher ups who viewed me as disposable."

The Detective chuckled humorlessly. "Given that we are very disposable in their eyes, that experience is going to come in handy."

"Any last bit of advice?" Leon asked.

Rogers grinned. "Cover your ears." He motioned to the bandage on the side of his head, and then turned on his heel to head to one of the back offices to hide.

Leon chuckled and shook his head, heading outside. The air horns stopped their incessant noise, and he watched a half-dozen heavily armed men creating a perimeter on the main drag around three black SUVs.

He took a deep breath and headed towards the cluster as a group of well-dressed men stepped out of the middle vehicle.

"You!" A tall man pointed at Leon as he approached. "Are you the man in charge of this… whatever the hell it is?" He waved his hand around above his head.

"Yup," Leon replied, crossing his arms. "And who might you be?"

"I am Tiago Rivas, head of the Rivas Cartel and the current ruler of El Paso," the man declared, his back ramrod straight.

Leon raised an eyebrow. "Ruler of El Paso?" he asked. "I wasn't aware we had elected a king."

"Kings are not elected, my friend," Tiago said, wagging a gold-adorned finger, "they seize power when the opportunity presents itself. I saw my opportunity, and I took it."

Leon gently clapped his hands together, as if applauding a good putt. "Well congratu-fucking-lations."

Tiago's eyes darkened. "You would be wise to show me respect."

"Respect is earned," the self-proclaimed leader of Fabens shot back. "So far you haven't earned a goddamned thing."

The cartel leader laughed. "Fine, if this is the way you want to go about things, I will happily oblige." He drew his shiny handgun and aimed it at Leon's forehead, his opponent not even flinching with the movement. "You have ten seconds to tell me why I shouldn't kill you and everyone in this town."

Leon shrugged casually. "Because we can do things your people can't do."

"Like what?" Tiago sneered. "Go out into the wasteland and get supplies? I have an army of people who do my bidding at my command."

Leon nodded. "That may be true, but I can guaran-damn-tee they don't have satellite surveillance."

Tiago pursed his lips and lowered his gun, contemplating.

Angel growled, stepping up beside his father. "Just shoot him and take his shit," he demanded. "We got people who can run it."

"Not without the codes that are in here," Leon singsonged, tapping his temple. "You touch me, or anybody in this town, and I'll punch my own ticket, and you boys get nothing. Now, I don't know who the fuck you are, but you need to sit your happy ass down and let the grownups continue talking."

Angel snarled. "How dare you speak to the son of-"

"Oh, he's your father?" Leon cut in, eyebrows rising to his hairline. "Well, if you take another step closer to me, I'm gonna make you call *me* daddy. Now sit your punk ass down before I embarrass you in front of your friends and family."

Angel reached for his knife, but his father smacked him in the arm.

"Enough," he snapped. "Back to the truck."

His son scowled, glaring daggers at Leon, who simply winked and blew him a kiss. Angel stormed back to the truck, slamming the door extra hard behind him.

In the distance, headlights appeared over the horizon, and Tiago raised an eyebrow as his guards turned, on high alert.

"Friends of yours?" he asked.

Leon nodded. "Scouts who were out in the wastes, collecting stuff for you."

"So my tribute has arrived," Tiago declared, spreading his arms.

Trenton got out of the car, carrying the case of tequila, and slowly moved past the guards, setting the box directly at the feet of the cartel boss.

Tiago's eyes lit up at the color of the caps, and pulled a bottle out to examine it. "This," he said as he tapped on the label, "is some fantastic stuff. Where did you get this?"

"Couple of hours down the road," Trenton replied stiffly. "Cost us quite a bit, too."

The cartel boss returned the bottle to the case, and raised a hand, palm out. "Tell me, how much?"

"Three people's lives, three dirt bikes and a dune buggy, all of which were our main modes of transportation," Trenton replied flatly.

Tiago chuckled, and turned to rove his eyes over his companions. "These people are willing to sacrifice themselves so I can get drunk," he declared. "Rodriguez, you have set up a fine source of entertainment for me."

Rodriguez shifted his weight as the cartel boss continued to laugh over the situation. Trenton clenched his jaw, and Leon nodded gently at him for reassurance.

"Juan Pablo," Tiago finally said, "first thing tomorrow I want you to deliver half a dozen bikes to them. Grant them access to the gas station on the south end of town. Hell, give them some weapons too. As long as it benefits me, what are a few guns and bullets?"

Juan Pablo nodded. "Yes, sir."

Tiago turned back to Leon, and stared down his nose. "Let me be very clear," he said, voice low and menacing, "while I do find this whole situation amusing, the *moment* you stop being useful to me, I will burn this town to the ground with everyone inside of it. I will make you watch as the people you protect burn alive. Are we clear?"

"Crystal." Leon stood still as a statue.

Tiago patted him on the cheek. "I'll expect something from you very soon." He grinned and walked off, waving his hand above his head to get the guards moving back to the trucks. "Let's go, I have some tequila to drink!" On his way past Rodriguez, he lowered his voice to a hiss. "You may think you've done good here," he said. "I assure you that you have not. If this town falters, *you* will burn with them."

366

Rodriguez nodded as he waved everyone into the truck, and glanced back at Leon. He touched his left ear, and Leon nodded slightly, affirming that the Detective was still alive. The cartel mole smiled faintly, and then jumped in the SUV.

Reed parked the cherry truck on the side of the road and got out to watch the black cartel vehicles speed off, and Leon approached Trenton.

"What happened to Clara?" he demanded.

"Nothing happened to her," Trenton replied. "I just didn't think the cartel needed to know she was alive."

Leon nodded and followed him back to the truck, where Reed was helping Clara out from under a blanket in the backseat.

"What did I miss?" she asked, hopping down to the ground.

Leon grinned. "Me taunting El Guapo to his face."

"El Guapo?" Clara raised an eyebrow, and looked back and forth between Trenton and Reed, who held equal confusion on their faces.

"The boss asshole who just left," Leon said.

Trenton raised a hand. "Tiago Rivas?"

"Who the fuck is El Guapo?" Reed added.

Leon sighed. "Because he reminds me of the bad guy from the Three Amigos," he explained, shaking his head at his obvious age. "And I may have to show some respect to his face, but I'll me goddamned if I show any to him or his bitch ass son behind his back."

Clara chuckled, shaking her head. "Three Amigos, huh? Never saw it."

"Well, then we'd better add a VHS player to the list of things to scout for, then," Leon declared, giving her shoulder a squeeze, and they headed back to the command center.

CHAPTER NINETEEN

"Holy shit." Rogers' eyes were as wide as saucers. "You really told Angel Rivas that you'd make him call you daddy?"

Leon laughed. "It seemed like the logical thing to do at the time." He shrugged. "Let El Guapo know I'm not backing down."

The Detective wiped tears of mirth from his eyes. "El Guapo! Like Three Amigos!"

"Finally another person among us who appreciates the classics," Leon raised his hands, and then shot a triumphant look at the other three.

Trenton rolled his eyes, and turned back to the map with all of the circles on it. "Man, some of these places are gonna be difficult to get to. Those spots way south of the I-10 won't be too bad, but Fort Stockton and Fort Davis are probably two day trips away."

"We're probably going to want to avoid Fort Stockton for as long as we can," Leon pointed out. "It's the biggest city between here and Junction. We're not going to have the manpower or the firepower to deal with that. Hell, we can't even clear our own backyard yet."

Rogers crossed his arms. "If they deliver on those weapon promises, we can start on that at least. But that's only half the problem." He rubbed his chin. "We really need able-bodied people. Right now these three are the only people who are able to venture out there."

Leon took a deep breath. "It's a long shot, but I'll start putting the call out to those military boys out in New Mexico," he suggested. "Our schedule chat isn't for a couple more days, but it couldn't hurt to try."

"That's a good idea, but the priority is finding supplies," the Detective replied, shaking his head. "So whenever we have satellite coverage, I'd like you to be scouring every inch of ground you can." He cocked his head, a mischievous glint in his eye. "If you don't mind, *Mister Mayor*."

"Oh good lord." Clara put a hand to her forehead.

Leon smirked. "Nah, I'm good with Mayor," he said.

"And on that note, I'm going to go find some food and a bed to sleep in," she announced, putting up a hand to stop him.

"You did good today, Clara," Trenton said softly, his voice sincere as he caught her attention. "You saved the town, really."

She shrugged, avoiding his gaze as if it wasn't a big deal. "It's my home now too," she said nervously. "Just trying to do my part to carry the load."

"Well, you get some rest, because tomorrow morning we're back at it," he replied.

She nodded and gave a little wave before hurrying out of the command center.

"We should be doing the same," Reed said.

Trenton nodded. "Good call," he agreed, and gave a salute to the duo in charge. "Don't stay up too late, *amigos*."

After a return wave, the two remaining Fabens citizens turned back to the laptop as it gave a beep.

"Looks like you're up, Mister Mayor," Rogers said.

Leon gave him a sly smile. "I'm on it," he assured him. "You should go get some sleep, Detective. I'll keep watch."

Rogers clapped him on the back. "Oh, be honest, you just want free reign of the coffee pot."

"Only a day in and you already know me so well," Leon replied with a chuckle.

The Detective stepped towards the door, but then turned back to give his new companion a sincere look. "Thanks for everything you did today. We might not still be here if it wasn't for you."

Leon shook his head. "Don't thank me yet. I get the sense this shit is just getting started."

END

DEAD AMERICA: THE SECOND WEEK

BOOK 4: CINCINNATI

BY DEREK SLATON

© 2019

CHAPTER ONE

Day Zero +10

"Fire! Fire!" somebody yelled as thick black smoke poured out of a storeroom at Cincinnati stadium. Screams erupted in the crowd, and several men in military uniforms rushed forward with fire extinguishers.

"Move!" one of them demanded, trying to avoid barreling over a young couple in his way. Two of his comrades reached the doorway first and sent a sea of foam into the large room, but the two extinguishers didn't do much to stop the inferno inside.

"We need water!" one of the men cried. "Now!"

One of his teammates tore off down the outer corridor, frantically searching for a fire hose. One of the straggling civilians waved him over in the distance, pointing to a hose box he'd spotted on the wall.

The man in uniform nodded his thanks and threw open the door, taking the long hose off of its hook. "You wait thirty seconds," he instructed the civilian, "then open this bitch up full blast, you got it?"

The man nodded sternly. "I'm on it."

The military man threw the coil of hose over his arm, making sure that it would unravel as he ran, and tore off back towards the storeroom. He held the nozzle tightly at the ready, anticipating a strong flow and kickback.

The hose tightened and straightened and fired almost as hard as a gun when the stream hit. The man grunted as he kept it steady, the water immediately hissing as it began to douse the inside of the storeroom. Steam wafted out the open doorway, and he stepped closer to try to aim farther into the room.

The smoke and soot soon overwhelmed him and he dropped to one knee, coughing as he tried to keep the hose steady.

A rough hand clamped down on his shoulder and pulled him back. Somebody took the hose and continued to spray the blaze while he gasped for air.

"What in the good goddamn is going on here?" a stern voice snapped, and the man recognized it as Captain Hopkins, the military leader at the Cincinnati stadium shelter.

"F-fire… in the store… storeroom… sir…" the man on the ground gasped.

The Captain paled when he realized that the black plumes were coming from the particular storeroom that had held six months of military rations. The supply that was supposed to last the fifteen hundred residents while they waited for the greenhouses to start producing food.

"Fuck," Hopkins muttered, and motioned for a nearby civilian to come over to them. "You, get this man to the field hospital. It's outside of section two-thirteen."

The man nodded and looped the gasping soldier's arm over his broad shoulders, helping him to his feet. Hopkins clenched his jaw as he watched two soldiers continue to battle the blaze, one with the hose at a safe distance and the other with a fresh extinguisher.

The Captain turned to a wide-eyed woman next to him. "You," he barked, and she jumped but turned to him, back straightening. "When that fire is out, you tell my men I need an immediate status report. Can you handle that?"

She nodded jerkily. "Yes… sir?" she replied.

"Good," he said. "Make sure they understand the *immediate* part. And they know where my office is."

"I'll handle it," she assured him.

Hopkins strode off quickly, snatching his walkie talkie from his belt as he moved. "Bud, it's Hopkins, come in."

There was a crackle from the receiver. "This is Bud."

"I need you to find Corporal Strickland," the Captain said, "and the both of you need to get to my office immediately."

Bud paused, and then came back, "I believe Corporal Strickland is leading a team training exercise at the moment."

"I don't care what he's doing," Hopkins snapped. "We have a situation and you two need to get to my office, now."

This time Bud was far more prompt. "Yes sir, we'll be right there."

Hopkins clipped the radio back to his belt and stepped up to the railing on the second floor. He leaned on both of his hands, clenching his jaw as he looked out over the city. The sun was just coming up over the horizon, bathing the skyscrapers in hues similar to the flames consuming their rations at that moment.

It would have been beautiful had it been any other morning. But this was the apocalypse. And it was often hard to find beauty in the apocalypse. Beneath the fiery glow of what would otherwise be a breathtaking sunrise were rotting corpses wandering the streets feasting on human flesh. It was enough to put a damper on such a peaceful sight.

As if on cue, moans and groans echoed up to the Captain, and he looked down at the sea of zombies pressed up against the concrete wall of the stadium below. His presence had excited them, it seemed, and they reached up, milky dead eyes unblinking, mouths open and bloody saliva running down their chins.

"I don't know how we're going to get past you motherfuckers," Hopkins growled, clenching a fist. "But we're gonna do it, one way or another."

CHAPTER TWO

Hopkins sat down at his desk, a piping hot cup of coffee already waiting for him. Thank the heavens for good secretaries, even in the apocalypse. He reached into the bottom drawer of his desk and pushed back some folders, rummaging for the large bottle of whiskey hidden there. He unscrewed the cap and poured a generous dollop into his coffee.

"That kind of morning, Captain?" Bud asked as he strolled in through the open door.

Hopkins took a long sip of his brew before returning the bottle to his desk. "Where's Corporal Strickland?"

"He's on his way," the older man replied, pulling out a chair to sit in. His chocolate skin shone under the fluorescent lights as he cocked his head. "What's going on? You look downright spooked."

The Captain reached over and hit the speaker button on his phone. "Cathy, can you please bring us two more cups of coffee?" he asked. "And leave room in them, please."

"Yes, sir," Cathy replied immediately.

"I appreciate the gesture, Captain," Bud said, leaning forward, "but you know I'm not a big drinker."

Hopkins shook his head. "You will be." He ran his hands through his thinning hair and sighed.

Cathy reached the office door at the same time as Corporal Strickland, a fit man in his mid-30s. He shot her an award-winning smile, his teeth blinding pearls behind cinnamon skin.

"Thanks, I've got those," he said, taking the two steaming mugs from her. She nodded her thanks and headed back to her post, and he entered the office, setting the cups on the desk. "Apologies for being late, Captain," he said gruffly. "I was in the middle of a training exercise and had to pass it off."

"Please, Corporal, sit," Hopkins said, waving to the empty chair next to Bud.

Strickland sat down, and the Captain pulled out his bottle again, topping up the coffee cups with whiskey.

The Corporal furrowed his scarred brow. "I've seen this movie before. How bad is it?"

"About twenty minutes ago, there was a fire in the MRE storage room," Hopkins said.

His two guests remained silent, and then reached for their mugs, each taking a long sip.

It was Bud who broke the silence, his face somber. "How extensive is the damage?"

"I'm waiting on the final report." The Captain shook his head. "But based on the smoke I saw pouring out of there, we're going to have to assume it's a total loss. If we are able to salvage anything, it won't be enough to sustain the people we have here for very long."

"What about the greenhouses?" Strickland asked, leaning forward.

Bud shook his head. "They're still weeks away from being able to produce anything meaningful," he said. "Hell, we don't even have them all built up yet."

"Well." The Corporal sighed. "What are you thinking, Captain?"

Hopkins took a deep breath. "I'm waiting to be patched through to D.C. My hope is that they can air drop us some supplies to get us through."

"And if they can't?" Strickland asked.

"You're gonna have to go out and get us some," Hopkins said. "Which is why I wanted you here. You're my field team leader, so you ask whatever questions you need to."

The Corporal nodded gravely. "Understood."

"Captain Hopkins," Cathy's voice came through the speakerphone, "I have John Teeter on line two for you."

He pushed the button to reply to her. "Thank you, Cathy," he said, and then flipped over to the phone channel. "Hello, John, are you there?" he asked.

"I am, Captain," John replied. "And you're also on the line with my top researcher, Whitney Hill."

"Captain," a female voice added.

"Miss Hill," Hopkins greeted her. "You are also on the line with Bud, the civilian manager of this facility, and Corporal Strickland who is my field team operator."

"Gentlemen," John replied. "So, Cathy has informed us that you had an emergency, but was sparse on the details. You wanna give me the nickel version? Because have a lot of fires we're trying to put out at the moment."

"Understood." The Captain sighed. "We had a fire in our store room. It's still being put out based on what I witnessed, I'm going off the assumption that it's a total loss."

John waited a beat before asking, "A total loss of what?"

"Food and medicine," Hopkins replied.

"What the fuck, Captain?" John exclaimed. "Why was everything kept in one storage room?"

"Because this is a small facility, and we're still in the process of setting things up," Hopkins snapped, unamused with the tone the man had taken with him. "Frankly, it doesn't matter at this point, does it?"

John let out a long breath. "No, I supposed it doesn't." He paused. "How can we help?"

"Well, we need food and medicine," the Captain replied. "Is an air drop in the cards?"

"I'm afraid not," John replied. "All of our assets are being moved to the northwest for an offensive. There isn't a ship or plane within a thousand miles of you."

Hopkins clasped his hands tightly around his coffee mug. "What about trucks? I know there are a lot of forces in Kansas."

"Yes, there are," John agreed, "and we're in the process of creating caravans to get supplies out to survivors. It would take us weeks for us to get anything to you."

The Captain scowled. "Why in the hell is it going to take weeks to get us supplies by truck?"

There was a shuffle and some muffled speech, as the two on the other end spoke quietly.

"Well," Whitney finally said, clearing her throat, "this has been kept under wraps for fear of destroying morale within our east coast facilities, so what I'm about to tell you does not leave the room. Are we clear on that point, Captain?"

Hopkins leaned back in his chair and took a sip of his coffee. "Depends on what you're about to tell me," he finally said.

She sighed. "A few days ago, the decision was made to seal off the east coast by destroying the bridges over the Mississippi River."

"What?!" Hopkins slammed his mug down on his desk, coffee sloshing over the sides as he leaned over the phone, eyes wide. "Who was the stupid motherfucker that came up with that bright idea?"

"I'm that stupid motherfucker," Whitney declared.

There was an uncomfortable silence between both parties, and the normally forceful Captain had no idea how to respond to that.

"Before you have an aneurysm trying to think of some way to recover from that outburst," Whitney continued, "let me assure you it was done so after careful consideration and a lot of debate. This was not a decision that was made lightly. We are in a very difficult situation and if we don't do everything just right, we run the risk of becoming extinct.

"Oh, and in case you think we're sacrificing you for the greater good, remember that *we're* on the east coast, too," she added.

Hopkins put a hand to his forehead. "Miss Hill," he said hoarsely, "you have my apologies."

"No apology necessary," she assured him. "Now, we did leave up a select handful of bridges so we can get supplies across, but they are all to the south, so it's going to take time to get stuff to you. How long do you think you can hold out?"

He shook his head. "I don't know yet, but possibly only a few days worth of food."

"In that case, we're going to have to find you a local source of supplies," John put in.

"I'll have my team pull up some current satellite imagery of the area and get it sent over within the next few minutes," Whitney said. "That should help you scout."

Strickland leaned forward, leaning his elbows on his knees. "This is Corporal

Strickland," he cut in. "What about the area military bases? I know they were pulling supplies for us. Surely they still have some left."

"It's unknown how much they may or may not have on hand," John replied, "however I do know they were both overrun by massive hordes. They were slated to be evacuated but only a handful made it out."

Strickland took a deep breath. "Well, this just keeps getting better and better."

There was another shuffle on the other end and some inaudible chatter in the distance.

"Gentlemen, my apologies, but we're getting pulled into a meeting with the President," John said. "Whitney's team will have those satellite images over to you in a few minutes. Once we're out of this meeting, we'll devote some time and resources to seeing how we can help you boys out further."

"Thank you John," Hopkins said, "and please give our thanks to Miss Hill as well."

"Will do," came the reply. "Good luck." There was a *click* as the line went dead, and all three men fell silent for a few moments.

Bud took a deep swig of his coffee. "So, we're on our own, huh?" he asked.

"Wouldn't be the first time the government's done this to us," Strickland muttered.

"Okay," Hopkins piped up. "While we wait on the sat imagery, I need you to do me a favor, Bud."

"What do you need, Captain?" the civilian leader asked.

"We sure as hell ain't driving out of here," Hopkins said, "so we need to know what those choppers on the infield are going to be able to do for us."

"I'll get one of the mechanics up here," Bud assured him, getting to his feet.

Hopkins put up a hand. "We're also going to need someone familiar with the area. It'll help immensely if we know what's inside the buildings we're looking at."

"I'll be right back," Bud promised, and left the office.

Strickland's shoulders straightened. "What do you want me to do, Captain?" he asked.

"Figure out who your team is," Hopkins instructed. "It's going to be a max load of six in that chopper if we want to bring back supplies. We may only have one trip if a horde gets wind of you."

"I can work with six," the Corporal said.

"I know you can." Hopkins nodded firmly. "Just be back in fifteen."

Strickland stood and saluted. "Yes, sir."

CHAPTER THREE

Fifteen minutes later, Strickland had returned and Cathy was just refilling his mug when Bud approached the office with two civilians in tow, a man and a woman.

"Captain, are you ready for us?" Bud asked, knocking on the door frame.

Hopkins stood up. "Please, come in. Who do we have here?"

"Gentlemen, let me introduce Paul Huffman," Bud said, stepping aside to reveal a stout man in his fifties with a quite prominent bald spot shining in the fluorescent lights. "He's my lead mechanic and has been heading up the maintenance on the two helicopters."

The Captain pursed his lips. "Why is a civilian working on military hardware?"

"Because the boys your higher-ups assigned to this facility know jack shit about helicopters," Paul said gruffly before Bud could answer.

Hopkins raised an eyebrow. "And you do?"

"Yes sir, I do," his guest replied, puffing out his chest a bit. "I've been flying for the better part of three decades, and I run Huffman's Sky Tours out in Harrison. Been working on choppers longer than some of these boys have been alive."

The Captain nodded, and extended his hand to shake. "Good enough for me," he replied, and motioned for the man to sit down. "And who is this young lady?"

"Jean McCormick," the woman said, stepping forward to offer her hand to him. She looked to be in her early thirties, her petite face framed by mousy blonde hair. "I grew up in Bevis, which is northwest of the city. I spent the last eight years running the shipping department for the SuperCenter chain, so I'm pretty familiar with everything in the area."

Hopkins nodded. "Good, pleasure to meet you," he said, and returned to his seat. "Has Bud filled you in on what's going on?"

"Yes sir, he has," Paul replied.

"Good." The Captain turned on the monitor behind him. "Then you know what we're up against."

Cathy filled coffee cups for the three latecomers and then retreated from the office, closing the door gently behind her. The monitor showed a map of the southern portion of the area on the other side of the river.

Bud furrowed his brow as he leaned against the wall, allowing Jean to take the last empty seat. "Why can't we see the interstate?"

"Because those things have completely clogged it," Hopkins replied. "I did a quick sweep of the surrounding areas down south and it pretty much looks the same, so we can mark out everything on that side of the river."

"Bevis might be a good target," Jean piped up. "It's north, northwest of the city, maybe fifteen miles as the crow flies."

"That's a little too close for comfort," Strickland put in. "Population is still pretty thick. We need to get out in the sticks if we're going to pull this off. You know of anything that's closer to sixty or seventy miles out?"

Paul barked a hysterical laugh, seemingly out of nowhere.

Hopkins shot him an annoyed glance. "Something funny?"

"Oh no," the older man ran a hand over his bare head, "it's actually quite horrifying." He took a deep breath to compose himself. "Whoever flew the bird last was not only a shitty pilot, cause let me tell you these babies are dinged up to hell, but they are also quite forgetful."

The Captain clasped his hands in front of him on his desk. "What did they forget to do?"

Paul gulped. "Fill it up with gas."

There was a tangible silence for a few moments as what he'd said sank in.

"So," Strickland finally said, clearing his throat, "let us in on your little secret. How bad is it?"

He shrugged. "I've pulled the fuel from both, and my best guess it that we have—maybe—eight minutes of flight time? Possibly less, depending on the damage."

The Corporal couldn't hold back his own bitter laugh, leaning back in his chair in defeat.

Bud shook his head. "Not to worry, though, we have gas pumps on site."

"But are they stocked with aviation fuel?" Paul asked.

Bud furrowed his brow. "Well. No."

"Well you might as well say you have a water hose, because it would be just as effective as the gas you have," Paul replied, letting out a deep whoosh of breath.

"Christ," Strickland hissed, "do we even have enough to get us to Bevis?"

Paul nodded. "Yeah, we do, however if y'all don't mind, I have another suggestion."

The Corporal waved for him to continue. "By all means, go ahead, we're making this shit up as we go anyway."

"Captain," Paul prompted, turning to face the monitor again, "can you please pull up the I-74 and 275 interchange?"

Hopkins slid the remote for the monitor across the desk to the aviation specialist. Paul picked it up and raised an eyebrow, confused.

"Consider yourself promoted," the Captain declared, and leaned back in his chair with his coffee cup to watch.

Paul turned the remote over in his hand. "But I'm not in the military."

"Consider yourself drafted, then," Hopkins amended, waving a flippant hand.

Paul shook his head in bewilderment. "I can work with that." He fumbled with the remote, and then finally figured out how to move the arrows to properly scan the map. He zoomed in on the intersection he'd been looking for. "We need to find a landing zone somewhere south of here. This intersection is halfway between Bevis and my town of Harrison. Now, while some of you boys head up to Bevis and the SuperCenter, I can lead another group to my workshop."

"Two teams?" Strickland cut in. "You know we can only take six people with us, right? Splitting up is incredibly dangerous. What do you have in your workshop that's so important?"

Paul stared at him. "An aviation fuel truck."

Hopkins smacked a hand down on his desk. "Okay, two teams it is, then. Bud, please radio to Horowitz and have him ready to fly."

"Yes, sir," Bud replied, pushing off of the wall.

"Whoa, whoa!" Paul put his hands up. "Was he the dingus that flew in here? Because that boy shouldn't be going anywhere with y'all."

Hopkins shrugged. "The other pilot was bitten during one of the restocks, so Horowitz is our only viable option."

Paul rolled his eyes. "You've got me."

"*You* can fly a military chopper?" the Captain asked, blinking at him.

"Hell yeah I can," Paul replied, almost sounding defensive. "I've had a few in my collection over the years. Not only that, but I have more flight time than your boy. I've also done less damage to my equipment in three decades than he's done in the last three fucking days."

Strickland clasped his hands in front of him and leaned forward, facing the older man with a stern expression. "Paul. I need you to be straight with me. Can you handle yourself out there?"

"I mean, I can shoot a gun with halfway decent accuracy," Paul replied with a shrug. "I ran a couple five k's last year, albeit at a slow pace. As long as y'all aren't expecting me to parkour over walls and shit I should be able to keep up."

Strickland took a deep breath and turned to the Captain. "From what I know about our pilots in this unit, I think we'd be hard pressed to find one with a better resume."

Hopkins laughed and nodded, giving another wave as he took a long sip of his spiked coffee.

"Okay, you're in," Strickland said, turning back to his new pilot. "Whenever we're done with this meeting, I want you to find us a good landing spot. But for the time being, can you please shift the screen over to Bevis?"

Jean motioned with her thumb, indicating he should move the map down as Paul tried to navigate the city.

"The shopping center is just off the interstate to the north," she said, and when he centered on it, she pointed. "The building on the right there is the SuperCenter. Before evacuating, we were in the middle of a shipment, so with any luck those trucks are still there."

"Any of them have food?" Hopkins asked. "Medicine?"

"There was some fresh stuff that is worthless now," she replied, "but pretty sure we had a few pallets of canned goods."

"Better than nothing at the moment," the Captain admitted. "Might buy us a day or two. Corporal, just make sure you have somebody who can handle a big rig on your team."

Strickland nodded. "Yes, sir."

Jean raised a delicate hand. "I can do it."

The Corporal took a deep breath. "Jean, I appreciate the offer." He paused, seeming to choose his words carefully. "And before I say another word, let me *assure* you that what I'm about to say I would say to anybody, regardless of gender. So please don't think I'm a sexist prick because you just happen to me a woman." He fixed his gaze on her. "But there is no way in fucking hell I'm taking another civilian on this excursion. Because if he wasn't an experienced helicopter pilot I'd be leaving his ass here, too."

"That's not all I bring to the table, Corporal," she said, raising her chin.

Strickland chuckled and shook his head. "Okay, let's hear your story too, then."

"I'm the shipping manager for the SuperCenter," Jean began, "not just for that store, but for the district. I have files on every truck in the region, including GPS coordinates and shipping manifests. Not to mention store inventory for fifty-five stories in the immediate region. If Paul is successful in getting us a fuel truck, I can lead us directly to the supplies we need.

"And before you ask, I've spent the better part of a decade dealing with trucks and stock room guys, so I can handle my own."

Strickland pursed his lips. "Why can't we just grab these files for you?" he asked. "Seems easy enough."

"Well, there's a laptop and two USB keys that may or may not be where they're supposed to be," she explained. "If you want to take the chance at bringing back the wrong thing, I totally understand."

Hopkins put his hands up as Strickland shot him a questioning stare. "It's your operation, Corporal, entirely your call."

Strickland grunted. "Fuck it. This is a hail Mary mission anyway, might as well go for broke, right?"

"That's kind of my feeling on it as well." Hopkins laughed, and took another long sip of coffee.

"Okay, you're in," the Corporal said, waving in Jean's general direction. "Bud, please escort them to where they need to go. Just have them on the landing field in thirty."

Bud nodded. "On it, sir." He led the pair from the office, closing the door behind him.

"So, Corporal, who do you want on your team?" Hopkins asked.

"I want Becker as my second-in-command to head up the Bevis team," Strickland replied immediately.

The Captain furrowed his brow. "You want a Private to be your second?"

"He wasn't always a Private," Strickland explained. "He got demoted from Corporal last year when we were deployed. Admittedly, he pulled some needlessly stupid shit, but in his defense it was his seventh deployment in eleven years. That kind of action can drive any man a little loopy."

Hopkins pursed his lips for a moment. "Do you trust him?"

"If I didn't, he'd be sitting here doing guard duty," Strickland said.

The Captain shrugged. "Fair enough. Who else do you want?"

"I'll take Private Yates," the Corporal continued. "He was with me in the sandbox last tour. Very capable and resourceful. I get the sense that's going to come in handy this mission."

"We need that for this whole fucking situation," Hopkins muttered.

"No shit," Strickland agreed. "And for my sixth, I'd like Private Goodman."

"Goodman?" The Captain furrowed his brow. "Isn't he a bit inexperienced?"

"Yeah he is," the Corporal admitted. "He's only been out of camp for six months. But in the entire time he's been assigned to my squad, he's done everything I asked with precision, and he's eager to prove himself. Plus, I figure having someone with youthful exuberance who hasn't become disillusioned with life itself might be of some benefit on this mission."

Hopkins chuckled and raised his coffee in a mock *cheers*. "Looks like you have yourself a team," he said. "When you load out, take as much ammo as you can carry. No use in rationing it, since if you fail this mission we're all gonna starve to death."

"Starving to death sounds better than being zombie chow," Strickland mused as he got to his feet.

Hopkins took a deep breath. "Here's hoping we'll never find out. Good luck, Corporal."

"So did they tell y'all what this is about?" Private Goodman asked as he pulled his boots on, voice echoing in the locker room.

Private Yates shook his head. "Nope, we got the same order you did," he replied as he clipped his ammunition belt on. "Just come down and gear up."

"Well, it's gotta be big if they're giving us the green light to take whatever we want," Goodman said, eyes wide with excitement as he picked out a large rifle from one of the lockers.

Private Becker snorted as he shrugged into his bulletproof vest. "Or they know it's a suicide run."

That put a damper on Goodman's mood, and he turned to his companion, brow furrowed. "Surely they aren't sending us out there to die, are they?"

"Do you see any high ranking troops here, rook?" Becker sneered. "Cause I sure as shit don't."

Yates shot him a steely glare, and then turned to the younger man. "Don't worry, Becker here is just a salty motherfucker who's lost faith in the system, what… two, three deployments ago?"

"That's cute that you think I ever had faith in the system," Becker shot back as he laced up his boots.

Yates clapped Goodman on the shoulder. "Don't worry kid, we'll be fine," he said, and the younger Private nodded, shoulders relaxing a bit.

Strickland walked in, flanked by Bud and two more civilians. "All right, you boys geared up and ready to go?" he barked.

Goodman stood ramrod straight and saluted. "Yes, sir!" he cried.

"What's the mission, if there are only four of us headed out?" Becker asked as he got to his feet.

Strickland stepped aside. "Well, there's going to be six of us. Meet Paul and Jean."

The newcomers gave a small wave, and Becker eyed them for a moment before shaking his head, turning to stuff more ammo into his belt.

"Oh boy," he muttered, "an escort mission. These always go well."

"It had better go well," Strickland said firmly, "because if it doesn't, everybody in this facility is going to starve to death."

The three Privates froze, even Becker, who straightened and turned to his Corporal.

"Fucking hell," he blurted.

Yates swallowed hard. "So the rumor going around about the fire was true?"

"If anything, the rumor wasn't as bad as the reality of the situation," Strickland explained, crossing his arms. "This facility only has about two days of food left. The fire also destroyed most of the medicine and seeds for the greenhouses."

"Well, I guess it could be worse," Becker scoffed. "At least we aren't walking."

"You say that," Paul said with a chuckle.

The Private's eyes widened. "You've got to be fucking kidding me. Are we walking out of here?"

"Oh no, we're flying out of here," Paul assured him, putting up his hands, "just not very far. I found us a landing spot at a construction site halfway between our two targets."

Yates cocked his head. "Two targets?"

"That's right," Strickland cut in. "The helicopter is almost out of fuel, so Paul, Goodman, and myself are going up to Harrison to get a refueling truck. While we're doing that, Becker's team is going to head up to the SuperCenter in Bevis to get supplies." He pulled a small stack of maps from his back pocket and handed them out to the proper teams, with highlighted routes. "We've checked the latest satellite imagery and the route to Bevis along the interstate looks pretty clear. So when we land, you are to secure transportation at the apartment complex here and proceed up to the target. It's a high-end place, and they typically have branded concierge vehicles. We figure the keys will be in the manager's office."

Yates raised an eyebrow, glancing up from his map. "That's one hell of an assumption there, isn't it?"

The Corporal raised his chin. "I mean, if you want to go door to door in the neighborhood nearby hoping someone left their keys there, you're free to do so," he said with a flippant wave. "We're just going with our best guess about the easiest way to find transportation. And this seemed like it."

"I can live with that." Yates sighed. "Plus all that tree coverage in the neighborhood next door makes me nervous."

Becker nodded. "Yates is right. It looks like a hell of a lot of civilization around that complex." He drew in a breath. "How do you know it's not overrun?"

"Didn't see much in the way of movement, although the trees do make it more difficult," Strickland admitted. "Although the apartment community is gated, so if you can get inside, you should be okay."

Yates sighed. "Famous last words," he muttered.

"Hey, if you want to swap missions with us, you can," Strickland said, more than a hint of amusement in his tone. "*We're* headed through the woods and across the river on foot."

Becker's eyes widened. "Why in the fuck are you doing that?"

"Because we spotted a horde on the interstate close to our target in Harrison," the Corporal explained. "They won't be much of a problem when we're in a big-ass fuel truck, but could give us issues in a civilian vehicle."

"Okay." Becker let out a sharp *whoosh* of breath. "Apartment complex it is, then."

Strickland nodded sharply. "Thought so. Any other questions?" He waited a beat, and then raised a hand and twirled it in the air. "Okay, finish getting ready, and be at the chopper in five." He headed for one of the lockers and started pulling down gear for himself.

Becker approached, lowering his voice. "Hey, can you level with me?" he asked quietly. "What am I doing here? Jackson is your second in command now, isn't he?"

"You're here because I know you're a leader," Strickland replied as he kicked off his shoes and pulled on a pair of combat boots.

Becker crossed his arms. "My *rank* suggests otherwise."

Strickland sighed and looked up at him. "Rank doesn't correspond with being a leader. I know what you went through in the sandbox, and I know what you've accomplished. This is a do or die mission, and I need someone I can count on. That's you. Not Jackson."

The Private gave a solemn nod. "Thanks, Strickland," he said in a rare moment of sincerity.

"You're welcome," the Corporal replied, bending back down to lace his boots. "Just don't make me regret it."

Becker barked a humorless laugh. "Well, from the sound of things, if you do have regrets it won't be for very long."

CHAPTER FIVE

The blades began rotating on the chopper, and Paul slid his headset on, checking his gauges. "All right boys and girl," he declared into the mic, "strap your asses in and hold tight. This is gonna be a short ride that could end very quickly if my math on the gas is off."

"Please tell me you at least got a quality education?" Becker joked.

Paul grinned back at his motley crew. "Best school in rural West Virginia."

Becker blanched. "Fuck."

There was a round of chuckles as the helicopter lifted off, and within seconds they had a full view of the city. The streets were packed full of zombies, rotting, shambling corpses looking for meat.

"Think anybody is alive down there?" Goodman asked, eyes wide with awe.

Yates shook his head. "If they are, they probably aren't enjoying life very much."

They cleared the downtown area quickly, but within view of the landing zone, the fuel alarm began to bleat angrily.

Strickland leaned forward. "Are we good, Paul?"

"Gonna be close," the pilot replied.

"Are we good?" the Corporal demanded.

"Yeah, I see the landing zone up ahead," Paul snapped. "Just shut up and let me focus."

Strickland nodded and tightened his grip on his restraints, the rest of the team doing the same as the beeping intensified. None of them had any background in aviation, and didn't know whether the thing was going to drop out of the sky or not.

Paul stabilized the vehicle as the engine began to sputter, and at about fifteen feet above the ground, they dropped. He landed evenly, though not without a good jostling, and quickly shut everything down before turning to give the Corporal a thumbs up and a grin.

Strickland simply glared at him.

As the blades slowed, the trio of Privates jumped down first, rifles raised to create a loose perimeter around the bird. A few zombies staggered from the construction zone towards the hubbub.

Becker lowered his weapon and drew a machete, heading towards them at a brisk pace. He casually beheaded one, and then waited for the second to get within arms reach. He stabbed the blade into its face, and then swept the area with his gaze once more.

"We're clear," he announced, and headed back to the group.

Strickland jumped down and stood aside for Jean and Paul to clamber to the ground. "Okay, you all know your mission," he said. "The rally point is here, two hours before sundown. If the mission isn't complete by then, we're gonna need to come up with a plan B before it gets dark."

"Any idea what that might be?" Becker raised an eyebrow.

"No clue," Strickland admitted brightly. "Although, if those apartments look nice you're welcome to pick up a brochure."

The Private barked a laugh. "Consider it done, Corporal."

"All right, let's move out," Strickland said, raising a hand, and the two groups of three split off in their respective directions.

CHAPTER SIX

Strickland glanced over at Goodman as they moved through the woods on a dirt bike trail, noting the young Private's white knuckles around his gun. "You need to relax some, kid, all that stress is going to burn you out."

"Just want to make sure I'm ready for anything, Corporal," Goodman replied.

Strickland nodded. "I appreciate that, but I'd rather have to relaxed when we encounter some of those things," he said. "Odds are, we're not going to find any runners out here in the wilderness, so if some zombies do pop up, we'll have plenty of time to react. And react quiet and smart."

The younger soldier nodded, his shoulders lowering a little, but his eyes still scanning the trees intently.

"So how much further have we got?" Strickland asked, catching up to Paul, who studied a printout as they walked.

"Should be a clearing about a hundred yards ahead," the pilot replied. "There's going to be a small trailer park and a drop-off point for inner tubes. There's a popular place a few miles up river and this is where it ends."

Goodman offered a small smile. "So we're going tubing?"

"Well, I'm kinda hoping there are some canoes as well." Paul chuckled. "But we'll take what we can get."

Strickland nodded. "Are we going straight across?"

"We can, if you want, but might be a better idea to ride the current for a half mile or so," Paul replied, motioning vaguely with one arm. "There's a drag strip on this side of the river. Once we see that, if we get off on the other side, it's a straight shot north through fields to my shop."

The Corporal nodded thoughtfully. "Sounds like a plan to me. Could use a lazy river ride, the way this day is going."

As they reached the edge of the woods, they peered around the thick trees to survey the field and street ahead. There were six trailers lined up in two rows, about thirty yards from the river. A few zombies lumbered about, but a cluster of them banged on the side of one of the far trailers.

Strickland raised his binoculars, scanning the area. "I'm not seeing a boat, raft, or even a single tube," he whispered. "You sure we're in the right spot?"

"Positive," Paul replied quietly. "This is where we came out last time we went."

The Corporal lowered the binoculars. "Then where are the boats?"

"Could be down by the river," the pilot replied. "It's a good thirty, forty yards from the trailers."

Goodman squinted as he peered around the tree. "Could be some behind the trailers, too."

"Okay, this is what we're doing," Strickland said as he clipped the binoculars back to his belt. "We move quickly across the road and get to the outside of the trailer on the left. We hug the outside of it and then make a dash for the water's edge, grab anything that floats, and hop on."

Goodman raised an eyebrow. "And the zombies?"

"Don't engage unless you have to," the Corporal replied firmly. "We make any sort of noise, and we're going to have a crowd."

Paul gripped his handgun tightly and nodded. Goodman gave him a pat on the back and held his own rifle at the ready, loosening his stance to get ready to move.

Strickland gave them a wave and then darted out of the tree line, leading them quickly across the street. They managed to make it behind the first trailer unseen, moving silently with their backs against the fiberglass.

Paul suddenly hissed, leaping away from the lineup and firing underneath the trailer. The shot missed completely, a zombie flopping out from underneath, moaning and reaching for him. Goodman, figuring the gunshot had fucked them already anyway, aimed down and put a bullet in the back of the corpse's head.

"We've gotta move," Strickland said as Goodman grabbed Paul's arm to get him back into formation. The moans and groans of the nearby zombies rose as they abandoned their posts and focused on the source of the new noise.

As the Corporal reached the end of the trailer, a zombie staggered around the corner, and without hesitation he fired right into its forehead, taking it down. He peered around the corner, and took a deep breath at the sight of at least a dozen creatures heading between the two trailers.

"Find us a boat!" he barked, and then leapt into the space, firing a volley of automatic gunfire at the mini-horde.

Goodman jerked Paul past Strickland, hurrying down the side of the second trailer. He stopped short as a door flung open, a clumsy zombie getting tangled in the stairs and falling face first into the dirt. The Private dispatched it quickly and jumped over the limp form, skidding at the corner to look around the front of the trailer.

There were even more creatures coming out of the thick brush by the river, and he stepped forward to fire, dropping a handful of them with well-placed headshots.

"Goodman!" Paul cried, clapping him on the shoulder.

The Private looked to where he pointed, at a canoe leaning against one of the far trailers. He pursed his lips, not liking the distance, but upon looking up and down the riverbank he didn't see anything else they could use.

"Corporal!" Goodman yelled.

Strickland stopped firing long enough to dart over to them as he reloaded his rifle.

"Found a boat," the Private explained, and pointed, "but it's twenty yards that way."

Strickland took a moment to look and sighed at the cluster of zombies in their way. "Unless you want to swim, let's do it," he said.

"Not a big fan of shrinkage," Goodman replied, "so let's get that boat."

The two of them marched forward between the trailers, Paul staying close behind them to avoid straggling. He held his gun tightly, watching the two soldiers take down zombie after zombie with terrifying precision.

When Goodman's gun gave a dull *click*, there was only a trio of corpses left guarding the canoe. He lunged forward and kicked the front one squarely in the chest, knocking the other two back and giving him a chance to reload. He took them out quickly as Strickland whipped around behind Paul's back to cover their path back to the river.

"You two get the boat, and I'll clear the way," he said as he reloaded his own rifle, taking down the zombies staggering in from the far end.

Goodman pulled the boat down from its perch, and lifted one end. Paul grunted as he picked up the other, struggling a little, but then managed to get a decent grip and they shuffled after the Corporal. He moved slowly towards the river, aiming carefully but only firing on the immediate threats as they got closer and closer to the water.

He jumped into the brush on the bank, making sure it was clear of waterlogged corpses before waving them in. They shoved the boat into the water, and Goodman held it steady while Paul scrambled inside. Strickland covered the bank as Goodman pushed off and hopped in, and then the two helped the Corporal clamber up.

A few runners reached the bank, just close enough to grip the side of the boat, and Goodman fired wildly from the hip, bullets tearing into the zombie's torsos. They weren't kill shots, just sending them staggering back, but it was enough for the canoe to reach the safe center of the river.

The three men caught their breath as the boat caught up in the current, carrying them along their destination.

"Is everybody okay?" Strickland finally asked, tearing his eyes away from the corpses clustering at the river's edge.

Goodman clapped the winded pilot on the back. "You gonna make it, bud?"

"If I… if I ev… ever say I can keep… up with you boys again…" Paul huffed, "I want someone to… smack me…"

The two soldiers burst out laughing, partly in amusement but partly just in joy that they were still alive.

"Good god, this is a fucking hike, man," Yates huffed as he followed Becker through a field. They could see the small neighborhood next to the apartment complex in the distance.

Jean raised an eyebrow at him. "Not afraid of a little cardio, are you?" she teased.

"I mean, I guess all things being equal, I'd prefer to be here than back in the desert," he admitted. "Pretty sure I'd prefer the walking dead to a hundred and twenty-five degree days."

She wrinkled her nose. "Yeah, my grandmother lives in Phoenix and I used to spend summers out there growing up, so I know all about that."

"Last time I checked, Phoenix doesn't get up to one-twenty-five," Becker cut in, glancing over his shoulder.

"It gets closer than you might think," Jean replied. "Plus, there's blacktop wherever you go, so you get baked from the top and bottom at the same time. Kind of an extreme heat spitroast."

Becker chuckled. "Extreme heat spitroast. I like that one."

They continued quietly towards the neighborhood, crouching in some knee-high brush to survey the area. Becker looked through his binoculars and studied a few zombies roaming around a cul-du-sac. There was a huge open field between the group and the highway, away from the cluster of houses.

"It's a little out of the way, but I think we should head south a couple hundred yards before crossing over," Becker said, lowering his binoculars. "Anything we can do to not draw attention to ourselves is worth it in my book."

"Agreed." Yates nodded. "I get the sense we're going to be fighting enough of those things today without going and looking for it."

Becker cocked his head. "Jean?"

She blinked at him, looking surprised that he wanted a civilian's input. "I'm with you," she replied. "I'm in no hurry to kill more of those things."

"*More* of those things?" Yates asked as they got up to move away from the neighborhood.

"Like anybody who has survived this long, of course there is a story." Jean rolled her eyes. "I'm not really keen on talking about it, but if you promise to keep it between the three of us, I'll share."

The Private held up a hand. "Scout's honor."

"Yeah, let's hear it," Becker agreed.

Jean took a deep breath and let it out slowly as they strolled through the open field. "Okay, well, when this thing really started to kick into gear, I heard my neighbor screaming for help. I looked out my window and could see two of those things fighting to get into his apartment. And I'll be honest, if it had been any other neighbor I'd had throughout my life I'd have just cracked a beer and waited for them to shut up."

Yates barked a laugh. "Damn, that's cold."

"You haven't met some of my neighbors," she insisted.

He raised his hands. "Fair enough."

"This kid was sweet," she continued, "even helped me move a washer and dryer into my apartment when I got fucked by the delivery guy. So against my better judgement, I grabbed a knife out of the kitchen, snuck out my front door, and stabbed one of the zombies in the back of the head.

"I had just enough time to pull the knife out before the other one turned on me. It came at my so fast I didn't even have time to stab. I just aimed and got lucky when it rammed its eyeball through the tip of the blade."

Becker let out a low whistle. "Two runners with a single knife. That's pretty impressive."

"Yeah," Yates added as he ran his fingers through the tall grass, "why wouldn't you want to share that story?"

"Because of what happened next," Jean said, swallowing hard. "He helped me up and took me inside his apartment to get cleaned up, and was extremely grateful that I had saved his life. Just thanking me profusely. I tried to tell him it was nothing, but he was adamant about making it up to me one day. Turned out it only took about two minutes."

Becker's eyebrows rose in amusement. "You know that story sounds like *he* wouldn't want it told. Being a two minute man isn't good."

"Nah, it's not like that," Jean replied with a laugh, waving her hands in front of her face. "I was still in the process of removing the gore from my hair when there was a knock at the door. It was some of you boys, there to take him to the stadium. Turns out he was some sort of science geek, and deemed vital to national security. As they started pulling him away, he stopped them and demanded that I be allowed to come too, since I was his top research assistant and vital to his work.

"I'm not certain I could even tell you what his last name is, let alone what kind of research he does, but he convinced them. I don't know if it was because they believed him, or they didn't want to take the time to fight about it, but a minute later we were in an armor-plated vehicle rushing towards the stadium as the world descended into chaos around us." She paused, and took a deep breath, glancing up at the sky for a beat. "If I hadn't opened that door when I did, I have no doubt I would be dead right now."

There was a moment of silence, until Yates shook his head. "Pure kismet," he said quietly.

"Don't you mean karma?" Becker asked. "She did a good thing and was rewarded for it."

"No, kismet," Yates corrected. "Fate. He saved her life so she could be in a position to save all of ours."

His companion snorted. "That just sounds like the ten dollar version of the nickel word I used."

"You know, the military will pay for your college education," Yates teased, a sly twinkle in his eye. "They'll teach you fancy words like that."

"Hard to go to school when they keep stop-lossing me and sending my ass back to the desert," Becker replied, though it sounded good-natured enough.

"This is true," Yates agreed. "Well, when we're looting the SuperCenter, I'll see if I can't find you a philosophy book or something."

His companion barked a laugh. "That'll work, I hear Ohio winters can be brutal. It'd be nice to have some emergency kindling laying around."

The trio shared a chuckle as they emerged from the grass onto the road. Busted cars dotted the area, but the only zombies were a few about fifty yards away, staggering around an overturned truck.

Becker nodded in the direction of the apartment complex, where they had a clear path with no ghouls in their way. "All right, let's do this."

As they closed in on the front gate, they realized just how tall it really was. The eight-foot-tall slotted iron looked to be on a motor, held together by tough stone walls running the perimeter of the property.

Becker cocked his head as he peered in at the machinery. "Yates, you think you can get that thing going?" he asked.

"Should be able to," his companion replied. "Those bad boys usually have a manual release in case the power goes out.

Can't be having rich folks be stuck in their apartments, after all."

Becker crouched down and laced his fingers together. "Okay, let's get you over, then," he said.

Yates planted his boot in his cupped hands and easily sprung up over the gate, landing gracefully on the other side with a loud *thud*. The noise attracted a few zombies from the highway, and Jean pursed her lips in concern as she noticed them turning and ambling in their direction.

"Hey, Becker, we've got company," she said.

He glanced over and then waved them off. "I wouldn't worry about them." He shook his head. "They're gonna have trouble getting over the guard rail. And even if they did, the fall down the hill would cripple them anyway."

She kept a wary eye despite his reassurance, watching them struggle with the guard rail. One of them let out a screech of frustration, and they both began to moan loudly in anticipation of a meal. Both Becker and Jean froze as moans echoed from inside the complex in response.

"Should we worry about *that*?" she asked.

Becker leaned over to look at Yates. "Hey, buddy, how's that gate coming?"

"Slow, some dumbass put a padlock on the motor cover," the Private replied. "Trying to pick it."

There was a rustling in the bushes about twenty yards from the gate, and Becker gripped the iron bars. "Pretty sure you can just shoot it off," he called.

"You sure?" Yates asked, brow furrowing.

As a few zombies emerged from the bushes, Becker drew his handgun and aimed. "Really sure!" he cried, and then fired three times, dropping the first three corpses quickly.

The echoing moans from inside the complex grew louder, drawn by the noise, and Yates' eyes widened.

"Holy shit," he breathed, and took a step back, firing several times into the lock. It finally *pinged* open and he dove forward, studying the motor for the manual release.

"Forget the fucking gate!" Becker cried as he holstered his gun, and laced his hands together again. "Help me get Jean over!"

Yates ran back to them as she put her foot securely in his companion's hands.

"Just roll over and he'll catch you," Becker explained.

She nodded firmly, bracing her hands on his shoulders. "Got it," she said.

He tossed her up, and she pushed off
of him like a springboard, catching the
top of the gate with her arms and using
the momentum to propel her body upwards.
She planted her foot on top and managed to
swing over, holding on and glancing down
nervously.

"Let go, girl, I got you," Yates
encouraged her, and she took a deep breath
before letting go. He caught her waist and
her feet touched down softly.

Becker whipped around and drew his
rifle, switching to three round bursts to
try to hold off the horde that was now
growing into the dozens. He emptied the
magazine and then turned back to the gate.

"Jean, catch the gun," he said, and
without waiting for a response, he tossed
the assault rifle over the top.

She jumped forward and barely caught
it, and watched with wide eyes as Becker
took a run at the stone wall. He leapt
against the one side, planting his foot
into the pillar to give him more lift, and
sprung up to grip the top of the gate with
both hands. He let out a loud grunt as he
pulled himself up, vaulting over and
flopping back onto the other side.

Yates caught him, though they
stumbled back a little bit. "You all
right?" he asked.

"Yeah," Becker replied, letting go and brushing himself off. "Let's get a move on."

CHAPTER EIGHT

Jean handed Becker his gun, and he reloaded it as they backed away from the gate. Leaving it closed was the only option, as it was now completely covered in moaning, rotting corpses. It bowed and creaked a little but held.

"Good thing you didn't get it open," Becker said.

Yates nodded, eyes wide. "Never been more thankful to fail a task in my life."

They turned and headed through the complex, keeping their weapons at the ready. There were only a few cars in the parking lot, definitely a lot less than would have normally been around for all of the residents.

"Looks like those who could, picked up and got the fuck out," Yates said.

"This thing hit pretty early on a work day," Jean replied, shaking her head. "A lot of these people are probably dead on the interstate."

Becker clucked his tongue. "Ironic."

"How so?" Yates furrowed his brow.

His companion shook his head. "All those people sitting in rush hour traffic day after day after day, probably wishing for death a thousand times. And now they got their wish."

Yates shivered. "You know what, that one's close enough."

A loud clang echoed in the distance, and Jean swallowed. "What the hell was that?"

The soldiers glanced at each other with concern.

"That sound like the gate to you?" Yates asked.

Becker nodded. "Let's get to the office."

They picked up the pace, jogging across the parking lot to the front office. In the employee parking spots, there were two black SUVs with the Shady Grove Apartment logo branded on the side in swirly gold lettering. Directly behind them, the office door was slightly ajar, but there was no movement in the floor-to-ceiling windows.

Becker stepped inside cautiously, sweeping his gun back and forth as he headed into the dim office. Jean stayed close behind him, and Yates brought up the rear, closing and locking the door behind them.

He stepped up beside the other soldier. "Bring 'em to us?" he asked.

Becker nodded. "My legs hurt, I'm game."

Yates knelt and smacked the butt of his rifle against the marble floor, echoing sharp cracks through the building. It was a large open area, and almost immediately moans carried back to them from the offices on the far side.

The soldiers led the way in that direction. All of the office doors were closed, and they found the one that was vibrating with smacks of zombie hands. Yates stood off to the side, and reached over to turn the knob and throw the door open.

Becker couldn't see anything in the darkness, but fired a few shots at head level. The moaning stopped in favor of the sound of bodies crumbling to the ground, and he stepped inside to make sure that he'd gotten them all. Yates knelt and smacked the ground again, but there were no answering noises this time.

Jean pulled out two little flashlights, and held one out to Becker. "Ready to go find us some keys?" she asked.

He clicked it on and offered her a smile. "I appreciate the eagerness, but let me do a quick sweep just to be safe."

She nodded and stayed behind with Yates as their leader made quick work of running through the last few rooms.

"Okay, we're good," he declared as he strode back to them. "Yates, I want you to keep an eye on the front. That horde already took down a metal gate, and while those giant windows are beautiful, I doubt they have much load capacity. If they show up here, we need to be ready."

"On it," his companion said, and hurried back to the front door.

Becker turned to Jean. "Let's start the hunt," he said, and they headed to the first set of desks.

They rummaged through drawers, pulling out every one and digging for anything even resembling a key. They checked in filing cabinets, in the pockets of any clothes strewn over chair backs, on the floor beneath in case anything got dropped.

"Nothing but fucking apartment keys," Becker grunted as he tossed aside yet another set he'd found.

Jean finished with the desk she was going through, feeling equally deflated, but then spotted a purse sitting on the windowsill nearby. "Oh, please tell me you were a naughty manager," she murmured, and hurried over. She dumped the purse out onto the desk, rummaging through random candy wrappers and makeup, she found a set of car keys on a Shady Grove keyring. "I think I've got them!" she declared, holding them up above her head like a precious artifact.

"Thank fucking christ," Becker replied, "cause I haven't found *shit*."

She held them out to him as he approached her, and offered a grin. "I mean, unless you want me to chauffeur you two around?"

He returned it as he took the keys. "Tempting thought, but I got this."

They headed back to the front, and Yates held up a hand to stop them. He put a finger to his lips and waved them forward to a crouch behind the front desk.

"Those bastards are out there," he said, motioning to the parking lot. There were at least three-dozen zombies milling about, in and around the cars. At least they hadn't clustered around the door, but it still wasn't an ideal situation.

"Goddamn they just keep multiplying," Jean groaned.

Becker held up the fob on the car keys, hitting the lock button. One of the SUV's lit up and gave a happy little *beep*, agitating the zombies nearby.

"What the hell did you do that for?" Yates hissed.

Becker took a deep breath. "Well, if we're going to fight our way through these things, I wanted to make damn sure we have the right set of keys."

"Now that you're sure," his companion said with a shrug, "how do you want to play this?"

"Fuck man, I don't know," Becker admitted. "You got any bright ideas?"

The trio looked around the room for anything to give them a lightbulb moment.

Yates motioned to the furniture in the lobby. "Maybe we can pull that couch into the doorway here and use it as a stopgap? Then we can pop those things in the head as they get close?"

Becker pursed his lips. "But if the noise we make attracts more, we could run out of ammo."

"True," Yates admitted, "but at the moment that sounds like our only solid plan A."

"Let's put it on the back burner as plan B, and keep working on a plan A," Becker suggested.

Jean ducked back into the office she'd found the keys in, and snatched a map of the property from the wall. She spread it out on a table out of sight from the front windows, waving for the soldiers to come see. She stared at it, illuminating it with the flashlight, and tapped her finger on the community pool area.

"Hey guys, I think I've got a plan," she said as they approached.

"We've got nothing but shit ideas on our end," Becker admitted with a shrug. "What you got?"

"Okay, we're in the office here." She pointed to the map. "And all the zombies are in the front parking lot, right?"

Yates nodded. "And we definitely do *not* have a safe way of getting out there."

She took a deep breath. "So we let them in."

Yates raised an eyebrow and turned to Becker. "My plan B ain't looking so bad now, is it?" he joked.

Jean scowled at him. "I'm not finished."

"Sorry." The Private put up his hands in surrender.

"So, once again," she continued, "we let them in. We keep their attention as long as we possibly can. Once it starts getting too close for comfort, we open the doors to the pool behind us. As long as we keep their attention, they're going to follow us. We get them into the pool area, and we take this side walkway around the building, right up to where the SUV is."

Yates furrowed his brow, leaning over the map. "Won't they just follow us?"

"Nope," Jean replied, tapping on that section of the map. "There's chest high gates with a magnetic lock, so it'll work even without power. We get out, they're trapped in."

The soldiers glanced at each other and chuckled.

She frowned. "What's so funny?"

Yates put his hands up again. "Trust me, we aren't laughing at you."

"We just think it's funny that a SuperCenter shipping manager has more tactical sense than half of the superior officers we worked under out in the field," Becker added.

"So… you think it's a good plan?" Jean asked.

Becker nodded. "It's fucking brilliant. Let's do it."

After doing a quick sweep of the pool area and making sure the magnetic gate was as secure as they'd assumed it was, they gathered in the community room.

"All clear," Yates declared. "We're good to go."

Becker motioned to the front windows. "Jean, would you like to do the honors?" he asked.

She grinned. "Absolutely." She aimed her gun at the front floor-to-ceiling glass, and pulled the trigger. It shattered, shards raining down onto the sleek marble floor of the ritzy apartment office. The zombies in the parking lot immediately swarmed the lobby, excited by the sudden turn of events. Jean shot out two more windows to give them a good pathway to the pool, and the horde screeched as they poured inside.

The trio backed into the pool area, and Yates rushed to the gate to make sure it was ready to go. Jean and Becker continued to move slowly, hoping to draw the horde as best they could. They picked up patio chairs and tossed them into the path of the oncoming zombies, sending the corpses stumbling over each other. A few of them fell into the pool, but the rest continued to gain on the trio.

"Close enough for my comfort," Becker said when the gap between them closed to about ten yards.

He threw up a hand and Yates opened the gate. The three of them slipped through and then slammed it shut behind them. They stood there as bait for another few moments, making sure that as many creatures as possible poured into the pool area.

"Let's get to the SUV," Becker finally said, and they darted up the side walkway. They reached the corner of the building, and he peered around the corner, seeing two zombies still in the parking lot. "Two left, apparently not impressed by our show," he muttered. "Be ready to move," he said, and then stepped out, popping both zombies in the head. "Next stop, SuperCenter!" he declared as they jogged across to the SUV.

"Shotgun!" Jean said brightly.

Yates grinned at her as he opened the passenger door and waved her in. "Hell, girl, after the way that plan went off, it's all yours!"

"Such a gentleman," she replied as she clambered up into her seat. "Your momma would be proud."

Yates closed the door and hopped into the back seat. "I'd like to think so."

Becker fired up the engine and peeled out with a satisfying screech of tires, taunting the zombies one last time before leaving them in their pool prison.

CHAPTER NINE

Strickland handed his binoculars over to Paul as the trio crouched in the grass within 50 yards from the main Sky Tours building.

"How we looking?" the Corporal asked.

Paul pursed his lips as he surveyed his old place thoroughly. "The refueling truck is going to be parked in front," he explained. "Keys are going to be in the main office, so if we take out that trio of zombies on the landing pad we can go in through the back door without much trouble."

"What about on the inside?" Strickland asked. "Are we going to have any nasty surprises when we go in?"

Paul shook his head, lowering the spectacles. "Doubtful," he replied. "Only had one employee and they came to the shelter with me. Doors were locked tight and I can think of about a hundred better places to take shelter."

"Okay, let's do it then," the Corporal declared. "Goodman, silent kills only, we don't need any unwanted attention. While we handle that, Paul, you're on door duty. You got your keys?"

He pulled a keyring from his pocket and gave them a little jingle before handing back the binoculars.

Strickland nodded and clipped them back to his belt. "Okay, let's move," he said, and pushed up to a bent-over position and began the jog across the field. As they hit the blacktop, the noise of their boots on asphalt attracted the attention of the three zombies staggering about.

They were grouped together, so the Corporal rushed up and slammed his shoulder into the closest one's abdomen, sending it toppling back into the others. The three all fell to the ground, and flailed around in frustration to try to untangle and get back to their feet.

Goodman and Strickland made quick work of them with blades to the head, and soon the three corpses lay still.

Paul unlocked the door and stood at it as he waited for the other two to join him.

"Why aren't you going on?" Strickland asked as they approached.

Paul took a deep breath as he grasped the knob. "Because, I've been wrong before and it's bitten me in the ass," he explained. "If I'm wrong this time it could be a literal ass-biting."

The Corporal cracked a smile and motioned for him to go ahead. He raised his weapon and moved in quickly as Paul threw open the door, doing a quick sweep about the empty warehouse.

"We're clear," he said, and Goodman ushered Paul in before securing the door.

The pilot strode quickly for his office, easily locating his keys in the organized chaos. "Got em," he called as he reentered the warehouse, "let's get outta here!"

"Guys, that might not be so easy," Goodman declared from the front window. The others joined him, and froze, wide-eyed.

"Fuck me…" Strickland breathed, jaw dropping to the floor.

The refueling truck stood in the front parking lot, near the road. An SUV was plastered into the front of it, melding the two together into a spectacular mess. Two zombies in the SUV flailed and thrashed in the front seats, trapped by their seat belts and the hood of the vehicle crushing them in.

"Do you think it's drivable?" Goodman finally broke the silence.

Paul scratched the back of his head in bewilderment. "Given that the radiator is resting on the front windshield, I'm gonna go with *no*."

"Okay, time for plan B," Strickland said firmly. "Paul, what about one of your helicopters?"

"Only one I have operational at the moment is a two-seater," the pilot replied with a shrug, "so unless Goodman here wants to hang on to the bottom…"

The Corporal groaned. "Yeah, not sure our liability insurance would cover that."

"What about a two truck?" Goodman piped up.

His two companions blinked at him, the idea sinking in quickly.

"That's actually pretty brilliant," Strickland replied with a nod, and turned to the pilot. "You think that'll work?"

Paul chewed his lip in thought for a moment, and then let out a deep breath. "Gonna need one hell of a tow truck," he said, crossing his arms, "but I know exactly where one is. Buddy of mine has an industrial strength one at his hangar at the airport. It's a big ole bitch too, could move my ex-wife and her mother in one trip."

"A shame he wasn't around when I got divorced." Strickland chuckled. "Could have saved me a bundle."

"So, where's the airport?" Goodman asked.

Paul motioned towards the back door. "A couple miles away," he said. "Shouldn't be that difficult to get to, since we can head through the fields."

"Well, it is a beautiful day for a hike," Goodman declared.

Paul shrugged. "We'll have to come back on the roads, but we can worry about that in a bit."

The Corporal pursed his lips. "Let's hope that the other group is having better luck than we are."

The SuperCenter stood tall amidst a horde of about seventy or eighty zombies, a whirling mass of rotting flesh around the bright blue building. The *Lowest Prices, Everywhere!* sign was covered in blood, making the smiling cartoon dog on it look that much more macabre.

"Must be a hell of a sale going on at the SuperCenter," Becker said, leaning on the railing of the I-275 bridge.

Yates nodded and stroked his chin. "Double coupon day, maybe?"

"Ah yes, zombie hoarders of the world, unite." Becker spread his arms.

Jean chuckled and shook her head. "Well, the good news is that they're congregating at the front. Hopefully, the back should be open."

"Is there another road that leads to the back?" Becker asked.

"No," she explained, "all the deliveries had to come in through the front and go around the building. They'd started to put a dedicated delivery entrance, but apparently the developer didn't think it was worth the investment."

Yates groaned. "But it was *so* worth the investment."

"So we're going through them?" Becker asked.

The other soldier turned away from the side of the bridge and pursed his lips at the SUV. "That's a thick-ass crowd of zombies," he said. "You think this thing can make it?"

"I mean, if we get up a head of steam," Becker mused, "the four wheel drive should kick in and get us over any bumps in the road."

Jean wrinkled her nose. "Uh, Becker?" She pointed to the side of the vehicle, where, next to the brand name was a *2WD* sticker.

The Private shook his head in disgust. "Who in the fuck would buy a *two wheel drive* SUV?" He threw his hands up. "That's like paying for a hooker who only gives your junk a few tugs! Completely pointless!"

"You've never met my ex-husband," Jean replied. "He probably could have gotten change back."

The soldiers winced and shook their heads at her plight.

Yates let out a low whistle. "I'm afraid this philosophical debate will have to wait for another day," he said, crossing his arms. "We need to figure out how we're getting in there."

"I still vote we run the fuckers over," Becker declared.

The other soldier turned back to the railing. "Is there a straightaway long enough for us to get up to speed?" he asked.

Jean nodded. "There's a residential street that leads into the parking lot," she said. "It's about three, maybe four blocks?"

"Alright, let's do this!" Becker cracked his knuckles.

"Wait," Yates interrupted, putting his hands up to stop his overzealous companion. "What do we do when we get to the back? How are we getting in?"

"I'll need ten seconds, maybe," Jean replied thoughtfully. "The door has a keypad locking system. Just gotta punch in the code, and we're in."

The soldier furrowed his brow. "Powered key lock?"

"Mechanical," she assured him.

He nodded. "Well, that's good at least. What about once we're inside?"

"The loading dock runs the length of the store," she explained.

"Are the doors to the main store open?" he asked.

She shrugged. "There's one set of double doors in the center. It locks from our side, but I have no idea if it's open or not."

"Which means we could be walking into a shitshow," Becker cut in.

"Given the size of the crowd out front," Jean added, "I'd almost bet on it."

He let out a *whoosh* of breath. "Okay then, once we're inside, the priority is securing that door. Yates, do you want to be the runner or the gunner?"

"Hey, I went first last time," Yates protested.

Becker shook his head in amusement. "That's what I get for asking instead of delegating."

"Yeah, you're a little rusty there, bud," his companion teased.

"I'll shake it off, provided I live through the next fifteen minutes," Becker assured him. "Come on, let's saddle up."

CHAPTER ELEVEN

Becker lined up the SUV in the middle of the street, back tires resting against the curb a few blocks away from the SuperCenter. He took a deep breath and tightened his hands on the wheel.

"Jean, when we get to the back, I want you to focus on nothing but the door," he said firmly. "Get it unlocked but do *not* open it. We might have a fight on our hands, and I'll be damned if I'm going to drag a civilian through all of this just to lose them at the destination."

She smirked. "Yeah, if you do that I'd haunt your asses."

"Fair enough," he replied with a nod. "Yates, as soon as I slam this bitch into park, you cover the rear and I'll take the front. When we get the signal from Jean, you take the door and I'll lead us in."

Yates raised his gun and nodded. "Ten-four."

Becker looked in the rearview mirror. "And Jean, if you wouldn't mind securing the door while we clear the storeroom, that would be greatly appreciated."

"Not a problem," she assured him.

He took another deep breath and revved the engine. "Here goes nothing."

He punched the accelerator and peeled out, the engine screaming as it redlined and built up speed through the residential neighborhood. By the time they hit the parking lot, he was going about sixty miles an hour, and the passengers braced for impact.

When the grill hit the zombie horde, the first corpse practically exploded in a fine crimson mist. Everyone jolted forward as the SUV plowed through about two-thirds of the throng before significantly slowing down. Becker hit the windshield cleaner to try to wash away the guts and rotting flesh blocking his vision as the engine whined.

"Fuck, fuck, fuck!" he cried as the SUV struggled to move any further.

Yates threw open the sunroof, and surveyed the area in front of them. "We're almost through, floor it!" he yelled, and his companion did so.

The vehicle surged forward slightly and then stalled out. Becker snarled more choice words and tried to start it again, but after a screech and a sputter, smoke began to billow out from underneath the hood.

"It's dead!" Yates barked. "We gotta go!" He pulled himself up through the sunroof and stood on the top of the SUV, raising his assault rifle to try to take care of the few rows of zombies clustered in the direction they needed to go.

Becker clambered up and slid down the windshield onto the hood, immediately opening fire. The zombies began to thicken, pressing up against the sides of the vehicle from all sides.

"We're gonna burn through a ton of ammo doing this," Yates declared as Jean climbed up onto the roof next to him.

Becker clenched his jaw, still firing, and then shook his head. "I'm open to ideas. This is the safest option right now."

"No it's not!" Jean cried.

The soldiers turned and saw dozens more zombies pouring out from the surrounding neighborhood, staggering excitedly towards the noise in the SuperCenter parking lot.

"Fuck," Becker spat, "so much for that plan."

Yates raised his hand. "I've got a plan."

"I love it, let's do it," Becker replied.

His partner raised an eyebrow. "You haven't even heard it yet."

"Well, it's better than mine, and we're out of time," Becker explained. "So what are we doing?"

"When I say go, unload everything you have on the back line," Yates pointed where the zombies were the thinnest. "Once they drop, we jump over the front line and run like hell."

Becker lowered his gun, eyebrows reaching his hairline in shock. "*That's* your plan? Jump over them?"

"Is it still better than yours?" Yates asked.

"Fuck sakes," his companion muttered as he reloaded his gun. "Jean, you ready?"

She nodded. "Tell me when."

The soldiers took aim, and Becker swallowed hard. "Say the word."

Yates took a deep breath. "Go."

They opened fire, thinning the back line of zombies as quickly as they could, rapidly dropping corpses to the asphalt. The fallen flesh created a landing pad of sorts on the other side of the eight or so zombies still trying to get to them against the hood of the SUV.

"Jean!" Becker cried, and she leapt to action.

She slid down the windshield and sprung off of the hood, leaping over the outstretched hands of the zombies. She landed on the pile of bodies and stumbled forward, but caught herself enough to run down the little hill and tear across the parking lot.

The two soldiers gripped their weapons tightly and pushed off from the windshield simultaneously, managing to clear the hungry corpses and land safely on their fallen brethren on the other side. They tore off after Jean, resisting the urge to look behind him as the entirety of the throng turned to pursue the trio.

Jean skidded to a stop before the back alleyway, taking it wide to make sure she didn't run into any unexpected foes, but it was surprisingly empty. The soldiers caught up and the three of them tore towards the loading dock, and Becker sprinted ahead of the back to fire at two zombies hanging out at the bottom of the short stairwell that led up to the door.

"Take the door," he huffed, "and *wait* when you get it unlocked."

Jean nodded and took the steps two at a time. "You got it," she said.

Yates and Becker turned back to see the horde coming around the corner, squeezing into the alleyway like a tidal wave. They had less than a minute before they'd be zombie chow, and they backed up the steps as Jean punched a ridiculously lengthy code into the keypad.

It gave a happy *beep* and she turned the handle but didn't open the door.

"We're in," she said, and then the door smacked into the side of her face.

She regained her footing quickly, and Yates threw himself against the door to try to shut it again as zombie arms flailed about, pinned between door and frame. Becker pulled his handgun and fired through the crack several times in rapid succession until there was nothing but a pile of bodies on the other side.

He reloaded as he yelled, "Open it, let's move!"

Jean didn't waste any time, and the two soldiers burst in so she could slam the door behind them just as the rest of the throng caught up to the staircase in the alleyway. She locked the door and leapt back from it as hands thundered against the metal from the outside.

Yates and Becker spread out a little, moving together through the storeroom. There were pallets of boxes and skids of merchandise lining the walls, some splattered with blood and some shining in the sunlight as if the apocalypse wasn't literally beating down the door outside.

Yates spotted the double doors to the store first, and rushed forward when he saw they were wide open. Zombies milled about the aisles of the women's clothing section beyond, and it almost would have been comical had it not been a life or death situation. He slammed and locked the doors, securing them before the corpses could make a mad dash for their location.

Becker came around a tall skid and two zombies were suddenly on him, grasping for his face. He wedged his head into the crook of one's jaw, and pressed the side of his handgun against the chest of the other to keep it at arm's length and away from chomping distance. He struggled against the first one, avoiding the teeth snapping against his hair. He managed to maneuver the gun so it was pointing upwards, and fired three shots into the bottom of the second zombie's head before aiming over his head and pressing the barrel into the soft flesh of the first one's eye socket and pulling the trigger.

As the corpses crumpled to the concrete floor, he wiped a hunk of rotted goo from his forehead with a cry of triumph.

"Try to sneak attack me, will you bitches?" he bellowed, kicking one of the fallen zombies. "Yeah, that's what you get."

"Ah, you okay, man?" Yates asked as he skirted the skid of goods, brow furrowed in concern.

Becker nodded with a maniacal grin. "Yeah, I'm good. *This* motherfucker tried to get the drop on me." He kicked the corpse again, baring his teeth. "Didn't work out so well for you, did it?"

"You really should consider switching to decaf," Yates chirped. "All that tension is gonna blow our your heart, man."

Becker rolled his eyes. "Yeah, like I'm going to live that long."

They shared a grim chuckle and patted each other on the back, turning back towards the back door.

"Where'd she go?" Becker's eyes widened.

"Jean?!" Yates cried.

"I'm in the office!" Her voice floated back over to them in the distance.

The two soldiers headed towards the tiny shipping office at a brisk pace.

"Man, the apocalypse hit this place hard," Becker said as he entered the small room. Papers were everywhere, binders and pens strewn across every surface in the place.

Jean laughed. "Nah, it's always looked like this."

"How did you ever find what you were looking for?" Yates gaped.

She shrugged as she rummaged through the bottom drawer of the desk. "I got paid by the hour, so I wasn't in a hurry." She pulled out a scuffed laptop that looked like it weighed a ton. "All right, got the main shipping computer."

"Christ, that thing is older than I am." Becker wrinkled his nose.

"What can I say?" Jean shrugged again and tucked it under her arm. "The owners were more concerned with buying their fifth yacht than providing us with adequate equipment."

Yates shifted his weight from one foot to the other. "What else do you need?"

"There's a USB key, somewhere in here," she said, tapping her chin as she looked around. "It's black and red with the company logo on it."

Becker nodded. "That can wait a minute," he said. "You want to walk through the storeroom with us so we can figure out how to get out of here?"

"Sure thing," Jean agreed, and led the way back out to the storeroom.

Yates patted the side of a skid of canned peaches. "Looks like this thing hit on grocery day," he said. "We lucked out on that one."

"Yeah, with a store this size, there was never a shortage of canned goods," Jean replied. "That's not going to be our problem."

Becker raised an eyebrow. "Wait, we have a problem?"

"Well, we can get the goods on the truck," she explained, heading towards the cargo hold. "But getting to the driver's seat is going to be a bitch since we're going to have trouble getting out the door."

Yates knocked on the side of the truck. "How's this store's hardware section?"

"Surprisingly robust," Jean replied. "Ever since that mega chain store across the street shut down, we beefed up our selection."

The Private raised an eyebrow. "So you should have a metal saw in stock, right?"

"It's probably going to be a non-powered handheld variety, but yeah, we should have a few," she replied.

Yates shook his head. "It's all good, we don't need that big of a hole."

"What, you gonna go out the side?" Becker asked.

Yates pointed up to the ceiling of the truck. "Go out the top, then in through the window. Easy as can be."

"What about the truck keys?" His companion wondered.

"Company policy is that the driver has to leave them in the cab while they unload," Jean replied.

Becker raised his eyebrows and nodded slowly. "Well, goddamn if we don't have a plan."

"Don't get too excited," Yates shot back. "We still have to hit the pharmacy and the garden center."

His companion clucked his tongue playfully. "Can't you just let me have one moment of joy today?"

"Well, while you celebrate, *I'm* going to start looking for a way into the main part of the store." Yates winked.

Becker let out an overly dramatic sigh. "No, the moment has passed. Come on, let's go." He turned to Jean. "Let us know if you need our help with anything."

"You got it," she replied with a little salute. "And if y'all have any questions, just give me a shout. I know this store like the back of my hand."

CHAPTER TWELVE

"Man, this place is a ghost town,"
Goodman said as he followed Strickland and
Paul across the tarmac. The repair hangar
loomed ahead of them, and there wasn't a
single zombie in sight. "Why can't
everywhere be like this?"

Paul shrugged. "Doesn't surprise me
that nobody's here," he said. "Those who
could, fueled up and took off as soon as
this thing started. The closest
neighborhood is nearly a mile away. No
reason for the zombies to stick around if
there's nothing to eat."

"Make sense I guess," the Private
agreed, but raised his gun as they
approached the hangar. "But just in case
there's something in there…"

There was a padlock holding the large
sheet metal door shut, and Paul pulled out
a few hairpins he'd stashed in his pocket
just for the occasion. He knelt down and
began to fiddle with the lock.

Strickland raised an eyebrow. "You
know, we can just shoot it off."

"Nah, it's all good. Wouldn't want
you to waste the ammo on-" he said as the
padlock popped open, "-something so
simple."

The Corporal blinked at him. "I'm
impressed."

"Well, when half your day is waiting on clients to show up, you gotta do something do keep your hands busy," Paul replied with a shrug as he slid the lock from its hole. "Figured I'd do something useful with my time."

He glanced at Strickland, who nodded and then Paul flung the door open. The Corporal and Goodman entered first, doing a quick sweep of the area to make sure it was as barren as outside.

There was a rusted vintage car up on the lift at the far end of the room, surrounded by tools strewn all over the floor. The soldiers turned towards the huge wrecker tow truck, a massive hulk of a vehicle that looked like it could drag a two-story house across town.

"You definitely didn't oversell the tow truck," Strickland said blankly as Goodman let out a low whistle.

Paul clapped his hands together. "No sir, I did not. If this thing can't get the refuel truck to the chopper, then nothing will."

"Keys?" the Corporal asked.

"Let's find out," Paul replied, and approached the driver's side door. He clambered up into the cab and then leaned over, rummaging around in the center console. When he sat back, he held a shiny set of keys. "I do believe we're in business, gentlemen," he said with a grin.

"Fantastic," Strickland declared. "All right, Goodman, hop in. You get the bitch seat."

The Private wrinkled his nose. "Why me?"

"Rank has its privileges," the Corporal quipped.

Goodman rolled his eyes. "Yeah, all right," he grumbled, and climbed up into the large cab.

Strickland followed as Paul started the engine, the large truck rumbling to life.

"Oh yeah," the pilot purred, "that'll work. You boys ready?"

"Have at it," Strickland said as he closed the door.

Paul put the truck into gear and they rolled out of the hangar and down the only road out of the airport. Soon they came upon a small neighborhood, and he had to slow to a stop upon reaching two cars parked in the middle of the road. It looked like someone had set up a barricade at some point, with the vehicles nose to nose.

"What do you want me to do here?" Paul asked, noting the deep ditches on either side. They wouldn't be able to drive around.

The Corporal waved to his companion. "Goodman and I can get out and move 'em."

"Don't think that's going to work," the Private commented, and motioned past the cars where zombies staggered out from around the houses towards the rumbling truck.

"Fuck," Strickland muttered. "Okay, that's not going to work." He paused, pursing his lips in thought. "Paul, how close are we to your shop?"

The pilot shrugged. "Maybe half a mile at the most," he replied. "The turnoff is just up ahead and then we're on the main road back to it. It's a straight shot."

"How long do you need to hook up the fuel truck?" Strickland asked.

Paul scratched the back of his head. "Depends on how badly that SUV is wedged up into it. Could be five minutes, could be half an hour, I honestly can't tell you."

"Well, let's hope it's the five minutes," the Corporal said firmly, "because we're going to have to drive through those cars, and those zombies are going to follow us back."

"If there's only a couple dozen, we can handle them," Goodman piped up.

Strickland sighed. "With the way today is going, I doubt we're going to be that lucky."

"One way to find out," Paul declared, and threw the truck into gear. He punched the accelerator and the beefy vehicle rumbled loudly before finding its footing and crashing into the two cars.

The sedans shrieked from being crushed by such a large vehicle but slid fairly easily out of the way, one tumbling down into the ditch, taking a few zombies with it. The grill of the truck tore through a few more corpses, sending others that ran at it flying back into nearby lawns on impact.

As they picked up speed through the neighborhood, Strickland focused on the rearview mirror, his jaw tightening more and more as zombies continued to emerge from the houses into the street.

"Yeah, this is not going to be good," he muttered.

"Holy fuck!" Paul exclaimed as he turned onto the main road.

In the middle of the street was a horde of easily a hundred zombies waiting for them, staggering as one along the main drag. He continued to accelerate, plowing through them like butter.

"Where's the shop?" Strickland asked.

Paul wrinkled his nose as a severed hand smacked into the windshield and left a gooey handprint there. "Three more blocks up," he said.

The Corporal studied the rearview again, taking a deep breath as the remaining zombies turned to follow them up the street. "Let's do this shit quick," he said.

They reached the smooshed SUV and the trio scrambled out as fast as they could. Strickland fired twice to take out the two thrashing zombies inside, and Goodman took a defensive position horde-side. Paul examined the wreckage.

"What do you see?" Strickland called.

The pilot threw his hands up. "A tangled fucking mess! I can't tell anything else."

"Fuck it, just hook the truck up and pull," the Corporal said. "We'll just have to hope for the best."

Paul nodded. "I'm on it." He rushed back to the two truck and pulled out two heavy chains. He laid down on the road and squirmed his way beneath the SUV to hook them up. Goodman took a deep breath and glanced at his companions and then at the oncoming horde.

"We're never going to make it," he murmured to himself, and took a deep breath. He walked away from the truck

towards the road, and crossed it to the
field on the other side. He aimed his
assault rifle at the corpse parade and
fired a few rounds. "Come and get me!" he
roared, spreading his arms.

Strickland startled and leapt up from
where he was supervising Paul, head
whipping this way and that to locate his
teammate. His blood ran cold at the sight
of the Private walking backwards through
the field, and he immediately raised his
walkie-talkie to his mouth.

"Goodman!" he barked. "What in the
hell are you doing?!"

His companion raised his own radio,
firing off a few more rounds before
answering. "Buying time for you to get the
fuel truck free."

"How, by sacrificing yourself!?"
Strickland cried.

"I looked at the map, and there's a
huge wooded area to the east of us,"
Goodman assured him. "I'm going to lure
them into it and lose 'em there."

The Corporal clenched and unclenched
his jaw. There nothing he could do
about this now. "You remember where we
parked, right?" he asked, defeat in his
voice.

"Yes sir," Goodman replied, and
saluted him from the grass.

Strickland took a deep breath. "Well, then hurry your ass up, because we ain't gonna be waiting on you for long."

"Don't worry sir, I won't be late," the Private promised. "Now you boys just lay low until I get these things clear."

"Thank you," Strickland replied, swallowing a hard lump in his throat. "Be safe."

"Always, sir," came the reply, and then more gunfire to attract the significantly distracted horde.

The Corporal ducked down and clapped Paul on the leg to get his attention. He put a finger to his lips to encourage him to stay quiet, and the pilot fell still, letting go of the chains. He rolled over to see what was going on, and Strickland peered around the back of the SUV to watch as the horde shambled into the grass after a whooping and hollering Goodman.

The Corporal took a deep breath. His partner had been right. Had he not done what he did, they wouldn't have made it.

"All right Paul," he said firmly as the last of the zombies dragged their way across the field. "Let's get this done. If Goodman doesn't make it back, I don't want his actions to be in vain."

Paul nodded and returned to his work. "I'm going to make damn sure that it's not," he said.

Strickland kept watch, gun at the ready, just in case any of the horde decided to make their way back. He saluted the field.

"Good luck, kid."

CHAPTER THIRTEEN

Becker pulled the empty dolly back
out of the truck. He parked it behind
Yates and leaned on it, watching the
Private pace back and forth in front of
the wall that separated them from the
store proper.

"Dude, what are you doing?" Becker
finally asked. "You look like one of those
seventy-year-old grandmothers who walk
around the mall."

Yates shook his head, but didn't stop
pacing. "I'm trying to figure out how to
get us into the main portion of the store
without being eaten."

"Oh yeah?" Becker raised an eyebrow.
"And how's that going?"

His companion finally stopped moving.
"Pretty sure I got us something that will
work." He pointed up to a small window at
the top of the wall and off to the side.

"Uh, do we need to go by the eye
center so you can get some glasses?"
Becker blinked at him. "Because if you
think I can fit through that…" He motioned
to the two foot by three foot window.

"No, no, that's not for us," Yates
replied, waving his hands in front of his
face. "That's for Jean."

Becker nodded as the insinuation sunk
in. "Okay, I'm tracking you now. We get

her up there, she creates a diversion to draw them away from the door. Wham, bam, thank you ma'am, we're in business."

"And?" Yates asked, crossing his arms. "What do you think?"

"I think it's going to be a bitch and a half once we're in the store, since we have no idea how many of those fuckers are in there," his companion admitted. "But at least the plan will get us in, so that's something I suppose."

Yates wrinkled his nose. "Yeah, it's a work in progress."

"Maybe Jean has a map of the store we can use to plot our attack," Becker said, and waved for the other soldier to follow him towards the back office.

As if on cue, Jean emerged from the door, a grin on her face. "Fucking found it!" she declared, holding up the USB key in triumph. "We're in business, boys."

"Good job," Yates commended with a grin of his own.

She slid the USB key all the way down into her deepest pocket for safekeeping. "So, y'all found a way into the store yet?" she asked.

"Yeah, he came up with a plan," Becker replied, inclining his head towards his comrade, "but we need some help. Do you have a store map we can use?"

"Sure," Jean replied, and disappeared back into the office, rummaging around for a moment. "Here we go. Come in."

The soldiers approached and they leaned over the desk, studying the large map. Everything was clearly labeled by department, complete with a self-contained garden center.

"First things first," Becker said, tapping the map at the bottom, "we have to shut those front doors. Jean, do we need a key for it?"

She shook her head. "No, they have simple deadbolt locks you can throw," she explained. "Should be good enough to keep those things at bay, at least long enough for us to get what we need and get out."

"What about the garden center?" Yates piped up. "It looks like it's in a separate building."

"It's separate from the main store, but it's a self-contained outdoor environment," Jean explained. "If memory serves, the seeds we need are on aisle seven, which is about halfway down on the right."

Yates pursed his lips. "Are those doors locked?"

"They should be." She nodded. "The garden center was only open during the daytime, so it wouldn't surprise me if the opener never made it in when this stuff started."

Becker turned to the other soldier. "Well, what do you want to do about the rest of the zombies in the store?"

"Why are you asking me?" Yates asked, a mischievous glint in his eye. "I thought *you* were in charge."

"Well, all good superior officers look for talent to promote," Becker teased. "Your plan has gotten us this far, so let's see if you can finish it."

Yates chuckled and then took a deep breath. "Okay. Well, hopefully Jean can keep the majority of them entertained back here in electronics while we shut the doors. After that, I say we take up position in the main walkway in the center of the store." He pointed to the area and tapped. "We clear the aisles around us, and then take our shots. When they get too close for comfort, we retreat to the main walkway at the front of the store and just keep 'em moving until we take them all out."

"Just your basic run to the store," Becker said casually, "only with more bullets and rotting flesh. Sounds like a plan to me. Let's do it." He glanced at Jean for confirmation.

She nodded and grinned. "All set," she declared.

"Hey zombies!" Jean cried from the little window, balancing on a few pallets to stick her head through. "We have an amazing sale on big screen TVs here in the electronics department! Why don't y'all come check it out?"

Moans rose up in response as the dead shoppers came to have a look at the TVs. She watched as a few dozen corpses moved towards her, clustering to the electronics section. She craned her neck to survey the storage room door, and then pulled back in to address the soldiers waiting on the other side of it.

"You've got two zombies within five feet of the door who don't seem interested in the sale," she called. "Looks like that's as good as it's going to get."

Becker nodded and turned to his partner. "You ready?"

Yates pulled out his machete. "I'll handle them, you secure the door."

"On three then," Becker said, and put his hand on the knob. "One. Two. Three!"

He threw open the door so that his companion could rush through, catching the first zombie easily in the face. As the second zombie turned, Yates kicked it in the chest, sending it tumbling backwards into a mobile phone display. The soldier tore his machete from the first opponent's skull, and then knelt onto the flopping corpse, sliding the tip right between its eyes as Becker secured the door.

They immediately raised their assault rifles, making sure that the clattering phones hadn't distracted from Jean's declarations of discount Blu-Ray players. Becker nodded and the duo moved towards the front of the store. They moved as quietly as they could, so they wouldn't attract any unwanted attention from stragglers in the parking lot.

Becker stopped short at the front of the aisle, peering around. "Shit," he muttered.

"How many?" Yates asked quietly.

"A dozen or so," his companion replied, surveying the zombies milling about the checkout lines. "Pretty close to the doors, too."

Yates chewed his lip. "How do the doors look?"

"Doesn't look like any of those things are near it, so closing them shouldn't be an issue, Becker replied. "But as soon as that first lock clunks, we're going to be made."

His comrade nodded thoughtfully. "I saw we both tackle the doors, get in and get out before they can make it over to us," he said. "Then we retreat back over here and regroup."

"Agreed," Becker said. "You take the two on the left, I take the two on the right?" After receiving a nod, he peeked out again to make sure their opponents were in the same place.

They rushed out of the aisle, tearing silently for the center doors. They made sure to close and lock them at the same moment, the *clunk* echoing loudly. The zombies snapped in their direction as the two soldiers separated, each taking the opposite outer doors. Becker had the farthest one, securing it easily, but Yates didn't quite beat a zombie to his, slamming it shut on an arm.

Becker rushed over, shoving at the rotting arm as Yates struggled to hold the door closed, but the checkout lane zombies were closing in fast.

"Fuck it," Becker grunted and stepped back, aiming his gun through the hole to shoot the offender in the head. Yates shoved the corpse out of the way and got the door closed and locked. The soldiers had no choice when they whipped around but to open fire on the oncoming zombies, regardless of the fact that the electronics department horde was likely on its way.

"So much for plan A." Yates sighed as the last corpse fell, leaving a gooey mess all over the nearest conveyor belt.

"Plan B it is, then," Becker replied.

His companion raised an eyebrow. "Wait, we have a plan B?"

"Yep," Becker declared as he checked his weapon. "Run and gun."

Yates let out a deep whoosh of breath. "I was hoping for something a little more thought out, but desperate times and all." He checked his own gun and they moved to the main aisle.

As they reached the open area there were about thirty zombies ambling up the aisles towards them. The duo spread out a little and took aim, carefully placing their shots. Corpse after corpse fell, but even with the precision shooting the horde seemed never ending.

"Fall back to the front door," Becker said as the wave grew closer.

As they turned, another dozen or so zombies flooded towards them from another aisleway. They fired, dropping about half of them before they both ran out of ammo. Yates swapped his magazine as Becker grabbed hold of a shopping cart from the cash.

He ran towards the smaller group, smacking into the lead zombie, the momentum flipping it forward into the cart. He plowed the remaining moaners, sending them tumbling back to the linoleum. As they floundered around, struggling to get up, he pulled his handgun and quickly executed them before finishing off the one in the cart.

Yates caught up to him, taking a defensive position as Becker reloaded his rifle.

"Solid move," he huffed.

"Thanks, used to watch reruns of Supermarket Sweep with my mother," Becker replied as he clicked a fresh magazine into his gun. "Taught me a thing or two about proper cart mechanics."

They turned towards four zombies emerging from an aisle to their right. They raised their weapons and took them out quickly before turning back to the main group coming from the center aisle.

"We're burning through way too much ammo," Yates worried.

Becker waved for him to follow. "I've got an idea, come on," he said, and led him down the opposite side of a large freestanding metal display. "Start rocking this bitch so we can tip it over."

Yates caught on and they wrenched it back and forth. The noise coupled with their grunts caused the zombies to stay on the other side of it, slapping the metal instead of streaming around to the back.

"Push!" Becker screamed, and the soldiers both heaved with all their strength, finally pushing the beastly unit over. It crashed down onto the horde, crushing skulls and bones. A few towards the rear simply fell back, but Yates opened fire, taking them out with precise headshots before they could get up and clamber over their fallen brethren.

Becker listened to the moans and groans coming from beneath the display, and pushed against it with his boot. It didn't budge an inch.

"Well, they may not be dead," he said, "but I don't think they're going anywhere."

Yates nodded. "Agreed."

"Let's do another quick sweep of the store to make sure there aren't any stragglers," Becker suggested. "Then we can get what we need and get the fuck out of here."

"I'll do the sweep," Yates replied. "You hit hardware and get that metal saw to Jean so she can start opening up the truck."

Becker nodded. "Sounds good. Meet back at the garden center in five."

CHAPTER FIFTEEN

Goodman sprinted through the trees, bobbing and weaving around trunks, brush scraping against his legs. He fired a few shots over his head with the assault rifle towards the horde behind him, but didn't stop to see if he'd hit anything. He was doing an okay job outrunning them, considering he had a lot more maneuverability what with his being alive and all.

He slowed to a jog as he pulled the map from his pocket, along with a compass. *That hiking trail has got to be pretty close to here…* he thought, scanning the paper.

His eyes flicked up at the echo of moans in front of him, and he quickly pocketed his gear, taking aim at two zombies in the direction of the hiking trail.

FUCK, they're in front of me too! he thought wildly, fighting to keep his breathing steady. He marched forward at a brisk pace, and when they were about ten yards away, he took them down with two quick shots. He double checked to make sure they were fully dead, and scanned the area ahead for more surprises.

"That had better be it," Goodman muttered as he headed towards a bit of a clearing in the trees.

The snarls behind him grew closer and he sprinted forward, bursting into the clearing. The hiking trail ran right through it, and he turned in the direction he needed to go, seeing eight zombies staggering towards him in the dirt.

He raised his rifle and managed to drop three of them before running out of bullets. He ejected the mag, but when he reached for another, his pouch was flat beneath his hand.

Fuck.

The ammo bag was in the tow truck.

He threw his now useless assault rifle over his back, pulled out his handgun and machete, and darted towards the remaining five zombies in his way. Just before reaching them, he ducked under the arms of the one to the side and darted into the brush to get around them.

Something gripped his belt and he swung wildly with a scream, slicing down with the machete into a rotted wrist. It didn't come completely free of the arm it was attached to, and the hand still held fast. He fired point blank into the elbow, freeing himself and staggering back onto the trail.

He sprinted along the trail, pumping his legs harder than ever before. His heart pounded in his ears, nearly drowning out the moans of the zombies coming through the woods to converge on the path. He passed a wooden marker that declared 1 mile until the end, and knew he wouldn't be able to keep this pace for much longer.

He slowed down to a more manageable jog, just fast enough to keep the distance between him and the horde consistent. Occasionally a straggler would wander onto the path from the trees, but Goodman dodged them easily, not wanting to waste precious time stopping to fight.

He finally came to the end of the trail, reaching a parking lot filled with several cars and even more zombies. He skidded to a stop to catch his breath for a few moments, spotting the interstate in the distance. He just had to get there and then it would be a straight shot to the landing site.

He took a deep breath and jogged to the left, giving the parking lot zombies a wide berth. They turned to stagger after him, but most of them just bonked around the cars like rotted pinballs, giving him enough time to tear to the on ramp.

"Fucking hell," Goodman huffed at the sight of several hundred zombies packing the road. They were likely the horde that had followed the tow truck rumbling by earlier. He looked at his handgun and then holstered it. There would be no use. He didn't have near enough rounds to deal with a horde this size.

He turned to run back down the ramp, but the zombies from the woods had caught up to him, filling the road quickly. A frustrated scream tore its way from his throat and he ran to the edge of the ramp, leaning over the concrete edge to look down. There was a steep embankment filled with thick brush, and he couldn't tell how deep it was.

Yeah, this isn't going to feel good, he thought, and sheathed his machete. He hopped over the concrete wall and slid down into the brambles, sharp branches slicing open his arms and face. He covered himself as best he could, falling into a roll at the bottom.

His knees hit the asphalt of the frontage road hard, sending jolts of pain up his thighs. But he had no time to think about that as moans echoed around him, closer than the ramp. He staggered to his feet, shaking his head to stave off dizzy exhaustion, and spotted a sign pointing down a side street that boasted *River Access*.

"Guess I'm going for a swim," Goodman gasped the words to himself, and hobbled down the road as the moans behind him crew louder and denser.

He finally spotted the water, and only two zombies stood in his way. He drew his handgun and fired twice, putting a bullet in each skull, and glanced over his shoulder at the ocean of rotting flesh pursuing him.

He holstered his weapon and splashed into the water, the cold a welcome boon to both his overheated body and his exhausted brain. He flipped over onto his back and began a nice lazy backstroke, enjoying the relative safety of the water as the creatures lined up on the bank.

"Fuck each and every last one of y'all," Goodman declared, giving the zombies the finger. He let out a laugh, a note of hysteria in his voice at how he'd managed to survive this far.

CHAPTER SIXTEEN

Yates strolled up to the garden center door, having completed his sweep. "You okay?" He furrowed his brow.

Becker sat on the floor, head buried in his arms resting on his knees. He raised a hand without raising his head, and motioned to the door before letting his arm flop back down.

"Just… just take a look," he said, voice muffled by his arms.

Yates stepped up, pressing his face against the small rectangular window looking out over the outdoor center. "What the hell?" he breathed, eyes widening. The place was jam-packed full of nearly a hundred zombies. "How are there so many of them in there?"

"Fuck if I know, man," Becker moaned, finally raising his head to look helplessly at his companion. "It almost looks like someone decided to use this as a storage facility for the sick once people started to turn. Regardless of why they're in there, I have no idea how we're pulling this one off."

Yates cocked his head, stepping back from the door. "I've got an idea, give me a minute." He headed off back into the store, and Becker stared up at the ceiling, fighting to control his breathing.

In the distance there was a beeping noise, and it got closer and closer until Yates came around the corner, riding a small forklift. He slowed to a stop and opened the driver's door.

"What do you think?" Yates asked.

Becker threw his hands up. "What do I think about what?" he snapped. "You want me to compliment your ability to drive one of those things?"

"No, we can use this to get past those zombies and get the seeds," his companion replied.

Becker blinked at him. "Okay. Um. How, exactly?"

"Well, the cab is well protected, so they won't be able to get in," Yates said, patting the open door. "And we can grab a pallet out of the back so you have a platform to ride on."

Becker shook his head and then blinked at his companion again, face ashen. "So," he began, and cleared his throat before continuing, "your plan is for me to *surf…* on a fork lift… above a sea of flesh-eating zombies."

"And grab the seeds, yeah, just like that," Yates confirmed, and cocked his head as his friend massaged his temples in shock. "I mean, if you have a better idea,

I'm all ears." He shrugged. Silence. "Well?"

"No, I don't have a better fucking idea," Becker growled. "I'm just trying to delay the inevitable of me pallet surfing over a sea of death."

Yates grinned. "I'll go get a pallet, then."

"Goddammit," Becker muttered as his companion put the forklift into reverse.

A few minutes later, Jean stood beside the garden center door, ready to throw it open. "You ready to do this?" she asked, raising an eyebrow at Becker, who bounced back and forth on the balls of his feet, testing his footing on the wooden skid.

"Fuck no, I'm not ready to do this," he grunted.

"I think he's about as good as he's going to get," she said.

"Agreed," Yates replied, leaning out the forklift door. "When I give the signal, you throw open the door. As soon as we're through, you slam it shut. When we come back, we'll be coming in hot, so be ready."

Jean nodded. "I will be." She snapped her fingers. "Oh, I almost forgot." She reached into her back pocket and grabbed a bright pink canvas bag, holding it out to Becker.

He took it, a look of distaste evident on his face as he unfolded the offending fabric, complete with smiling purple flowers printed on the side.

"You know, for the seeds," Jean explained, and scratched the back of her head nervously under his death glare. "Yates, you'd better head out before he strangles me," she joked.

"On your mark," the driver replied and settled into his seat, closing the door securely. He cracked the window just in case he needed to talk to Becker.

She nodded at him before jerking the door open, and he floored the accelerator, picking up a head of steam as they sped into the garden center proper. The door slammed shut behind them and Yates paused, getting the lay of the land.

"Holy fuck, there are runners!" Becker cried, motioning to a few fast moving zombies approaching them.

Yates shrugged. "As long as they aren't climbers, you should be okay," he called as he moseyed the forklift along the aisles.

"Motherfucker, don't even *joke* about that," Becker snarled as the zombies reached them.

They smacked against the sides, leaving bloody handprints along the outer edge of the vehicle, but otherwise parting as it bumbled happily along the aisle.

"The next one is ours," Becker pointed, keeping a wide-legged stance and trying not to look down at the sea of hungry monsters waiting to devour him if he fell.

Yates drove slowly, allowing Becker to grab handfuls of seed packets and stuff his pink canvas full to bursting with various fruits and vegetables.

"I think we're good," he called back, tying the handles securely so nothing would fall out. "Let's get the fuck outta here."

Yates pointed past him. "There are still more seeds that way."

"We're past the food and into the flowers, now," Becker replied.

Yates cackled as he sped up to outrun their followers. "Don't you think some roses would brighten up the stadium?"

"I'll draw you a fucking picture, now let's *go*!" Becker demanded, bracing himself against the roof of the forklift as they turned the corner at the end of the aisle. They put some distance between them and the horde, but three runners had pushed through the main group and were catching up.

Becker wedged the bag of seeds securely between his feet and drew his rifle, leaning on the roof to aim. He managed to drop one, but couldn't manage to hit the other two with their erratic speed.

"Fuck, I can't get them!" he cried.

Yates slammed on the brakes and drew his handgun, rolling down the window. They reached the driver's side, screeching, and he quickly dispatched them at point blank range, blowing rotted brain matter all over the garden hoses.

He dropped the gun into his lap and floored it again, speeding towards the door. Jean opened it to allow them to speed through, and then slammed it again behind them, clear of the disappointed zombies on their tail.

Yates lowered the pallet so that Becker could jump off, and he let out a deep sigh of relief as his boots hit the floor.

"Did you get what we need?" Jean asked, double-checking the door before heading over to him.

Becker grinned, holding out the ridiculous pink bag. "I hope you like salad."

"Well, I always said it would be the end of the world before I went on a diet," she replied with a relieved laugh. "Turns out I was right."

Yates jumped down from the forklift and the trio headed for the storeroom, in significantly better spirits than when they'd traveled the other way.

"Are we loaded up?" Becker asked.

Jean nodded. "Loaded up and got the hole in the roof cut," she confirmed. "We're ready to head back to the chopper."

Becker let out a deep sigh of relief. "Let's head out, then."

CHAPTER SEVENTEEN

Jean drove slowly along the interstate so that she could weave around the random broken down cars strewn along the highway.

"The turnoff to seventy-four south should be just up ahead," she said. "Then, just a hop, skip and a jump away from the landing site."

Yates took a deep breath. "Hope the other group was able to get the fuel."

"Well, if not, we got enough food to start our own little colony together," Becker piped up.

Jean rolled her eyes. "No offense boys, but that doesn't sound too appealing to me."

"What, you don't want to play den mother to a couple of rough and tumble soldiers?" Becker teased, and then lashed out to brace himself as she slammed on the brakes. "Damn, sorry, didn't realize it was that bad of a suggestion."

"No," she snapped, "look."

The soldiers stared down the interstate, seeing a shambling horde of hundreds of zombies just past the turnoff to the seventy-four.

"Fuck," Becker breathed, "if we turn of now, then they'll just follow us to the landing site."

Yates leaned forward. "Jean, if you would please pull up to those cars just by the turnoff."

"What the fuck are you going to do?" Becker demanded.

His companion reached into the ammo bag and pulled out a block of C4, wiggling it in the air with an excited grin on his face.

Becker scoffed. "You've had that this whole time?"

"Just saving it until we really needed it," Yates replied with a shrug.

His companion threw his hands up. "Yeah, I mean, it's not like we've been trapped and surrounded by zombies how many fucking times this trip."

"It just goes to show how much confidence I have in your abilities, oh leader," Yates drawled.

Becker glared at him. "We're having a chat once we get back to the stadium."

Yates chuckled as Jean stopped beside a large pileup of cars. He hopped out and attached explosives to several areas of the vehicle wreckage, and then clambered back up into the cab.

"Okay, we're good," he declared.

Jean popped the truck back into gear, and took the ramp to the seventy-four. About a half mile or so down the road, Yates grinned and hit the detonator.

The explosion was immediate, and so powerful that the truck rocked on his tires.

"Christ!" Becker cried. "How much of that stuff did you use?"

Yates shrugged. "I don't know, a couple of blocks?"

"Felt like you used enough to *level* a couple of blocks," his companion muttered.

"Just wanted to make sure the zombies stayed attracted to that, and not to us," Yates explained.

Becker let out a low whistle. "Well, if that doesn't do it, then nothing will. Holy fuck."

As they pulled up on the landing site, the mood in the cab rose to significant heights at the sight of a tow truck with a fuel tanker attached to the back of it. Strickland and Paul were in the midst of gassing up the helicopter, and the Corporal turned to the trio as they bustled out of the transport.

"What in the hell was that explosion?" he demanded. "Was that you?"

Becker pointed both hands at his companion. "That was all Yates," he said, and raised his palms. "He decided we needed a diversion for the horde on the interstate."

"Good to know they don't teach subtlety in basic anymore," Strickland said, raising an eyebrow.

Yates simply grinned. "Didn't seem like a subtle kind of moment, Corporal."

"Apparently," Strickland replied dryly, and then glanced back to Becker. "Did you get what we needed?"

"We have enough food on the truck to last us a couple of weeks," Jean cut in, "seeds to start growing, and I have all the information we need to keep us stocked until we become self sufficient."

The Corporal let out a deep sigh of relief. "That is fantastic news."

Becker furrowed his brow. "Hey… where's the youngster?"

Strickland clenched his jaw and frowned. "He led a group of ghouls away from us so we could secure the fuel," he said. "Been trying him on the radio, but I haven't been able to get a hold of him."

"He's a tough kid," Yates piped up. "He'll be alright."

"I hope so," Strickland replied somberly. "But nothing we can do about it right now, so let's get this chopper loaded up."

Becker nodded. "Yes, sir."

They pulled canned goods from the truck and loaded the cargo holds of the chopper until Paul declared them near dangerously overweight. As he closed the hatches, there was a rustle in the bushes behind them.

Becker and Strickland spun around, aiming their rifles at a smirking Private Goodman.

"You weren't going to leave without me, were you?" he asked as he trudged towards them, soaking wet.

A huge smile broke out on Strickland's face as he clapped him on the back. "Wouldn't dream of it." He frowned at the sight of crimson lines criss-crossing the young man's skin. "Good lord. Is that your blood, or zombie blood?"

"Little from column A, a little from column B," Goodman admitted. "Took a nasty trip through some brush on the side of the interstate."

The Corporal gave his shoulder a light squeeze. "When we get back, your first visit is to the infirmary."

"Yes, sir," Goodman replied.

Paul leaned out of the chopper. "Hey, y'all ready to get the hell outta here?" he asked. "I know I am."

Strickland nodded, and waved the Private forward. "After you, Goodman."

The young man went up first as the helicopter whirred to life, the rest of the team following. They secured their belts and hope soared in their chests as

the chopper began to climb into the air,
full of food and seeds and gas.

From the air, they watched the fire
raging on the bridge at the interstate,
hundreds of zombies massed around it, some
flailing in the flames. The landing site
was completely clear, hopefully leaving
their fuel supply safe for the time being.

The sun hung low on the horizon as
the bird headed back for their stadium
home, each team member thankful in their
own way that they'd fulfilled their
mission of keeping all of the survivors
back there alive.

END

DEAD AMERICA: THE SECOND WEEK

BOOK 5: HEARTLAND - PT. 3

BY DEREK SLATON

© 2019

CHAPTER ONE

Day Zero +11

The landscape was vacant beneath the midday sun, the Missouri River flowing along the east side of the chugging train into a large reservoir.

Bill focused hard on the tracks, plugging at a brisk pace but keeping a keen eye out for anything out of the ordinary. Even in the middle of nowhere they had to stay vigilant; something could pop up at any moment.

"Can somebody explain to me why we're trying to get up to Seattle instead of just settling down here?" Private Johnson asked from the window, waving a hand at the beautiful scenery. "Look at this, ain't nothin' for days."

Sergeant Kersey didn't look up from the map he was holding. "Because the U.S. military is a thirsty beast that requires all manner of resources, most notably oil," he explained flatly. "And not only are the Canadian oil fields within reach, but Washington state has the fifth highest refinery capacity of any state in the union."

"Interesting," Johnson replied, stroking his chin, "but how in the hell did you know that random-ass factoid?"

Kersey shrugged, still staring at the map. "Because General Stephens told me that when I suggested the exact same thing you just did."

"Great minds, huh?" Johnson chuckled.

The Sergeant shrugged. "Yeah, something like that."

The soldiers pitched forward as Bill hit the brakes on the train.

"Goddammit!" Johnson cried as he fell down onto one knee. "What is it now?"

Bill motioned out the window. "Pickup truck on the tracks," he replied.

Kersey folded up his map and they surveyed the cluster of houses on the west side of the tracks. To the east were three nondescript buildings.

"Are you fucking kidding me?" Johnson threw his hands up. "There's like twenty people in this fucking town. How does a truck end up on the tracks?"

Bill shrugged. "Not sure, but we still gotta take care of it."

"Probably for the best," Kersey replied. "We're getting really close to Helena. Might do us a bit of good to regroup before hitting that."

The engineer nodded. "Probably a good call, as it's the fifth largest city in the state."

"What, did General Stephens tell you that one, too?" Johnson groaned as he brushed himself off.

Bill smirked. "Nope, I just paid attention in college."

Kersey barked a laugh as the train came to a full screeching stop. The three men clambered down from the engine car, and the first box car opened, revealing the rest of their team.

Private Kowalski jumped down first, rubbing his squinting eyes in the bright sun. "Damn Bill, any chance you can get a slow rolling stop next time?" he moaned. "I was firmly in dreamland, then the next thing I know Baker and Mason were laying on top of me."

"Sorry about that," Bill replied, hooking his thumbs into his belt loops. "I figured we were fine out here in the middle of nowhere, but it appears as though I was mistaken."

"How big's the job?" Private Baker asked as he stretched his arms above his head.

Kersey motioned to the front of the train. "Single pickup truck on the tracks."

"Ah, well, I'm going back to bed then," Baker replied.

The Sergeant shook his head. "You might as well stay up. We're getting close to Helena and need a game plan."

"Fifth largest city in the state!" Johnson declared proudly.

Private Mason raised an eyebrow in confusion. "Good… good to know there, Johnson."

Bill chuckled and shook his head at Johnson's wide grin, enjoying the look of glee on the Private's face at looking smart in front of his comrades. He patted him on the shoulder as they began to walk towards the truck.

"Mason, Johnson, make sure that truck is clear," Kersey instructed.

The soldiers raised their weapons, keeping guard even in such a tiny town. They did a quick sweep around the vehicle, but found nothing suspicious.

"We're good," Johnson said, and reached in to pop the gear shift into neutral.

It didn't take much effort for them to push the truck up over the tracks, and it rolled easily into the grass off to the side.

"So, what's next?" Mason asked.

Kersey lowered his gun. "We need to talk about Helena."

Corporal Bretz cleared his throat, rubbing the last of the sleep from his eyes. "Sergeant, if I might make a suggestion first."

"What is it?" Kersey asked, turning to him.

Bretz pointed to one of the three buildings across the street, boasting B-A-R in big block letters. "I think we should stock up on some, ahem, vital supplies before discussing our next impossible task."

The Sergeant grinned. "Two drink maximum, boys. We'll get the rest to go."

The soldiers whooped as they headed across the street in a pack, guns at the ready to breach the door to the happiest building in town. Kowalski and Bretz took up position on either side, the former giving a nod before turning the handle and throwing it open.

The Corporal rushed in first, swinging his gun around the dim space. It looked to be in fairly good condition despite the apocalypse, and only a single figure moaned and jerked behind the bar.

Bretz pulled out his flashlight and shone it in the direction of the undead bartender, who was missing the bottom of his jaw, tongue dangling down its neck.

"Clear the back rooms," the Corporal instructed. "I'll handle this guy."

Kowalski nodded. "On it." He jogged off as Bretz casually approached the bar.

He sat down on a stool, peering behind into the small space. The zombie staggered over, gargling all the way, and the Corporal pulled out his knife, stabbing into the creature's forehead without even standing up.

"That's the problem with these small town bars," Bretz said, shaking his head. "It's almost impossible to find quality help."

"We're clear back there," Kowalski announced as he came back in from the rear room.

Kersey led the rest of the soldiers inside. "Baker, Mason, see what you can do about getting us some light in here. Johnson, why don't you set us up something to drink?"

"Coming right up, sir," Johnson replied with a grin, and hopped over the bar. He kicked aside the corpse and got to work, setting up a line of glasses and pouring a double-shot of whiskey for each of his comrades. He held up his own glass, prompting everyone to do the same. "To the best damn group of rail riders I've ever known," he declared.

There was a smattering of *hell yeah's* and *damn straight's*, and Bill let out a laugh.

"Well, you guys haven't gotten me killed yet," he said, "so yeah, y'all are the best in my book as well."

Everyone clinked their glasses together and took sips of their drinks, relishing in the delightful burn of the alcohol so long denied them.

"Bill, can you join Bretz and I over here?" Kersey asked, waving him to a table in the center of the room. "We could use your expertise."

"Sure thing," the engineer replied, leaving the others to cheers a second time.

"Remember, two drink maximum," the Sergeant said firmly, pointing at the Privates. "I don't want to end up getting shot because one of y'all is drunk shooting."

"I'll keep 'em in line, Sarge," Kowalski said with a wink.

Kersey shook his head with a chuckle. "I'm sure you will." He turned to the table and sat down next to Bretz, who laid out a road map of the area.

"Bill, what do you know about the tracks in Helena?" the Corporal asked as he drew his finger along the rail line.

"There's a small yard there, I think maybe five, six tracks worth," Bill replied, leaning forward on his elbows to look at the map. "With any luck, it'll be empty and we can just roll right through."

"And if it's not?" Kersey asked.

The engineer clasped his hands together and took a deep breath. "We may want to consider abandoning this train and finding something at the other end of the yard."

"Kind of defeats the purpose of clearing a path, doesn't it?" Bretz raised an eyebrow.

The Sergeant puffed out his cheeks and then cocked his head. "Well, there's seven of us, including Bill, and I doubt we have more than a hundred rounds left between us. We haven't been through any town this big yet, and it's not going to take much for us to get overwhelmed."

"I'm not sure the General is going to be particularly happy with it," Bretz replied, and then shook his head, raising his glass. "But fuck it, he isn't here."

Kersey laughed. "Cheers to that."

CHAPTER TWO

Bill slowed significantly about two miles from the city. He and the soldiers were on high alert, ready to stop at a moment's notice. Mason and Baker stood on the outer railing while the rest of the team were packed inside the engine car.

"What in the holy hell?" Johnson breathed as they came around the bend towards the city.

There were piles and piles of dead bodies on either side of the tracks. Bill eased the train to a stop.

"Didn't expect to see this," Bretz said, taking in the walls of rotted flesh. "Sarge, what do you think?"

"It's like someone is making a mass grave," Kersey replied, motioning to the excavation equipment off to one side.

Johnson blinked a few times. "There's gotta be what, a few thousand bodies there?"

"Easily," Bill replied, and stifled a gag as the scent permeated the cabin. "Judging by the smell, I'd peg it even higher than that."

Kersey clenched his jaw. "Let's keep moving. We need to see what's going on in Helena."

The engineer nodded and eased the throttle forward, inching them forward into the city. As the skyline came into view, the soldiers leaned forward in confusion.

"Sarge, are those lights?" Bretz asked, eyes widening.

Kersey pulled out his binoculars, stepping right against the window to peer at one of the buildings several hundred yards ahead. Even in the late afternoon sun it was clear there were floodlights on.

"Unless I'm going blind," he replied, "those are indeed lights."

Bill slowed to a gentle stop again, staying short of a makeshift barricade blocking the tracks. Somebody had put up a fence, and it extended on either side of the tracks in either direction. A trio of pickup trucks approached up the railroad, and Kersey stepped out of the cab to join Baker and Mason on the front, weapons at the ready.

"Lower your guns," the Sergeant said, "but keep them ready. Given that pile of bodies we just passed, whoever is in charge of this town has some firepower. Might be a good idea to get on their good side."

The trucks stopped on the other side of the fence, in a V formation, and a short fit white man with black hair jumped out of the front vehicle. He strolled up to the barricade, as casual as if it were a normal summer day.

"Well howdy," he greeted, hooking his thumbs into the pockets of his jeans. "If I had to venture a guess, I'd say y'all aren't from around these parts."

Kersey chuckled. "What gave us away?"

"Not to insult yer sneaking ability, but riding into town on a big ole train is a dead giveaway," the man replied with a toothy grin. "Plus, as much as I hate to admit it, tourism has been a bit down the last few weeks. In fact, nobody has come through here in quite some time. So anybody new is gonna be raisin' my suspicion."

The Sergeant spread his palms slowly. "Well, if you'll have us, I have a few boys here who could use some quality R and R."

"Definitely a possibility," the man said, and cocked his head. "But first, why don't you tell me who y'all are and what y'all are doin' here."

"My name is Sergeant Kersey, U.S. Military," Kersey explained. "I have a team of five plus my civilian train engineer and we are clearing a path to the Northwest so the bulk of our men in the Midwest can make their way up there."

The man raised his chin thoughtfully, shifting his weight to one hip. "The Northwest, huh? Something big going down?"

"That's the current rumor," the Sergeant replied, with what he hoped looked like a noncommittal shrug.

"All right, good enough for me," the man replied, and gave a thumbs-up to the trucks behind him. "Why don't you boys lock up your train and your rifles and I'll take you to meet Mayor Hogan."

Kersey took a deep breath. "You don't honestly expect us to go with you unarmed, do you?"

"Not at all," the man said with a shake of his head. "Sidearms are just fine. In these difficult times, we are trying our best to live in town the way it was before all this. And frankly, having a group of army men walking around with assault rifles isn't the best way to be achievin' that."

The Sergeant nodded. "Fair enough. We'll be right down." He stepped back into the cab, followed by the Privates outside. "Leave the rifles in the cab, sidearms only."

"That's leaving us awfully light," Bretz replied, pursing his lips.

Kersey shrugged. "Not like we really have the ammo for them anyway."

"This is true," the Corporal agreed bitterly, and unslung the large gun from his shoulder.

"All right, everybody on their best behavior," Kersey said firmly, looking each man in the eye in turn. "Bill, no matter *what* happens, you're with me. Always. We clear?"

Bill nodded. "Yep."

"Okay," the Sergeant said, letting out a deep *whoosh* of breath. "Let's go check out the mysteries of Helena."

CHAPTER THREE

Kersey and Kowalski rode in the backseat of the main man's truck, Bill nestled comfortably between them. The dark haired man—whose name had turned out to be Seth—drove across the outskirts of town and then onto the road and into the heart of it, his companion in the passenger's seat stoic all the way.

The soldiers gawked at the stores along the street fully lit up with power, the town almost looking normal.

Kowalski did a double take at the sight of a man at the grocery store helping an older lady load up paper bags into her car. "I have so many questions," he blurted.

"In due time, sir," Seth replied with a chuckle. "Mayor Hogan will gladly answer all of yer questions."

"But I'm just… how?" Kowalski stammered. "It doesn't look like anything has even happened here. It's like the apocalypse jumped overtop of you."

Seth took a deep breath. "As I'm sure you noticed when you rolled in, the apocalypse most certainly did *not* skip us over."

"I'm… I'm sorry." Kowalski's face drained of all color. "I'm truly sorry for

saying that. I really didn't think before
I spoke."

"It's alright," their host replied.
"I know you didn't mean any harm. And I
can only imagine what y'all have seen out
there. We only got a brief glimpse of it
before the TV went dark. I can see how our
town is a bit of a shock to you."

Bill let out a low whistle between
his teeth. "That's an understatement."

"Look, I know that Mayor Hogan is
going to explain everything to us."
Kowalski leaned forward, eyes wide. "But I
just gotta know. How in the world do you
have power?"

Seth nodded in defeat as they turned
a corner. "Since I'm the one who headed up
the project, I can answer that one," he
said. "The Canyon Ferry Dam is just up the
way on the Missouri River, and is a prime
source of hydroelectricity. Once we got
the town secure, I led a team up there and
we were able to get everything stabilized
and running smoothly. We have to ration
the power a bit since it's not at full
capacity, but based on your reaction to
it, I'm going to assume we're doing better
than most other places."

Kersey shook his head slowly. "This
town is certainly a marvel. You should be
very proud."

"We are, sir," Seth replied firmly.
"We are."

The trio of trucks pulled up to an old courthouse. It was two stories and built of stone, easily a heritage building in the city.

"Come on," Seth said as he put the vehicle in park, "I'll take you to Mayor Hogan."

It was quick for Kersey's team to mobilize, following Seth inside, as they all were burning with questions about this interesting town.

Their dark-haired host led the way across the marble floors of the courthouse. People scurried about here and there, and it was surreal to see such a flurry of normal-looking activity underneath the tungsten glow of lightbulbs.

"Oh, Seth, you're looking good today," a little old lady said as she approached the group. "You and your wife need to come by so I can cook you a proper dinner."

He grinned fondly at her. "We would be honored, Miss Lindsey."

"Oh, that's so good to hear!" she exclaimed, clasping her hands together. "And your new friends are invited too. Been a good while since I've had a mess of hungry boys to cook for!"

The soldiers smiled at her enthusiasm and waved to her with a chorus of *ma'am's* as she wandered past.

"She seems nice," Johnson said as they continued their walk. "Reminds me of my memaw."

Seth chuckled. "She cooks a mean meat loaf, too."

"Sarge, just to let you know," Johnson declared," I may go AWOL if we're not here for that."

Kersey laughed. "You and me both."

They headed up a flight of stairs to the second floor offices, and Seth opened the door to a large conference room. There was a massive oval table, and on the far end an oak desk where a middle-aged man stood up from his chair.

"Come on in," he invited, and gave his thick white mustache a swipe as he approached the group. "Seth my boy, how are you?"

The dark-haired man smiled. "I'm doing well, Mayor, and you?"

"Oh you know, just another day in the apocalypse," Mayor Hogan replied. He surveyed the group of soldiers and clasped his hands in front of him. "These must be the military boys I heard about over the radio."

Kersey stepped forward. "Yes, sir."

"Oh, don't call me *sir*," Hogan replied with a wave of his hand. "Way too formal. Mayor is just fine."

The Sergeant nodded. "All right, Mayor," he replied. "I'm Sergeant Kersey, and these are my men." He introduced everyone in turn, and Hogan went down the line, shaking everyone's hand with a surprisingly firm grip.

"Welcome to our little slice of heaven," he said when he was finished, motioning for everyone to sit at the large table. "And given the look on your faces, y'all look as confused as a chicken in a whorehouse. So what would you like to know?"

Kersey took a seat and swiveled towards the white-haired man. "For starters, how did you manage to secure a city this size?"

"We had a crazy amount of luck," Mayor Hogan admitted. "The day all of this started spreading, we had a fierce pop-up thunderstorm. Lightning ran in on the control tower at the airport and blew out everything. Had to shut it completely down for a full day. So while the rest of y'all were dealing with those critters running wild, we just had a whole mess of sick folk. We got just enough national news to know what was happening, so we were able to get people quarantined." He paused, swallowing hard at the memory. "It… it was difficult putting our neighbors down like animals. But just like when a dog turns rabid, you gotta do what you gotta do."

Kersey nodded somberly. "I think I speak for everyone in my group when I say we know how you feel," he said. "We've all had to do things that will haunt us, but like you said, we gotta do what we gotta do."

"Thank you Sergeant," Hogan replied. "Anyway, once we were able to pacify the zombie uprising, it wasn't too difficult to do the rest. Seth here got us set up with power, we have several farms in the area that we were able to keep running and get set up with greenhouses, and we mostly neutralized the threat from Missoula by blocking up the interstate."

Bill blanched. "What's wrong with Missoula?"

"Let me guess, that's the next stop on this trip?" Bretz groaned.

The engineer nodded. "Yep."

"Missoula got hit hard," the Mayor explained. "We were able to evacuate a few hundred people from there, but it was a slaughterhouse."

Seth drummed his fingers on the edge of the table. "And unless you are finding another mode of transportation, there's another complication."

"Let me guess." Bill raised a hand. "Tracks are blocked?"

"With an overturned fire truck," Seth replied.

Bill scrubbed his hands down his face. "Jesus fucking christ. How in the hell do you flip a goddamn fire truck?"

"My brother works out at the airport," Seth explained. "As this was going down, he was in touch with his friend at the Missoula tower, so he got the play-by-play. They had a plane crash after the pilot turned as they were in their final descent. Somebody at the fire department who was way too dedicated to his job drove out there and got attacked. He lost control, and the next thing you know, instant train block."

Kersey turned to the engineer. "Can we go around Missoula?"

Bill rubbed his temples and sighed. "There's only one path through the forest, and it runs through Missoula," he said. "I mean, I suppose we could swing a couple hundred miles south and cut through Idaho, but then we'd have to go through Boise which is considerably larger. And god only knows what kind of shitshow that's gonna be. I mean it's already going to be a shitshow when we hit Spokane, but hopefully by then we can get some support from the General."

Kersey took a deep breath. "I don't know about you, but I'd rather face a difficult situation while knowing what I'm in for, rather than walking into something blind. Let's figure out a way to get that fire truck moved."

"I'm pretty sure there's some C4 left," Baker piped up. "Let's just blow it off the tracks."

Bill shook his head. "That would most likely destroy the tracks in the process."

"What about a tow truck?" Bretz asked.

Johnson shook his head. "Nah man, we're gonna be hard pressed to find anything with the kind of horsepower that can move a fire truck."

"Would a dump truck work?" Seth asked, and shrugged as the soldiers all turned to him. "I mean it's not like you have to worry about the wellbeing of the fire truck, you just need it moved, right?"

Johnson nodded thoughtfully. "Yeah, them dump trucks got some power behind them. I think that could work."

"There's a landfill in the north part of town, about a mile or so from the airport," Seth explained. "Should be easy enough to get to."

Johnson clapped his hands together. "City landfill it is!"

"Don't say I never take you anyplace nice," Kersey quipped.

"I do have a couple of requests for you, if you wouldn't mind," Hogan cut in.

The Sergeant swiveled to face him. "Of course, Mayor."

"There are still some survivors holed up in a church downtown," Hogan explained, folding his hands together on the table in front of him. "We haven't been able to reach them, and they're low on food. Would it be possible for you to get them out?"

"I think we can manage that," Kersey agreed. "What else can we do for you?"

"Despite our barricades on the interstate, we're still fearful of an exodus from Missoula," the Mayor replied. "Second largest city in the state, and it wouldn't take a lot of them leaving to cause us some problems. I know you don't really have any control over what they do, but if you could try to lead some of them out into the forest we would be appreciative."

The Sergeant nodded. "We'll make as much noise as we can while leaving town," he said.

Hogan raised his hands in thanks. "The fact that y'all are willing to try is good enough for me."

"Corporal Bretz, would you please take over the planning on this raid?"

Kersey asked. "I'm going to go radio the General and see if we can't get some reinforcements up here to help us out with Missoula."

Bretz nodded. "Yes, sir."

"Pardon me, son, but did you say reinforcements?" Hogan asked. At Kersey's nod, he cocked his head. "How many are we talking about?"

"For now?" Kersey shrugged. "As many as they can spare. But once we finish our mission, there's going to be a couple hundred thousand that will be working their way through here and up to the Northwest."

The Mayor clucked his tongue. "Seems like you boys are planning quite the party."

"Something like that," the Sergeant replied.

Hogan leaned forward. "Well, you tell the General we're here to help. Probably can't handle all two hundred thousand of y'all at the same time, but we'll do what we can."

"Thank you," Kersey said, and headed out of the office into the hallway.

CHAPTER FOUR

"Excuse me," Kersey said to a pair of women exiting a small office, "may I use that office to make a call?"

One of them nodded and held the door open for him, cheeks pinking slightly as he smiled his thanks and headed inside. Once he had privacy, he keyed in the proper frequency.

"Heartland base, please respond," he said. "This is Sergeant Kersey."

The response was almost immediate. "This is Heartland base, we read you loud and clear Sergeant Kersey."

"I have a priority alpha message for General Stephens," he declared.

"Please hold, I will get him for you," came the reply.

"Thank you," the Sergeant said, and leaned against the desk behind him while he waited.

"Sergeant Kersey, what's your status?" the General asked.

"General, we're in Helena, and it's unlike anything we could have predicted," Kersey gushed. "The city is fully functional. It's secure, has power, it's like nothing ever happened."

There was a momentary silence. "How in the hell did they pull that off?" Stephens finally asked.

"The short version is that the airport was knocked out the day the virus spread, so they had time to prepare," the Sergeant explained.

"Better to be lucky than good, I suppose," the General replied.

Kersey nodded. "Without a doubt, sir."

"When are you and your team heading out?" Stephens asked.

"Depends on how quickly you can get some reinforcements to me," the Sergeant replied. "We've run into a situation in Missoula and it may be too much for us to handle on our own."

"I'm sorry," the General replied, "but your orders are to push onwards. D.C. is breathing down my neck to get the army to the Northwest for their invasion. We've had some issues with getting the caravan up and running on our end, so we're behind schedule. I'm going to have to move Heaven and Earth just to get your some reinforcements to raid Spokane."

Kersey sighed before hitting the button again. "I understand General, and we'll figure out a way to accomplish our mission. But you are correct that we will need some help with Spokane. What kind of reinforcements can we expect?"

"I've been able to get fifteen hundred men to Moorcroft as an advance team," Stephens said. "Since I know you are close to Spokane, the next shipment to Moorcroft will be supplies. Should be able to spare a thousand men to send your way."

The Sergeant cocked his head. "Twenty-five zombies to every man. Sounds like a challenge."

"Well, it's better odds than you currently have in Missoula, so consider yourself thankful," the General replied.

"That I do, sir," Kersey replied sincerely. "That I do."

"When you clear the way through Missoula, contact me," Stephens said.

The Sergeant glanced out the window. "The sun is setting low here sir, so we will be tackling this at first light."

"Understood," the General replied. "Be safe."

"Thank you, General," Kersey replied, and then turned off his radio and promptly threw it down onto the desk. "Fuck my life."

CHAPTER FIVE

Kersey headed back into the Mayor's office, where Seth was showing the soldiers where the trucks would be located on a large map.

Hogan straightened. "Did the General have some good news for you?"

"Well, we should have reinforcements," the Sergeant began, "for when we take Spokane. We're on our own for Missoula."

Kowalski scoffed. "Great. So if we somehow survive tomorrow we'll get some help. Fantastic."

"Can we not just wait for the Spokane group to get here?" Bretz asked, brow furrowing.

Kersey shook his head. "D.C. is up his ass to get the troops moved up," he explained. "We have orders to clear the tracks."

"Suddenly, going AWOL for that meat loaf is sounding a lot more appealing," Johnson muttered, leaning back in his chair.

"Sergeant, is there anything we can do to help you?" the Mayor asked, clasping his hands in front of him. "We can't really offer you men as we're stretched thin between the farms, the power station and the barricades, but…"

Kersey cocked his head. "Could you spare some ammo?"

"Absolutely!" Hogan replied. "Just jot down what caliber you need, and Seth will bring you a care package later in the evening to the Bed and Breakfast on sixth."

The soldiers all perked up at the sound of that.

It was Mason who raised his hand, eyes alight with excitement. "Bed and breakfast?"

"Yes, sir," Hogan replied with a grin. "You boys look like you've been through the ringer since this shindig got started. Thought you could use a little R and R, so I'm gonna get you set up at the best little B and B we've got. Y'all have got a full day tomorrow, so I figure a good night's sleep followed by coffee and bacon and eggs would be in order."

Johnson locked his fingers together and waved his clasped fists at the sky, tilting his head back. "Grilled meat, thank you Jesus."

Hogan chuckled. "So you're a meat man, are you?"

"Only in his private life." Kowalski smirked.

The room erupted in laughter, even the man himself.

"My apologies on the phrasing there, son," Hogan amended, and reached out to clap Johnson on the back. "What I mean is, are you the time of man that appreciates a perfectly seasoned and cooked slab of beef?"

The Private's mouth practically watered at the question. "Oh, yes, sir."

"I thought you might be," the Mayor replied. "Seth, once you get these boys settled in, head down to Big Bubba's and tell them to set up a table of seven. Have ole Bubba send me the bill."

Seth grinned and nodded. "Consider it done, Mayor."

"Thank you so much for your hospitality," Kersey said, and extended his hand to shake. "I don't know what else I can say."

"Nothing else is needed, Sergeant," Hogan replied, shaking his hand cordially. "Now, you boys enjoy your stay here in Helena. And you let ole Mayor Hogan know if you need anything else." He shook everyone's hands in turn again, waving them off at their *thank you's*, including Johnson, who was near choked up at the thought of grilled meat.

Seth led the group outside and up the street, springs in their step despite their exhaustion. The promises of good food and comfortable beds were exciting, to say the least.

"Man, this is something else, isn't it?" Baker gaped at the open shops around them.

People milled about lazily, enjoying the evening. A group of kids tossed a football around in the middle of the road, laughing and running together like they didn't have a care in the world.

Kowalski nodded. "Have those kids playing stickball and this is a snapshot out of the fifties."

"I loved playing stickball growing up," Bill said, a wistful edge to his tone.

Kowalski raised an eyebrow. "Dude. I thought you were in your twenties?"

"Yeah, but I grew up in the rural Midwest," the engineer replied. "The nineteen-fifties didn't hit our town until sometime in the mid-nineties."

The Private snorted. "Just wait until you get MTV, it's going to blow your fucking mind."

"You should have seen our reaction to color TV," Bill teased.

After a chuckle rippled through the group, Baker took a deep breath.

"Y'all think we can rebuild like this?" he asked. "I mean, if we're successful in Seattle?"

Bill shrugged. "I don't see why not. If a bunch of civilians in Helena, Montana can do it, I'd like to think the full force of the U.S. Government would be capable."

"Well, given our recent history, nation building hasn't been one of our strong suits," Kowalski quipped.

Bretz glanced over his shoulder from the front of the pack. "What's so funny back there?"

"Oh, nothing Corporal," Kowalski replied innocently, "just laughing at our collective shortcomings."

"We're guests here, Private," Bretz replied with mock sternness, "please keep the flashing to a minimum."

Kowalski pouted. "Oh, you're no fun."

"Well, here are your digs for the evening," Seth declared as he stopped in front of the Bed and Breakfast. "If y'all want to go in and take a load off for a bit, I'll go get dinner set up. Give me an hour or so and then head on over there. I'll have everything ready for you." He motioned across the street to an old building that looked like it had been there since the dawn of time. Inside the big front windows lay a family-style diner that added to the fifties' feel.

"Thank you," Kersey said, holding out his hand to their guide. "I really appreciate the hospitality. We all do."

"It's our pleasure, Sergeant," Seth replied. "I'll see you soon."

The soldiers turned towards the Bed and Breakfast, lingering on the street collectively for a moment.

It was Johnson who broke the silence. "Anybody else feel like this is too good to be true?" he asked.

"You should stop worrying and just be thankful we have a reprieve," Mason replied, clapping him on the back. He stepped forward and they all bustled into the building, taking in the surreal sight of the happy street once more before entering the coziness inside.

CHAPTER SIX

Johnson practically dove on the plate of pancakes in the middle of the breakfast table. "These are mine, Kowalski!" he cried.

"Dude, you eat any more and that belt of yours is going to commit suicide," Kowalski said with a shake of his head.

The charming old lady that had brought the food wagged a finger at the soldiers. "Boys, no need to fight," she declared. "I've got another batch on the griddle as we speak."

Johnson and Kowalski both blushed and ducked their heads, shoulders relaxing under the scolding. Bill took the opportunity to reach over and spear his fork through the whole stack, liberating the pancakes over to his plate.

"Whoa, what the hell, man?!" Johnson yelped, eyebrows shooting up to his hairline.

Bill grinned as he cut a large bite of the sweet treat. "What are you gonna do, court marshal me?" He shoved the gigantic hunk of dough into his mouth and the two soldiers glowered at him.

"Morning boys, did y'all sleep well?" Seth asked as he strolled into the dining room.

There was a series of nods, and a few mumbled responses around mouthfuls of eggs and bacon.

"This breakfast is awesome," Johnson blurted, spitting a hunk of yellow scramble onto Bretz' cheek. "Sorry, Corporal."

Bretz shook his head and wiped his face, simply putting a finger to his lips to shush the boisterous Private.

"You ready to hear the plan, Seth?" Kersey piped up, setting down his cutlery and leaning back with his mug of coffee.

Seth nodded and took a seat. "Whenever you are, Sergeant."

Kersey produced his map, spreading it out over the open part of the table nearest their guide. "Okay, I've been studying this map for the last couple of hours and this is the best plan I've come up with. If anybody has questions, concerns, or a brighter idea, I'm all ears." He glanced around the table, eyes sincere, and his team nodded. "Bill, you're going to give us a ride past this neighborhood on the north side of town, and drop us off. There's nothing but empty fields between there and the landfill, so it should be an easy hike to get there. Mason, you are on Bill guard duty."

Johnson swallowed his mouthful and raised his hand. "Why not just have Bill drop us off there?"

"Because that train is going to make a hell of a lot of noise, and the last thing we want is to draw attention to the fact that we're at the landfill," Kersey explained.

Baker furrowed his brow. "Won't we just lead the neighborhood zombies there, though?"

"Nope," the Sergeant replied, tapping the map, "because as Bill backs his way out of town, he's going to lay on the horn to make sure they follow."

Seth's eyes grew wide. "Whoa, wait a minute. The last thing we want to be doin' is to draw those things in our direction."

Kersey raised a hand. "He's going to be stopping on the bridge over the river, so none of them will get through. And I promise that once I lay out the rest of the plan, you'll understand and be good with it." He turned to Mason and cocked his head. "One more thing. You boys are going to be our communication hub. We're not going to have any direct contact between the teams because the last thing we want to do is inadvertently alert nearby zombies that lunch is here."

Seth's shoulders relaxed and he smiled as the old lady returned and set a cup of coffee in front of him, and a fresh stack of pancakes in front of Johnson. He gave Bill the side-eye on her way out of the room, and he chuckled, sitting back from his plate as a sign of good faith.

"Okay," Kersey commanded the room once again, "once we get to the landfill, we're going to break into two teams. Bretz and Johnson, you'll be heading south into town to rescue the people trapped in the church. Once secure, you'll get up to the train and hand off the truck to the civilians. Again, Bill, will lay on the horn to keep the zombies occupied. A few stragglers may continue their pursuit, but it won't be anything to take care of them with your barricades." He moved his finger across the map. "Kowalski, Baker and I are going to head to the airport to figure out a way to get the fire truck off the trails. With any luck it'll be a simple push."

Kowalski took a deep breath. "And if it's not?"

"Then you'd better have an itchy trigger finger," Kersey replied, "because there's gonna be a lot of zombies to kill while we figure out how to move it."

Seth raised a hand. "I can actually help on that one," he put in. "Ammo for yer assault rifles were a bit lacking, but I was able to dig up a couple hundred

rounds for each of you. For my sniper
friend, however, plenty of hunters in the
area were more than happy to be donatin'
some rounds. So I got you set up with
about a thousand more shots."

"Holy fuck," Kowalski breathed.

"Language!" the old lady snapped as
she returned with a pot of coffee to
refresh everyone's mugs.

Kowalski blushed again, lowering his
chin. "Sorry, ma'am," he said. "Holy
fudgesicles."

She nodded as she refilled his cup.
"That's better."

"You think you can do some damage
with that?" Seth asked.

The Private grinned. "Without a
doubt."

"Once we have the route clear, Bill,
you're going to come pick us up, and Baker
is going to set up some C4 to attract
every zombie we can," Kersey continued.
"Then we're off towards the forest and
Spokane. Anybody got any other questions?"

There was a collective shaking of
heads, and the Sergeant nodded, draining
the last of his cup. "All right, well
hurry up and finish your breakfast. We've
got a long day ahead of us."

CHAPTER SEVEN

Bill brought the train to a stop on the outskirts of east Missoula, about a half mile away from a large neighborhood that stretched to the north. Kersey peered through his binoculars, and took a deep breath at the sight of dozens of shambling figures on yards and streets.

"Bretz, get the team ready to go in the box car," he instructed. "From the looks of things, we're going to have to burst out and hit the ground running. I'll stay up here and pick our stopping point."

"Yes, sir," the Corporal replied, and jumped down from the cab, heading to the back.

"Mason, once we're clear of the train, I want you to shoot at anything on our side of the tracks that is even *thinking* of looking in our direction," Kersey continued. "And Bill, as soon as we're clear, I want you heading back."

The engineer nodded. "Not a problem, Sergeant."

"Okay, take us to the landing spot," Kersey said.

Bill inched the train forward, picking up a little bit of speed. The noise of the wheels on track drew out zombies from what seemed like every possible nook and cranny. They emerged from alleyways, bushes, behind houses. Of course they weren't smart enough to stay away from the train, and bounced off of the moving vehicle like a rubber ball off of asphalt.

Kersey stepped out onto the outer railing so he could keep an eye on the terrain behind them. Hundreds of zombies flooded the tracks, and easily thrice that congregated in the neighborhood, heading their way.

"How much time do you need to stop this thing?" the Sergeant called inside the door.

"Speed I'm going?" Bill replied. "Maybe forty-five seconds?"

"Start slowing down, then," Kersey instructed. "We wait any longer and we might get overrun."

Bill hit the brakes, the train screeching its deceleration.

The Sergeant lifted his radio to his lips. "Forty seconds, Bretz," he declared. "And you boys get ready to hustle, because goddamn if we don't have a horde on our asses."

"Copy that," Bretz came back.

Kersey bit his lip as he stared at the horde behind them. There was about a hundred yards between the train and its pursuers, but it shortened as the vehicle slowed. He shook his head and raised the radio again.

"Fuck it, we gotta go *now*," he demanded. "Get out and start running. Mason, you start popping them, and Bill, lay on that horn as soon as we're clear." He slid down the ladder, and dropped onto the ground, stumbling from the moving vehicle.

"Gotcha, Sarge," Johnson grunted, grabbing his bicep and hauling him back to his feet.

Kersey's eyes widened at the sight of the veritable sea of zombies pursuing them from the horizon, and quickly folded into the soldiers' formation as they fled across the dusty terrain.

Bretz led the group, moving quicker than the slowing train. Mason hung out the door of the engine cab, the constant *pop pop pop* of his gun echoing before Bill set off the whistle. The wail was near deafening as he began to move it in reverse, drawing the attention of the horde.

The soldiers ran as hard as they could for a few hundred yards before finally slowing, gasping for breath and leaning on their knees.

"Way too early in the morning for that much cardio," Kowalski huffed. "Holy hell."

Bretz laughed, taking in their empty surroundings. "Not getting soft on me, are you?"

The Private rolled his eyes. "Well I do have five times the ammo y'all do," he said. "That shit adds up."

"Suck it up," the Corporal replied, clapping him on the back. "We still have a couple miles to the landfill."

Kowalski grunted and stretched his arms above his head. "A hike and a mound of garbage," he declared brightly. "Life is indeed good."

The soldiers headed at a significantly slower pace across the field, not a single building in sight from the neighborhood. The air was eerily silent, after the deafening moans of the horde, but the train had been a sufficient distraction for the group.

As they approached the landfill, Kersey motioned for everyone to take a knee beside the lone building at the entrance. There was a single metal bar, not even automated, but one that would have been lifted by whoever was manning it.

"Baker, Johnson, check out the inside," the Sergeant instructed. "See if there are any keys."

They rushed the door, quickly slipping in to sweep the small front room.

There were a few chairs and a messy desk with papers everywhere. Johnson kicked the only other door open, finding an empty back office.

"You check the desk, I'll check in here," he said, and the sound of drawers opening and closing echoed as he swept the small area. On the wall there was a metal box, and he twisted the handle, finding several sets of keys hanging inside. "Hey, I got 'em," he called, and when his companion sidled up next to him, he shrugged. "Which ones we taking?"

Baker shrugged back, and grabbed all of them. "Looks like we each get our own truck," he replied with a grin.

"Any luck?" Bretz asked as they emerged from the building.

Johnson held up three sets and jingled them. "Got six sets o' keys. Now we just need some trucks."

"I think I got some," Kowalski said from the roof, peering through his scope.

"What about resistance?" Kersey asked.

"Couple of shamblers, but nothing we can't handle," the sniper replied. "Apparently, this wasn't a popular destination to ride out the apocalypse."

Johnson snorted. "Hard to imagine why." He waved his hand back and forth in front of his nose. "With that stench? Yum."

"All right, let's move," Kersey said, and Kowalski jumped back down to the ground.

The group moved out at a deliberate pace, guns at the ready regardless of the quiet.

"Any idea how to tell what keys go to what truck?" Baker asked as he patted his pocket to make sure his three were secure.

Johnson shrugged. "Well, they got numbers on the keychains, so one can only hope."

They rounded a corner of garbage to find six old style dump trucks, each with an open top and an empty sticky back bucket. Each one had a bright yellow number on the side, and Johnson grinned, motioning to the closest one with a flourish.

"Johnson, Baker, find us two trucks and make sure they have plenty of fuel," Kersey said. "Bretz, you and Kowalski take care of our friends over there."

The sniper and his companion headed over to the duo of zombies staggering around the farthest truck. Though blood-soaked, they wore matching coveralls, with the city crest on the shoulder.

The soldiers pulled their knives to silently dispatch the creatures, and then turned as two of the trucks roared to life.

"Oh yeah, got a full tank of gas right here!" Johnson bellowed.

Baker gave a thumbs up from the driver's seat of his. "We're looking pretty good here too, Sarge!"

"Okay, we know the mission, so let's get it done," Kersey raised his hand to round up his men, and the four left split between the two trucks into teams of three.

CHAPTER EIGHT

Bill kept a slow pace, enough so that the zombies could keep up, and pulled the whistle again. "Hey, Mason," he called, "I think you can stop shooting. Our boys should be far enough away now that nobody else is going to break away."

"Yeah, you're probably right," the soldier replied and ducked back inside the cab, sliding the door shut. "So, how much further do we have until we get to the bridge?" he asked as he took a seat beside the engineer.

"Should only be about five minutes or so," Bill replied, and offered his companion a smirk. "Not too long. You in a hurry?"

Mason chuckled. "Nah, just thought we might be able to get a nice breeze going off the river."

"Might help with the smell, that's for sure," Bill agreed.

The Private sighed as he watched the thousand or so zombies ambling after them, arms outstretched and bloody mouths open. "So much wasted life out there," he mused. "Don't know whether to cry or be pissed."

"I say neither." The engineer shrugged. "Dwelling on it won't change it, and whoever is responsible for this is probably long dead."

Mason's eyes darkened. "At least they damn well better be."

"All you can do is keep moving forward, which is ironic given our current direction," Bill replied brightly.

The Private barked a laugh, and shook his head. "You're all right, Bill," he said, clapping his companion on the shoulder.

"Hey, you've only known me for a week," the engineer replied. "Might want to reserve judgement on that one." He winked.

The train rattled a little bit, signifying that they'd reached the bridge. As the cab backed into the bottleneck, and zombies jostled and fought for position to follow. Several of them toppled over the edge or were trampled, flailing bodies everywhere.

"Man, they really want us, don't they?" Mason asked.

Bill nodded. "Yeah, I wouldn't worry though, there's no way they're getting up here," he said. "Even if they could climb, it's a hard time squeezing in between the train and the bridge railing."

The vehicle screeched to a stop.

"So, what now?" Mason wondered.

Bill grinned and reached up, pulling the whistle again, another wail echoing through the area. "We keep drawing them

in, and hope our boys can get the job
done."

The soldier nodded and leaned back in
his seat, putting his feet up. The duo
relaxed and watched even more corpses
stagger over the horizon, dumbly excited
to try to eat a locomotive.

CHAPTER NINE

"That… does not look good," Baker said as they headed down the last stretch of road towards the airport.

Zombies staggered out from the side streets, ambling up onto the road towards the noise.

"No, it does not," Kowalski agreed, leaning forward to peer out the windshield of the large truck. "Hopefully the airport isn't anywhere near as crowded."

"Even if it isn't," Baker replied, "how much time are we going to have to get this thing moved?"

Kersey raised his binoculars. "Drive to the end of the next street and stop," he instructed.

"What?" Baker blurted. "Those things are going to be on us in a matter of minutes if we do that."

The Sergeant motioned ahead. "There's a dozen of them around the fire truck."

"Shit," the Private muttered.

"Exactly," Kersey replied. "Kowalski, I need you to pick some off from here so we can silently kill them when we move up. We start shooting at the fire truck we're going to attract anything that might be at the airport. At least here, it might be out of earshot."

Kowalski nodded. "Let me slide by you, Sarge," he said, and ducked under his companion to switch seats. Just after Baker slammed on the brakes, he threw open the door and clambered up on top of the cab.

He lowered himself to one knee, and raised his rifle, steadying his breath to line up his first shot. The bullet ripped through his target's soft head, dropping the rest of the corpse to the ground.

The crack of the gun echoed loudly, and the rest of the zombies hanging out around the fire truck turned and headed slowly towards the dump. Kowalski kept himself steady and fired again and again, taking out each creature one by one.

As he paused to reload, Baker unrolled the driver's side window. "Kowalski, we gotta get rolling, man," he urged, motioning behind them.

Kowalski glanced quickly, noting the large horde heading up behind them, looking to be in the hundred strong.

"Twenty more seconds," he said, and fired more rapidly, barely taking the time to aim. His shots were true, however, taking down as many as he could before diving back into the cab and slamming the door shut. "Got 'em down to three, Sarge."

"Good job," Kersey replied, "let's go!"

Baker hit the gas, screaming towards the fire truck and putting at least fifty yards between them and the approaching horde.

"Stop here," the Sergeant instructed as they approached the trio of zombies still staggering up the tracks. "When we're out, start getting into position to move that fire truck."

"I'm on it," Baker confirmed, and slammed on the brakes. The passengers leapt out and drew their machetes, jogging out of the way so the dump could scream by them.

"Go left, I got the right," Kersey said, and Kowalski nodded as the two branched out. The Private slashed and took the first zombie's head off with a clean swing, whereas the Sergeant stabbed directly into the forehead of his corpse.

As both fell, Kersey motioned to the remaining zombie. "Would you like the honors?"

"Oh please, Sarge, be my guest," Kowalski replied with a flourish.

The Sergeant jogged up and swung hard, catching the creature in the temple. It gave an almost surprised-sounding gurgle before it slumped to the ground.

"Do a sweep around the fire truck and make sure we don't have any surprises,"

Kersey instructed. "Then I want you keeping an eye on that horde."

Kowalski nodded. "Yes, sir," he replied, and rushed around the overturned truck. He was thankful that there were no more zombies hanging around, and unslung his rifle again to take stock of the airport.

The wreckage from the plane was a couple hundred yards away, charred debris dotting the landscape. Black corpse-shaped blobs were strewn everywhere, but none were moving. The hangars looked zombie-free, as well.

"Hey, Sarge, we're good," he called over his shoulder. "Doesn't look like anything is going on at the airport, either."

Kersey nodded. "Good, keep an eye on the horde. If they get within a hundred yards, you shout."

The Private saluted him and jogged over to the road, taking a knee and looking through his scope to size up the situation. There was an overturned car on the side of the road that he estimated as his hundred yard marker.

In the meantime, Kersey waved Baker in, inching him up to the bumper of the fire truck. He stopped him when the dump barely kissed the vehicle.

"Okay, you're looking good," he said, taking a few steps back. "When you hit the gas, floor it. Keep an eye on me and I'll let you know if you need to lay off."

Baker nodded and dropped gear, then punched the gas as hard as he could. The tires caught on the dirt and slammed into the overturned truck, whining and straining with every last ounce of horsepower.

"Hell yeah, keep it moving!" Kersey cried, waving to the Private to keep going as the fire truck began to slide off of the tracks. As the cab crossed over the first rail, however, it came to an abrupt stop, and he put his palms out, darting forward.

"What the fuck happened?" Baker cried as he let off the gas.

The Sergeant shook his head. "I don't know, hang tight," he replied, and laid down on the tracks to get a better view. He noticed on the side of the cab that was facing downwards, a hunk of one of the metal braces had broken free and wedged into the rail. "Something metal is caught on the tracks," he called, and got up onto one knee.

Baker muttered a curse under his breath and sighed. "Ideas?"

Kersey thought for a moment, and then studied the lever on the side of the dump truck that allowed the back to rise and empty its contents. "I've got an idea, but we're going to need some chain," he said.

"Sorry Sarge, but I'm fresh out," Baker replied.

"Maybe in one of the hangars?" the Sergeant asked.

"Sarge!" Kowalski shouted from the road. "Whatever you're going to do, it's gotta be in the next two minutes, cause these boys are getting close."

Kersey scrubbed his hands down his face. "Fuck." He glanced back at the horde and skirted around to the passenger's seat. "Kowalski, on me," he demanded, and the Private followed him up into the cab.

"Thanks for taking bitch seat, Sarge," the Private quipped.

Kersey shook his head. "Don't thank me yet, you haven't heard my plan."

"Fucking hell," Kowalski muttered.

"Where am I going, Sarge?" Baker asked.

"Go up a couple more blocks," Kersey instructed, motioning away from the horde. "Turn towards the interstate, then head back to the east. There was a two-story hotel by a roundabout a few blocks back."

Baker shifted into reverse. "Here's hoping they have a mini-bar." He glanced in the rearview. "Should I be getting them to follow us?"

"Nope, that's Kowalski's job," Kersey replied.

"Sarge, I know I got a lot more ammo, but…" the Private in question trailed off.

"Don't worry, you'll be on the roof," the Sergeant explained. "And you get to spend the rest of the day picking off as many as you want. Not to mention you'll have the unit record for most kills in a day."

Kowalski brightened. "Really now? Okay, I'm in."

Baker rumbled up the mostly empty street, and sped towards the hotel parking lot. There was a burned-out car upside down in front of the main entrance, and most of the windows on the ground floor of the scuzzy building were broken.

"Christ, Sarge, you couldn't have found me some better digs?" Kowalski quipped. "This looks like the kind of place that charges by the hour and comes with a dead hooker in every room."

Kersey wrinkled his nose as he imagined a zombie hooker flopping about on a hotel bed. "Good thing you don't have to go inside, huh?"

Kowalski barked a laugh and grabbed his ammo bag. He hung out the door and climbed up the side of the truck, making an easy leap over onto the second floor railing. He leaned over as Kersey grabbed the door handle.

"You boys don't forget to pick me up, now," he called.

Baker offered a grin. "Don't worry sunshine," he yelled back, "wouldn't dream of missing out on weeks upon weeks of you bragging about the most kills in a day!"

"As soon as you're in position, start shooting," Kersey said as he shut the door, leaning out the window. "Don't stop until we come back. And stay tuned to channel eight on your radio. I'll let you know when we're headed your way."

Kowalski saluted. "Good luck, Sarge." He watched as the dump rumbled away, back in the same direction it had come. He turned his attention back to the main road, and the flood of zombies flowing into the streets and parking lots nearby.

He ran to the end of the exterior hallway to the maintenance room, and kicked open the door. There was a ladder there that led up to the roof, and he burst inside, securing the door behind him.

The roof was slightly slanted, but easy enough to navigate the metallic shingles. Kowalski took position at the top center, straddling the gentle peak and settling onto the rounded center. He wedged his ammo bag in front of him and unslung his rifle.

"Okay, who wants to go first?" he asked, and scanned the crowd. He focused on what looked like a bodybuilder, missing large chunks of muscled bicep. "Sorry bud, but you remind me of my high school bully. Here's a little payback."

Kowalski pulled the trigger, and the zombie's head exploded in an array of crimson, splattering the corpses shambling around it.

"And, there's one," the Private said brightly. He took aim again, this time firing on a short blonde valley-girl with milky dead eyes. "Yeah, take that, Karen!" he cried.

He lowered his rifle and raised his eyes to the clouds, taking a moment of self reflection. "Yeah, I may have some lingering issues from my formative years," he said to himself, and then chuckled.

Kowalski raised the rifle and fired again and again, the cracks drawing even more moans to the hotel. "All right Sarge," he said with a grin, "I got 'em occupied. Do your thing."

CHAPTER TEN

Johnson studied the map of the south side of town, but was drawn out of his reverie at the *thunkthunk* of zombie flesh hitting the grill of the truck.

"Goddamn, Bretz, could you hold off on ramming these sons of bitches?" he demanded. "Making it difficult to hold my train of thought."

"I mean, I could always lay on the horn," the Corporal replied, "but I don't think they're going to get out of the way."

Johnson sighed and pointed out the windshield. "When you get up to the next intersection, slow down so I can see where we are," he said.

Zombies poured out of every opening, attracted to the rumbling of the dump. Bretz pulled up in front of the charred remains of a building, and the sound of hands smacking against the sides of the truck intensified as they stopped.

Johnson looked at the street sign and then back to the map, lips pursed tightly.

"You know, it's okay to admit when you're lost," Bretz teased.

The Private growled. "I know where we are!" he snapped, and after another moment finally tapped on the paper. "There, found us!" He grinned, leaning back in his seat, satisfied.

"Uh," the Corporal began, raising an eyebrow, "are you going to share with me, or do I have to guess?"

Johnson shook his head as if to clear it. "Oh, sorry. It's two more blocks up, then turn left. We should see the church after that."

"I think I can manage that," Bretz replied, and put the truck back into gear. He easily steamrolled over the hundreds of zombies surrounding them, parting the horde as they headed for the turn.

The side street only had a handful of corpses milling about, but the church in the distance was surrounded by a horde of easily a hundred strong.

"That's gotta be it," Johnson pointed.

Bretz pulled up to the side of the church, and as they approached, a pale arm hung a white flag out of one of the windows.

"Looks like they've been expecting us," the Corporal said. He pulled closer and rolled down his own window, leaning out as if he were in the drive-thru.

A man in classic black pastor's clothes surveyed the soldiers. "Well, it's not an Ark, but I think given our current situation that might be for the best."

"Especially when you consider ole Johnson here gets seasick," Bretz replied.

His passenger scoffed. "It was *one* time!"

"Well I appreciate you boys coming," the pastor replied, putting a hand over his chest. "I'm Pastor Dave."

"Good you meet you," Bretz replied. "I'm Corporal Bretz, and this here is Private Johnson."

Dave nodded to each of them. "Pleasure to meet you," he said. "Seth gave me a heads up that you boys were coming, so I got everyone moved into the rec center around back. It's got a flat roof, so I figured that would be easier than having people jump out of windows."

"Sounds good," the Corporal replied. "We'll meet you around back."

He pulled away as Dave closed the window, and the truck rumbled around to the back, drowning out the excited moans.

"Man these critters are hungry," Johnson said as they pulled up as close as they could to the side of the one-story building.

Bretz slithered up into the driver's door window. "Come on, let's get up there and help out," he said.

They pulled themselves up onto the top of the truck, and a tall man in jeans

and a polo shirt rushed over to the edge
to give them a hand over.

"Be careful now," he said. "That
isn't a fall that you're gonna be coming
back from."

"Appreciate the hand there," Bretz
replied as he jumped the gap.

The man smiled and helped Johnson
across as well. "I'm George, the youth
pastor here."

"Thank you," the Corporal said, and
introduced himself.

Johnson did so as well, shaking the
youth pastor's hand. "So, what's the deal,
here? Where's everybody at?"

George pointed at a hole in the far
end of the roof, where a balding man
reached down to pull a young woman up.

"They're still in the rec center," he
explained. "We have some elderly people in
the group, so we thought it best to wait
for you to get here before bringing them
outside."

Bretz scratched the back of his head.
"Don't suppose you have some ladders we
can use, do you?"

"Yes sir, we do," George said with a
grin. "We'll bring one up right now so we
can start getting people loaded in."

The Corporal nodded. "How many people
are we looking at?"

"Thirty-seven, including myself, sir," the tall man replied.

"Okay, give me half a dozen able bodied men to get down into the truck first," Bretz instructed. "We're going to have a couple on the edge and the rest in the bed to help the less abled."

"Sounds good," George agreed. "You wait here and I'll get them rounded up and over to you."

Johnson sighed as he stared down at the sea of hungry corpses below. "Loading elderly people into a trash truck as an army of dead things bang on the side of it."

Bretz couldn't help but chuckle. "Yeah, they left this one out of the recruitment brochure, didn't they?"

Several minutes later, they had four burly young men inside the back of the truck, with two more standing at the top of the ladder.

"Okay, let's start loading in some of the elderly," Bretz said, he and Johnson stationed at the edge of the roof.

George approached with a woman who looked to be in her mid seventies. "Come on, Miss Mary, let's get you down there," he said gently. The soldiers helped her over to the men on top, and the ones in the bucket braced her as she climbed down.

"Christ, we're gonna be here for days," Johnson muttered under his breath.

Bretz shrugged. "At least we're up here, nice and safe," he said. "We could be dealing with that fire truck."

"*Or* we could be like Mason with our feet propped up on the train listening to Bill tell stories," the Private shot back. "I mean, how does he keep getting that gig anyway?"

"You should take it as a compliment." Bretz grinned. "Just shows that Sarge has a ton of faith in you."

Johnson barked a laugh. "Well, remind me to fuck something up next time I'm around him."

All of a sudden there was a metallic screech.

"What in the fuck?" Johnson breathed, and the soldiers turned to see the back of the dump truck opening up, the front end rising. The people already inside scrambled to hold on to whatever they could, screaming.

"Oh my god, what's happening?" George cried.

Johnson let out a growl of frustration as she spotted the zombies hanging off of the release lever for the bucket. He pulled his rifle from his back and released the mag, making sure the chamber was empty.

"What are you doing?" Bretz snapped.

"One of them fuckers hit the lever, and we gotta hit it back," Johnson replied. "You two are gonna lower me down as low as you can so I can hit it with my rifle."

The Corporal glanced at the fearful faces in the bucket as it raised even higher on its ascent.

"Fuck, let's do it," Bretz said, and motioned to George. "Get his leg."

Johnson laid down on his stomach and they each took a leg, lowering him down over the side of the roof. "Bretz, if you drop me, I swear to christ I'm going to haunt your ass."

"I might not if you weren't such a fatass," Bretz grunted.

In the back, the men were able to grip the sides of the truck, but one struggled to hold himself and keep hold of the elderly lady in his grasp.

"It's okay," Miss Mary whispered.

He shook his head, his hand loosening on the side of the bucket. "I'm so sorry."

She wiggled out of his grip and slid down the bed towards the throng of hungry creatures. He watched in vain, able to solidify his grip now that he had the use of two hands. One of the young men closest to the bottom caught her to stop her descent, but her momentum caused him to lose his grip and they both went tumbling into the horde.

Miss Mary went headfirst into the asphalt, the zombies descending upon her immediately to snuff out her screams.

The young man cried out in disappointment and fear as he kicked off of the shoulders of a corpse to try to scramble back into the rising bucket. He almost managed to get a fresh grip on the metal but shrieked in pain as teeth tore into his calf.

His screams and pleas for help spurred Johnson on, the soldier desperately stabbing at the lever with his rifle. A zombie grasped hold of the butt of it, and they began a vertical tug-of-war.

"Let go, motherfucker!" Johnson yelled, and pulled out his handgun with his free hand, firing into the zombie's face. The creature's grip went slack, and Johnson stabbed once more, finally catching the lever.

The gears shifted pace and the door began to close, the bucket returning back to its prone position. A few men joined George and Bretz in hauling the soldier back up onto the roof, and he flopped over onto his back in a sweaty heap.

"Holy shit, that sucked," he huffed.

Bretz clapped him on the shoulder. "Could be worse, you could have been on my end. You're going on a fucking diet, that's an order."

Johnson gave him a playful salute while he caught his breath.

Screams arose inside of the truck, and the Corporal joined George at the edge of the roof to watch in helpless horror as the door came down on the young man whose legs were being feasted on below.

The life drained from his eyes as the door severed his thighs, and Bretz took aim. "Everybody stay back and cover your ears," he said, and the other civilians in the truck complied, turning their faces away as well. He fired once, putting a bullet into the back of the young man's head.

"Why did you do that?" George cried, grabbing his arm.

Bretz shook him off. "If I didn't, then he would have become one of them. And we've lost enough lives today."

Johnson got to his feet. "We're going to have to keep a watch, make sure they don't hit the lever again."

"Won't be an issue," Bretz replied, and took aim again, firing a single shot that severed the lever directly from the truck with a metallic *cling*. "That should do the trick. Even so, keep an eye on it."

Johnson nodded and reloaded his gun, slinging it back over his shoulder. "If it means I don't have to be dangled over them like a fish at one of them Sea World shows, I'm all about it."

Bretz pulled out his walkie talkie and moved out of the way as they began to move people across into the truck again.

"Mason, come in," the Corporal said.

There was a quick crackle and a click. "Mason here."

"You boys getting along okay?" Bretz asked.

"Yessir, just watching zombies tumble down the embankment into the river," came the reply.

The Corporal rolled his eyes. "Sounds like you're working hard."

"Always, sir," Mason replied easily.

"Mission update," Bretz continued, "we're at the church getting people loaded into the truck. At the pace we're going, we should be headed your way within the hour."

"We'll be waiting and ready for you, sir," the Private said.

Bretz straightened. "Have you heard from Sarge?"

"Yes sir, they had some complications on their first run, but they're gearing up for another go at it," came the reply.

The Corporal sighed and nodded. "Okay, I'll contact you when we're loaded up. If we need to delay transport so we're on their timeline, let me know."

There was a moment of static before another click and Mason declared, "Yes sir. We'll see you soon."

CHAPTER ELEVEN

Baker sped across the tarmac.

"That hangar looks like our best bet," Kersey said, pointing to one with an open door and a half-dismantled plane inside.

Baker eased to the right, scoping out their target as he drove. "Yep, looks like maintenance." He slowed a little to avoid a hunk of metal from the crashed airplane. "Not saying I'd wish that fate on anybody... but given the way this town ended up, they probably got off easy." He inclined his head to the charred corpses everywhere, some still strapped into their seats.

"That may be true," Kersey said thoughtfully, "but I'd much prefer to go down fighting. I like the thought of taking some of those things out with me if I have to go."

Baker snorted. "I'll remember that the next time we're in a dead end situation." He slowed to a crawl and stopped about fifteen feet from the hangar door and killed the engine.

"Okay, no shots unless *absolutely* necessary," the Sergeant said as he drew his machete. "Let's find some chain, secure it to the back, and get out."

His companion nodded. "Lead the way."

As they walked to the open door, they heard the crack of gunfire in the distance.

"Sounds like Kowalski is still having a good time," Kersey said, shaking his head.

Baker grinned. "He really wants those bragging rights, doesn't he?"

"Just doing what I can to keep him motivated," the Sergeant admitted, and they entered the hangar. They scanned the large space and didn't see anything moving in their immediate area, but there were several shadows and dark corners.

Kersey reached over and smacked the handle of the machete against a metal table, sending a loud *clang* through echoing through the space. There were no answering moans, but there was definitely sounds of movement coming from one of the offices to the left.

"You get the chain, I'll check it out," he said, and after Baker's nod, headed over to the office. It had a giant bay window as one wall, and he cringes at the sight inside. There was an overturned desk along the far wall, pinning a pissed-off looking zombie behind it from the waist down.

Next to the desk sat a corpse in coveralls, a large chunk of his face missing, a double-barreled shotgun sitting in his lap. Kersey shook his head, not envying the series of events that had likely led to the moment this man decided to take his life. He noticed a large box of shells next to the limp man, and drew his bottom lip between his teeth in deliberation.

"Couldn't hurt to have a little more firepower," he muttered, and slipped into the office, careful to stay out of reach of the pinned zombie. He grabbed the shotgun and the shells, securing them to his belt, and then vacated the area quickly.

"Found some chain?" he asked as he approached Baker.

The Private stood over a workbench with a whole mess of industrial tools scattered across it. "Yeah, there's a whole mess of it over there."

"Well grab it and let's get going," the Sergeant urged.

Baker crossed his arms and turned to his superior. "I was thinking, Sarge," he began, "I don't know if it's going to be enough to just hook the chain up to the center of the truck back. Too much of a risk it's going to snap under the weight."

"You got a better idea?" Kersey raised an eyebrow.

Baker wrapped his hand around a giant drill and held it up, the thick bit

glimmering as he tilted it. "Give me
twenty minutes and let me drill a few more
holes through the hull," he suggested.
"Then we can hook up several chains and
distribute the weight evenly."

"I like it," the Sergeant agreed with
a nod, and held up the shotgun he'd found.
"And while you do that, I'm going to make
this a little more dangerous."

As Baker headed off with the drill,
Kersey moved over to a large metal saw. It
was battery-powered, and he fired it up,
laying the shotgun barrel down to line up
his cut. The saw went through it like
butter, and he held up his brand-new
sawed-off shotgun, blowing gently on the
cut tip.

A half an hour later, the soldiers
ran the last of the chain through the
holes on either side of the center hitch.
Baker attached large hooks to the ends
that they could use to affix the fire
truck.

"Well, what do you think?" Kersey
asked as he took a step back from their
handiwork.

Baker grinned as he piled the excess
chain into the back. "I think that's as
good as it's going to get."

"All right, let's do it," the
Sergeant said, and they clambered back
into the cab. As they approached the fire

truck, they rumbled through a pothole, sending the chains clanking against the metal frame.

A dozen or so zombies staggered out of a nearby broken-down store, and Baker shook his head. "Shit, that woke some of 'em up."

"How much time do you need to hook up the chains?" Kersey asked.

"Five minutes, max," the Private replied.

The Sergeant checked his assault rifle, and put his hand on the door handle to get ready to jump out. "You get that truck moved. I'll handle them," he said.

Baker nodded as he hit the brakes. "Yes, sir."

Kersey threw open the door and jogged to the center of the street, heading away from the trucks and the other direction of the pack of corpses. He waited until he was at least twenty yards away from Baker before taking aim and firing.

"I'm over here, boys! Come and get me!" he yelled as he dropped two zombies in quick succession.

He continued to walk backwards, drawing the group of rotted flesh away from the trucks, brow furrowing as more zombies came out of the woodwork and staggered up onto the road between him and Baker.

"Well, this isn't good," he muttered, and jogged down into the ditch into a vacant parking lot in the direction of the airport. He turned around again and continued to fire, dropping more corpses to get trampled by the growing horde in pursuit of him.

His rifle gave a dull *click* as the zombies matched his pace, about ten yards away from him, and he pulled out his new shotgun, firing a spray of metal pellets. The blast sent bits of gooey flesh and bone flying, tripping up a few of the horde.

The metallic grinding of metal on metal echoed in the distance, and he glanced over at the trucks to see the back of the dump lifting up.

"Fucking hell," he cursed as he noticed some stragglers heading in that direction. "Baker, you'd better be back in that truck." He broke into a sprint, angling himself so he could skirt around the pursuing corpses. He managed to get a bit of distance before reloading his rifle and firing at the zombies heading for the trucks.

He paused to line up a shot on one of them, but its head exploded before he could fire. Baker gave him a thumbs up from the front of the dump before clambering up into the driver's seat.

Kersey took off in the direction of the airport, hitting the runway and pounding pavement towards the wreckage, moving parallel along the train tracks. The piercing screech of metal on metal as Baker floored it in reverse, and caused a good chunk of the horde to switch gears, but with the Private safely in the truck Kersey focused on his own safety.

He continued to fire and run, fire and run, and then checked back on the trucks through his scope. "What the fuck are you doing?" he murmured when he realized that Baker was pulling the fire truck this time. The screeching was near deafening, even from so far away, but then he realized it was actually working.

Except the noise had drawn the entire horde.

CHAPTER TWELVE

"Oh no you don't!" Kersey roared, and fired with the shotgun some more, but the metallic squeals drowned him out. He once again sprinted around the horde, back up the tracks towards the trucks, hoping to beat them there.

He threw his rifle over his shoulder and pumped his arms as well as his legs, heart leaping as the fire truck cleared the tracks. Baker jumped out and hit the lever to lower the door, and then looked up at his Sergeant with easily a hundred zombies in close pursuit.

"Get the chains!" Kersey screamed.

Baker got to work unhooking the fire truck, and the Sergeant reached him, huffing as he struggled to undo a chain that had gotten crushed by the twisting metal frame.

"That worked better than expected," the Private said brightly, unhooking three of the five chains.

Kersey shook his head. "Let's avoid getting eaten before you make that proclamation," he said, still struggling to get it free.

Baker grasped the other one on his side, finding the same problem that the chain was completely stuck in the busted fire truck. He looked up at the approaching horde, only about fifteen yards away.

"We're not going to make it, Sarge," he warned, eyes widening.

Kersey looked over his shoulder and grunted, kicking the fire truck in frustration. "Fuck!" He shook his head and ducked under the chain to get to Baker's side. "Head towards the hotel, now!"

They took off down the road a bit before turning north onto a side street, skidding around the corner at the sight of more corpses in the middle of the road. Two zombies staggered out of the open door of a house to the right tumbling ass over tea kettle as they tried to navigate the stairs, and Kersey shoved Baker in that direction.

They swept past the tangled creatures and thundered up the front steps, hurtling inside and slamming the door behind them. The soldiers dropped to the floor and pressed their backs up against the wall, staying out of sight and silent as possible.

The moans and groans outside seemed to be moving past them as opposed to circling the house, but there was a shuffling echo from the living room. Kersey looked over at his companion, putting a finger to his lips. Baker nodded and the Sergeant drew his machete, heading silently down the hall.

He jumped into the room, prepared to strike high, but the zombie was short, and dove for his midsection. He thrust down into the top of her head, leaping back, her face bouncing harmlessly off of his torso that she'd wanted to devour just a millisecond before.

He tore the machete from the teenaged corpse's head, and let out a deep sigh of relief over having narrowly escaped death, once again.

Baker entered the room, shoulders a little more relaxed. "The bulk of the horde's past the house, now," he said. "You okay, Sarge?"

"Heart's going like it's keeping the beat at a rave, but other than that, I'm good," Kersey replied.

Baker nodded. "I think if we give it five minutes or so we should be able to sneak out and get back to the truck."

The Sergeant shook his head. "I don't think that's going to work," he said, crossing his arms. "I don't know what you did, but that hook on the chain I was working on is completely embedded into the frame. It's going to take a fuckin' torch to get that off."

"So how are we getting Kowalski?" the Private demanded.

"Maybe Bretz and Johnson can get him before heading to the train?" Kersey asked as he pulled out his walkie-talkie. "Mason, come in."

The response was near immediate. "Mason here, Sarge."

"What's the status on Johnson and Bretz?" Kersey asked.

"We're fine Sarge, thanks for asking," Bretz replied. "All done."

Kersey sighed. "Fuck."

"I'm going to assume that wasn't in regards to our safety?" the Corporal joked.

"Sorry," the Sergeant replied, "we have a bit of a situation here and could have used your truck."

Bretz came back, "Sarge, if you need us to, we can go get another one."

Baker waved the Sergeant over to the window.

"Hang on, I think Baker has an idea," Kersey said, and lowered the radio to go have a look. "What have you got?"

"There's a Humvee at the house across the street," the Private said. "Should be good enough to get us through the crowd." He motioned through the curtains at the bright yellow Humvee proudly displayed in the driveway across the way.

"You think you can hot wire it?" Kersey asked.

Baker grinned. "Might kill the resale value, but yeah, I can do it."

"Bretz," the Sergeant said into the radio, "getting another truck isn't going to be necessary."

The Corporal let out a sigh of relief. "Good to hear that, because we really don't want to run from these fuckers any more than we already have today."

"You and me both, brother," Kersey replied. "Mason, can you put Bill on?"

There was a pause before the engineer said, "What can I do for you, Sergeant?"

"How long do you think it would take you to get to the airport?" Kersey asked.

"We can be there in fifteen minutes."

"Okay, you boys get ready to move and wait for our signal," the Sergeant instructed. "We might not have much of a window to hop a ride."

"Ten four, I'll be ready," Bill replied.

Kersey turned the dial to channel eight, and raised the radio once again. "Kowalski, you still having fun?"

Yet another gunshot echoed in the distance, and then there was a *click*. "Absolutely, Sarge!" the Private replied. "I've taken out a few hundred of these boys! This record is going to stand until the end of the war!"

"I'm glad you're excited," Kersey said, smiling. "I'll need you to change gears a bit, though."

"You on your way to come get me?"

"Yeah, but there's been a change in plan," the Sergeant said, taking a deep breath. "We're going to need you to find a way down off the roof so we can pick you up at ground level."

There was a long pause. There were a few clicks, as if he were starting to speak and then thought better of it. "I'm sorry Sarge," Kowalski finally said, "can you repeat that? My radio had the bullshit filter turned on."

"No. You heard me correctly," Kersey declared.

"Are you fucking kidding me?" the Private cried. "I've spent the last hour attracting every zombie in the city to me, and currently have half the goddamn population of this shitberg surrounding me. And you want me to get down to the *ground*? What the fuck happened to the dump truck?!"

Kersey gave him a moment to calm down, and then replied, "It's permanently fused to the fire truck."

"Just…" Kowalski stammered, anger clear in his tone, "fine… goddammit. Give me a minute."

"I don't think he's happy," Baker quipped.

Kersey shook his head. "Yeah, wherever we stop next we'll have to raid a trophy shop and make him an award for his daily kill record."

"I'll add it to the shopping list." The Private laughed.

"Sarge, I just checked the way I came up, and the room is filled with zombies," Kowalski came back. "Even if I could get by them, the entire upper floor is clogged with those things. So unless you want me to go full frat boy and jump into the pool, I don't know how I'm pulling this off."

The soldiers shared a sly glance.

Kersey raised the radio to his mouth. "A pool, you say? Where's it located?"

"Sarge, we need to work on your sarcasm detection," Kowalski snapped.

"Well, if you didn't want to do it, then you shouldn't have suggested it," the Sergeant shot back. "Didn't you learn anything from the Istanbul mission? Now where's the pool?"

"Goddammit," Kowalski growled in defeat. "It's in the back of the hotel."

Kersey cocked his head. "Are there many zombies around it?"

"A couple dozen, but it's gated so I'll have a safe landing zone."

"Okay, you get read to move," the Sergeant instructed. "Baker and I have to jack a ride, and then we'll be over."

Kowalski sighed audibly. "Fine. I'm shooting a couple more zombies just on principle before you get here."

CHAPTER THIRTEEN

"How are we looking?" Kersey asked as he joined Baker at the front door.

The Private peered through the curtain. "Still about half a dozen, but nothing we can't handle."

"How long to hot wire it?" the Sergeant asked.

Baker shrugged. "Two, three minutes max."

"Okay," Kersey said with a nod, "you make a beeline to the vehicle. I'm on zombie duty." He pulled out his machete, gripping it tightly. "Gonna be as quiet as I can be."

They took up positions on either side of the door, and shared a look before the Sergeant threw the door open.

Baker sprinted across the street, drawing the attention of the six shambling zombies, and they turned to follow him, moaning with excitement. Kersey leapt quietly down the steps, coming up behind them, executing a surprise attack. He brought the weapon down hard on the back of the first one's head, caving in the skull. He immediately spun and thrust, catching the next one in the side of the face with the blade, and as they both crumpled to the ground, Baker reached the Humvee.

Kersey slashed at a third zombie, but the echoes of more moaning rode to him on the breeze, and he turned to see a good portion of their old pursuers heading back towards them up the street.

"So much for stealth," he muttered, and pulled out his handgun. He rapidly dropped the last three zombies still heading for Baker, who popped his head out of the vehicle in surprise. "I got it under control!" the Sergeant yelled. "Keep working!"

Baker ducked back into the vehicle as Kersey brandished his assault rifle, firing into the oncoming fleet. He dropped as many as he could in the front, sending them stumbling over their fallen brethren as he reloaded.

"How we looking?" he yelled.

Baker stuck his hand out the door, keeping his head under the dash. "Thirty seconds!" he shouted back.

Kersey ran up next to the passenger door, firing again to try to trip up more of the staggering dead. The gap rapidly closed, and when the horde was about twenty yards away, the vehicle roared to life.

"Got it, let's go!" Baker cried and jumped up into the driver's seat.

Kersey dove inside, and the Private reversed and then floored it, sending corpses flying in every direction as he barreled up the street.

"Man, I miss this kind of power behind the wheel," Baker groaned as the vehicle mowed through the zombies like they weren't even there.

Kersey chuckled. "Thank god for overcompensating civilians," he replied, and raised the radio to his lips. "Mason, tell Bill to hit it."

"Copy that," Mason replied.

Kersey switched back to channel eight. "Kowalski, we're on the way. Be there in sixty seconds. You ready?"

Click. "No."

"That's the spirit," the Sergeant replied brightly. "We'll cover you."

"Damn well better," the Private muttered back.

Baker drive around the corner and onto the main road leading to the hotel. There were easily a thousand zombies stretched along the street, swarming the parking lot and the building proper.

"He wasn't kidding about his kill record, was he?" Baker asked breathlessly at the sight of unmoving bodies piled up in big stacks amongst the still walking ones.

Kersey shook his head. "I've known him for years, and he takes those very seriously. Got super pissed when Johnson took his record in Iraq." He looked up towards the roof and spotted the Private running across it. "I see him, he's on the move."

Baker floored it, skidding around the corner and slamming zombies out of the way as they circled the building. There were a few dozen creatures hanging out around the pool gate, and he skidded to a stop as close to the latch as possible.

Kowalski came flying down from the roof, splashing into the deep end, and Kersey popped up out of the sun roof, opening fire on the zombies clustered near the door. As they fell, Kowalski hauled himself out of the water, limping a little as he made his way to the gate.

"I got you, just head towards us!" Kersey yelled, and continued firing, picking off any corpse that even looked in the direction of the path the Private needed to take.

Kowalski unlatched the gate and hobbled to the Humvee, throwing open the back door to fall inside in a dripping heap. "I'm in! Go go go!"

Kersey slid back into his seat just as Baker hit the gas, the force of them peeling out closing the back door behind their refugee.

"Holy shit, that was epic," Baker blurted as he hit the main road, glancing at his companion sprawled out across the backseat. "You okay?"

"Fucking banged up my leg on the bottom of the pool," Kowalski groaned. "Goddamn safety regulations keeping everything shallow. Let a few kids drown, I needed the deep end!"

"Well, if it's any consolation, that was without a doubt a nine-point-eight on the dive," Kersey piped up.

"Nine-point-eight?" the Private cried. "What in the hell do I have to do to get a ten?"

"Probably not come up injured?" Baker asked.

Kowalski let out an exasperated laugh, just happy to be alive. "Yeah, I'll buy that."

CHAPTER FOURTEEN

"How bad's your ankle?" Kersey asked and he and Kowalski stood next to the train tracks. They'd driven a good mile from the airport, leaving the horde far behind. The train slowly made its way towards them, a veritable army of creatures behind it.

"Eh, just sprained it pretty good," Kowalski replied. "Nothing a day or two off of it won't cure."

The Sergeant nodded. "Lucky for you, we have some downtime in our future. No way in hell we're tackling Spokane without some major backup."

"Did the General tell you how many troops he's sending us?" Kowalski asked.

Kersey scratched the back of his head. "Yeah, he did, but you've had a rough enough day already. I don't want to depress you with specifics."

"Oh, great, so nowhere near enough to get the job done safely," the Private moaned.

The Sergeant stretched his arms above his head. "Don't you just love being bright enough to read between the lines?"

"Oh, yeah, it's a joy all right," Kowalski replied.

"So, how high did you get your kill streak?" Kersey asked.

"Day's not over yet." The Private smirked. "But at the moment, I topped out at two hundred and eighty-three."

His superior's eyes widened. "Damn man, that's gonna be a tough number to beat going forward."

"Thanks, Sarge." Kowalski puffed out his chest with pride. "Feels good to be back on top again."

Kersey chuckled. "Johnson leaving Iraq with the title eats you up, doesn't it?"

"Man, I still call bullshit on that." The Private scowled. "Calling in an airstrike shouldn't count."

The Sergeant cocked his head. "Well, if you want to play it that way, then the remote drone pilot should get credit, right?"

"Well, all I care about is the record is now *mine*," Kowalski replied, clenching a victorious fist.

Kersey's walkie-talkie crackled to life.

"Hey, Sarge, you there?" Bretz asked.

Kersey raised the mouthpiece to his lips. "Yep, I'm here, what's up?"

"Got us a bit of a following here, and Bill doesn't think it's a good idea for us to stop," the Corporal replied. "I mean, unless you want to fight off a couple thousand of those things."

The Sergeant pursed his lips. "Not really at the top of my list of things to do today."

"I didn't think so," Bretz replied. "So how do you boys feel about hopping a moving train?"

Kersey took a deep breath. "How fast are we talking?"

"Not very, just enough to keep pace ahead of the zombies," Bretz said.

The Sergeant looked over at his limping companion. "Think you can make it?"

"I've run through worse," Kowalski replied. "But I *am* going to complain about it."

Kersey barked a laugh. "I don't doubt it." He raised the walkie-talkie to his mouth. "Yeah, Bretz, we'll be good to go."

"All right, we'll be on your position in about a minute," the Corporal confirmed.

Kersey turned to the Humvee. "Baker, time to go."

The Private emerged from the vehicle, arming the switch on the C4 he'd rigged up inside. He jogged over to the duo, holding the detonator above his head.

"You read to blow up that behemoth?" Kowalski asked.

Baker grinned. "There's enough C4 in there to get it into orbit."

"Think it's going to actually attract those things?" the sniper wondered.

"Well, since we have quite the following already, I was going to wait until we're up the line a bit before triggering it," Baker explained. "Maybe get lucky and get a second wave following us."

Kersey nodded. "Not a bad idea."

The train closed in, moving at only a few miles an hour. A sea of zombies lumbered behind with only a few feet of space between.

"All right, here's our ride," the Sergeant said. "Kowalski, you're up first." He clapped his limping friend on the back.

Kowalski hobbled along the rail, looking back as he moved for the ladder to catch up to him for the engine car. He grabbed it and hauled himself up with his arms, Kersey and Baker jogging behind him. He slipped into the engine car, and Baker leapt up next, quickly sliding out of the way so Kersey could jump up with relative ease.

"All aboard and ready to get rolling," the Sergeant declared as he entered the cramped engine cab.

"Well, get comfy," the engineer bellowed from the console. "We have a long ride ahead of us. I'm gonna keep it about this speed for an hour or so to make sure we're deep in the woods with these guys behind us."

Baker set his watch for twenty minutes. "Okay, my timer is set to detonate the Humvee, which will hopefully give us a second group."

"Did anybody think to bring beer?" Johnson raised his hand.

"I wish," Kowalski cut in as he lowered himself to a sitting position on the floor. "It would be nice to have my daily kill record celebrated properly."

"What are you talking about?" Johnson's eyes narrowed. "You know *I* have the squad record."

Kowalski grinned up at his comrade. "Not anymore. Got two-eighty-three today."

Johnson paled, and scrubbed his hands down his face. "I'm never going to hear the end of this, am I?"

The sniper crossed his arms. "Did you let me hear the end of it after your little airstrike?"

"Well… no," his companion stammered. "But that was totally different!"

"How?!"

"Well, I mean… it was *my* record!" Johnson said, looking ever the petulant child. "So it was different!"

The group burst into laughter, even the two arguing soldiers. Partly because

of the argument, but also just in relief
at surviving the day.

CHAPTER FIFTEEN

Kowalski muttered a few choice obscenities under his breath, and ducked back inside the engine car. "Sarge, we've got a problem."

"Let me guess, they aren't breaking away?" Kersey sighed.

"I watched them for give solid minutes and maybe a half-dozen broke off from the pack," the sniper explained. "Even if we leave them in the dust, there's a good chance they're just going to follow us down the tracks."

"We have enough ammo to take them out though," Mason piped up. "Why don't we just set up a firing line and start taking them down?"

Bretz shook his head. "Because we don't know what's ahead of us. We can't burn that much ammo."

"Maybe get a couple decoys?" Kersey asked. "Fan out into the woods and draw them in?"

Johnson crossed his arms. "Sarge, that's all kinds of risky. Doesn't look like there are any sorts of paths in the woods out there. Gonna be way too easy to get tripped up."

"I still have a couple blocks of C4," Baker cut in. "We can get ahead of them a bit, I can run out and plant some, and get back to the train before they get close."

Kersey cocked his head. "How much do you have left?"

"Three blocks," Baker replied, as Bill increased the accelerator behind him.

The Sergeant nodded. "That's not a bad idea, but I just hate the idea of using it-" he paused when he realized they were moving faster. "Bill… why did you accelerate? We're not doing Baker's plan."

Bill clucked his tongue. "You want to clear out those zombies, right?"

"That's what we're discussing," Kersey said.

The engineer waved him off. "Then hang tight and I'll take care of it."

The train picked up speed, putting several hundred yards between the box car and the ambling horde. Bill rode the momentum all the way up a half-mile incline before screeching to a halt at the top. He triggered the emergency brakes and pulled a crowbar from under the console, whistling as he headed to the door.

"Pardon me, boys," he said, and Mason and Baker glanced at Kersey.

The Sergeant nodded his approval and the soldiers opened the door, getting out and sweeping the immediate area as Bill jumped down. The rest of the group followed, curiously watching as the engineer stretched his arms above his head, bouncing on the balls of his feet for a moment before strolling down the train towards the box car.

The soldiers followed, and at the second to last car, he hopped up onto the back and began to fiddle with the coupler. He paused, and stuck his head out to survey the group.

"Hey Sergeant," he said, "you boys don't need anything in the box car, do you?"

Kersey glanced around at his men. "Everything we need is in the front couple of cars, right?"

There were nods all around and he turned back to Bill. "Yeah, we're good."

"Fantastic," the engineer replied brightly, and then disappeared back between the cars. He pulled the pin on the coupler and stood up, giving the hitch a few good stomps with his foot.

Gravity began to take hold, and the free-roaming box car began to roll slowly away from the train, taken by the hill. It picked up speed, and sliced right into the decomposing flesh of the oncoming horde like butter.

Zombies parted like the red sea, leaving crimson tracks behind, thousands of mutilated zombies flying everywhere. The car whizzed out of sight on the horizon, and a mere hundred corpses remained, many missing limbs.

Johnson turned to Bill and began a slow clap, his mouth agape in awe. The engineer still stood atop the coupler, and gave a playful bow as the rest of the soldiers joined in the applause.

"Well," Johnson said as he clapped Kowalski on the back, "looks like your daily record lasted all of an hour."

The Private's eyes widened. "Son of a bitch!"

"What do you think there, Sarge?" Johnson teased. "Call that an even thousand?"

Kersey chuckled. "Unless you want to go count the body parts."

"Yeah, I think a thousand sounds good," the Private replied.

Kowalski began stomp-hobbling back towards the engine car, muttering under his breath. "You just wait until I get more ammo…"

"Does this mean I'm officially part of the squad?" Bill asked as he jumped down to the ground.

Johnson grinned. "Brother, you just killed a thousand zombies with a box car. You're one of us without a doubt."

"Glad to be part of the team," the engineer declared, holding up his crowbar with triumph.

Mason shook his head as they wandered after Kowalski. "I can't believe one train car did that much damage."

"It's thirty-two tons of rolling steel," Bill explained. "It probably hit them going forty, forty-five miles an hour. Nothing organic is going to react real well to that kind of impact."

Baker raised an eyebrow. "Do we need to go get it?"

"Nah, it'll be fine," the engineer said, waving flippantly behind him. "It'll just keep going until it runs out of steam. Sergeant, you'll just have to let the next team coming up know about it. They can latch it the front of their engine and bring it back."

Kersey nodded. "I can handle that. Plus, the General will get a kick out of that story. I have to admit, that was pretty fucking awesome."

"So, what do you say?" Bill cracked his knuckles. "Should we keep on trucking and find us a nice place to stay for the night?"

The soldiers let out collective noises of appreciation, and clambered back up into the engine car. Kersey looked back at the remaining survivors on the blood-soaked tracks, aimlessly staggering to their feet in disoriented arcs, mostly dispersing into the woods.

He let out a deep breath, finally
feeling like they'd completed their
mission.

CHAPTER SIXTEEN

The train coasted along at a comfortable five miles an hour, within view of the Lake Pend Oreille at the northern tip of Idaho. The soldiers took in the sight of the setting sun glinting over the water, sparkling away and almost feeling like the town of Hope was a fitting name.

"This is one hell of a sight," Johnson breathed. "I can see why people decided to settle here."

"Let's be honest," Kowalski said, "the only reason anybody settled these parts is because their wagons broke down and they didn't have the ability to keep moving. Let's come back here in another month or so and see if you like it with ten feet of snow on the ground."

Johnson grinned. "I don't know, I could go for some sledding."

"Hey Sarge," Bill piped up, "looks like there are some buildings up ahead. Want me to stop?"

Kersey turned to the engineer. "How close are we to Spokane?"

"Best guess is about ninety miles, but it's not going to be too much longer before we start hitting real patches of civilization," Bill replied.

The Sergeant nodded. "That's all I needed to hear," he replied, and raised his hands. "See if you can't find us someplace nice."

"You got it." The engineer turned back to the console, and began to slow down.

Kowalski hung out the door and raised his rifle, scanning the area. "Doesn't look like there's anything moving up there," he said. "And unless my eyes are playing tricks on me, looks like there is a nice lakefront resort in our future."

"God knows we've earned it," Bretz added.

The soldiers all checked their weapons, readying themselves for one more sweep once the train stopped. Bill screeched the vehicle to a halt right in front of the three-story resort. A billboard facing the tracks boasted *Hope Full Service Resort!*

"I guess it would be too much to hope that the masseuses are still around?" Baker joked.

"Yeah, you're going to have to take care of that happy ending all by yourself," Kowalski quipped, and then raised his hand. "On that note, I call not bunking with Baker."

Bretz and Johnson hit the ground first, doing a quick sweep of the

immediate area as the rest of the soldiers
leapt down, save Kowalski who carefully
climbed. Bill walked to the door and sat
down, letting his legs dangle over the
edge.

"Yeah, yeah, I know the drill," he
declared. "Just make sure y'all don't
forget me once you clear the place."

Kowalski snorted. "Don't worry mister
record holder, we won't forget you."

Kersey led the group across the
parking lot, everyone at high alert. There
was no movement anywhere, not even a
single car parked there. They reached the
front doors, and he motioned for Johnson
to deal with the lock.

The Private knelt in front of the
lock with his picking tools, and fiddled
with it for a moment before stopping and
leaning back on his haunches.

"What's the problem?" Kersey asked.

He shook his head and opened the door
that had been unlocked all along. "Gotta
love small towns." He held it open with a
flourish, waving his teammates inside.

The front lobby was massive—a huge
open concept with a hunting theme. Animal
heads dotted the walls, various fur skins
lining all of the furniture. The soldiers
fanned out, surprised not only to find no
zombies, but no signs of any struggle
whatsoever.

"This is a hell of a nice place,"
Mason said.

Kowalski poked a stuffed bear head
with the barrel of his gun. "As long as
you're not a member of PETA."

Johnson moved into a room off to the
side and then emerged almost immediately,
a huge grin on his face. "It's clear in
here, and there's a restaurant. With a
full bar!"

"Hallelujah!" Baker exclaimed.

Kersey flopped down on a cow-skin
couch in the lobby and put his feet up.
"Bretz, can you go get Bill? I think we're
in good shape here."

The Corporal nodded and headed back
outside to collect the engineer.

"Johnson, Baker, Mason, I want you to
do a sweep of the rooms, make sure every
inch of this place is zombie-free," Kersey
said, and the three soldiers nodded,
heading up the stairs quickly.

The Sergeant rubbed his hand down the
black and white upholstery. "Little odd
for my tastes, but if it works for you,
have at it," he muttered, shaking his
head. He raised his walkie-talkie to his
mouth. "Heartland base, please respond.
This is Sergeant Kersey."

There was a pause. "This is Heartland
base, we read you loud and clear Sergeant
Kersey."

"I have a priority alpha message for General Stephens," he said, and then waited while the operator informed him they would get him the General. He wrinkled his nose, more than a little creeped out by all the decapitated animal heads staring at him. He avoided the gaze of a snarling wolf.

"Sergeant, please tell me you have good news," Stephens came through the radio.

"Yes sir, we have cleared the path through Missoula and are currently in Hope, Idaho," Kersey explained. "Ninety miles from Spokane."

"How much further are you going to be able to push on?" Stephens asked.

Kersey took a deep breath. "Realistically general, this is as far as we can go without significant backup," he admitted. "We're going to be hitting civilization soon, and we can't risk compromising our current position. It's a good staging area for the Spokane assault." He paused. "How soon can we expect our reinforcements?"

"I don't have a specific timeline for you," the General admitted, "but three, maybe four days for the train convoy to reach you/"

The Sergeant let out a deep sigh of relief. "There's no rush on our part," he assured him. "We're all beyond exhausted and could use an opportunity to rest up. Oh, and when the convoy gets going they need to contact us. There are a few things they'll need to be aware of on their trip up."

"I have to say, Sergeant," Stephens began, "you have exceeded any and all expectations I had for this mission. The speed at which you completed it, and all without a single casualty among your men. You should be very proud."

Kersey smiled. "I am, and I appreciate the compliment."

"Kersey, I need you to be frank with me."

The Sergeant leaned forward, brow furrowing. "Yes, sir?"

"Do you feel like you are up to the task of leading the assault on Spokane?" Stephens asked.

Kersey blinked at the mouthpiece for a moment before responding. "You want *me* to be in command of a thousand men?"

"Not just be in command," the General amended, "but draw up and lead the operation."

The Sergeant flopped back against the couch, mouth agape. "I… with all due respect, that sounds like a huge step up."

"I'll be blunt," Stephens said immediately. "This virus hit our command structure hard. We've lost well over half of our leadership, and some of those who are still in charge aren't equipped to deal with this new type of battle we're waging. You have proven yourself more than capable in combating the enemy, and if you feel as though you're up to the task, I will give you the opportunity."

Kersey drew in a deep breath. "Yes, sir. I can handle it and won't let you down."

"At this time, I'm giving you a field promotion to Captain," Stephens declared. "In a few days time, you will have the command of a thousand troops for the assault on Spokane."

"Thank you… thank you General," Kersey stammered, still stunned.

"Don't let me down, Captain," Stephens replied.

The new Captain sat up ramrod straight and nodded. "I won't, sir."

He stared at the walkie-talkie in his hands long after it went silent, stock still on the hideous couch until the trio thundered back down from upstairs.

"Hey Sarge, we're all clear here," Johnson bellowed. "Everyone's gonna get their own room, too!"

They approached the stunned soldier, who didn't move or acknowledge their presence.

"Sarge?" Mason asked as Bretz returned with Bill in tow. "You okay?"

"Huh?" Kersey snapped out of his reverie and shook his head, setting down the radio. "Yeah, sorry. The General just threw me for a loop."

Bretz approached, brow furrowed. "What's going on, Sarge?"

"Well for starters, it's now Captain," Kersey said, and his men erupted into applause. He scratched the back of his head as they hooted and then put his hands up to calm them down. "It also means that I'm in charge of the assault on Spokane."

The Corporal saluted him. "Sir, I think I speak for everyone here when I say we're behind you. We couldn't be happier about following you into battle."

Another round of whoops and hoots.

"So, *Captain*," Kowalski said with a grin, "what's your first order as a newly promoted man?"

Kersey finally relaxed, leaning back and curling his hands behind his head. "I think we've been through enough today, and we have more than enough on our plate for tomorrow," he said. "For tonight, my orders are to secure the building, find something in that kitchen to whip up, and unlike the last bar we were at, tonight it's a two-drink *minimum*."

The squad blew up into even louder cheers, hauling their new Captain from the couch to hustle him into the restaurant proper. It would be a celebration for them all, a minor reprieve from the hell they'd be facing soon enough. For that night, however, they had each other and they had safety and relaxation, and they were going to make the most of it by carrying out their new Captain's orders.

END

DEAD AMERICA: THE SECOND WEEK

BOOK 6: THE NEVADA CARAVAN

BY DEREK SLATON

© 2019

CHAPTER ONE

Day Zero +11

"How much further we have to go?" Private Ortega asked, running a hand through his dark hair and squinting out the passenger window of the big rig.

Private Hickman stared down his nose as he took in the barren wasteland that was rural Nevada. "About ten miles closer than we were the last time you asked that," he snapped.

"No need to get bitchy," Ortega growled. "I'm just trying to stay on top of things.

Harlan clucked his tongue, not taking his eyes off of the road. "Now now kids," he said brightly, "if you don't cut that out I swear I'll turn this truck around."

The two soldiers chuckled, tense mood evaporating, and Hickman spread out the haphazardly folded map a little more across his lap.

"Now, that being said," Harlan continued, "are we close to a town or anything? We're still running real low on fuel. And I don't know about you, but I could certainly go for a room temperature energy drink right about now."

Hickman pursed his lips and studied the map closer, tapping it with his finger. "Looks like there's a little town called Schurz a few miles up the road here," he said. "But god only knows if it's going to be big enough to support a gas station."

"Well, you boys better hope it does," the driver replied, "cause if not, y'all are gonna be pushing this big bitch the rest of the way."

As they rolled into town, they studied the handful of houses and single story buildings. There were a few cars strewn about, but no life (or unlife) whatsoever.

"Well, this doesn't look promising," Hickman muttered.

Ortega shook his head. "Looks like this town just up and vanished."

"Or, given the size of it, this town could be in the midst of rush hour," Hickman scoffed. "Not sure we could tell the difference."

"There we go," Harlan said, pointing to a large gas station sign on the horizon. "Thank fucking christ." He pulled up alongside the lone diesel pump off to the side.

"Hang tight while we sweep the area," Ortega instructed, readying his gun.

The truck screeched to a stop and the two soldiers hopped down from the cab, giving the immediate area a once-over. It was as clear and barren as the rest of the town.

Ortega waved for their companion to join them, and then turned to his partner. "You want to check around the back of the building for the generator? I'll check the inside."

"Yeah, I got you," Hickman replied, and jogged off.

"Hey, pick me up a few of those energy drinks," Harlan inclined his head to Ortega. "Original flavor, none of that fruity shit."

The Private gave him a thumbs up and strode towards the convenience store. Just as he reached for the glass door, a few zombies smashed into it from the inside. He leapt back and raised his weapon, but the door held fast, locked.

"Sorry, but looks like you're going to have to go without," he called over his shoulder.

Harlan wrinkled his nose. "Motherfucker."

Ortega peered in through one of the windows, taking stock of the store. There were nearly a dozen zombies inside, all very excited to see a fresh meal through the glass. Hickman came back around the corner and had a look for himself.

"Don't worry bud, we've got you covered," he waved to the driver.

Harlan grinned. "My man!"

"You really want to risk our lives for some energy drinks?" Ortega raised an eyebrow.

"No, but if we want the gas, we're going to have to get inside," Hickman explained, "because the generator switch is in there."

Ortega sighed, rubbing the bridge of his nose. "Of course it is." He stepped back from the window. "So, how do you want to play this?"

"If we both start shooting from here it could cause a rush and overwhelm us," Hickman replied, stroking his square chin.

His companion cocked his head. "Wanna do a little yo-yo?"

"Uh, sure?" Hickman replied, pursing his lips in confusion.

"We yo-yo them," Ortega repeated, holding up his hands. "You get around to the other side, fire off some rounds and take a few out, then when they get to your side, I do the same. While I'm shooting, you come around to this side, and we have plenty of time to finish them off."

Hickman nodded thoughtfully. "All right, I can dig it," he said. "You keep 'em occupied while I get in position."

They shared a fist bump and split up.

Ortega stood in front of the glass door, waving and pounding on the glass. "Yeah, you fuckers want to turn me into tacos, don't ya? Well that ain't on the menu today!" He peered past the significantly more excited zombies and saw Hickman through the other side in position. At a thumbs up, Ortega ducked behind the brick, out of the way of the glass.

His partner took aim from the other side of the store, firing into the window in front of him. The glass shattered, and a zombie's head exploded like an M80 stuffed inside a cantaloupe. The mini-horde turned their attention towards the shooter, grunting their delight at the broken barrier between them and a fresh meal. Hickman took the opportunity to fire several more rounds, easily dropping half of them onto the now blood-soaked floor.

As they reached the halfway point, he yelled for his companion, and Ortega leapt out from behind the wall. He took aim at the back of the group and pulled the trigger, destroying the window on his side and taking out his enemy's head. He lined up another shot and another, taking out two more, while Hickman fired again into the confused group of corpses.

After ten seconds of sustained shooting the store fell silent, a pile of rotted flesh seeping goo across the linoleum tiles.

"Yo-yoing, huh?" Hickman commended as he strolled around to his partner's side. "You need to patent that shit and sell it back to the military. That needs to be in the new field manual."

Ortega snorted. "With my luck, they'd think it was a great idea and want to drop me into every godforsaken place to implement it."

"Because that would be a huge change from our current predicament." Hickman rolled his eyes.

His partner couldn't help but laugh. "True fuckin' story, bro."

"I'll check behind the counter for the switch, if you want to get our chauffeur his energy drinks," Hickman said, motioning with his thumb.

"I heard that!" Harlan barked. "And just a fair warnin', you call me chauffeur again and I'm gonna start callin' you Miss Daisy!"

The soldiers chuckled.

Hickman cocked his head. "Fearless leader, then?" he asked.

The driver put a hand to his chin in mock thought, and then raised his hands in the air. "I humbly accept your designation."

The duo stepped through the broken bay window and into the store proper. Ortega danced around the thick blood creeping across the floor to scan the long-dormant coolers on the far end.

"You want anything?" he asked.

Hickman stepped over a corpse behind the counter. "I'll take some water, and some nacho chips if there are any left," he replied, and felt around under the register for some kind of switch. He knelt down and found it, labelled clearly, and flipped it. A low rumbling started up on the other side of the far wall, signifying success.

Ortega emerged from the window, arms full of snacks and drinks, and furrowed his brow at the sight of Harlan struggling with the pump.

"You all right?" he asked.

"Fuckin' thing ain't workin'," the driver replied brusquely. "I'm squeezin' the handle and it's comin' out dryer than an eighty-year-old's cumshot."

Ortega winced. "There's a visual I could have done without," he muttered, and then popped his head back inside. "Hey, the pump ain't working."

"Well it's on," Hickman replied with a shrug.

"See if there's a secondary generator," his partner suggested. "Or maybe the pump isn't turned on?"

Hickman ducked back behind the counter again, searching for more switches. He found the board for the pumps, and then his shoulders slumped in defeat. He pulled a post-it note off of the board and walked over to his companion, sticking it to his chest and walking right on by without another word.

Ortega tilted his head and stared down at the note, reading *First diesel delivery on Friday!*

The Private sighed. "Fucking hell."

Harlan cocked his head as the soldiers sauntered over to him, and dropped the nozzle at the sight of their forlorn faces. "We fucked?"

"Yup," Hickman replied, and pulled out his map, holding it up against the grill of the truck. "Okay. We're here, and it's just a straight shot up the highway to Yerington." He pointed to the paper.

Harlan nodded thoughtfully. "That's what, twenty, twenty-five miles?"

"It's a good a guess as any," Hickman replied. "The high school is on the north end of town, so right as we come in. According to our intel, that's where the survivors are."

Ortega cracked open the beverages and handed them around, taking a long swig of his water as he studied the map. "We going to have enough fuel to make it?"

"We've been ridin' on empty for a while now," Harlan said. "There might be enough fumes in there to get us to town. Only thing I can guarantee is that we ain't goin' much further than that."

Hickman took a deep breath and folded the map. "This is *such* a well thought out operation."

"Hey, I'm doing the best I can, here." Harlan bristled.

"Ain't your fault," Ortega assured him. "We're just not a fan of this whole *let's send out some disposable assets without proper intel or resources.*"

Hickman pocketed the map with a sigh. "Especially when *we're* the disposable assets."

CHAPTER TWO

The truck rolled into the north part
of town, still chugging away despite
running on fumes. There was only one lone
zombie lumbering along the edge of the
street, and it looked up dumbly with milky
eyes as they passed.

"The school should be three, four
blocks up on the left," Hickman said,
pointing through the window.

As they got closer, zombies began to
stagger out of everywhere. They stumbled
down lawns, bouncing off the sides of the
truck and tumbling back into the grass on
the side of the road. As they reached the
football field, Harlan slammed on the
breaks, the three men's jaws dropping at
the sight before them.

"What the hell happened here?" Ortega
breathed.

The school was a smoldering wreck.

The football field crawled with
zombies, the fence completely down. There
was a massive hole blown into the side of
the building proper, and the second floor
collapsed into the first along the entire
back half of the building.

They'd been told this was a survivor
camp. But there didn't seem to be a single
living thing left.

All of a sudden a high-pitched buzz echoed in the cab, as the fuel light blinked rapidly. Harlan immediately threw the truck into gear and floored it.

"What are you doing?" Ortega cried.

The driver shook his head. "Tryin' to get us the fuck outta here before we run outta gas. If I can't get us clear we're gonna be in a heap of trouble if we're surrounded by those things."

The soldiers shared a grim look, silently conveying that this was the only logical solution. In front of them was a modest downtown area filled with one and two-story buildings. Two blocks up stood a wall of zombies, at least a thousand clogging the street.

"Can we punch through them?" Ortega asked.

Harlan dropped gear and punched the gas. "We're gonna try!"

As he smacked several corpses staggering around on the road, flinging them harmlessly to the side, Hickman opened his map.

"It's a straight shot out of town, maybe a mile and we're clear," he said.

And then the engine sputtered.

Hickman clenched his jaw. "So much for that."

"Hang on boys, this is gonna be bumpy!" Harlan bellowed, and jerked the wheel to the left. They bounced up onto the sidewalk, screeching along the first building on the block which was a clothing store with shattered windows. They ran over a good amount of zombies, crunching them beneath the tires as the rest swarmed around the open sides of the truck.

"Get to the roof!" Ortega barked.

He rolled down the passenger window and pulled himself out, careful not to let any part of his body dip low enough into the sea of rotted fingers reaching up to grab him. He knelt on top of the cab, and then reached down to help Hickman up. Harlan struggled to get through the window, his belly catching on the sill. He twisted around to sit there and reached up, screaming as a zombie managed to brush up against his ass.

"Holy fuck they're getting me!" he cried.

Ortega grasped his wrists tightly. "Stay calm, man, I got you," he said firmly, and pulled.

The larger man struggled to find his footing, and then pushed off of the window frame to wiggle his way up onto the roof. He flopped over onto his back, chest heaving.

"Why the fuck did I volunteer for this?" he huffed.

Ortega clapped him on the shoulder. "Could be worse. You could still be in Kansas."

"Well played, son," Harlan wheezed. "Well played."

Hickman stood on top of the transport container, and turned to look down on his two comrades. "Once you boys catch your breath, we can get up on the roof of this store," he declared. "It's clear up here."

Harlan nodded and sat up. Ortega helped him his feet and they clambered up onto the back, making their way up to the roof. The trio stood at the edge and stared down at the street below. There were at least a thousand zombies covering every inch of the road, a sea of moaning flesh clogging the space between every building.

"Don't think the yo-yo technique is gonna work this time," Hickman said.

Ortega took a deep breath. "No shit, brother."

As they stared at the sea of death below, a sharp whistle cut through the air. They looked around and then saw a flash of blonde hair on a roof four buildings down from them. The figure waved at them.

"Think they're friendly?" Harlan asked.

Hickman shrugged. "Given their current situation, I don't think they have a choice." He didn't want to add that they were in the same boat, and led the way across the buildings to get closer to the waving man.

Upon approach, they realized it was a young man that couldn't have been older than seventeen. He stood at the edge of his roof, about eight feet of groaning alley separating the two buildings.

"Man, are we glad to see you guys," the young blond gushed. "Are you here to help us?"

Ortega scratched the back of his head. "Well, that was the original plan, but it doesn't look like we made it in time."

"Yeah, what the hell happened at the school?" Hickman asked.

The young man shook his head. "I'm still not a hundred percent sure," he admitted. "Some of the others inside can fill you in better than I can. Why don't you jump across and I'll introduce you to the rest of the group?"

Harlan glanced down and immediately backed up, raising his hands in surrender. "Man, I got a better chance of bein' kidnapped by porn stars who have a thing for truck drivers than makin' that jump."

"We got you covered," Ortega assured him. "Hickman, you go ahead and jump across. I got an idea."

His companion nodded and took a run at it, springing across the gap with ease. He turned around and took a wide-legged stance.

"Okay, I want you to do the same thing he just did," Ortega continued, motioning to Harlan. "Only I'm gonna give you a boost, and he's gonna pull you in."

The driver gaped at him, mouth opening and closing twice, before he scrubbed his hands down his face and shook his head in defeat. He took a deep breath and lined himself up in front of the soldier, psyching himself up for a jump that he was sure would kill him.

He leapt, with Ortega timing a significant shove to his back, and managed to land on the side of his ankle.

"Motherfucking goddamn fucking son of a fuckin' whore bitch!" Harlan cried as Hickman caught his stumbling form, lowering him down into a sitting position.

The soldier took a close look at his ankle and then patted his knee. "It ain't broke, just gonna be sore for a couple of days."

Ortega jumped across and they helped their now-limping friend to his feet.

The young man waved for them to
follow him. "Come on, the ladder inside is
this way."

CHAPTER THREE

Harlan muttered obscenities under his breath as he descended the ladder, trying not to put too much pressure on his smarting ankle. Ortega caught him at the bottom, and Hickman followed close behind, the three of them turning to face the room.

There were about twenty people in the furniture store, all ages and shapes and sizes strewn about.

"I told you I heard something, Ryan!" a red-headed woman that looked to be in her early twenties cried as she approached the blond.

He rolled his eyes. "And I believed you," he replied, putting a hand on her shoulder. "If I didn't, I wouldn't have climbed up. Gentlemen, this is our spitfire, Audrey."

"Welcome to our very own little slice of heaven," she said, extending her hand. The trio shook it in turns.

"Nice to meet you," Ortega said. "I'm Private Ortega, this is Private Hickman. And this big ball of joy is Harlan."

The redhead furrowed her brow at the wincing truck driver. "Are you okay?" she asked.

"Yeah, he's fine, just twisted his ankle up a bit," Hickman replied.

"Oh, well the Doc can take a look at him as soon as he's done with Jordan," Audrey said, motioning over her shoulder. An older man sat, wrapping a bandage around a younger man's leg.

Ortega pursed his lips. "You know bites are contagious, right?"

"No fucking shit, dude," the redhead snapped. "Just because we're in a small town doesn't mean we're morons. It also doesn't mean we haven't been dealing with the same world-ending bullshit that you've been dealing with. Or did you happen to miss the thousand rotting corpses on your way in?"

The soldier raised his hands in surrender, shaking his head. "Whoa, whoa, I wasn't implying that," he assured her. "It's just when I enter a room and see someone bandaged up, I just like to check."

"Yeah, well, we're still alive and kicking so it should be a safe bet that we figured that one out," Audrey scoffed, crossing her arms.

Ryan stepped closer to her, interjecting himself between the two. "Jordan broke his leg when we escaped from the school," he explained.

"Come on," the redhead said gently to Harlan, holding out her hand to support him and lead him over to the doc. "Let's get you taken care of."

"Thanks girl, I appreciate it," the big trucker huffed.

"Hey, Ryan," a mid-thirties soccer dad greeted as he walked over with a middle-aged black man in a janitor's uniform. "We got the last big dresser moved over to the windows.

The blond nodded. "Are the curtains working?"

"Hard to say." The janitor shrugged. "They're still leaning up against it, but I can't tell if they're pushing as hard."

Ryan's brow furrowed. "Is somebody watching it?"

"Yes, Miss Becky is on window duty," he replied.

The soccer dad motioned to the soldiers. "So, did the military come to rescue us?"

"Not really," Ortega replied, scratching the back of his head. "We were actually coming to help you solidify your survivor camp, but it appears we got here a bit too late."

Hickman sighed. "And Ryan here wasn't any help in filling in the blanks for us. Either of you know what happened at the school?"

The two men glanced at each other, and the younger man motioned to the older.

"You knew it better than any of us, Ruben," he said, "be my guest."

"I mean there were, what, a hundred and fifty, two hundred of us in there, Garrett?" Ruben replied, rubbing his chin thoughtfully.

The soccer dad nodded. "About that."

"Well regardless, we were able to secure the old school and the football field before things got too bad out here. And things were going pretty well." Ruben paused, taking a deep breath and putting his hands on his hips. "We had plenty of food, plenty of room, and that generator was nice and full so we had heating and air. I thought we had enough to keep us going until somebody like you showed up, but then yesterday happened." He motioned around the room. "See, pretty much everybody here now was out by the concession stand, turning part of the field into some farm land when it went down. I didn't see what caused it myself, just heard this horrific scream coming from the gate. One of the younger kids had apparently wandered off from whoever was watching them, and they walked up to the horde. I looked up just as the lock gave out, and hundreds of those things swarmed onto the field." He paused and blinked a few times. "That little kid was swallowed up whole. And the woman wasn't far behind.

"Some of the people here wanted to run to the school, but I stopped them, knowing we wouldn't make it in time. We took cover behind the concession stand and watched as the field flooded with those things. They were able to get the school locked up tight, but the problem was the generator. It was exposed and close to the door. The zombies must have been attracted to the noise, and got caught up in it or something because it didn't take long for the smoke to start.

"When we saw that, we got moving, running out of the football field and heading towards downtown. Not long after that, we heard the explosion." He swallowed hard, and looked to the ceiling, taking a deep breath before composing himself. "Somehow we were able to fight our way in here, and we've been here ever since."

"And unfortunately for us," Ryan added, "enough of those things saw us getting in here that they stuck around and attracted the crowd that's out there now."

Ruben leaned forward. "But you fellas went by the school, didn't you?" he asked. "Were there any survivors?"

"Most of the building collapsed in on itself," Ortega said, shaking his head sadly. "If there are any survivors under there, we don't have a way to get to them or get them out. I'm sorry."

The janitor nodded in somber acceptance.

"So, have y'all thought about getting out of here?" Hickman piped up.

"We tried yesterday, before the crowd outside got too big," Ruben explained. "One of the local boys thought he could lure them away and give us a chance. He got down to the end of the street and started making a ruckus, but that only attracted more zombies. Before he had a chance to react, he was surrounded. Ever since then, all we've done is lay low."

Garrett shifted his weight from foot to foot. "So what about that truck?" he asked, eyes wide with hope. "Can it get us out of here?"

"We ran out of gas as soon as we pulled up," Ortega said.

"Damn." Garrett winced. "Is there anything useful in there?"

"Yeah, it's filled with useful stuff," Hickman replied, rolling his eyes. "It's kind of the entire reason we're here."

The portly man narrowed his eyes. "I mean, is there anything useful to our current situation?"

Hickman sighed. "Yeah, plenty. There's a shitload of guns and ammo in there, but it's behind about fifteen pallets of other stuff. So unless you want to start unloading the truck, we ain't getting to it."

"What about diesel?" Ortega cut in. "Is there a gas station in town?"

Ryan wrinkled his nose. "There is, but we drained it and and took everything to the school."

"Great, so no diesel anywhere in the general vicinity," Hickman declared. "This mission keeps getting better and better."

Ruben suddenly gasped. "Hey! What about ole Charlie Russell?"

Garrett furrowed his brow. "Crazy Charlie down there in Mason?"

"Yeah, him and I go way back," the janitor replied, waving his hands around. "I mean, we kinda lost touch when he… well…"

His companion raised an eyebrow. "Went survivalist nut-job?"

"I probably wouldn't have put it that way, but yeah," Ruben said.

"A survivalist might have diesel on hand," Ortega cut in. "How survivalist are we talking?"

"A couple years back, he decided to turn the trailer park he owned into a compound for like-minded individuals," Garrett explained. "Didn't take long before he was the only resident left."

Hickman nodded. "How far away is Mason?"

"A couple miles due south of here, just on the other side of the river," Ruben replied.

Hickman raised an eyebrow and turned to the other soldier. "I mean, if we can get some fuel up here, we could employ the biggest goddamn yo-yo this world's ever seen."

"It'll give us a chance to refuel and get the fuck outta here," Ortega agreed.

"Would you fellas mind joining us on the roof?" Hickman turned to the others. "We have some plans to make."

Ryan nodded. "I'll grab Audrey. If she finds out we're making a plan without her, she'll cut me."

The Private barked a laugh. "After their last conversation, there's a better chance she'd cut Ortega."

CHAPTER FOUR

"Okay, just give us a lay of the land," Hickman said as the group congregated on the roof. The zombies below sounded excited as all hell, reaching up to try to get to the moving fresh meal above.

"To your right is the north side of town with the school," Audrey began, motioning up the street. "Straight ahead to the west, about three quarters of a mile up, you'll run into the river. Don't let the name fool you, it's more like a glorified creek if anything. Most places it's going to be waist deep at best. And to your left is south, where after a couple miles you'll hit the bridge that will take you right into Mason."

Hickman nodded. "And how big is Mason?"

"Maybe a hundred people?" Garrett replied. "Honestly, I'd be surprised if anyone is still left there."

The Private shook his head. "Well, with the way today's going, let's assume it's going to be full. Even so, I think we can handle a hundred."

"Y'all have that much ammo?" Ryan's eyes widened.

"I got a hundred for my rifle, and another twenty or so for my handgun, pretty sure Ortega has the same," Hickman replied, and motioned to his partner. His brow furrowed when he realized how silent his companion was, staring down at the sea of zombies with a steely gaze. "You all right there, man?"

Ortega drew in a deep breath. "Just thinking," he said flatly.

A few awkward moments later, Hickman held up his hands. "You, uh, wanna fill the rest of us in?"

"The way I see it, we have a variety of problems," Ortega replied. "We can't go south to Mason because we run the risk of a lot of these things following us, which means we'll be overrun."

The other soldier shrugged. "So we head north and cross the river."

"If we go that way, we can hit the sporting goods store a couple blocks up," Ruben suggested.

Ryan's brow furrowed. "Why?"

"Cause they just got in the new four-wheelers," the janitor replied. "Figure it's going to be easier to outrun those things on those than on foot. Plus, I don't know about you, but I really don't want to swim then hike a couple miles to Mason."

"I take it there's a bridge close by?" Hickman asked.

Audrey nodded. "Yeah, just head due west from the sporting goods store. It's blocked off with cars, but we should be able to get around them."

"There!" the Private exclaimed. "Problem solved!"

Ortega sighed. "It's only part of the problem," he said. "When we come back with the fuel, we need a major distraction. How are we going to accomplish that when we don't have any explosives?"

Hickman crossed his arms. "How well stocked is that hardware store?"

"I worked there over the summer." Ryan raised his hand. "It's got pretty much anything you could need."

"Propane tanks?" the Private asked.

The young man nodded emphatically, eyes lighting up when he realized what he was getting at. "Yes, sir. A cage of them up front. There are keys for the cage at register one. Blue plastic keychain."

Hickman turned to his partner and clapped him on the shoulder. "So, you think you can lead this group down to Mason without me?"

"Where are you going?" Ortega asked.

"I'm gonna take up residence at the hardware store," Hickman replied, motioning across the street.

Ortega shook his head. "Nah brother, we can deal with that once we get back with the gas."

"I need to get over there and get prepped for when you come back," his partner countered. "Plus, once I'm over there, I can keep these things occupied and focused on me, meaning fewer are going to follow you."

Ruben raised a hand, much like Ryan had just moments before. "Sir, I'm not meaning any disrespect towards your abilities and whatnot, but how exactly are you planning on getting over there?"

Hickman pointed towards the end of the block where a car had crashed into the corner of the building. "Gonna use that," he said. "I can get up to the banister on the second floor, work my way across, and get in through the upstairs."

"I... don't know if that's going to work," Ryan said slowly.

Hickman grinned. "Trust me, kid, it'll work. The Army trained me well."

"I'm sure they did," the young man replied, and crossed his arms in indignant defiance. "But that second floor is a residence. The store owner and his family live there, and if I know him, he barricaded himself inside when this thing started. You may be dealing with some resistance."

Hickman sighed. "Fantastic," he said brightly. "So I'm either going to get shot at, or there's a family or zombies living there. Good times."

"Only question left is, who all is going to Mason?" Ortega asked. All four of the civilians raised their hands immediately, and he nodded in appreciation. "Looks like we have a raiding party. Are you sure nobody wants to stay behind to make sure the survivors downstairs are ready to move?"

Ryan shook his head. "The Doc and a couple of the others are capable of that," he assured them. "They aren't really fit enough to get out here, though."

"Garrett, you sure?" Ruben put a hand on the portly man's shoulder. "What about your girls?"

"I'm going because of them," Garrett replied firmly. "The more able bodies we have out there, the better chance we have at pulling this off."

"Can't argue with that," Hickman put in.

"Okay, it's settled then," Ortega said. "If you have weapons, guns or otherwise, grab them."

Ryan took a deep breath. "We're low on guns. I think there might be two down there, I'll go get them."

"Good deal," Ortega replied. "While you're down there, inform the Doc what's going on and tell him to be ready because we aren't going to have much time when we come back. Does he have a radio?"

The young man nodded. "Yeah, there's one down there."

"Good, tell him to monitor channel seven," Ortega instructed. As the civilians headed back down the ladder, he stood next to his companion on the edge of the sea of death below. "You ready to do this?"

"Nope," Hickman replied, popping the *p.*

Ortega chuckled. "That's my boy."

CHAPTER FIVE

Ortega led his team to the southern edge of the furniture store, and they started a riot. They clapped, whistled and yelled, making noise to attempt to draw the horde's attention to them as much as possible.

Hickman crept to the far northern end of the block, staying as low as he could. He lined himself up with the back of the truck, taking a few deep breaths to steady his heart rate and be ready for what he was about to do.

His radio crackled quietly, and Ortega's voice came through at the lowest volume. "Hey, you read me?"

"Yeah, how am I looking?" Hickman whispered back into the receiver.

"I think it's about as good as it's going to get," Ortega replied.

Hickman chuckled quietly to himself. "Doesn't sound promising," he said.

"There's about forty or so between you and the car," his partner said, "but they're spread out pretty good."

Hickman scrubbed a hand down his face. "Oh, forty, is that all?"

"Well, it's better than the couple hundred that were there a few minutes ago," Ortega assured him.

"Can we give it a few minutes?" his partner asked, swallowing hard.

"Negative," Ortega replied. "I don't know how much longer the front windows are going to hold under the pressure."

Hickman sighed. He crawled to the edge of the building, peering out over the street. "Are there any directly beside the truck?"

"There are a couple, can't tell how many though," Ortega came back.

Hickman got up on one knee, shaking out his hands to psych himself up. "When I go, try to take out the ones that are closest to the car," he said, keeping his eyes on his path between ambling zombies.

"I got you, brother," his partner promised.

"And for the love of Christ, don't shoot me," Hickman said.

Ortega chuckled. "Wouldn't dream of it. Good luck."

Hickman tucked his radio away, and took another deep breath before pushing off the roof. He hopped down onto the top of the truck, the thud fairly insignificant but loud enough to attract the attention of the corpses closest to him.

He took a run at the back of the truck, hopping down to hang from the edge, dangling a few feet above the street. He made sure there were no gnashing teeth directly below him, and then dropped to the asphalt. As soon as his boots hit the ground, a zombie lunged at his shoulder, and he planted his foot into its chest to shove it back before sprinting in the direction of the car.

Zombies turned towards him, but heads began to explode. Ortega took out corpse after corpse, the cracks of his rifle from his vantage point serving to draw the attention to him instead of his running friend.

A pack of a few dozen began to close up the clear path Hickman had planned on heading through, and Hickman dashed forward, putting his shoulder down. He barreled through the mini-horde, ducking under outstretched hands and shoving back and forth like a running back through the secondary. When he emerged from the pack, two creatures came at him from either side, snarling and snapping. He reacted without thinking, snatching one arm and flinging one zombie into the other, knocking them both off of their feet to the street.

Hickman tore for the car anew, only one zombie left in his path. As he approached it, its head came clean off, and he used the falling corpse as a springboard to jump up onto the truck of the wrecked vehicle. He steadied himself on the roof, and glanced over his shoulder. The remaining zombies converged on his position, and he knew that if he didn't act fast that they would easily be able to reach him on the roof of the mangled car.

"I hope this shit is well built," Hickman muttered under his breath, and squatted down before leaping straight up, grasping the lip of the second floor balcony. He grunted loudly as he pulled himself up and swung a leg up over his head, giving him just enough leverage to pull himself out of the grasp of the zombies angrily swarming the area he'd just vacated.

He struggled for a moment, his fingers straining to hold his weight, and he gave one last heave to propel himself up onto the ledge. He rolled over onto his back, huffing and puffing as the zombies below moaned in frustration at their lost meal.

"Man, that was amazing, brother!" Ortega's excited voice came through the radio. "I knew it wasn't going to be that bad!"

Hickman lazily raised the mouthpiece to his lips. "Do me a favor, and don't talk to me for a minute, will ya?"

"I understand you," Ortega replied with a chuckle. "You take a moment while we get into position."

Hickman sat up slowly, shaking his head. "Ten-four," he said. He grunted as he got to his feet and made his way across the wooden awning above the street. He kept his eyes ahead of him, focusing on his footing instead of the hungry corpses below.

A loud *thunk* on the window to his left startled him, and he lashed out to steady himself on the siding. He studied the zombie behind the glass, once a young girl in her late teens, blood-soaked blonde hair matted against a deep wound on her cheek. She gnashed her teeth against the glass, clawing fruitlessly with broken fingers.

Hickman shook his head and continued to move, taking a knee beside the first window of the residence above the hardware store.

"I'm in position, are you ready?" he asked quietly into the radio.

"You tell us," Ortega replied. "How are we looking down there?"

Hickman unslung his assault rifle and looked through the scope, staring back at the zombies swarming the furniture store. "It's a similar situation to what I had. But if you give me a minute…"

He began to fire on the zombies near the truck, heads exploding and splattering crimson along the cab. The *crack* of his gun attracted not only those zombies, but a lot of the furniture store ones as well, relieving the pressure on the weakening windows.

"You're good," he said. "Go now."

"On the move," Ortega came back. "I'll be in touch."

Hickman continued to fire for a while, clearing out a few more zombies for the group as they made their way to the truck. He monitored them jumping down to the ground and then heading up the road away from the main horde. Once they were safely away, he slung the rifle back over his shoulder and pulled his knife out of its holster, turning to work at the lock on the window. He jimmied the blade underneath and pried hard, and the latch *snicked* open.

He opened the window as quietly as he could, and slid into the apartment, bracing his knee on the edge of a sink full of grime-covered dishes. He pulled his second leg in and bonked one of the plates, grimacing at the echo of rattling ceramic. He jumped down to the floor and took a defensive stance, holding his knife out in front of him.

"If anybody is in here, I'm not looking for trouble," he called. "Just want to do a little shopping at your store."

He tensed at the sound of footsteps from the other end of the apartment, and then whirled in the opposite direction at the pantry crashing open. Two female zombies descended upon him, and he immediately reacted, stabbing downward into the shorter one's head, burying the blade into her skull. He jerked it back, but instead of the knife coming free, the girl's head detached from her body, leaving him with a bloody lollipop.

"Oh fuck," he breathed, and dropped it to the linoleum before reaching for his handgun, but the other zombie lunged for his shoulder. He braced his forearm against her chest, trying to keep her teeth out of his shoulder, leaning back as he fumbled for his weapon.

A male zombie entered from the other side, letting out a loud excited moan at the sight of fresh meat. Hickman backed up against the kitchen island, flipping himself backwards and pulling the female zombie with him. He rolled, scattering utensils everywhere, and flung her down to the other side, landing on her chest with his knees.

She flailed around, arms smacking against the kitchen chairs, and the flimsy table buckled, knocking a set of salt-and-pepper shakers to the floor. He saw the kitchy lighthouse shape and grabbed one, jamming the tip of it into the zombie's eye. He punched down on it twice to lodge it into her brain, and she finally went limp.

He leapt back up to his feet and pointed his handgun at the remaining zombie, who stupidly caught himself against the other side of the island, shrieking in frustration. Hickman pulled the trigger and point blank put a bullet into its forehead.

As the corpse fell limp, he froze and strained his ears for any more movement in the apartment, and after a few beats he did a quick sweep of the space. His shoulders finally relaxed and he checked himself for any wounds as the adrenaline and shock wore off. He let out a deep ragged breath on an exhausted laugh, happy just to be alive.

CHAPTER SIX

Ortega led the group down the mostly clear road towards the sporting goods store. Zombies began to emerge from the side streets, and Ryan turned to aim at one as they ran.

"Save your bullets and keep going!" Ortega barked, and the young man complied, sprinting to keep up.

The Private reached the door first, taking a knee with his rifle, his back to the front of the store. "Somebody get that door open!" he cried, and began to fire bursts of bullets into the oncoming creatures from around the corner. Several zombies fell under his *spray and pray* approach.

"I can't get it!" Garrett barked in frustration as he tried to pick the lock.

Ortega leapt to his feet as about eighty zombies headed their way, drawn to the sound of gunfire. "Move!" he instructed, and the middle-aged man jumped out of the way as the soldier aimed his rifle at the bottom pane of glass. He fired once, shattering the door, and Garrett quickly reached in to unlock it through the jagged hold before pulling it open.

Ortega went first, the rest of the group piling in behind him. Audrey clicked the lock once they were all inside, and her and Ruben immediately grasped a nearby chunk of shelving to block off the bottom panel of broken door.

The Private motioned for Ryan and Garrett to each take an aisle on either side of him, as they were the only ones with guns, and the trio made their way quickly through the store. Two creatures staggered out from behind one of the four-wheelers at the back, and Ortega dropped one. Ryan took out the other with a near-perfect headshot, and the Private clapped him on the shoulder.

"Good shot, kid," he said, receiving a nod of appreciation. "Both of you finish doing a sweep, make sure we're alone in here," he instructed as he headed over to the trio of four wheelers.

They were up on a central display, and he blinked at the keys dangling out of the ignition. "This must be a very trusting town."

"Not really," Ruben replied as he walked up behind him. "Everybody just knew the owner was a gun-toting maniac, so they didn't want to press their luck."

Ortega chuckled and shook his head. "Cheaper than an alarm system. I like it." He climbed up onto the vehicle and turned the key to start the engine thrumming. It had half a tank of gas, much to his pleasure, and he glanced at the others as Ruben fired up one, and Audrey hopped on the third. "Everybody good on gas?" he asked.

"Little less than half a tank," Audrey reported.

Ruben held up his hand in a thumbs-up. "Got three-quarters over here."

Ryan headed over as he holstered his gun. "We're clear in here, but it's not looking good outside."

"How close are they?" Ortega asked.

"A few of them are at the window right now, and the rest aren't far behind," Ryan said, motioning over his shoulder to the front of the store.

Ortega got down from the four-wheeler and stepped to the side, peering down the main aisle of the store. There was a large bay window to the left of the front door, with four zombies smashed up against it, teeth gnashing at the glass.

The Private pursed his lips for a moment, and then glanced at the helmet display next to him. He grabbed a bright yellow one and knocked on the top of it before heading back over to his vehicle.

"Should we get helmets too?" Ruben asked.

Ortega shook his head as he got back into his seat. "Nah, brother, I'm leading

the charge through the glass, so I wanted
that extra bit of protection."

Audrey patted the seat behind her.
"You coming or not?" she asked Ryan, and
the young man shrugged before clambering
onto the back, tentatively wrapping his
arms around her slender waist.

"Hey, you look good riding the bitch
seat," Garrett teased.

Ruben sneered. "Are *you* ready to go,
big boy? Or should I say *bitch*?" He patted
his own passenger seat, and his middle-
aged friend visibly deflated as he
reluctantly climbed up.

Ortega clipped on his helmet and
pushed the visor up so he could address
the team. "Give me a three-second head
start," he instructed. "I'm going to hit
that window hard, and that should be
enough time for the glass to hit the
ground. As soon as we're out, head down
the side street next to us and don't stop
until you hit the bridge. If we run into
trouble, hit the field to the south and
meet out by the river, where we'll
regroup. Questions?" At the round of *no*'s,
the soldier checked his rifle to make sure
it was on three-round burst mode, and
slammed down his visor. "This is a bad
idea," he muttered under his breath, and
then dropped the four-wheeler into gear.

He tore down the main aisle towards the zombie-reinforced plate glass window, steadying his gun on the handlebars. About fifteen yards away from the front of the store, he fired into the glass, leaving big cracks along the surface. He grabbed the handles and put his head down in anticipation, and hit the glass.

The force of the impact sent the quartet of zombies flying, glass exploding in all directions. He skidded to a stop in the street and took quick stock of the swarm headed towards them, and then peeled out towards the side street.

As he made the turn he heard the other two vehicles keeping pace with him, and they roared down the side street, a mostly clear road ahead. He couldn't help but crack a smile at the sound of Audrey's hoot, something charming about the young woman enjoying the wind in her hair despite the circumstances.

CHAPTER SEVEN

Hickman opened the pantry door, relieved to find a case of bottled water inside. He used one to wash his blood-soaked hands and face, wiping himself clean with some paper towels before chugging the rest of the water and then letting out a deep breath.

"That was way too fucking close, man," he muttered, shaking his head at the trio of corpses on the floor.

He stuffed two water bottles into the side pockets of his pants and headed towards the door he'd found during his sweep that led to the stairs down into the hardware store. He stayed silent, noting that it was an open staircase into the store proper, and inched towards the landing.

He had a pretty good birds-eye view of the large space, glancing over four rows of metal shelving. The plate glass windows and door at the front were secure, despite the small army of zombies milling about outside.

He scanned the dim store, noting a brief glimpse of movement at the far end, but nothing jumped out at him. He took a deep breath. Firing was out of the question. The chances of ricocheting against the shelves was too great, not to mention the loud noise would attract the now-docile zombies outside.

He drew his knife and pursed his lips. *Looks like it's the blade again*, he thought, shaking his head. It was less than ideal, but it was his safest of the unsafe options. He ducked low and moved as quietly as he could down the stairs, choosing an aisle he'd noted as empty so he could hopefully sneak up on his enemies.

As he reached the end, he peeked around ever-so-slowly, where two corpses were fixated on a cardboard cutout of some more-than-likely deceased celebrity hawking car wax.

Hickman darted out and planted his blade deftly in the back of the closest zombie's distracted skull. He tore it out and stabbed the other in the side of the head before the first one even hit the ground, and then whipped around in a defensive stance to wait.

"Come out, come out, wherever you are," he murmured, and strained his ears. He stepped forward and banged the handle of his blade against one of the metal shelves, causing a bit of a ruckus but not enough to echo to outside.

Hickman waited again, but there was nothing. *Either I'm alone, or these fuckers have learned to play possum*, he thought, and then immediately shuddered in fear at that thought. The one saving grace any survivors had was that the zombies were dumb. If they got smart, then the world was even more fucked than they'd initially thought.

He shook off the thought and walked over to the register, heading behind the counter. Just as Ryan had said, there was a padlock key in the drawer below. He crept by the windows, not wanting to attract any attention, and ducked behind the propane cage as he unlocked it.

There were at least a dozen inside, and he gently rolled each one to see which ones were full. With a stroke of luck, eight of them were, and he grinned.

Eight of these things going off at once is going to cause one hell of an explosion, he thought, and then tapped his chin. *But I need to get these far enough up the road before I can set them off. Guess I'm doing some shopping.*

Hickman walked down the aisles, looking for something he could use to transport the heavy tanks. He cocked his head at a rope display, and rolled a thick piece around his fist.

"Let's see," he murmured, ignoring the fact that he was now talking to himself, "run the rope through the opening, create a propane tank backpack…

653

forty some-odd pounds a piece… yeah, fuck that." He dropped the rope and continued up the aisle, turning the corner display to find a set of large plastic wagons.

He reached out and fingered the price tag, reading the specifications. *500 POUND CAPACITY!* The tag boasted, and he grabbed the back end of the wagon easily, noting how lightweight it was.

"This," he declared, "this, I can work with." He turned and spotted a wall of open-ended hooks. "All right, I got a plan."

A little while later, Hickman stood at the end of the lip on the building where he'd climbed up from the busted car. He attached a hook to one of the propane tanks and lowered the attached rope carefully down into the wagon on the ground. Once it was situated, he lowered the rope a little more to free the hook and then retrieved his rope.

There were several zombies milling around the car, but they weren't particularly interested in the wagon. He stood up and set the rope down before walking back along the canopy to grab another propane tank from the load he'd hauled up the stairs. He paused to wink at the teenage girl zombie in the window that had startled him the first time.

"What do you think, girl?" he asked, puffing his chest out. "Am I a genius, or what?"

She groaned into the glass, still attempting to chew through it.

"Yeah, you're right," Hickman replied thoughtfully. "It's still going to be a bitch and a half to move that thing up the road." He shook his head, realizing he was now having a conversation with a corpse, and continued on his way to get another tank.

CHAPTER EIGHT

Ortega led the trio of four wheelers down the highway towards Mason. It was almost peaceful, a nice breeze and no zombies in the immediate vicinity. The ten-foot-wide river stretched out parallel to the road, with just open field beyond.

Audrey swerved back and forth playfully, causing Ryan to grip her waist in fear and squeeze his eyes shut. The two men on the vehicle beside her chortled at the young man's plight.

Ortega slowed to a stop as they reached the outer edge of town, pulling up in the middle of the road. The other two vehicles came to a stop on either side of him, and they all cut their engines to save on gas as they took in the tiny town.

"Man, this place does not look big at *all*," the soldier said.

Ryan finally relaxed, leaning back on his hands. "It's like six blocks by ten blocks."

"I used to work at a mall up in Carson City that was bigger than this place," Audrey added.

Ortega turned to Ruben. "So, where does your buddy live?"

"Far end of town, by the river," the janitor replied, pointing. "Literally the last lot."

"Okay, I don't want to take any chances," the soldier said. "We'll ride up four blocks and then walk the rest."

Garrett cocked his head. "You think he's still alive?"

"If anybody's capable of it, it's ole Charlie," Ruben replied with a nod. "He planned for the end for years. Almost breaks my heart to think he didn't get a chance to show everybody he was right."

Ortega took a deep breath. "Well, if he's there, let's hope he's open to some visitors." He turned the key in the ignition to bring the four wheeler back to life, and moved a lot slower this time, keeping an eye out for zombies. To their surprise, as they moved through town, there was not a single movement. He slowed to a stop and killed the engine a few blocks down from the trailer park, and the others followed suit.

"It was awfully quiet riding through town," Audrey said when the vehicles were quiet. "You'd think there would be at least a zombie or two, right?"

Ryan shrugged as he swung his leg over to dismount. "Maybe they got bored and left?" he asked. "No sense in sticking around if there aren't snacks to be had."

"Snacks?" she snapped and smacked him on the arm. "Really? They're people, dipshit."

657

The young man ducked his head, putting his hands up in surrender. "Sorry, sorry. That was tactless," he admitted. "But you get my point. If people aren't here, why would they be?"

Ortega checked his weapon. "Well, if they *are* here, we'll be ready," he declared. "Come on, let's go see if Charlie is home." He led the group on foot towards the trailer park.

Ruben quietly directed him down a side street a few blocks up, so that they wouldn't be within line of sight. They didn't want to surprise him, but they didn't want him to peg them from too far away just in case he was volatile before he realized they were friendly.

They pressed themselves up against the last house on the block, and Ortega peeked out around the corner, taking in the trailer park.

"Ruben, it looks like your buddy was alive at one point, because there are a hell of a lot of dead zombies on the road," he said. There was a six-foot-tall chain link fence surrounding the park with barbed wire on top, and at least sixty corpses motionless in the street.

"Well in that case, we need to be careful, so we don't spook him," Ruben replied.

Ortega shrugged. "What do you suggest-"

CRACK! The sound of a rifle cut through the air, and a brick just above the soldier's head exploded from the wall, spraying red chunks everywhere.

"That was your one warning shot, soldier boy!" a man screamed. "You just wander on back the way you came! Ain't nobody here interested in what you peddlin'!"

Ortega took a deep breath and bellowed, "Charlie, I'm Private Ortega and we need-"

CRACK! This shot didn't hit anything, but it was effective in cutting his plea short.

"How the hell d'you know my name?!" Charlie screamed. "Goddamn government! I knew it! I knew they had me on a list! Dead people risin' and the government cain't leave a God fearing patriot alone!"

Ortega let out a low whistle and glanced at Ruben. "Any thoughts?"

"Yeah. One." The janitor raised a finger, and then yelled, "Charlie! It's me."

"Ruben?" the man cried, incredulity in his voice. "Is that you?"

"Yeah, it's Ruben," his friend called.

Charlie blurted a string of curses. "Don't tell me the government got you too, man?"

"You are one dumb motherfucker, you know that?" Ruben called back. "The government didn't get me, and they didn't come all this way to take out some old man in a trailer park. They sent a couple soldier boys with a big-ass truck filled with food and other good stuff to help us survive. We here because we need your help!"

There was a pause, and then with less conviction, Charlie asked, "You… you mean the soldier there isn't trying to kill me?"

"Well, if you fire another shot in his direction, I'm guessin' he's gonna start takin' it personal," Ruben replied. "But as long as that doesn't happen, I think we cool."

Another pause. "Okay," Charlie declared. "I'm comin' out."

"You might want to keep your weapon lowered," Ruben said quietly to the soldier. "I'll go first to make sure he's cool."

Ortega nodded. "Gotcha." He lowered his rifle, and waited for Ruben to step out first, the rest of the group cautiously following behind him. As they approached the gate, a decrepit-looking

man with scraggly white hair unlocked a
padlock on his front gate. He pulled the
gate open, his wild snowy beard parting in
a smile at the sight of his friend.

"Good to see you, you ole coot,"
Ruben said, and they embraced. "I knew
you'd still be alive out here."

Charlie put a hand over his heart,
partially covering his black Skynyrd tee.
"Man, I been preparin' for this day my
whole life. You think I was gonna miss
it?"

The two shared a laugh, and then
Ruben motioned to the rest of the group,
keeping an arm around the older man. "I'd
like to introduce you to some of my
friends. This young buck here is Ryan. The
distinguished-looking man here is Garrett.
The lovely young lady here is Audrey, and
I emphasize *lady*, so you keep that filthy
tongue in check, ya hear?"

"Don't listen to him," the redhead
quipped with a grin, "I could tell him
things that would put him in an early
grave."

The old man chuckled. "I like her."

"And last, but not least, this here
is Private Ortega, who I believe you owe
an apology to," Ruben finished, and stared
down at his friend sternly.

Charlie extended his hand, head bowed like a scolded child. "I… I hope there's no hard feelin's there?"

"No harm, no foul," Ortega replied, and shook his hand firmly. "I can't say if the situation was reversed that I wouldn't have done the exact same thing you did."

Charlie smiled. "Well, that's so good to hear. I tell you what, let's go to my place and have us a little fence mending celebration. I have some cold ones in the fridge that I would be more'n happy to share with y'all."

"Not really in a position to party at the moment," Ruben admitted. "We got us a bit of a situation up in town we need some help dealing with."

Charlie nodded slowly, putting up his hands. "Okay, okay. Well, I tell you what, let's go to my place and have us a little brainstorming session about how to best deal with the problem at hand. I have some cold ones in the fridge that I would be more'n happy to share with y'all."

"Charlie…" Ruben scrubbed his hands down his face.

Ortega put a hand on the janitor's shoulder. "You know, I believe the man would like us to have a beer with him," he said. "It's the least we can do while we talk about what we need to do."

"Well, what do you know?" Charlie declared proudly, punching his friend in the shoulder. "I like this soldier boy already! Come on in!" He laughed and re-secured the padlock behind them, a skip in his step as he led the group further into the trailer park.

CHAPTER NINE

The group gawked at the setup as they headed to the middle of the lot. There were trenches dug all around the lone trailer in the center, filled with barbed wire and wooden stakes boasting death to whatever stumbled in.

"Now, y'all mind your step," Charlie cautioned. "You don't want to be gettin' caught up in any of that."

Ortega raised an eyebrow. "Preparing for the worst, huh?"

"Yes sir," the old man replied firmly. "My perimeter isn't as strong as I would like, so if any of them ever got through I wanted to make sure I'd have a fightin' chance." He led them across the trenches and around to the front of his double-wide, where he had quite the setup with an outdoor bar and grill area.

"Damn, man, I'm impressed," Ruben breathed as he patted the wooden counter.

Charlie grinned. "Oh, you ain't seen nothin' yet, old friend," he said, and headed over to the grill. Next to it there was a large outdoor recliner, and he shoved it out of the way to reveal a steel door with a digital keypad. He knelt down and punched in a few numbers, allowing the door to slide open. "Come on in," he said, stepping down the flight of stairs beneath.

"Well goddamn," Ruben breathed as they got to the bottom and entered a twenty by twenty room. "How the hell did you afford all this?" He gaped at the floor to ceiling shelves full of food and goods.

"Remember about a decade ago when you were givin' me hell about cryptocurrencies?" Charlie turned and stuck his thumbs innocently into the belt loops on his cutoff jeans, puffing out his chest. "How you said I was throwing my money away? Well, I hate to say I told you so… but I told you so." He walked over to the large refrigerator in the corner and opened it up, pulling out a six pack.

He started handing them out, the group all gawking around at the room as they absently took a can.

Ryan, however, furrowed his brow and shook his head. "I'm only seventeen, sir," he said politely.

"Did you go to high school around here?" Charlie raised a white eyebrow.

The young man nodded. "Yes, sir."

"Well, then sorry it's not somethin' a bit more potent," the old man replied. "I knew some of the people whose liquor cabinets y'all raided for your parties."

Ryan blushed and took the beer, cracking open the can without another word.

"All right, y'all come on up and make yourselves at home," Charlie said. "Let's see how I can help you out." He ushered them all up from the basement and they got comfortable on all of the patio chairs adorning his large deck. He cracked open his own can and reclined in his chair, putting his feet up. "Okay. Lay it on me."

Ortega leaned forward, resting his elbows on his knees. "We have a transport truck that's stuck downtown," he began. "It's full of things to help the survivors here become self-sufficient so that we can all ride out the apocalypse. Problem is, it's out of gas."

"Okay." The old man shrugged. "I don't see how I can help."

"Are you dense?" Ruben rolled his eyes. "We need some of your diesel so we can get that thing running again."

"Are you friggin' kidding me?" Charlie cried. "I barely have enough to keep me going for the next three months. Why don't y'all just hit up the gas station and call it a day?"

Ruben glared at him. "Did you not hear the big explosion the other day?"

"Uh, yeah?" the older man replied.

Ruben threw his hands up. "Well, there ya go."

Charlie sighed, rubbing his beard and shaking his head. "Man… I don't know."

"We got people trapped inside one of the shops up there," Ruben said, his eyes softening. "If we can get that truck going, then we can get them outta there."

The old man pursed his lips. "And where are you plannin' on takin' them?"

"Looks like you have plenty of vacant houses around here," the janitor replied, motioning to the empty trailers.

"No, no, no," Charlie said, raising his empty palm. "I know we go way back, but man, it takes a set of wheelbarrow-sized balls to come into *my* house, drink *my* beer, want *my* fuel and then tell me you want a bunch of people to move in! Jesus, man, come on!"

Ortega took a deep breath. "What if I made you deal?"

The old man regarded the soldier for a moment, eyes narrowed. "All right, given that I took a couple of potshots at you, I suppose part of my apology can be hearing you out," he said. "Let's hear what you have to say."

"Okay," Ortega continued, "you give us some fuel and help us secure the town, and I'll set you up with your own private solar-powered generator. The rest of us

667

will be sharing, but you'll have your very
own."

"Solar panels?" Charlie scoffed. "You
mean that commie hippie bullshit that
ain't worth a damn? Why in the hell would
I want that?"

The soldier regarded him calmly. "I
promise you, it's worth quite a bit. With
what I'm going to set you up with, you'll
be able to run everything you have, above
and below ground. And remember. The sun
isn't going to run out of power. Your
diesel, however, will."

"I ain't convinced." Charlie set down
his beer and crossed his arms defiantly.
"But you are right about my diesel being
in short supply." He stroked his beard,
letting out a deep sigh. "But you seem
damn convinced it's gonna work, so I'll
give you the benefit of the doubt. That
said, this is the *last* part of my apology
for shootin' at ya."

Ortega nodded, and put a hand over
his heart. "Apology accepted." He extended
his hand, and the old man shook.

"So how secure do we need to get this
place?" Charlie asked. "What you thinkin'?
Forty, fifty of them critters coming our
way?" He snatched up his beer and lifted
it to his mouth once again.

Ortega and Ruben shared an uneasy
glance.

"Well," the soldier said slowly, "we have a plan to distract the ones near the truck so we can refuel, but there could very easily be a thousand to fifteen hundred following us down there."

Charlie choked on his brew. "Fifteen fuckin' hundred?!" he sputtered. "Are you fuckin' kiddin' me? Did you see an arsenal down there? Because I sure as shit didn't!"

"We've got plenty of weapons and ammo in the truck," Ortega assured him. "We just need to get it here and unload enough to get to them."

The old man drained the rest of his beer, and sat back in his chair thoughtfully. Finally, he took a deep breath.

"Okay." He ran a wrinkled hand over his hair. "There are a few cars in the neighborhood that we can use to block off that bridge. Ain't got no clue where the keys are, but there's enough of us that we can push 'em up. We'll get 'em in position so we can move 'em on to the bridge once you're across."

Garrett cocked his head. "Do you have anything we can dig a trench with on the other side of the river?" he asked. "Even with all those guns and ammo, it's going to be tough to take out a thousand of those things."

"Nah, you leave that to me," the old man replied. "Ole Charlie's got a plan."

Ruben snorted. "Last time I heard you say that, I ended up in County for a few weeks."

"That was a hell of a night though, wain't it?" Charlie grinned.

The janitor shook his head and chuckled. "From what I remember of it, yeah."

"All right, let's get down to business," the old man said with a groan, and got up from his seat. "I'm pretty sure I've got a couple of five-gallon canisters around here somewhere. Private, if you wouldn't mind giving me a hand with that."

"I can do that, brother," Ortega said, and got to his feet. "In the meantime, Audrey and Ryan, if you two wouldn't mind running one of those four wheelers up to the bridge and dropping it off for Hickman? He's gonna be coming that way and would probably appreciate it if he didn't have to walk all the way here."

Audrey pointed at Ryan. "Just so we're clear, you're riding with me on the way back."

"I guess I should just be happy that I get to drive one of these for a little bit," the young man replied.

She clapped him on the back. "That's a good attitude. Come on, let's get this done."

"Just go as quick as you can," Ortega said, "because Ryan, you're gonna have to come with me into town."

The young man ruffled his hair. "Man, my day just keeps getting better," he said playfully.

"And I'll take ole Garrett here and we'll start tracking down those vehicles," Ruben said, and stood up, knees crackling. "Judging by the size of that bridge, I'm thinking three might do the trick?"

"Four might be better," Garrett replied. "Two end to end and two more shoring them up? You get enough of those fuckers all pushing in the same direction and they can move some cars."

"And if we have a vehicle in the rear, we'll have a firing platform," Ortega added.

Ruben nodded. "Four it is, then."

The group headed off, and Ortega put up a hand, taking his radio from its clip. "One sec, I just gotta let my partner know what's going on."

"Have at it, sir," Charlie replied, and collected the beer cans to dispose of them.

Ortega pushed the button on the mouthpiece. "Hey, Hickman, you still alive

671

up there?" he asked. There was no
response. He swallowed hard. "Hickman, you
copy?" Still nothing. Heart pounding, he
clenched a fist and looked to the sky
before asking desperately, "Come on, this
isn't funny, brother."

"Man, you are impatient," Hickman
came back. "I'm working over here and
can't drop everything at your beck and
call."

Ortega let out a relieved laugh.
"Apologies, brother. How we looking up
there?"

"I've got seven canisters loaded in,
one more to go," came the reply. "It's
gonna be a big-ass boom when it goes off."

"Good to know," Ortega replied. "I
figure we're about thirty minutes out.
Will you be ready by then?"

"Yeah, I can work with that," Hickman
said. "I'm going to be doing a deadass
sprint through these things, so you let me
know when you're in position."

Ortega nodded. "Ten four," he said.
"Oh, and I'm having some transportation
arranged for you up at the bridge. We're
dropping off a four wheeler as we speak."

A noise of intense satisfaction came
through the speaker. "Much appreciated!"

"Okay, hang tight," Ortega said.
"I'll be in touch soon." He returned his
radio to its clip and turned to the old

man. "All right, Charlie. Let's see about getting us some fuel."

CHAPTER TEN

Hickman stood in the window of the apartment and took a sip from a bottle of water as he looked out over the street. There were still hundreds of zombies outside the furniture store, but at least they weren't banging on the glass anymore, having forgotten about the fresh meat inside.

His radio crackled. "Hey, you ready to roll?" Ortega's voice came through.

"As about as ready as I'm ever going to be," Hickman replied, his voice monotone.

His partner snorted. "If that's not the voice of overwhelming enthusiasm, I don't know what is."

"Well, I'm about to get chased through the streets by a thousand zombies while pushing nearly four hundred pounds of propane," Hickman said flatly. "This wasn't exactly on my list of things to do today, you know?"

There was a short pause. "I'm sorry brother, I'd switch places with you if I could."

"Yeah, I know man, I know," Hickman replied.

"So, where you setting this thing off at?" Ortega asked.

His partner pursed his lips. "I'm thinking the sporting goods store. Only thing I Have to light this with are some flares, so I need a way to keep the gas relatively contained so it filters out to the flame. Kind of hoping there are some tents or something set up."

"I'm pretty sure there wasn't one set up," Ortega replied. "But there was a small office behind the customer service desk."

"You think that's going to cause enough of a distraction?" Hickman asked. "Going off that deep inside the building?"

Ortega came back immediately. "Yeah, it'll be plenty loud, having several of those things go off at the same time. At the very least, it'll blow out the windows. Although it wouldn't hurt for you to fire off a few rounds."

"Trust me, as soon as I hit that pavement I'm going to be weapons hot," Hickman assured him. "None of this stealth bullshit."

His partner laughed. "Hard to argue with that. And you know where you're headed, right?"

"Yep, side street then straight on to the bridge." Hickman nodded firmly at his reflection in the window.

"Just be careful," Ortega warned, "we had a couple of stragglers follow us out

of the sporting goods store. They've
probably wandered off the main road, but
you never know."

"I'll save some shots for them,
then," his partner promised.

"Be safe, brother," Ortega said.
"We'll see you soon."

Hickman took a deep breath. "Looking
forward to it." He put his radio away and
crept back outside onto the awning as
quietly as he could.

He inched his way along to the end,
and took a knee to look over. There were
two zombies within ten yards of the wagon,
but they were too stupid to bother looking
up at him. He turned and gave a hard tug
to the thick rope he'd previously secured
to a drainage pipe.

This is way too close for comfort, he
thought bitterly as he gave the rope
another strong tug to make sure it would
for sure withstand his weight going down.
*If I pop off from here, that'll give me
about ten seconds to get down and get
moving… this had better be fucking worth
it.*

He drew his handgun with one hand and
gripped the rope with the other, taking a
loose-legged stance to be ready to spring.
He aimed his gun at one zombie head, and
then practiced swinging quickly over to

the other a few times before taking a deep breath.

He fired, taking out the closest one, and swung to take out the second before it could even react. He shoved his gun back in its holster as the bodies hit the asphalt, and repelled himself down the building. He landed right next to the wagon and braced himself against it, giving a great heave to get it rolling.

A dozen or so zombies shambled towards him from about thirty yards away, and he grunted as his hamstrings burned and his back muscles pinched.

"There we go," he grunted to himself as the momentum began and the wagon picked up its own speed, "there we go!" As it gained speed, he pumped his legs harder, jogging to keep up with the propane projectile. A corpse staggered into the street but the wagon knocked it clean out of the way, sending it into a face plant on the ground.

Hickman glanced over his shoulder, noting that the dozens have turned easily to hundreds, and he drew his handgun again as he continued to push. He fired a few shots into the air, just to draw more attention to himself.

As he approached the sporting goods store, he dug in his heels and pulled back on the handle to slow the wagon's progress. He managed to maneuver it up onto the sidewalk and bumbled over the broken glass.

"All right, I'm in business," he chirped as he spotted the small office on the far end, and began to shove across the store. Moans filled the air to his right, and he immediately unslung his assault rifle, unloading into the few corpse shoppers.

He continued to push the wagon down the aisle towards the office, and then jerked back on the handle to keep it from bumping too hard against the door. He threw it open, gun raised, giving a quick sweep to make sure he was alone. The room was small, about ten feet by ten feet, and thankfully empty.

Hickman shoved the wagon in and against the far wall, and then started opening valves. After the top row, snarls and moans echoed through the store.

"That's gonna have to do," he muttered, and rushed back to the office door and away from the hissing canisters. He produced a few flares from his pocket and lit them up, dropping them just inside the door and slamming it shut.

The front of the store was flooded with zombies, blocking off his escape. He looked around frantically for some kind of fire door, but couldn't find a single one.

"Oh, come on!" he bellowed. "Even small towns have building codes!" He spotted a storage room and ran for it, the clock ticking on both his enemies and the propane. He went in, rifle first, and scanned the small empty room before finding an unmarked door at the back.

He ran over and turned the knob, and the door opened about six inches before stopping. Sunlight teased his face and he grunted, looking down at the chain on the outside, padlocking the door shut. He stepped back, braced his foot against the door to hold it taut, and fired half a dozen shots into the eye the chain was wrapped through on the wall.

The anchor tore off, the door smacking open into the alley, and Hickman tore towards the street, firing wildly at the few zombies milling about in his way. The corpses dropped and he made no move to check them, his only goal to get as far away as possible as fast as possible.

Legs pumping pavement as hard as they could, he ran, taking a sharp turn towards the bridge and away from the corpses piling into the volatile store. The smattering of slow-moving zombies were sparse on this end, and he didn't bother to slow down to fire, keeping a keen eye on the prize as he ran full-tilt.

A block or so later, the store went up in a massive *BOOM*, and Hickman skidded to a stop to look back, gawking at the smoke billowing up into the air. "All right Ortega, let's hope that worked," he muttered, and then continued towards the bridge.

His immediate task was completed, but the day was nowhere near over.

CHAPTER ELEVEN

"You think Hickman did it?" Ryan
murmured quietly to Ortega, who was
crouched next to him by the edge of a
building about a block away from the
furniture store.

As if on cue, a loud *BOOM* rattled the
earth.

The Private smirked. "If I had to
venture a guess…"

The younger man shook his head and
smiled, patting his new friend on the
shoulder. "Sorry for doubting you," he
said. They watched as the horde in front
of the furniture store turned its
attention towards the commotion, and began
to wander off in search of the explosive
noise. "Hell yeah, it's working!" Ryan
hissed, pumping a fist into the air.

"Don't get excited yet," Ortega
warned quietly. "Not all of them are
moving."

He clenched his jaw as a half dozen
or so stubborn zombies stayed fixated on
the furniture store, unmoved by the epic
barbecue happening up the street.

"How do we handle this?" Ryan asked.

Ortega drew his knife. "We gotta do
it silently."

"But it's six on two!" The young man
paled.

"Which is why we gotta hit 'em quick," Ortega replied. "You got your blade?"

Ryan pulled out a large hunting knife, nodding as beads of sweat broke out on his forehead.

"Okay, you follow my lead," the soldier said. "We walk—not run, *walk*—as quietly as we possibly can, up to them. I'm going to take the one closest to us, and I want you to focus on the second one. If you don't drop it with the first blow, I want you to grab on to its chest and hold them at bay. I got your back, so I don't want you to panic. You understand?"

Ryan nodded stiffly. "Yes, sir."

"Let's do it, then," Ortega replied, giving the young man's shoulder a reassuring squeeze. "Leave the gas here, when we clear 'em out, you run back and grab it."

At another sharp nod, the soldier led the two of them out, walking softly to the sidewalk. In the distance, the tail end of the horde moved past the back end of the truck, leaving just the six zombies between them and their goal.

The first corpse had mashed itself so hard into the glass with excitement that its cheek was caught in a crack, and as it turned to look at Ortega it left half its face hanging in the window. He stabbed it quickly in the eye socket before it could make a noise, and Ryan strode past to the next one.

He made a stab for the forehead, but the blade skidded off of the top part of its ear. His heart leapt into his throat, but he took Ortega's advice and braced his arm against its chest, holding it at bay. The soldier quickly stabbed it in the eye on his way by.

"Aim for the eyes, not the forehead," he whispered. "Easier to penetrate."

Ryan nodded and focused on the remaining four corpses shambling towards them. They were, at least, spaced out with a few feet in between, giving the duo a tactical advantage. The young man lunged forward and stabbed into the first one's eye, dropping it easily.

Ortega grabbed the next one by the shirt and shoved it into the one behind, stabbing twice in quick succession to take them both out. Ryan darted around to the final creature, but he hesitated at the sight of the rotting young woman. He couldn't help but feel that he knew this girl, that they'd shared a class together, or something, and now here she was, about to make a move on eating his flesh.

He snapped out of it just in time to end her suffering, planting the knife into her face.

As her body hit the street, Ortega approached. "Did you know her?"

"I'm not sure," Ryan admitted, rooted to the spot as he stared at the lifeless corpse.

"You good?" Ortega asked, brow furrowing.

The young man took a deep breath and nodded. "Yeah."

"All right, back to work, then," Ortega instructed, and they headed back for the door of the furniture store. The soldier did a light *shave and a hair cut* knock to make sure that those inside knew they were living beings. Soon enough, the barricade on the inside began to shift, and two older men revealed themselves on the other side, eyes wide with relief.

"Man, are we-" one began, and Ortega quickly shushed him.

"Quiet," he whispered. "We need to get everyone out of here now, *quietly*. Get ready to move."

The man nodded without saying another word.

Ortega turned to Ryan. "Get the gas and fill the tank, I'm going to clear us some space." As the young man trotted back off to get the fuel, the soldier snuck up to the truck. As he peered around the front grill, he had a clear view of the horde congregating around the burning sporting goods store.

Unfortunately, the novelty was wearing off, and some of the zombies were losing interest in the flames that weren't providing fresh meat.

"What's wrong?" Ryan asked as he approached with the gas cans, a few civilians trickling out behind him. "Why aren't you moving?"

"Because the bait is starting to wear off," Ortega replied. "We gotta open up the back of this truck and throw some stuff out to make room for everyone. As soon as that door goes up, we're on the clock, brother."

"I'll let everyone know to move up and be ready," Ryan said.

"Get anyone who is even remotely able-bodied up here to help me," Ortega instructed. "I need two people to help shove stuff off and pull people on."

Ryan nodded and took off. The soldier kept a close eye on the horde, chewing on his lip as he attempted to make calculations on their situation.

Worst possible case, forty-five, maybe fifty seconds before they get here, he thought, and shook his head, glancing over his shoulder at the older people shuffling out of the furniture store. *That's gonna be tight.*

Ryan jogged back up with two middle-aged men in tow. Ortega simply raised an eyebrow at the rotund men, who looked like they'd get winded hopping out of a recliner.

"Best we got." The young man shook his head.

"Gonna have to make do," Ortega replied with a shrug. "You boys know what we're doing?" At their nod, he turned back to the kid. "Okay. Where's Harlan?"

The man in question hobbled up to them, ducking in behind the grill of the truck. "Good to see you're still alive and kicking," he said quietly.

"Good to see you're at least doing one of those things," Ortega replied. "Your ankle good?"

"Stings like a bitch, but I can drive us out," Harlan replied with a little salute.

"Okay, when we go, you get in that cab," Ortega instructed. "As soon as Ryan gets it fueled, you start it up. And as soon as I fire a shot you start driving south. Kid, I want you in the cab with him so you can tell him where to go." Both men nodded, and the soldier turned to the group. "Okay, let's do this."

He led his two helpers around to the back, with the civilians following. The doc carried an injured Jordan at the front between him and another man. Ortega waited until everyone was clustered around, and then threw open the door latch, shoving it upwards. It screeched to the top, slamming against the roof, and the soldier winced before leaping up inside.

The back edge of the horde turned excitedly towards them, wandering their way. One of his helpers gaped at the zombies in fear as Ortega and the other man began tossing things out into the street.

"Get to work or people will die!" the soldier screamed.

The frightened man snapped out of it, and grabbed a box, throwing it out. The truck was packed relatively tightly, pallets stacked floor to ceiling, and Ortega managed to create a shelf for people to climb up on without having to haul the heavier stuff.

"Start getting people up, we're almost good," he grunted, scrambling to clear a path as his helpers began to pull people up into the bed. He got down on one knee and hauled one person up, keeping a mental count in his head of how much longer they had before the horde reached them.

The truck rumbled to life, sitting idle and waiting for his signal.

"This is gonna be tight," he muttered.

They hauled as fast as they could, but the horde was closing in. One woman screamed as they got close, prompting an elderly man to step forward to try to protect her from the oncoming corpses. The creatures easily overpowered them both, descending on the screaming civilians and drowning it out with snapping teeth and tearing flesh.

Ortega waved to the two remaining people on the ground, and pulled his handgun, firing once before tossing it behind him and reaching down for a hand. His helpers grabbed the other man, and the truck began to move as they dragged the final two civilians to safety.

The soldier sat back on his haunches, watching with a pang in his chest as the zombies chowed down on the two unlucky people. He hadn't wanted to lose anyone.

But as the thousand-strong horde began to lumber after the truck, he had a feeling that losing two elderly was going to be the least of his worries that day.

"All right, the turnoff is just up a bit more on the right," Ryan instructed, pointing through the windshield.

Harlan nodded. "Any idea where they want me to park this thing?"

"Just put it right in the middle of the road, right after you get across the bridge," Ryan instructed. "We gotta get these guns."

The driver shook his head and let out a low whistle. "The fun never stops." He turned towards Mason and rumbled across the bridge, waving at the trio waiting for them. As soon as the truck cleared it, Audrey, Garrett and Ruben began pushing the first car into place as a blockade.

Ortega was first off of the back, rushing over to the group. Ryan followed soon after, having dismounted from the passenger's seat as fast as he could.

"Any sign of Hickman yet?" Ortega asked.

Audrey shook her head. "Not yet."

"Okay," the soldier replied, pursing his lips for a moment. "Hopefully he gets here soon. In the meantime, let's get that other car on the bridge."

"How much time do you think we have?" the redhead asked.

Ortega let out a deep *whoosh* of breath. "Fifteen, maybe twenty minutes. It's not that far of a walk."

Charlie strolled out of the gate from the trailer park, holding a beer and whistling a jaunty tune. "Hey, before y'all block off that bridge, let me get a couple of ya for somethin'."

"Dammit, how can you be drinking at a time like this?" Ruben snapped. "Ain't nobody got time for your shenanigans!"

"Oh yeah you do," the old man shot back, raising his furry white chin. "Gimme three and I promise it'll be worthwhile."

Ortega shrugged. "Ryan, Garrett, Ruben, give the man a hand. Audrey and I will help with the truck unloading. If we don't get these guns, it isn't going to matter what Charlie has up his sleeve."

Ruben sighed and waved for the others to follow him after a still-whistling old man. Charlie stopped beside two fifty-five gallon drums sitting on moving company grade hand trucks. He leaned on one of them, casually taking a long sip of his beer.

"Whatcha got there?" Ruben asked.

The old man grinned and smacked his lips together. "A hundred and ten gallons of the best diesel fuel money can buy."

"I guess a better question is," Ruben replied impatiently, "whatcha plannin' on doin' with this?"

"Well ole buddy," Charlie said, "we got a shitload of guests comin', seems rude not to get a barbecue goin'."

The janitor cracked a smile, a lightbulb going off in his head. "I'm trackin' now. Garrett, give a brother a hand."

Garrett nodded and they heaved the giant drums one by one onto their sides, rolling them back to the bridge. Once they got across to the road, the cylinders took up about a third of the pavement side by side.

Charlie pulled out his large hunting knife and slammed it down into the side of one of the drums, twisting it to create a decent sized hole. He punctured it a second time for air flow, and then repeated the process on the second cylinder.

"All right, roll 'em forward a bit," he instructed, and then put out a hand to stop them again, putting a few more holes in each. Once the drums were nice and swiss cheesed, he tossed his empty beer can and helped push the drums along the road. "Okay, slow and steady boys, we wanna make sure this stuff pools up nicely."

Ruben nodded as he used a bit less elbow grease. "How are you plannin' on lighting this thing?"

"Oh, don't you worry about it," Charlie drawled. "Your ole buddy has got you covered."

"Well, it better be hot as hell," Ryan piped up, "because in my chemistry class we did an experiment on fuel types and diesel has a higher flashpoint than regular old gasoline."

Charlie clucked his tongue. "Well, what do you know, those government indoctrination centers actually taught you something useful."

"Government what?" Ryan raised an eyebrow.

"Nevermind," Charlie replied with a shake of his head. "You are correct that it takes a higher flashpoint to get this baby going. But a sustained flame on it will do the same trick. Like I said, don't worry about it."

Ryan wrinkled his nose and took a deep breath. "All right."

"Now now, ole Charlie here still has a ton of alcohol to drink," the old man declared. "I ain't gonna just let all that go to waste by getting us killed, now."

About a hundred and twenty yards along the road, the last of the sticky black fuel oozed out of the holes in the drums.

Ryan gave his a little shake. "What do we do with the barrels?"

Charlie turned and kicked his and Ruben's into the ditch, and turned back to the group, swiping his hands together. "What?" He shrugged at the blank stares from his companions. "It's not like the EPA is gonna come fine me or anything."

Ryan shook his head as Garrett kicked theirs off of the road, and started back towards the bridge. Charlie and Ruben moved with him, but they quickly realized that their fourth hadn't followed.

"Yo, Garrett, you comin', man?" Ruben asked, pausing. The three of them turned to see the middle-aged man, stock still in the middle of the road, staring at the front edge of the zombie horde cresting the horizon.

"I… I can see them," he stammered.

Charlie rolled his eyes. "All the more reason to get your ass in *gear*, boy! We got work to do!" He clapped his hands together, and this seemed to snap the pale man out of his deer-in-the-headlights stare.

He jogged to the group, shaking his arms as if to bring life back into them, and the four civilians walked briskly back to the bridge. Charlie headed over to the truck as the other three got back to work on the car barricade.

"Yo, army boy!" he bellowed. "We got company!"

Ortega hopped down from the back of the truck, brow furrowed. "How close are they?"

"Fuck if I know, all I know's we can see 'em on the horizon," Charlie replied. "So they gonna be here sooner rather than later."

Ortega took a deep breath. "Goddamn they got here quick." He glanced around at the people he'd rescued from the furniture store, and crossed his arms. "I need another favor."

Charlie crossed his arms as well, matching the soldier's stiff posture. "These solar panels better be worth it," he muttered.

"Oh, don't worry, they are," Ortega said.

The old man sighed. "What do ya need?"

"These people aren't going to help us in a fight," the soldier explained. "Can you get them into your compound?"

Charlie nodded. "Yeah, I got you covered." He turned to the civilians and spread his arms, waving them in his directions. "Okay, y'all, follow me! I got a nice cozy little place all set up for y'all. Just *one* rule: don't touch my shit!" He managed to keep a stern expression for all of a few seconds before he barked a laugh. "Just playin' with y'all. There's plenty of food and water down there. Come on."

He led the group away towards his bunker, and Ortega approached the truck, clapping Harlan on the shoulder. "Hey, you go with them."

The driver narrowed his eyes. "Fuck you. You boys are gonna need my help. Just prop my plump ass up against the car and hand me a weapon."

"All right man," Ortega replied, raising his hands in surrender, "if you wanna me on the line with us, you'll be there."

Harlan nodded firmly with a noise of indignant pride, and both men turned at the sound of a four-wheeler engine screaming towards them.

Hickman skidded to a stop just short of them and hopped off with a grin.

"About damn time you showed up," Harlan declared.

The soldier rolled his eyes. "Sorry, I had to blow up a sporting goods store."

"Well, these things take time, I guess," the driver replied, as casual as if they were discussing the weather.

"How we looking here?" Hickman asked.

Ortega took a deep breath. "Well, in about five minutes, we're gonna have a thousand zombies on us, and we're still waiting on weapons."

Hickman unslung his rifle, flipping the scope to long range. "I'll see if I can't slow 'em down just a bit." He jogged over to the car barricade, hopping up into the hood of one, and took a knee before aiming.

He squeezed the trigger and took the head of a zombie clean off. As it crumpled to the ground, the corpse tripped up a few of its brethren. The soldier didn't waste any time sending round after round into the horde. It wouldn't buy much extra time, but every little bit would help.

"Got them!" Audrey cried from the truck.

Ortega stepped forward as she set down a whole pile of assault rifles. "You find the ammo?" he asked.

"Yep," she replied, "that's coming next." She headed back into the dim tunnel.

The soldier began doling out weapons, and turned to his two civilian helpers that had stuck around. "Okay, crash course," he began. "Rule number one, only point them at zombies." He pushed on the barrels of both guns so that they were pointing at the ground. "Rule two, keep it

in three-round burst mode. I get the sense
you aren't going to be the greatest shots,
so while it'll burn through ammo, you'll
have a better chance at hitting the
target. And rule three, here's the release
button." He pointed to his own rifle to
show them. "Just smack in another mag, and
you're ready to go. Questions?"

Both men raised their hands.

Harlan snorted. "How in the hell did
you boys live in rural America and not
know how to operate a firearm?"

"I was a schoolteacher," one of them
replied.

"Hell, if that's the case, then you
should not only know how to operate it,
but be proficient at it!" Harlan rolled
his eyes.

Ortega shook his head. "You're not
helping," he scolded.

The driver hobbled over to one of the
men and snatched it from his grasp,
checking it over and getting it ready.

Audrey shoved the last of three large
boxes to the edge of the truck. "Got us a
thousand rounds, but they needed to be
loaded in."

"You know how to shoot?" Ortega
asked.

She nodded. "Yeah, I can handle
myself."

"Okay, get down here and get his weapon," he instructed, inclining his head towards the other civilian.

She jumped down and did as he asked, checking the weapon with expert grace.

"Help Harlan over to the cars, and start firing when you feel comfortable you can hit the target," Ortega continued, motioning to her. "I'm gonna get these boys going on loading ammo."

Audrey nodded and took the driver by the arm, heading towards the line of cars.

"Badass, girl," Harlan complimented her as he limped along.

"Okay, grab the ammo," Ortega instructed, leading his helpers to the bridge, carrying a box between them. "So you press down and slide. Press down and slide. Count to twenty-five, and move on. It's a tight fit when it's full, and we got plenty to spare so no need to fill the mags all the way up. Can you handle it?"

He handed an empty mag to each of them, and they quickly got to work. To the soldier's surprise, they moved at a decent speed, and he clapped them both on the shoulder in appreciation.

"Ortega, need you up here!" Hickman called, and his partner rushed over, climbing up onto the hood next to him.

"What do you think?" Ortega asked as he watched the stumbling horde, now within thirty yards of the bridge.

Hickman shrugged. "I think barring a miracle, we're fucked."

CHAPTER THIRTEEN

"So, how we pulling a miracle?" Ortega asked, squaring his shoulders as he sized up the oncoming horde.

Hickman shrugged. "Bottleneck them on the bridge?"

"If we can take out enough of the front line, it might give us a barrier so we can slowly take them out," Ortega said thoughtfully.

His partner grinned. "Good a plan as any."

They hopped down from the car in unison, and took up defensive positions behind the vehicles. Hickman moved to the far end and Ortega flanked the remainder of their group, everyone readying their weapons.

"Okay, as soon as they hit the bridge, start firing!" Ortega instructed as the zombies made the turn, some of them cutting across the grass to approach. "Aim straight down the line, and go for the head. When you need ammo, grab one mag at a time."

Ryan let out a deep *whoosh* of breath. "What happens if they breach the barricade?"

"Fall back into the neighborhood, and take shelter," Ortega replied.

"Fuck that!" Hickman shook his head. "If they breach, we're dead. Either from them getting us or starvation. Stand your ground and don't let them through."

The rest of the group looked to Ortega for confirmation, and he couldn't help but concede. He nodded. He'd wanted to give them some hope, but sober reality was the better play. He offered his partner a grim smile of thanks for being the voice of reason and honesty.

"Nobody fires until we do," Ortega said firmly. He turned towards the horde, holding his gun up and steady. He watched the zombies stagger towards them, gaping mouths drooling crimson as they moaned their excitement for a fresh meal. They were packed shoulder to shoulder stretching back hundreds of yards, an ambling sea of rotting death.

Hickman fired the first shot, and the group unloaded into the front line. Bullets tore into the horde, some on target and blasting skulls, some missing wildly. Torsos blew open, limbs fell to the ground, bodies spun and flipped and went down spectacularly, but only to be replaced by more mindless dead.

The bottleneck had reached the bridge, about twenty feet away, when the first *click* sounded.

"I'm out!" Ryan cried, breaking from the firing line to rush back to the two men packing mags with ammo. He unloaded his empty one and snatched up one of only eight that they'd filled. "You guys gotta speed up!" he urged, and then slammed the fresh bullets back in, running back to the line.

The men fumbled to go faster, spurred on by the panic in the young man's voice, but shaky fingers and hands made them inefficient in their task. Audrey and Ruben both announced their empties and tore over to grab more ammo.

Hickman switched from single fire to burst mode, firing at head level across the whole line of dead. Bits of blood and rotted brain matter flew into the air like little fireworks, the bodies slowing the flow of the enemies a little bit while they were two shooters down. Ortega followed suit, but his rifle ran out, and he jogged back to grab a fresh mag.

As he clicked it in, his ears perked up at the sound of splashes, and he ran over to the edge of the bridge to see zombies wading into the river. "We're being flanked!" he bellowed, and began to fire down at the corpses easily traversing the waist-deep water. "They're getting to shore! Breaking the line!" he cried, as two zombies easily replaced each one he took down.

He ran off of the bridge and stood on the road parallel to the shoreline, standing guard as he waited for the corpses to emerge from the bushes. He dispatched one, then another, switching to single-shot mode to play a deranged game of whack-a-mole. He continually took out those closest to him, but soon enough there were a dozen lumbering creatures moving towards him on the road.

He began to walk backwards, and then ran out of ammo. As he switched mags, the zombies stumbled within ten feet of him, and then rapid-fire bullets tore into the group of corpses, sending them to the ground. The soldier turned to see Charlie standing behind him holding a gold-plated AK-57.

The old man grinned maniacally, sporting two bulky satchels on his hips. He moved forward, taking out all of the immediate zombies.

Ortega smirked as he clipped in a fresh mag. "You know automatic weapons are banned, don't you?"

"Well why don't you go ahead and confiscate it, then?" Charlie quipped, and handed him the gun. He unclipped one of the bags and handed it over as well. "Five fully loaded mags in there, you should be good to go."

Ortega nodded his thanks, clipping the sack to his own hips. "What about you?"

"Gotta get this barbecue going!" Charlie replied, pulling a trio of roman candles out of the other bag. He wandered up to the bridge, whistling as he lit the fireworks, and stepped up next to Ryan.

"What are you going to do with those?" the young man asked.

Charlie grinned. "I told you we needed a sustained heat source to get that diesel lit, and this is gonna do it," he replied.

"Those aren't hot enough!" Ryan protested, continuing to fire into the horde.

"Just watch, boy," the old man replied, and aimed the candles in an arc towards the road.

The horde reached the barricade, the combined weight of the oncoming dead inching the cars slowly but surely across the bridge. The first poofs of the roman candles sent brightly-colored bits of flame floating towards the pallid faces. The corpses stared up with rheumy eyes as the little bits floated down, falling to the ground and extinguishing with little *hisses*.

"That was your plan?" Ryan grunted. "Jesus man we could have-"

"Just *watch*, boy," Charlie urged, and another volley of colored flame shot through the air.

This time, a few thicker embers landed on a few corpses, and smoldered against their clothes. One of them was wearing something particularly flammable, and burst into flames, igniting the zombies next to it.

"There we go!" Charlie threw a triumphant fist into the air, eyes wild, and snatched Ryan's rifle from his hand. He took careful aim and fired at the flaming zombie, striking it in the head so that it fell directly into the diesel-soaked road.

He handed the gun back to Ryan, and then leaned casually on the stone bridge support, crossing his arms as the fuel ignited. The flames spread quickly, engulfing the zombies, consuming them in under a minute.

Thick black plumes of smoke filled the air, coating the battlefield as the horde went up in flames.

"I can't see shit," Audrey said, squinting into the smoke, and lowered her weapon.

Ryan stopped firing as well, not wanting to waste the bullets. "Me either."

Garrett fired off one more shot, and then scratched the back of his head. "I thought I saw something, but I can't tell if I hit it or not."

"Save your ammo, let the smoke clear," Hickman instructed. "Those barricades are hold-"

A loud screech cut him off as the cars pushed against the concrete.

"Fall back to the edge of the bridge," the soldier instructed, and rushed back with the rest of the group hot on his heels. He moved to the center of the bridge, the rest of them flanking him on either side.

Garrett leaned forward. "How do we know when-"

"Be quiet," Hickman snapped. A few tense moments passed, and the tires continued to gently squeak. He held fast, straining his ears, and then as soon as the squeaking stopped, he opened three-burst fire at the center of the bridge. After a few moments he stopped and listened.

"What are you shooting at?" Ryan whispered.

"The tires stopped making noise," Hickman explained, "which means they were through the line. Hopefully I just plugged the hole."

A moment later, the squeaking began again, but this time louder. The soldier clenched his jaw, realizing that the weight was no longer distributed evenly along the barricade.

"Open fire, open fire!" he cried, and the group aimed wildly at approximate head-height.

The smoke began to thin out, the corpses pushing forward reduced to smoldering lumps of crispy moving flesh. They made it past the cars and ambled towards the group, arms outstretched.

"When do we fall back?" Ruben demanded, eyes wide as he fired into the seventy or eighty corpses left pursuing them. "Hickman!" he cried when he received no answer. "When do we fall back?!"

The soldier knew he'd have to give the order soon, or the zombies would be on them. But just as he opened his mouth, automatic gunfire filled the air, tearing a gruesome path through the horde.

Ortega stalked forward, unloading an entire magazine into the oncoming barbecue, cutting the front wave down by half. He quickly reloaded and loosed another thirty rounds.

With this joining the combined effort of the group, the entirety of the charred horde fell on the bridge.

When the last crack of gunfire died away, they stood there, chests heaving and hearts pounding, staring at the blood-soaked bridge piled with bullet-ridden barbecued corpses. The scent hit them in the face then, the sickening acrid bitterness of burnt rotted flesh stretching the length of a football field.

Hickman turned to Ortega, wrinkling his nose at the gold-plated gun. "Where in the holy hell did you find *that* gaudy masterpiece?"

"Well, once I told ole Charlie that automatic weapons are illegal in this country, he graciously allowed me to confiscate it from him," Ortega replied with a grin, resting the ridiculous gun on his shoulder.

Hickman barked a laugh. "Well, I gotta say, it suits you."

Charlie strolled over and snatched it off of the soldier's shoulder, cradling it in his arms. "Sorry there, sport, but I'm havin' some second thoughts about lettin' you confiscate her. But I won't leave you empty handed, I got some makeshift spears for y'all."

"What the hell are we gonna do with spears?" Ortega raised an eyebrow.

The old man inclined his head to the giant pile of death. "Chances are some of them chargrilled fuckers are still kickin' under there, albeit at a severely reduced state. Once this smoke clears, we're gonna have to do a little cleanup."

The two soldiers shared a glance and a chuckle.

"You are one hell of a character," Ortega said, patting the old man on the back.

Hickman cracked his knuckles. "Come on, let's go get those spears."

CHAPTER FOURTEEN

The sun was low on the horizon. Some of the group led civilians cautiously through the barbecued remains of the horde, making sure to stab each and every one in the head as they went. They kept rags securely tied over the bottom halves of their faces to protect from the abhorrent smell wafting up from beneath their feet.

At Charlie's place, Hickman tossed a cable down from the roof of the double-wide to Ortega, who plugged it into the battery box that would now run the power supply to his trailer.

"All right my friend, you are up and running," Ortega said as Hickman slid past the panels and hopped down to the ground.

Charlie flipped the switch on his fuse box, and the lights strung around his grotto came on. "Well, I'll be a monkey's uncle," he said, awe in his voice. "That thing got workin' in that little bit of time?" He gazed up at the panel.

"Yeah, these things are pretty legit," Ortega replied, but reached over and flipped the switch back off. "Although, you'll probably have to ride tonight out in the dark and let it get a full charge tomorrow. After that, though, you should have constant power with the battery backup."

Charlie stretched his back out, hands on his hips. "I think I can live one night without my stories," he said. "Plus, it's shaping up to be a *beautiful* evening. Might be a good night to get a bonfire going."

Hickman swiped his hands across each other and laughed. "You haven't had enough fire for one day?"

"Nah, you can never have too much fire." Charlie waved him off. "Plus, with what all them folks have been through the last couple of days, might do 'em some good to have a bit of a festive evening."

Hickman nodded. "I think you're right."

Ruben headed over and mimicked his friend's stance, hands on his hips. "I thought you boys would have had the power going by now?"

"They got it goin', just needs a little time to charge," Charlie explained.

Ortega turned to the janitor. "You get people settled?"

"Yeah, we got a few houses set up pretty good for 'em," Ruben replied with a nod.

"What about the road into town?" Hickman asked.

"I got Harlan all set up," the janitor said, and held up a walkie-talkie. "He's gonna radio if there's anything we need to be concerned with. But based on what we did to them over there, I'd be surprised if anything comes our way."

Charlie headed for the door. "Excuse me for a minute, will ya, boys?" he asked, and ducked inside.

Ruben took a deep breath and then turned to the soldiers. "Hell of a day, huh?"

"Ain't that an understatement," Hickman replied with an exhausted chuckle.

Ortega sighed. "Of course, if the rumors I heard are correct, today's gonna be a cakewalk compared to what's coming up."

Ruben's eyes widened. "What in the hell do you have planned for us?!"

"Relax, brother," Ortega said, raising his hands, "not talking about you. Talking about the military at large."

The janitor shook his head, putting a hand over his chest. "You tryin' to give me a heart attack, there?"

"Sorry," Ortega said, failing to stifle a laugh, "didn't mean to alarm you."

Charlie emerged with a six-pack in hand. "My friend here being overdramatic again?"

"This fool was talking about how today was gonna be a cake walk compared to what's ahead," Ruben explained as he took one of the cans for himself.

Ortega put up a hand in surrender. "Except I wasn't talking about *us*."

"Or really anything more than rumors," Hickman added.

"Well, we got some time to kill," Charlie said as he doled out beer to the two soldiers. "What did you hear?"

Ortega took a deep breath. "That's there's going to be an invasion in a week or so."

"Where?" Ruben's brow furrowed.

"I heard it was the Northwest," Ortega replied. "Something about it being a strategic location or something like that."

Ruben took a thoughtful sip of his beer. "So what's that mean for us?"

"Assuming it's true," Hickman cut in, "it means we're on our own until they pull it off and venture down this far to bring us into the fold."

Charlie smacked his lips together after a particularly long chug. "And what if they're not successful?"

"Then you should be thankful we brought greenhouse materials so we can become self-sufficient," Ortega replied, raising his cane.

Charlie raised his own in response. "I'll drink to that." The quartet all clinked their beers together, and stood, staring out as the sun set on a day that they were more than glad they were alive to see the end of.

END

Up Next: The action shifts back to the Carolinas as Terrell battles to secure his new home against threats both living and dead.